WHEN THE TREE CALLS

THE ATHEMONI CHRONICLES

KRISTIN WAHLNE

KRISTIN WAHLNE

ISBN 979-8-9881901-1-0

My mom always told me I should write a book. I don't think
this is what she meant, but I think she'd be proud of me,
anyway. I love you, mom. And I love how you supported me
in every creative endeavor.

—Kristin

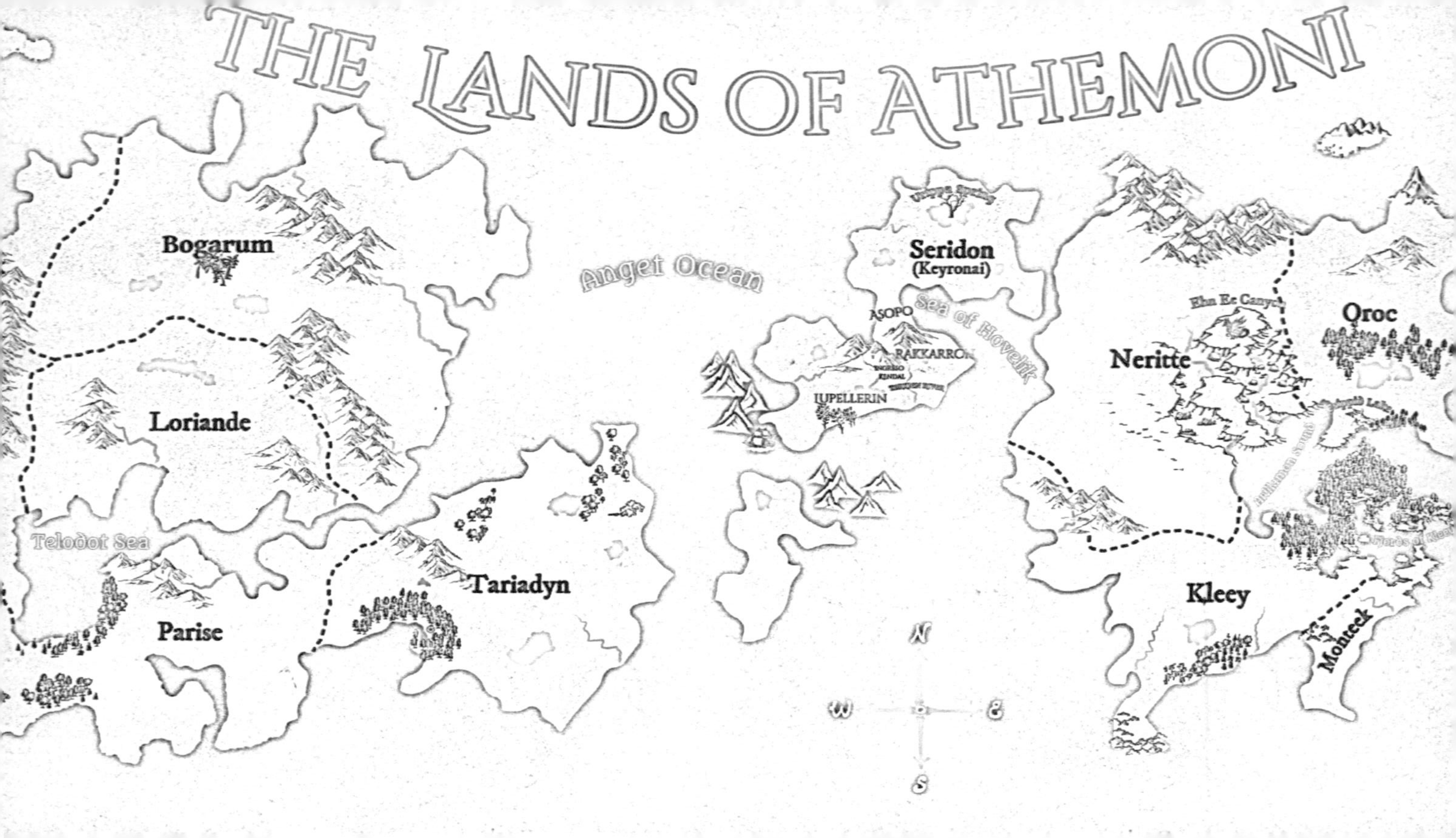

THE LANDS OF ATHEMON
Bogarum
Seridon
(Keyronai)
Anget Ocean
Sea of Hovelik
ASOPO
RAKKARRON
Ehn Et Canyon
Oroc
Neritte
KINDAL
IUPELLERIN
Loriande
Telodot Sea
Tariadyn
Kleey
Parise
Moneek
N
W
E
S

Urippa Spring
Seridon
(Keyronai)
cean
ASOPO
Sea of Hovelik
RAKKARRON
INGRESO
KENDAL
TENNREN RIVER
IUPELLERIN
Neritte

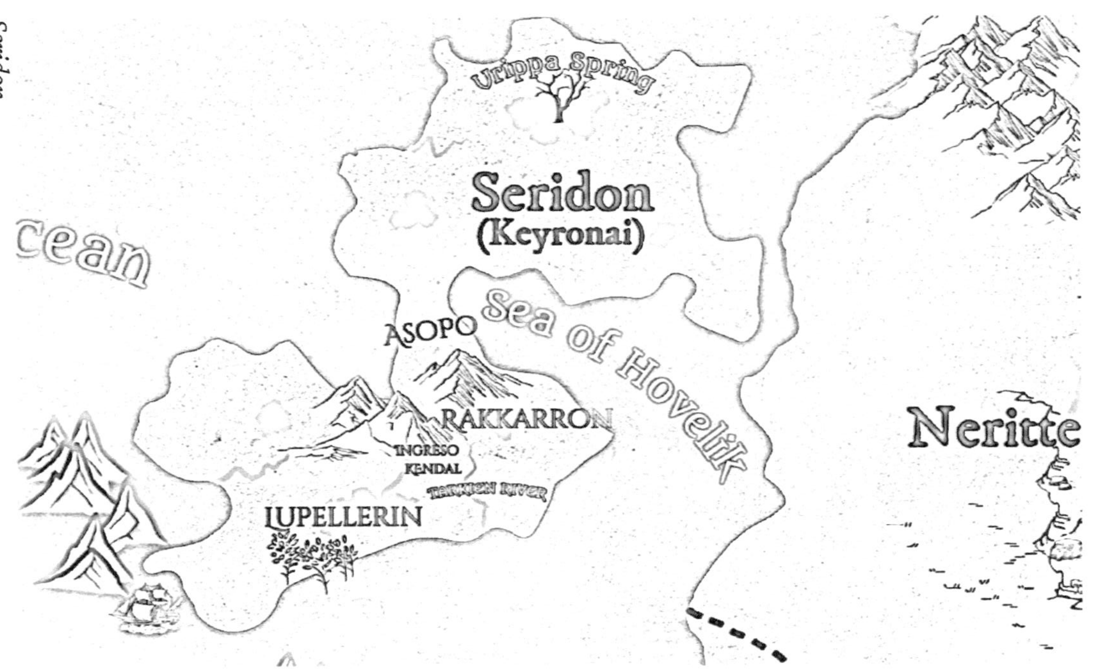

Seridon

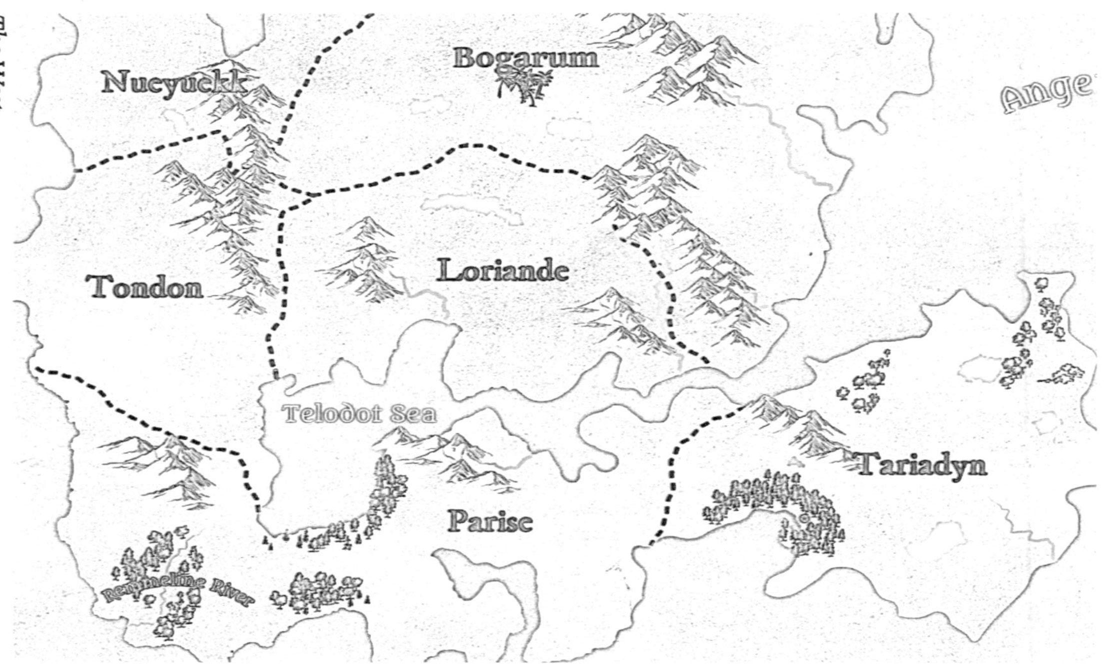

The West
Nucyuckk
Bogarum
Ange
Tondon
Loriande
Telodoi Sea
Tariadyn
Parise
Renimeline River

Sea of Hovelik
AKKARRON
Ehn Ee Canyon
Oroc
Neritte
Sippid Lake
Arlillion Sound
Fjords of Kleey
Kleey

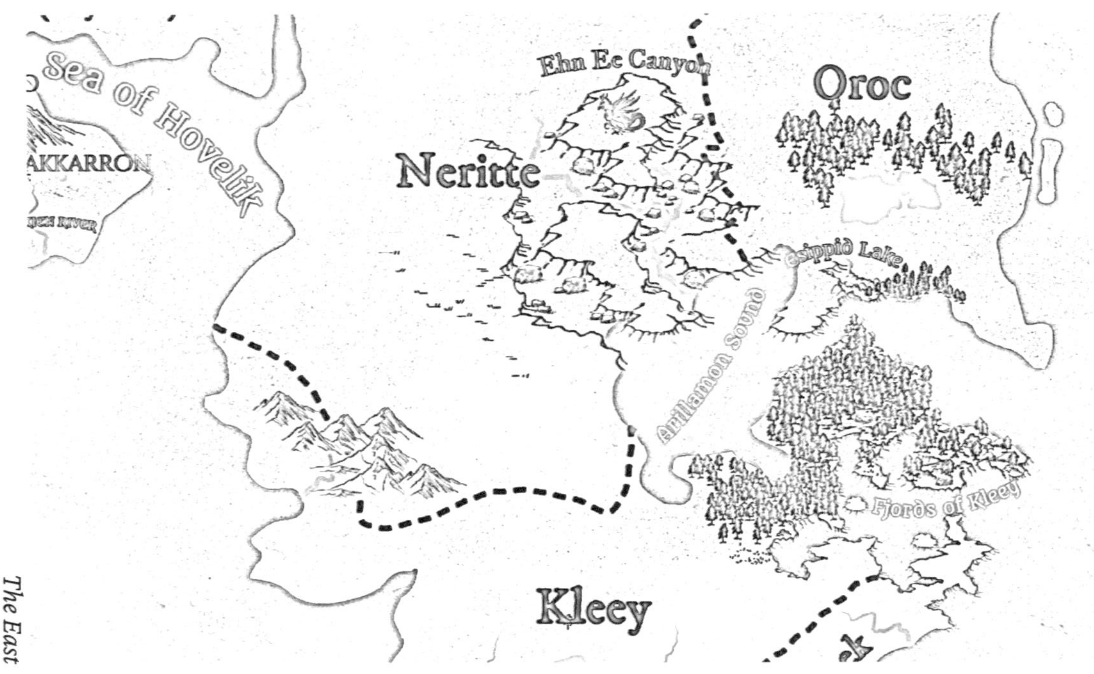

The East

Contents

Chapter One

I Hope This Is Heaven

They were gone. His squad; his brothers.

Aron trudged through the scorching heat as the desert sun beat down relentlessly, claiming any remaining strength from his damaged and bleeding body. Sixteen pounds of body armor, adding to the burden of the tactical gear, was tearing at his endurance. He'd left his rucksack in the brush over four miles back, but he dared not leave behind his M4.

Four miles back… it was a horrific scene Aron wouldn't soon forget. And now he was alone in enemy territory.

He crouched behind some abandoned wreckage to catch his breath as bloody sweat streaked down his dusty, chiseled face. Aron gripped his side where the shrapnel had cut into him, grunting in pain. *I could smell it*, he thought. *I could smell the carnage.* He had not anticipated that. He recalled the warmth of the sweet, pungent odor blended with the dryness of the air and the acrid, sulfuric scent of bomb residue that slithered into his nostrils. He had waited for three hours under the half-blown Humvee, his lifeless brothers surrounding him, before he was certain the enemy had evacuated. *Shit, this wasn't supposed to happen.*

Gunfire.

It was close. And there was more in the distance, half a mile maybe? Aron heard faint commands from the enemy. Although indecipherable, he knew they were close.

He tightened his grip on his bloody right side and stifled a groan. He lowered his head and squeezed his eyes shut as thoughts of home tore through his mind. *Maybe she was right. Maybe he wasn't built for this*, he thought, as a single tear slowly commingled with the sweat trails on his cheek.

He missed Tora, and it was tough not to be home with her during such an important time in their lives. But his leave was coming up soon, and by the time that was used up, this mission would be over and done with, and he'd be stateside. They'll get married, and all will be right with the world. *That'll make her happy for sure. Both of us, happy. Right?* As long as he made it out of here alive.

An explosion reverberated through the desert. *Gotta find cover.*

Aron scanned his surroundings and then pressed himself against the remaining rusted debris from the car bombed auto wreckage. The low concrete buildings about a quarter-mile in the distance appeared deserted. There was no movement; not even a breeze. To the rear of a block of vacant stores or warehouses rested the end of a line of freight cars engulfed in intertwining undergrowth; a clear indicator that they had been out of service for some time.

If he could maneuver his way to those buildings, the cover could buy him the time to evaluate his position. He noted the sun descending in the sky. It couldn't be much past 1600 hours. It would be a few more hours before darkness fell to conceal his presence.

Gunfire, again.

He was sure it was coming from the southwest. If they were headed this way, they'd close in on him, although the latest barrage of gunfire was a bit further out. But he couldn't be sure. *Is there more than one group?* As Aron carefully edged his body toward the front bumper, his throat tightened, and he gripped his rifle. He peered through the scope on his M4—no one. *Where the hell are they?*

Just ahead, about a hundred feet to his right, a twisted, metal guard rail wound its way a fraction of the distance toward the town. Lying low and crawling between it and the elevated rocky terrain would shield him relatively well. From there, camouflaged among the shadows, he could make his way to the gum trees and the stretch of boulders. He had to move.

Ignoring the sharp pain in his side, Aron wiped his brow with his dusty sleeve and low-crawled to his first target. His heart beat in his ears, and he froze. There were no sounds of birds. There was no rustling of branches. A slight, sharp clanging came from a piece of broken metal dangling from the wreckage he had just left. He listened.

And there it was. The muffled sound of a commander barking orders in the distance. *Had they seen him?* He saw no one, but like the gunfire, it came from the southwest, beyond the rocky terrain and further down. He pressed closer to the ground.

Silence.

He crawled forward again. Blood from his deep shrapnel wound soaked through the makeshift bandage he had twisted around his torso. He'd make it. And when he did, he'd have stories to tell his children and grandchildren, just like his grandfather. Just like his dad.

The boulders were straight ahead. Once he reached those last few with the single, small tree, there were about 150 yards of flat, open terrain before he would reach the rear of the nearest building.

A dull thump from behind compelled him to shift his position quickly. *Is that movement behind the first boulder?* He raised his M4.

Gunfire.

This was it. He had to make a run for the nearest building. Again, gripping his side, he bolted. There was a narrow alley behind the building, and he slipped into it, staggering through the debris to the other side. He was sure he'd heard someone following him not far behind. Rifle up, he turned and slowly retraced his path to the back corner.

"Canyon," came the challenge from the back of the building.

Aron lowered his rifle slightly.

"Nebraska," Aron responded, but did not lower the rifle until he saw his comrade's hands and then his face peer around the corner.

"Aron! Oh my God!" he whispered. "What the hell? How are you here?"

"I could ask the same of you! C'mon, Jerry. We need to get inside. We've got to find the other squad." Aron motioned to the front of the building.

The window on that side of the building was about forty feet away. After ensuring there was no one inside, they entered through the heavy side door and made their way to a back storage room.

The building was some type of textile manufacturing plant. Or at least it used to be. While the floor was littered with debris and most of the storage shelves had been torn down and destroyed, there were small remnants of fabric, a spool here and there, and broken equipment too large or cumbersome for looters to pilfer.

Jerry closed the steel door behind them and looked around. Light filtered in from the long, narrow window near the ceiling. File cabinets, storage shelves, and large plastic boxes lined the dull, dirty walls. There was no electricity.

"There's gotta be some needles around here. You got anything? My leg and side need sewing up. Shit, that gash on your head doesn't look good either," said Aron as he eyed the thick, bloody mess in Jerry's brown hair.

"Nah, it's fine. Here." Jerry handed Aron his med kit.

"You're doin' it, man," Aron said, pushing the kit back to him. He rummaged through the boxes on the shelf and quickly found several needles and thread. He watched as Jerry pulled out an ample supply of disinfectant wipes, which he used to clean the supplies before removing Aron's old bandages.

"Aw, yeah, dude. This ain't good," he said. "Too bad I suck at first aid. You may want to bite down on something."

Aron shook his head. "Just do it."

"Doesn't look like there are any pieces in there. I'll try to be quick."

The penetrating sting sliding through his wounds barely amplified the throbbing ache that was already there. So many hours in the desert had numbed his senses. His exhaustion was worse than the pain. Jerry wrapped clean fabric around his torso and leg and tied them in place.

"That should hold ya for a bit. Anything broken?"

"Nah, I don't think so."

Aron pulled out a map to analyze their position.

"The gunfire," he said, "did that come from the same squad that attacked our convoy? Or are there more?"

"From what I could tell, it's a separate one. IEDs too," Jerry said. "Not sure if they saw us. I didn't see you until right before you made a run for it over here. But they're headed this way."

"We're a few miles off-course. We need to veer a little to the east to catch up to Dan's platoon." Aron handed the map over to Jerry. "I say we lay low until nightfall."

"Best-case scenario is they change course or just move right through," Jerry agreed. "Meanwhile, we need to find a safer hideout than this place."

The men packed up what useful supplies they could find and cautiously exited the storage room to survey the small industrial district through the broken front window. The traffic lights were dark. There were several abandoned vehicles, and debris littered the streets. An old, rusted bike with only one wheel hung halfway inside the smashed window of the building across from them. It was desolate.

Through the scope of his M4, he had spotted a small door that almost appeared to be between two buildings, but, in fact, led into a narrow structure of its own.

"There," Aron said. "Nondescript, unremarkable, easily looked past. What do you think?"

"Yup, let's check it out." Jerry unlocked the heavy door, and Aron led the way to the far end of the street where they hoped to hole up and get a few hours of rest while the unforgiving sun continued its assault on the concrete and sand.

The narrow door was unlocked. With no electricity and no windows, they pulled out their flashlights to scan the interior. They moved through a tight hallway and entered a relatively large room. Across the room was a torn sofa that might have been the color of kiwi a decade ago, and the remains of a broken metal desk were pushed up against it. The walls were covered with wallpaper patterned in black, yellow, and dark orange rectangles. Large portions were bubbled and discolored from water damage, likely from the exposed rusted pipes.

At the northeastern end of the room, a black door sat propped open by a folded mat, and Aron and Jerry entered, weapons drawn. The door led to a narrow wooden staircase, and a stair runner muffled the sound of their footsteps as they descended into a smaller room with a distinct, musty odor. Metal folding chairs were stacked alongside the nearest wall to the left. Cracked wooden cabinetry lined the northern wall. They were empty. However, on top of the cabinets were several rolled-up, dusty rugs, which they unfurled and spread across the tiled floor.

It probably wouldn't get better than this. After bolting and securing the doors, Aron lay down to rest while Jerry took first watch.

It was quiet, other than the random distant explosions. *Had it faded? Had they changed course?*

The unimaginable events of the day, not to mention the sweltering sun, had not only taken his strength, it had stolen a piece of his soul. The memory of it all would forever remain vivid in his brain. His stomach turned as he recalled the brutal attack. The explosion. The blood. The commotion as the enemy soldiers littered the fallen bodies with bullets. And then the silence. How had he escaped? How did he get from inside the Humvee to underneath it? *This wasn't supposed to happen.*

Aron turned his head to Jerry perched at the foot of the staircase. He was relieved to have found him after the attack on their convoy. Although entering basic training concurrently, Aron was a few years older and had taken on a mentorship role for Jerry, with whom he had sensed an immediate kinship. They both came from a line of war heroes and had left their disapproving, significant others at home to follow in the footsteps of their fathers.

Aron's lineage was one of strong, confident, and fierce patriots who took great pride in serving their country. He recounted the many times he had listened to the war stories of his father, his uncle, and his grandfather. How at every holiday gathering, with stomachs full, the vets pushed their chairs back and reminisced, while his mother and grandmother cleaned up the dishes and prepared the desserts. It was the only time his mother allowed elbows on the table, as he leaned in, soaking up their memories.

His mother. She would have been so proud of him. Her passing, two months before his enlistment, just about broke him. But it had also given him the focus he needed to finally begin his journey to leave his own legacy.

He remembered the shadow box displayed in the family room filled with the medals earned by his family members, including two Silver Stars awarded to his father and uncle; the Coast Guard Medal, awarded to his cousin who tragically passed at the age of only twenty-eight, two Distinguished Service Medals, one for his father and one for his grandfather; and his grandfather's Medal of Honor took center stage. As a child, he dreamed of his own medal added to the family collection.

Now, here he was, living the dream. But this was not what he had fantasized. These were not the glory stories he had envisioned. Every last one in his squad except Jerry—dead. God dammit, this was not what he wanted. *Maybe she was right.*

Aron noticed Jerry was losing his fight to stay awake. Exhaustion was taking over as his head bobbed and nodded off to the side.

But it wasn't long before they both jolted upright at the sound of movement. They strained to listen as deep throated commands barked inside the wallpapered room above them.

They're here.

Aron hurried to the staircase wall and raised his weapon. The enemy struggled to pry open the door to the narrow stairwell. Aron nodded to Jerry.

There was more shouting, another command, and then an explosion. The sound was deafening, and the upper portion of the staircase shattered as wood and concrete launched into the room. Aron witnessed Jerry's body as it was thrown to the floor from the force of the blast before realizing the sudden sharp pain ripping through his gut. *God, no!*

Blood poured from his body as he collapsed to the floor. In the dark, he heard the enemy scramble to negotiate the collapsed staircase. And then the artillery fire.

Aron stretched to reach his M4.

Instead, his hand grasped a cold, hard stone. Or was it wood? His thumb and finger slid into the smoother recessions of the object, and immediately, his body dropped.

He felt an abrupt shock of iciness. The concrete walls, hard floor, and dusty rugs were gone. There was no more gunfire or explosions. The shouting had ceased.

He felt a cool, misty spray and realized he was lying on wet grass.

Grass?

Aron pushed himself onto his back, still gripping the unidentified object. The agonizing pain near his stomach made him cry out, and he grasped it with his left hand, which only made it feel worse.

"Jerry?" There was no answer.

The distinct scent of the grass peacefully conjugated with the sound of water spattering over rocks. He opened his eyes to soft rays of light filtering through the leaves of tall, stately evergreens. A cool, uplifting breeze tousled his hair.

I must have died, Aron thought. *I hope this is heaven. But since when did heaven hurt so much?*

With each refreshing rush of the wind that breathed through their needles, the trees appeared to speak to each other. Birds were chirping above.

It's OK. I can die here.

The sounds of nature lulled his eyes closed. He heard a bee not far off, busily gathering pollen from the surrounding wildflowers. *Yes, it's OK.*

Plink! Something dropped into the gurgling water.

He heard a rumbling, whooshing sound, and a wave of warm air passed over him. *Did the ground tremble?*

He got the undeniable feeling that someone was hovering over him. *If I open my eyes, they'll kill me for sure.*

A soft, small hand covered his forehead, and another checked for a pulse at his wrist. Aron struggled to open his eyes.

A pretty, delicate face with smooth, tan skin peered down at him.

"Just stay quiet," she said. "I got ya."

Aron felt another warm gust of air with a slightly charred aroma as her face faded and the world went dark.

Chapter Two

WILTING LILACS

"**I** just don't want you to go! Is that so difficult to understand?"

"Tora, we've been through this how many times now?" Aron couldn't hide his exasperation. "It's what I need to do."

"'Need to do.' Really?" She flung her book and blanket onto the couch. "You didn't 'need to do' it when you took the banking job four years ago!"

"That was *your* idea. *You* wanted me to work for your dad. That wasn't what *I* wanted! Your dad pays me a highly disproportionate salary to work a silly, boring job. How is that satisfying? I want more than money. Think of the opportunities the military can open up for us. We could travel, *and* honor our country!" The rain pelted the roof of their mid-size townhouse, where they resided in a friendly, gated community.

"Oh, so now you're so unhappy, and it's all my fault, right? Please," Tora dismissed his response with a wave of her hand. She turned to face him. Her tall, slender frame was tense, and her face beet red against her platinum blonde hair. "Running around with a gun, shooting at people? That's what you want? And what are you going to do when the shit really hits the fan? This is just... not you! You're just not that type of person. What about sky-diving? Wasn't that enough to satisfy your adventurous itch?"

"Not me? Did you seriously just say that? It's in my blood! I'm literally a freaking descendent of Stonewall Jackson! Practically my entire family fought to defend our country! It's what we do!"

"It's what your father did," she snapped.

"Not just my father. Every man in my family, and even a few women. We serve. And you and I have talked about this for as long as I've known you! Good God, Tora, we met when I was in high school ROTC! You even came with me and Seth to the gun range! How many more ways can I tell you? I'm beginning to wonder why you've stayed with me all this time." Frustrated, Aron slammed his fist against the door frame.

"Maybe I thought there'd be a ring someday!"

"Oh, here we go again." Aron rolled his eyes.

"When are you going to grow up, Aron? When? Always the adventures you have to do, first."

"Grow up? Is that what you think about all those who serve our country? You've always known who I was and what I wanted out of life. It's never been a secret. And you've done nothing but try to steer me away from my ambitions at every turn. I have put this off for so long, for you, trying to make you happy, Tora. But it's always what *you* want. For everything. You're never happy unless it's *your* way." Aron paused as Tora grabbed the blanket off the sofa to fold it, or rather, beat it into submission. "You don't think I have what it takes, is that it? Is it?"

"Have what it takes? What are you, a commercial now? And when have I ever told you it was OK with me? When? And by 'growing up', I meant that you'd stop acting like a kid in a theme park and maybe settle down, start a family. And the military would mean a major pay cut! And I don't want to move out of our house!"

Aron rolled his eyes again. "Of course, you don't."

"And what about your mother? If you don't care about me, you should at least care about her," Tora refused to let up.

He turned to face her. "What about my mother? She's always been proud that I've wanted to carry on the family tradition."

"She's sick, Aron!" Tora spat. "You mean to tell me you are so selfish that you would leave her when she is so sick? She's been practically immobile for almost two months now!" The repugnance in her voice softened Aron's resolve.

"OK, first of all, she is not incapacitated. Second, my mother has always been a strong woman, and I will see her through this. She knows, and you know, how much I love our country, and I want the chance to serve. I have put this off long enough, Tora. I had hoped that you would have come around and supported me by now, but I guess you never will." Aron started toward the door. *The same old argument rears its ugly head again*, he thought as he shook his head. "And no, sky-diving wasn't enough. And neither was the deep-sea diving trip. It goes a lot deeper than that, and I'm sorry you can't see that."

"Yeah, it does! You'll never settle down, will you!" Tora's eyes burned with anger as she stormed out of the living room to the upstairs and slammed the door.

"And there's her last word," he muttered to himself.

Aron loved Tora. He truly did, but sometimes he wondered what she really wanted out of a life with him. Did she genuinely love him? Or did she love what she wanted him to be? She had stuck with him through good times and bad. When his father died, right after they graduated high school, she had persuaded him to take a job at her father's bank. And while he was grateful for the opportunity and all that it provided, this was not the path he had envisioned for himself. But she had a point. Why hadn't he taken that next step with her yet?

The gentle roll of distant thunder prompted him to gather his keys, wallet, and gym bag and head out the door. As he drove, his thoughts centered on his mom. He would not leave her in the condition she was in. Her balance was getting worse, and she was practically skin and bones. Vomiting was a daily occurrence now, and the doctors hadn't been able to put a finger on what was causing it. Two weeks ago, her speech began to drag, and she spent most days in bed watching TV.

As he approached the stoplight, he decided it was more important to see his mother. He made a quick change into the left lane to make the turn. The gym would be there tomorrow.

The rain poured down, and for a moment, he felt a pang of sadness in his gut. His mother meant the world to him, and the thought of her—no, he did not want to think about it.

Aron's parents were both exceptional role models for him. They were loving parents who raised him with a sound moral compass. Losing his father when he was eighteen forced him to take on the role of head of the household, but he was more prepared than most at that age. His bank job certainly helped with the bills, but his mother soon pushed him out the door to get him to move on with his life. "I'm fine," she'd reassure him. "I don't need taking care of. You go do you."

Four years later, she couldn't get up and down the stairs without assistance. Aron had hired a live-in nurse to ensure she was getting the necessary care until they figured out what caused these symptoms.

The nurse opened the front door to the small but quaint house when she saw him coming up the walkway, and a warm, comforting aroma greeted him.

"Any changes?" he asked, peeking around the door to the kitchen.

"She's having a good day. She's upstairs," the nurse answered with a smile.

"Thanks, Gina. Smells good in here, by the way." He nodded toward the kitchen.

She laughed. "Are you staying for dinner?"

"No, just a quick visit today."

"Well, I'll pack some up for you then." Gina was a godsend.

Aron heard the TV from down the hall long before he entered his mother's room. She sat propped up in her bed, and she gave him a warm smile when he poked his head in.

"Aron! I'm so glad you're here!"

Gina had repositioned her TV onto a small folding table next to her bed, and her vase of wilting lilacs moved to the dresser. "So close, mom? Really?"

"Well, I just can't seem to focus on the picture too well lately. If I can't see the picture, might as well just have the radio on," she explained.

Aron sighed as he turned the volume down. "Why don't we get you up and walking around a little?"

"Gina took me for a walk earlier, before the rain. I'm fine. Now sit down and stop badgering me." She motioned to the wooden stool in the corner. "So, how's your job?"

"It's fine. You know, fine. Money is good, anyway," he said, brushing off the topic quickly as he moved the stool next to her bed and sat down.

"Mm-hmm. And the girl?" His mother's eyes narrowed.

"*Tora* is fine, and yes, we're still together, so no need to ask," he said sharply.

"Well, it's not that I don't like her, you know. I know you, and I'm just not confident she is the best fit for you. And I think you know it too, and it's not right to string her along. You want different things, Aron."

"Yeah. Well, it's not like we're engaged."

"And why aren't you, Aron?"

"Mom, come on." *I can't win today.* "Just listen, alright? I've been doing a lot of thinking," he began as his eyes met his mother's. He paused, considering whether this was the best time to bring it up. "Mom, you know how I've wanted to join the Army, like dad. And gramps. I feel like I've put it off long enough."

A smile crept across his mother's face. "Do it," she said. "It's about time. Oh, my son, I know this is what you've wanted."

"Yes, but I don't like the idea of being away when you're not well."

"Aron," she paused and cleared her throat. "You would make me so proud, make your father so proud. Follow your heart, son. All I want is for you to be happy, to follow your dreams, and too many... things... have gotten in your way. Please don't let me be one of your reasons for a longer delay."

"Mom, I can*not* leave while you're sick. I won't. So, I decided I will get things started once you show some signs of recovery."

His mother beamed. "I'm so happy for you, Aron. I think this is just what you need. I'll worry, but I'll be so proud. And I'll be back on my feet soon enough." Her arms opened to embrace him. She felt so fragile.

"So. How's Tora handling it? You've told her, right?"

Aron sighed. "You know. Same argument, different day."

"You need to be straight with her, Aron. If she's expecting something different, you find a way to make it work, or you end it. You should be with someone who supports you, someone who wants what you want, and so should she," she said before coughing into her sleeve.

"I've tried, mom. I've given her every opportunity to—"

"Stop. No more excuses. Figure it out. Is it going to work or not? Are you two right for each other? If not, quit wasting her time. Just figure it out. I want you to be happy, son. And she deserves that too. And ask yourself why things have not progressed further for you two. Don't run from the truth."

Why does everyone need to get married to be happy? Aron sighed as she reached out her hand to touch his arm. It felt cold. "Are you warm enough? You need an extra blanket?" He glanced around the room, looking for a warmer blanket, but there wasn't one.

"I'm fine," she insisted before another coughing fit set in. Aron handed her the water glass from her nightstand.

"Quick game of checkers, then?" he asked.

His mother smiled.

Aron arrived home to find Tora settled into her favorite oversized chair, reading her thick book that she'd been working on for over a week. She had pulled her platinum blonde hair into a ponytail, which fell almost midway down her back. She looked very studious with her glasses on. The soft glow of the lamp next to her emphasized her delicate features and now peaceful beauty. She barely looked up when he entered the room.

"Hey, hon'," he tested. "I've got dinner?" Aron held up the two bags that Gina had packed for him.

She returned the bookmark to the page with a sigh and made her way to the kitchen. She was wearing a short, pale pink nightshirt that exposed her long, graceful legs. As she brushed past him, he could smell a cool, enticing fragrance. Aron was slightly aroused but figured that now was probably not the time.

Tora ran her hand over his shoulders before sitting down at the table. *Is she done being angry?*

"You went to your mom's?" she asked quietly, without looking up.

"Mm-hmm. It's been a couple days, and I wanted to check on her." Tora smirked, and it did not go unnoticed.

Aron shook his head. "She's doing pretty well today. Thanks for asking," he snapped.

"Aron," she began with a sigh. "C'mon, let's not fight anymore. I'm glad she's doing well."

Several minutes passed as they ate in silence. He could still hear the soft patter of rain coming down outside.

"Aron, I'm sorry for arguing with you again. I know this is something that you've wanted, but I just... I just want you here, with me. I know it's selfish. I know I should support your dreams. But I can't help it. I just think if you—" Tora paused.

"I'm going to do this, Tora. You need to know that. I do want to make it work, though, with us. We're not the only ones to ever be in this situation. Couples make it work all the time," he said. "I understand how you feel, but I really would like your support."

Tora's gaze swept from his face to the table, then to her empty plate. Her lower lip trembled before attempting a half-smile. "I have something for you," she said as she rose from the table to place a light kiss on his cheek before disappearing into the next room.

Aron cleared the dinner plates from the table and wiped off his hands before following her. She pulled an envelope from her purse and handed it to him. His name was written on the outside of the light blue envelope. As he carefully opened it, Tora sat down on the soft couch and pulled him down to sit beside her.

He read the front of the card out loud. "Coming Soon!" it said in large fancy letters over two tiny footprints. The inside read, "Congratulations!"

Aron's mouth dropped open. A smile inched across his face. "Oh my God! Are you serious?" he asked, not quite believing what he was reading.

Noticeably relieved, Tora smiled and replied, "Yes."

"Wow! Tora! I can't believe it." Aron leaned over to embrace her and kissed her lips. The scent of her perfume aroused him again, and he scooped her up into his arms and brought her upstairs, where their king-size bed awaited them. He was going to be a dad. "We'll find a way to make this work, OK? We can do this."

When was the last time he had felt this good? *I'm going to be a dad!*

With Tora's legs wrapped tightly around him, he kissed her lips. Maybe this was the sign he needed, the nudge he needed, to make everything feel right. Exhausted, he cradled Tora in his arms as he fell into a peaceful sleep.

Aron awoke to the phone ringing. It was 3:30 AM.

"Aron?" It was Gina's voice on the other end. "It's your mother. She's taken a bad turn. You need to come. The ambulance is on the way." He was dressed and out the door in less than a minute.

His mother, fortunately, lived only a few minutes down the road. When he arrived, the paramedics were already there, lifting her onto the stretcher, an oxygen mask strapped over her nose and mouth. "What is it? Is she going to be OK?"

"Sir, can you step over here for a moment?" one paramedic said to Aron and led him to the hallway. "This is your mother?" Aron nodded.

"Sir, your mother is unresponsive. We're transporting her to Nipas Medical. You should probably meet us there."

Those words were like a brick thrown directly into his gut. *What had happened?* He was just here, and she was having a good day.

Gina quietly approached him and touched his arm. "I'm so sorry," she said. "I'll drive you." His mind was a haze of confusion. *She can't go now*, he thought. *I'm not ready for this. Please, not now.*

As his eyes followed the whirling red and white lights of the ambulance, he called Tora, who said she'd meet him there. They parked in the lot near the emergency room entrance, and Gina graciously offered to assist with the admission forms so that he could stay near his mother.

"Which way did they take her? My mom." The check-in assistant gave him the room number, and he nodded to Gina. "112P. Let Tora know when she gets here."

"I will."

Through the large window, he could see his mother. The nurses inserted an IV and attached several other pieces of equipment to her head, arms, and chest as she lay there, perfectly still. The pale skin on her hands and face was thin and blotchy. Aron's heart raced as the doctors worked to stabilize her. When they finally allowed him into her room, he sat down and cupped her cheek in his hand. "C'mon, mom," he whispered. "Please come back to me."

He glanced around, looking for Tora and then buried his face in his mother's cold hand. "C'mon, mom," he cried. His heart ached, as tears rolled down his face onto her hand and soaked the bed sheet. She would never know her grandchild. "I need you, mom. Please, not now."

For five hours, she lay there in silence. For five hours, Aron held and rubbed her hand. For five hours, the door swung open and shut as doctors and nurses rushed in and out to check on her. And after five hours, his mother took her last breath.

Chapter Three

A Neclu Pelri

Aron's muscles ached. *Is it morning?* Sluggishly, he opened his eyes. It was still dark. In fact, there was no light at all. He felt cramped and constricted. *Wait, where am I?*

He lifted his arm to turn over, but it immediately hit a solid object above him. Attempting to reposition again, he realized he was completely boxed in. The earthy scent of old wood enveloped him. Ice cold, his blood rushed through his body, starting from his face and moving all the way down through to his feet. *Was I captured?*

He slowed his breath to listen. Muffled footsteps and then the sharp clanging of metal pots. And water running?

Wait.

There was gunfire, he remembered. *Shouting, an explosion, shrapnel, more shooting.* It was coming back to him now. *I fell into... cool grass? Heaven...and an attractive girl.*

Then what?

"Alright, I'm done. So, you're not going then?" came a muffled voice.

"No, I have to take care of some things around here first, but maybe next week I'll come with you."

"You really don't do much with us anymore. Are you seeing someone again?"

Aron felt a bump against the box.

"No!"

"You're better off taking a bit more time for yourself. Trennel really did a number on you. Glad he's out of the picture and didn't last long. None of us liked him."

"He was company."

"Four months of 'company' is not worth what you went through."

"Well, he's gone now and has been for a while. And you should be too. I've got things to do, but tell everyone I said hi. I'll catch up with you tomorrow, maybe."

"Yeah, sure you will. See ya later."

A loud thud came from outside the wooden casket that encased him. Then a slight creaking sound. The lid of the box opened up, and bright light flooded in. Someone peered down at him and then slammed the lid shut.

"Hey!" Aron banged on the lid from the inside. "Hey! What's going on? Open it up!"

"Not yet," the girl said.

"Not yet? Open the damn lid! What are you doing?"

"Just promise me you won't hurt me." Her quiet voice was barely discernible.

"Why the hell would I hurt you? Just open the damn box!"

Aron heard the click of the latch opening, and he rammed his fist against the lid, slamming it into the wall. The girl jumped back, her eyes wide. She held a kitchen knife in her hand, poised to defend herself.

"So… you're finally awake," she stated, her arms shaking. "I just need your help. Don't hurt me. Here, just unlatch the sidewall there, and you'll be able to get out. Just don't be angry, OK? I don't want to stab you, but I will."

The earthy, wooden smell dissipated and was replaced by wafts of lilac. And it felt… familiar. Aron squinted as he unlatched the wooden side of the box, which was sitting on a low table, and climbed out. Simple and almost bare, the small, tidy room was inviting with wood floors, woven area rugs, and a rudimentary sofa and chairs with cozy cushions. A large window looked down onto a lake flanked by high cliffs, a thick forest, and mountains in the distance. An orange and pink sunset reflected off the lake's surface. On the other side of the tiny house, the kitchen window revealed only trees. It all had a bit of a cabin feel, and yet, different.

"What are you doing? Put that knife down," Aron demanded. "Who are you? And why was I in that box?"

"Just tell me what you did to Seriah!"

"Who? What are you talking about?"

"I know you all took him! Just get him back to us, and I'll let you go," the girl demanded.

"Get who back? From where?"

"Seriah!"

"I don't know what you're talking about! Who's Seriah?"

The girl backed away, still brandishing the knife in front of her.

"Don't lie. You all know what they do with us. Where is he?"

"I'm sorry. Maybe you have me confused with someone else. Why are you holding that knife? Put it down."

"Why would I trust you not to hurt me?"

"Why would you lock me in a box in your house?"

"I was helping you heal," the girl said, lowering her knife just a little.

"Heal?"

Aron stopped short. *Why am I not in pain? The explosion. I was just blown up.* He grabbed at his leg, his abdomen, searching for his wounds. *Where was the blood, the pain?* Without thinking, he raised his shirt. He saw a long, jagged crease along the lower part of his stomach below and to the left of his navel and another shorter one on his right side. Small pink dots lined either side of each line, the last remaining evidence of stitches removed.

"Exactly how long have I been sleeping?" he asked, almost afraid to hear the answer.

"I don't know. You'd lost a lot of blood. And if I was going to get anything out of you, I needed you alive. Took a lot longer to heal than I thought it would. Two and a half months, maybe?"

"Two and a half months? I've been out for two and a half months? What kind of hospital would release me to someone I don't know, let you bring me here, and stick me in a box while still in a coma?"

"Hospital? What do you mean by 'hospital'? I found you all the way out by the Remmeline River, remember? I brought you back here. I took care of you, and actually, the long rest was good for you. You were dying! Would you rather I'd left you to die? And you weren't always in the storage crate. I only put you there when I needed to. You are *a load* to haul in and out of that thing! But of course, I had to hide you. I can't have anyone know that I have you here. Everyone would panic!"

"Why? Who is everyone?"

"You can't be serious. What do you mean, 'why?'"

Aron shook his head, desperately straining to clear the haze. He recounted in his mind everything that he could remember. *Blistering dry heat, the attack on the convoy, Jerry, the explosion, falling, then the girl's face.* He strode to the window.

"What about Jerry? Did anyone find him? Has anyone notified my unit? Obviously, I'm not in the desert anymore. What country did they transfer me to? What about Tora? Does she know? Has anyone contacted her? My God, I need to call Tora!"

"I don't know who or where those people are. You were the only one I found. I didn't take anyone else. And I don't know where you came from or how you ended up by the river. I need you to tell me where Seriah is."

"I need you to tell me where I am!"

The two stared at each other, the girl's extended arm shaking with the knife. *This girl has no idea what she's doing. She's scared.*

"Look," said Aron, "please put the knife down. I'm not going to hurt you. Can I at least use your bathroom?"

The tiny brown-haired girl moved sideways two steps, and with her knife, motioned to the door in the hall behind him.

The door to one other small bedroom was next to the bathroom. They were the only ones in this small apartment. The shower looked like one of those outdoor showers, completely wooden. The toilet wasn't much more than a hole in a bench with a wooden cover, but pulling the chain overhead confirmed there was plumbing. Expecting a copious scruff, the mirror revealed a fatigued but clean-shaven face. His tousled hair was recently washed. *Did she give me a shave?* He opened the small cabinet, searching for the blade. Coming up empty, he turned on the cold water and splashed his face. Toweling off and blinking in the mirror, he saw he was dressed in a white cotton shirt and his ACU trousers; torn, but clean. *This is all so strange. Why won't she tell me where the hell I am?*

Aron returned to the living room and the girl, who had finally set down her knife on the roughhewn side table. Her unusually slight frame couldn't be five feet tall. She wore simple but scant clothes made of brown leather and some translucent gauzy fabric. Her long, dark, wavy hair was streaked with a lighter, reddish-brown. On her right side, her hair was pulled back in three narrow braids, while the left side draped freely around her shoulders and partially intertwined with a pendant hanging around her neck. It was an old and simple pendant with a unique symbol engraved on one side.

"If you sit over there on that chair, we can talk this out. You want some soup? I can get you some soup." She stepped back tentatively. Her eyes were a captivating shade of grey, and he could smell that familiar floral fragrance emanating from her. "I'm Iyla, by the way. You good now? I'm getting the feeling you're not remembering so well. Did you hit your head?"

No way this girl's got any military training. She's just some random civilian. Definitely not Iraqi. "Uh, yeah, thanks. And no. Or, I don't know. I'm Aron Coverstone," he replied, politely extending his right hand, into which she placed a glass of water.

Iyla wrinkled her nose as she hesitated before speaking. "Oh yeah, 'Coverstone, Aron.' I saw that on the metal tag you had around your neck. It's in a drawer, along with a few other things of yours." She reached for the knife and sat down in the chair across from him.

"You have my stuff? Where's my rifle? Look, where is this place? And why was I locked up in that box?"

She smirked. "It's a storage crate. And I told you, I needed to get you well, so I can get you to get Seriah back. You can't help me when you're dead. And I know I'm taking a colossal risk here, but I need to get my friend back."

"And like I said, I don't know your friend. And that still doesn't explain why you put me in a box."

"Look, you would've died. And I don't know what rifle you're talking about. And I know that you're a man. Hence, the 'box.'"

What? Aron raised an eyebrow. "Again, doesn't explain much. Is there a jealous boyfriend you were hiding me from?"

Iyla tilted her head with a confused smile.

"And no rifle," he added with a frown.

She hesitated and then shook her head.

"Look, Ella–"

"Iyla."

"Iyla, you seem like a... nice person, and thanks for... rescuing me. I think. I'm sorry I don't know about your friend, but where the hell am I? I can't stay here. I need to contact my platoon."

Iyla looked at him quizzically. "Platoon?"

"Look, I need to report back before I get thrown in the brig for going AWOL."

"I don't know what that means. But as for where you are now, you're in Tariadyn."

"But what country?"

"TARIADYN."

"That's the country?"

"Yes."

"Where the hell is that?" Aron exclaimed.

"What do you mean?"

Aron stood and paced the small room. Where was his rifle? His brow furrowed as his hands raked through his thick, brown hair.

"Ok, look," he said. "I was just fighting a war in the desert. There was an explosion, and the next thing I know, I'm here. I've never heard of a country called Tari, Tari—"

"-AY-din." Iyla finished.

"Tari-AY-din. My fiancée has no idea where I am. You say it's been two and a half months, which means I've quite possibly become a father by now. I need a map. Do you have a phone?"

Aron sensed that Iyla was almost as confused as he was, and he could see the apprehension in her grey eyes. She rose from the chair and rummaged through a drawer in a wooden cabinet near the kitchen. Everything was made of wood. Aron looked around for the door.

Should I know where Tariadyn is?

"Tariadyn is east of the Telodot Sea and Parise," she stated hesitantly. "No map, sorry."

"Paris?" Aron's face lit up.

"Puh-REES. Where I found you by the river."

Aron collapsed back into the chair, leaning forward with both hands to his head. *There must've been some memory loss,* he thought. *Head trauma, that's got to be it. I'm hallucinating.*

"Where are you from, then?" she asked.

"I'm an American, US Army. But I was stationed in Iraq before arriving here." Aron noticed her puzzled expression.

"Oroc?"

"Iraq."

"Iraq…" she contemplated. "But you're a man, no?"

"What? Uh, yeah. Is that not obvious?"

"Well, you're not a Sapin. But you said you were an American. Is that a specific type of man?"

Aron stared at her for a full minute as Iyla nervously stared back. It was only then that he saw, behind the wisps of brown hair framing her face, that her ears had an ever so slight point at the tip. Her petite frame, the way she seemed to glide when she walked; slowly, he was beginning to unravel the strangeness of his situation. *Shit. No, that's not possible.*

Is it? Aron ran his hands through his hair and again looked around the small room. *No, can't be. No way.*

He stood and walked over to her. He looked closely into her eyes. Iyla stepped back, caught her breath, and glanced at the knife she had placed on the counter. The sweet floral fragrance radiated from her.

"You don't know what an American is?"

Iyla shook her head.

"I'm from the United States," he offered, probing her eyes for her reaction. She offered no sign of recognition. "Earth?"

Iyla's lips parted briefly, and she took another small step back. "I've heard of Earth," she said softly.

"Oh my God," Aron whispered under his breath. *This can't be real. Definitely hallucinating.*

"Are you saying you traveled here from Earth?" she asked.

Aron blindly retreated to the chair and sank into it. *This cannot be happening. This only happens in books and movies. It has to be a dream.* And yet, it wasn't. His head was spinning.

"I'm not sure that 'travel' is the right word, but I was there, and now I'm here," he said. "Shit, what is going on?"

"Ugh, so you really don't know where Seriah is..." Iyla sighed and her body wilted. "Good moons! All this time wasted... ugh!" She drifted back to the counter and the knife. "But traveling isn't that outlandish, really. You've got a Sapin working for you, then?"

"A what? We are talking about teleporting between worlds, right? This happens all the time?"

"I wouldn't say *all* the time, but of course it happens. The Neclu Sapins, obviously. They usually come back with intelligence, ideas and things. Oh, crakes! They did bring you here, didn't they?"

"Neclu Sapins?" Aron asked.

"Yeah."

Aron paused for a moment. "I don't know what that is," he began. Again, Aron shook his head, trying to make sense of everything that was unraveling in front of him. He took a deep breath. "So, I have to ask, and don't take this the wrong way. You aren't... human, then. Are you?"

Iyla laughed nervously and sat down. "No." She watched him take it in.

Aron eyed the knife that she had reclaimed. "You don't need that. I won't hurt you. I really wish you'd put it down." Iyla hesitated and then set the knife down beside her.

Aron tried again. "So... you're an... elf?" he guessed, not believing he was even asking that question.

"No. Well, partially. I'm a Neclu Pelri," she stated.

"A Neclu Pelri," Aron repeated. "Neclu?"

"Yeah, 'Neclu', but we're not like the Sapins. We don't travel to other worlds. That's just them."

"How would you describe a Neclu Pelri, then?" he prodded.

"Well, we stay away from the humans, for one," she answered.

Aron chuckled. "Well, obviously *you* don't. So why is that?"

"Long story," she answered. "Humans. You know you're not a good sort. Dangerous to all kinds, but primarily to the Pelri."

"What? So, you have humans that live here? Did they come from Earth? Do they speak my language too? Is that how you learned it?"

"Not exactly right here. Most of the humans live in Seridon, which is across the Anget Ocean, but there are pockets of them in all the other countries as well. I thought *you* were from Seridon. I would assume at least some of their ancestors could be originally from your world, since this is how they speak. And no, they didn't teach me, at least, not intentionally. But I've learned a few languages. We Pelri have our own native language, too. Just seems kind of ancient and pointless to use it."

"Shit, they have to be from my world. How did they get here? And not all humans are bad, you know. We have plenty of great human beings where I'm from. Why do you think we're so terrible?"

"Of course, humans are terrible. The Seridon humans took my friend. And you, yourself, just said you were fighting in a war. Who were you fighting? Elves?"

"No, other humans! We only have humans and animals on Earth."

"Crakes! You're even terrible to your own kind!"

"It's not like that, really." *Or is it?* "What other species do you have here?"

"Just the usual ones, elves, dwarves, dryads and such."

"Oh, sure, the usual ones," Aron mocked. *This is insane.* "Well, apparently humans, being so evil, didn't stop you from saving my life and keeping me in your home for two and a half months. Just so you could find your friend."

"You were weak and dying. You were an easy capture. And besides, it wasn't just me. I had William with me. He saw you first. But apparently it was all for nothing since you're not even from here."

"William. He must be the boyfriend you were hiding me from." Aron rolled his eyes.

Iyla grimaced. "My... friend. He's the only one who knows about you. I hid you in the storage crate any time I left home or if someone came to visit. You just missed my friend, Belira. Good thing you weren't making any noise in there. If she knew you were here, everyone would know."

"And that would be bad because...?"

"No one knows I've been doing this."

"Shit, so you kidnap humans on the regular?"

"You're the first one I've actually succeeded at capturing. The first one I've talked to."

"Well, I'm sorry I can't help you. I've got to get back to my family, somehow."

There was a cool breeze blowing through the open windows, and he could hear the comforting sound of leaves rustling and the birds chirping. Wherever he was, it certainly was a beautiful place. His thoughts turned to Tora and what she must be going through, taking care of their new child, not knowing where he was. He had to get home to her and their baby.

He felt a small hand pat his leg. "I'm sure this is really difficult to take in," Iyla comforted. "I'm sorry you were taken from your family and your war. My place is small, but I can offer you shelter until we can figure out how to get you back. If I help you with that, do you think you could help me find my friend? You could scope out Seridon. You'd blend in, no problem."

"Get me back? Can you do that?"

"Well, I, personally, don't know how."

Aron sighed. "What about a Sapin-friend?"

"Uh, no. That won't happen. No Sapins. I really don't know what to do yet. Let me think on it," Iyla said.

"Whatever it takes to get me back home. My fiancée and my baby..."

"I know, I get it. Here, let me show you where I put your things. We can spread some blankets and make a bed for you, or you can even sleep on the sofa. Oh, and the storage crate is also available," she said with a grin. "But please don't go outside. We live here because it's a place where humans won't usually go." Motioning toward the window, Iyla continued, "The lagoon provides some protection for us. But if another Pelri sees you, we're probably going to have to move again, and I like it here. Just don't want to take any chances."

Aron followed her into her bedroom as she rifled through a drawer in her closet.

"Half elf, half pixie, by the way. And a bit of dryad in there too. That's me—a Neclu Pelri." Iyla volunteered. "And we're down to only 211 of us now. Here's your stuff." She pulled out a wooden container the size of a large shoebox and presented it to him. The outside of the box was colorful and imprinted with elaborate designs of trees, flowers, and fire. It reminded Aron of his uncle's tattoos.

Aron smiled and took the box from her. "Listen, Iyla. I don't think I thanked you properly for saving my life. I know your motives may have been ulterior, but I *am* grateful. I'm just... I need to get home."

"Think nothing of it. You'll repay me by helping me find Seriah and not killing me. We'll figure it out," she winked.

"Kill you? I just don't understand why anyone would do that." He sat down on the bed and placed the box beside him.

Iyla looked down at her feet, twirling her pendant between her fingers. "It's why there are only so few of us left, and it's why we are constantly on the move. If the humans find us, they would kill us or kidnap us, like my friend, and...worse."

"Worse?" Aron asked.

Iyla nodded and turned away. Aron thought he saw a teardrop in the corner of her eye.

"They experiment on our bodies. The humans want our abilities, and they think they can figure out a way to copy them in themselves by studying our genetic makeup, whether alive or dead and even—" Iyla paused and wiped at the tear that had escaped down her cheek. "They try to reproduce with us," Iyla explained. "So, we hide. And when we're found, we move. We always stay together.

"We're not the only ones," she added. "They do this to the others of our world too, just not as much."

The conversation intrigued Aron, and he was about to ask about these 'abilities' but figured that may be pushing it at this point. "With humans like that around, why would you take this kind of risk? With me, I mean. Why would you put yourself in this kind of potential danger?"

"They've taken too much. They've taken too many. They've got Seriah, and others. I've got to find a way to make it stop."

"Have they ever captured you?"

"No," she answered quietly. "Not me."

A heavy silence filled the room as Iyla wiped a tear and turned away from Aron. *What kind of horrible place is this, where humans prey on these seemingly innocent Neclu Pelries? This girl is brave and clearly a loyal friend.*

Aron had almost forgotten about the box of his belongings that Iyla had handed him. He opened it and found his boots, his dog tags, a knife, and a supply of disinfectant wipes.

"The rest of your clothes were torn and stained with so much blood, so I threw them out. Burned them, actually," Iyla said as he put the knife in his pocket and pulled his boots out of the box. "We'll have to get you some new socks." Aron chuckled at her mention of socks.

He reached into his right boot and pulled out something that was not familiar to him. "Here," he said, handing it to Iyla. "I think this is yours." It was a curious wooden object in the shape of a letter Y with a beautiful, deep red ruby embedded in the center. No, it was not embedded, nor was it merged or fused to the wood. The stone and the wood were somehow one solitary element.

"No," she said. "That isn't mine. You were gripping that in your hand when I found you. In fact, even after you passed out, I had to force your fingers apart to get it out of your hand."

Aron clenched it in his hand again, and it was only then that he recognized it. This was what he felt when he reached for his rifle on the dusty floor of the concrete room at the bottom of the narrow staircase amidst the thunderous explosion and shower of bullets. This was what he felt in his hand just before the drop into the cool grass—into this new world.

"This was it," he said. "This is what brought me here. I remember."

"Do you think?" Iyla asked, coming closer and taking the object from Aron to examine it. "I didn't pay much attention to it before when I was trying to keep you out of sight. But it's beautiful. Looks like Acacia wood. Wait, no… I don't think it is. It's really smooth, though."

"It has to be it," Aron exclaimed. "I reached for my rifle in the dark and grabbed this instead. Next thing I know, I'm lying beside the river."

"Well, there you go. We have a starting point." Iyla stared at the beautiful piece and turned it over in her hands. She tapped it against her palm a few times. "You know what? I have a friend who we can ask about this. He's been around for eons and knows everything about everything. I'm sure he'd have an idea."

"As long as he's not going to kill me. Why don't we go now? Or why don't you call him?" Aron asked, then realized he hadn't yet seen anything resembling a phone.

"No, he won't kill you, but he's not a Pelri. He's a regular elf. They don't like the humans either, but I've known him since I was a baby. He'll trust me. But he's pretty far away from here. We can leave in the morning if you like."

"Why can't we leave now?" Aron asked.

Iyla grinned. "Come on," she said. "Let's go down and get some stuff ready. We'll need William to take us there. And he won't be able to get here before morning. And he'll be nice to you, too."

Aron put his belongings back in the box and left them on the bed as they moved to the living room. He was surprised at the excitement he was beginning to feel. *Tora is never going to believe this!*

Iyla opened the door at the opposite end of the room and stepped outside. She scanned the surroundings thoroughly and motioned for Aron to follow.

He stepped out onto the porch and spotted the long, narrow staircase below him. Ivy was heavily entwined between the wooden rails, and the entire structure swayed as Iyla descended. The air was fresh and clean, and he inhaled deeply. He could hear the crickets, but the birds were now silent, aside from an owl in the distance. The lanterns surrounding the house brightened his path, and after taking several steps down, he looked back to where he began his descent.

"Uh, Iyla?"

"Yes," she answered.

"You live in a treehouse."

"Yes," she said again.

But this was no regular treehouse. The long, thick tree branches naturally curved to form the shape of the house. Each twig, each leaf, bent and merged to form the solid walls, floor, and roof. The house was completely camouflaged in the forest.

"How?" he asked himself quietly.

"How what?"

"I've just never seen anything like this. Who built your house?" Aron had constructed a birdhouse or two, but his father was a much better carpenter. Even he would have been stunned by this treehouse.

Iyla thought for a moment. "I guess technically, the trees built it."

Aron looked confused. "The trees? What do you mean?"

"Well, I told them what I needed, and they grew and bent themselves that way."

Aron was speechless. "You 'told' them?"

"Yeah," she said with a smile. "That's what Pelri do. We communicate with the forest. We learn everything from them. They're our friends. And flowers, bushes too, all the botanicals. We're very fortunate to still have a strong alliance with the trees after many years."

"This is incredible." Aron stood in amazement, surveying every inch of the beautiful treehouse.

"C'mon over here," Iyla urged. "We need to collect food for the trip. But let's be quick." She squatted down underneath the treehouse, pushing aside some large leaves, revealing some smaller, darker leaves and a cluster of round, dark blue fruit about the size of apples.

"What are they?" Aron asked.

"Blue tarthberries. Kinda like blueberries, just bigger and firmer. Do you know what blueberries are?"

"Yeah. Cool."

"I invented them," Iyla asserted.

"Seriously?"

"No, dummy, just pick them and put them in this bag." Aron chuckled at her teasing. "And don't pull the red ones," Iyla instructed. "Those aren't ripe yet, and if you eat them, you'll be sick for a week. They don't seem to bother William, but I'd rather not chance it. I'll signal for him to meet us here in the morning."

As she stood up, a gust of wind blew through the trees. The taller trees bent over near the top, and the ivy-covered staircase gently swayed.

"Iyla?" came a voice calling from a distance. "Iyla!"

She turned to Aron and motioned for him to get down. "Hide," she whispered, before running to meet her friend. Aron ducked behind the largest tree that held up her house—or rather, formed her house.

"I just passed Belira, and she said you weren't going tonight." This new Pelri had long black hair down to her waist. She was slightly smaller than Iyla and wearing similar clothes.

"Nope, I've got some stuff to do."

"Like what? I can't believe you're going to miss this dinner. Everyone will be there. And you haven't done much of anything with us for a couple months now. It's important. And we miss you."

"Aww, I know. I've just been preoccupied with a few things. I'll come to the next one, I promise." Iyla wrapped her arm around her friend's shoulders and escorted her in the opposite direction.

"The next one? C'mon, tonight's a big deal."

"The next one, I promise. Tell everyone I said hello."

"Fine." The Pelri sighed and headed back from where she came.

Iyla made her way back to her treehouse and pulled Aron out of hiding. "It's clear. Come on out."

"So, what are you missing tonight?" Aron asked.

"It's a dinner celebration."

"I hope you're not missing it on my account. You should go."

"Oh, my moons, not you too! Don't even worry about it."

"What's everyone celebrating?" Aron was curious.

"The birth of a new Pelri. Doesn't happen that often anymore. My friends, Neve and Sorett, they had a girl two weeks ago. I got to see her last week, and I held her."

Aron felt a pang in his stomach. He couldn't help but wonder if he was a new dad to a boy or a girl. Maybe Tora was late. Maybe he hadn't missed the birth. He had promised her he'd be back in time. Aron couldn't imagine what Tora was going through right now, not knowing where he was. He hoped Iyla's old elf friend would have some answers so that he could get back soon.

"You're oddly nice for a human."

"I told you, we're not all bad."

Moments later, Iyla stood quietly, listening, and Aron heard what sounded like soft music through the rustling of the leaves. Was the music coming from the trees or from Iyla? Or both? The wind blew again, and the trees swayed and shook.

Iyla's hands were now on her hips; her expression was abruptly serious. "Get upstairs!" she yelled to Aron. "Quick!"

Aron pulled his knife from his pocket. "What's going on?"

"Just go!"

The two of them hurried up the ivy staircase to the treehouse, the bag of tarthberries slung over Iyla's shoulder. "Go grab your box of stuff and hold on to it!" Iyla ordered as she ran to the kitchen to rummage through a cabinet.

What was going on? Back in the living room with his box under his arm, Iyla ran to him and grabbed his hand.

"We have to move," she stated.

"Why? Where are we going?" he asked.

"I don't know. Close your eyes!"

"IYLA! No! Tell me what's going on!"

"I will! There's no time! Close your eyes! It's going to feel like you're in water, but you're not. Just breathe. Do not let go of my hand."

"What?"

Before closing his eyes, he saw Iyla lifting a small object in front of her with her other hand. It was a pearly white, teardrop-shaped stone about the size of a golf ball. The glowing stone spouted a white flame that danced upward from the top. They stood in the middle of the living room for several minutes as the wind blew outside, and the gentle music grew louder and then faded away completely.

Chapter Four

WILLIAM

Aron was drowning, rolling in a sea of warm water. He felt Iyla's hand holding tight to his as he floundered, battling to find the surface. A quiet but clear voice cut through the undulating warmth. "Breathe. It's not water. Just breathe."

I can't! He reached for her with his other hand. *Which way is up?*

"Aron. Just breathe."

He cautiously took a breath. He did it. He could breathe. The rolling and struggling stopped, although the warmth of the non-water still surrounded him. He felt weightless, and his eyelids could not block out the fiery brightness all around him.

Two minutes passed, and he took several deeper breaths before realizing that the warmth had given way to an icy chill. With a thud, he collapsed onto the rocky terrain. It was dark outside now, except for the soft light of the stars and the moon—correction: the *three* moons. Two larger moons, both at least twice the size of Earth's moon, and one smaller one, all hung low in the sky. He could hear echoes of crashing water far below him and realized he was close to the edge of a high cliff. He felt nauseous, and he was no longer holding Iyla's hand. And he had dropped his tattooed box.

"Aron!" Iyla whispered as loudly as she dared.

"I'm here, by the cliff," he answered. "What the hell was that? Where are we?"

"Hurry, get behind that rock. I'm not sure where the others are."

"What others?" Aron reached for his knife. *Dammit! Knife is gone too.* He looked behind him and saw a massive boulder about two stories high. "Where are we now?"

"Just do it! Get down!"

He moved between several other rocks to get to the other side of the boulder. He didn't hear any other movement.

Iyla surveyed the new environment stealthily and then headed back towards him. *What 'others' was she talking about?* Aron's military training kicked in as he gauged the area for potential threats. A thick forest flourished beyond the grove of mammoth rocks, and the fresh pine aroma eased his nausea. Over his shoulder, the sea reflected the glow of the moons far down below the steep, rocky cliffs.

"OK, nobody else here," Iyla announced when she reached Aron. "Let's go."

"Are you seriously not going to explain to me what the hell just happened? Where is this, Norway? Are we back on Earth?"

"I told you, we had to move. A human must have spotted one of us, one of the Pelri, so we had to move. You didn't want me to leave you behind, did you?" Iyla explained. "I'm pretty sure we're in Kleey now."

"Are you saying we just teleported? You told me Pelries don't do that!"

"Pel-ree. No 's,'" Iyla corrected. "And no, I said we don't teleport to *other worlds*. We can do it here in our own world, but only as a group. Not on our own. Once all 211 of us connect, using our pearl drops, we move to a new location. The rest are out here somewhere, but I don't want them to see you, so we need to get moving and ask the trees to build another house. Our stuff will be inside."

"OK, yeah, sure. 'Ask the trees...'" Aron sighed, disappointed that this was not Norway.

Once they were about fifty yards into the forest, Iyla stopped. With her feet planted shoulder-width apart, she gazed upward. Again, Aron heard the faint, gentle music and rustling leaves. His adrenaline spiked as he searched for movement in the dark. He then watched, fascinated, as each branch of the trees in front of them grew and curved to form another beautiful house similar to the one they had just left behind. The trees and the Pelri communicated through music!

The surrounding trees retreated to form a wide clearing. Iyla pointed into the forest just past where the trees were building her new home. "Aron, we need more food. There's apples and strawberries here. Do you know what those are? Can you gather some more in a bag while I finish this?"

"Do I know what those are? The real question is, how is it that this whole new alien world also has apples and strawberries?"

Gathering fruit... are you kidding me? Aron watched as the trees slowly morphed until finally Iyla determined the house was ready to enter. And when they did, all of her belongings were neatly arranged inside as if nothing had happened. His tattooed shoebox, however, was strewn across the living room floor, with most of the contents, including his knife, scattered about the room.

While he picked up his things, Iyla unloaded the fruit they had harvested earlier into the cooler. "Does this happen a lot?" Aron asked. "This, 'moving'? And how the hell are you making that sound?"

"I'm not sure what 'a lot' means to you, but usually every couple of months or so. Although I think we made it almost half a year this last time, which was nice. What sound?"

"That music when you communicate with the trees."

"It's not just me. It's the trees too. And I don't know. We're connected. It just sounds like that when we are talking together." Iyla drifted over to the window.

"And how did our stuff get here? It's like we are in the same treehouse, but... somewhere else."

"Yeah, I'm sure this is Kleey. Those are the Fjords of Kleey out there," Iyla rationalized as she looked toward the cliffs. "It's a good spot for us. As for our stuff... hmm," Iyla paused as she contemplated Aron's question. "I guess it's a joint effort between our pearl drops, which know what things belong to us, and the trees, who communicate through each other where those things should go. Pretty sure it works that way. Haven't really thought about that much since it always just kind of happened. Looks like the trees didn't know what to do with your box of things."

"This is just unbelievable. Man, I wish I could do this stuff."

Iyla's eyes narrowed. "Yeah, I'm sure that's how it started with the Seridon humans."

"Hey now! I'm not them. I could never—"

"Just kiddin' with ya', settle down," she interrupted with a smile. "C'mon, it's late. We need to rest up for tomorrow."

"Are we still going to get to the old elf tomorrow? How far away is it now that we're here?" Aron asked, attempting to get his bearings. "I've really got to get home, Iyla. And how do you even know this Kleey-place is safe? Have you been here before? Why don't you have a map?"

"We're actually closer to my friend, now that we're here at the fjords. Not sure how long it'll take us, but it's northwest of here, across the Arillamon Sound. We'll still need William to take us there. And I don't need a map."

"Ah, yes. William. Did you tell him where you've moved to so he knows where to meet us? Bet he'll have a map."

Iyla rolled her eyes. "He knows where to find me."

"And we can't just teleport there? Not that I like drowning, but it's faster, right?"

"I told you, we can only do it as a group, when all the Pelri are going. It doesn't work just by ourselves."

Aron sighed. "So, what's this place like? Don't you carry any protection at all? No weapons, nothing? How do you know this place is safe? All I've got is my knife. What about a baseball bat?"

Iyla tilted her head slightly and wrinkled her nose.

"Ugh, good God, woman," he said. "I hope the trees put locks on your doors."

"Kleey is very remote. Who's going to try to get through the door?"

Aron shrugged and shook his head. "I'll take the couch."

Dreams of home filled Aron's mind for most of the night. He envisioned Tora sitting in a rocking chair in the living room, singing the baby to sleep. She was always a little off-key, but neither he nor the baby minded. The mouthwatering aroma of a home-cooked meal was making its way into every room of their townhouse. As he stood in the doorway of his dream, Tora looked up at him, smiled, and then handed him their child to kiss goodnight. *What was she thinking right now at this moment?* He wished he could tell her he was OK and was searching for a way back home.

Unfortunately, it wasn't long before the succulent aroma of dinner degraded into the smell of burned toast. "Tora," he muttered in his sleep.

The sound of a door closing awoke him. He grabbed his knife and sat up as he heard the shower turn on. The pungent, charred odor was coming from the kitchen.

Maybe I should make the breakfast, he thought as he stood up, stretched, and made his way to the kitchen. The kitchen was clean, and all the dishes were neatly put away. There was no sign of any recent food preparation. He put his knife on the table, opened the cooler, and pulled out a few eggs. They were a little bigger than what he was used to. When he closed the door, he again caught the pungent odor coming from the open kitchen window.

There was a loud crack of a log splitting outside and then a forceful, rumbling thud. Aron heard the sounds of smaller twigs snapping and dry leaves crackling, followed by a heavy *whoosh* sound before noticing a thin column of smoke winding upward directly in front of the window.

Someone or some*thing* was lurking outside the house. Grateful that he was perched in the trees, Aron slowly moved closer to the window to observe the prowler. At the exact moment that he moved his head in front of the open window, an enormous, round, grey eye met his.

Aron jumped back, knocking over two chairs and dropping the pan he had commandeered for protection. Now with the table between them, he crouched low and watched as the large eye scanned the rooms inside, blinked, and then dropped down out of sight.

The water turned off in the bathroom. "Iyla!" he whispered loudly. "Do not come out of the bathroom!"

The door promptly opened, and Iyla strode out, wrapped in a towel.

"Stay in there!" he ordered.

"Why?" she asked.

"There is something huge wandering around outside. I don't know what it is, but it's huge. Stay in the bathroom! Get back!"

Ignoring Aron completely, she walked over to the kitchen window and peered out. She looked to the left, turned to face Aron, and then nearly doubled over in laughter.

Aron stood up slowly. "Is it gone?"

"C'mon," she said, motioning him to follow.

Iyla led Aron to the front door and out to the tiny deck. He stopped short. What he saw about fifty feet away from him took his breath away.

Lying peacefully on the ground below was a massive, fire-breathing dragon. His head was the size of a sofa, and large, formidable teeth jutted from his ferocious jaws. His narrow, sharp ears pointed backward, each one pierced with a large, sparkling gemstone, and his long neck stretched into a muscular body armored with iridescent scales. He was dark green, similar to the pine trees surrounding them, which then shimmered into a deep indigo tone when he moved. A spiked tail extended and then curled around several trees while his enormous leathery wings folded close to his body. The dragon's head rose when they stepped outside, and curls of smoke released from his black nostrils. He was terrifyingly beautiful.

Aron grasped the ivy-covered railing at his side. "Holy shit," he uttered under his breath.

"Aron, meet William," Iyla said.

His mouth opened in disbelief. "*This* is William?" Aron asked. His eyes were wide, and his knuckles turned white on the handrail. "This is William," he stated, trying to force his acceptance of what he was seeing in front of him. "OK, then. OK... Not a boyfriend."

Iyla giggled. "I thought you said you had animals where you're from."

"Animals do not include dragons! So," he began. "You're a dragon-rider." This new awareness made Aron smile in surprised admiration. William grunted and exhaled loudly. The fallen leaves and dried pine needles blustered into the air and then danced back down, some settling onto the deck where they were standing.

"Well, *technically*, so are you. How do you think I got you from the Remmeline River to Tariadyn?" Iyla laughed.

"Holy shit," Aron shook his head. Two thin smoke curls rose again from William's nostrils and disappeared into the fresh pine air. "Do you all ride dragons? All the Pelri? I mean, how could you possibly lose a fight against men when you've got a sky full of dragon-riding Pelri?"

"No, we don't all. Just me now. There were two others in our group, but the humans took Seriah as I've said, and Kenrick's dragon died last year. I've known William since he was barely more than a hatchling. He was a gift from my mother."

Aron could hear the loving wistfulness in her voice. "So how does one go about finding and purchasing a dragon? And do they have any holiday specials going on?" Aron smiled at her confused expression.

"Well, that's where we're going. The dragon trainer lives in Ehn Ee Canyon. He's the old, wise elf I told you about who might be able to help us figure out what to do with you."

"Dragon trainer... now, that's what I call a cool job. How is it we'll be able to travel there without being noticed? I mean, your 'friend' here is no small potato." There was another grunt from William, and this time Aron felt the warm, smokey breath.

"Small what?" Iyla asked.

"Never mind."

"OK, well, there's something about a dragon's chemistry. For some reason, when it blends with the aura of a Pelri, we both disappear. Completely invisible, along with everything touching us. Takes about a minute or two to kick in but comes in quite handy," she said. "I can go anywhere I want with him and no one can see us. Anywhere he fits, of course."

"Wow," Aron pondered the thought of what it would be like to own a dragon. "So, if it were just me riding William, we would not disappear then," he surmised.

"Correct. Unless you have some ability that I don't know about."

"Nothing as cool as that! Amazing."

"Let's give William a few tarthberries, and then we should get going," Iyla said as she opened the door to head inside.

Aron followed behind her, but not before taking another glance at William relaxing on the ground below.

"Unbelievable," he said to himself.

After eating an egg-sandwich breakfast, Iyla pulled out a few brown leather satchels and packed one full of tarthberries, apples, carrots, and dark bread. In another, she packed blankets, clothing, and toiletries. The third satchel was for Aron, and into it, he packed his meager belongings, several canisters of water, and, most importantly, the wooden ruby amulet.

"You're going to need a cloak. And try to cover your hands. The wind gets chilly when we're high up there," Iyla pointed upward as she handed him a sizable thick wrap. "Doubles as an extra blanket."

After closing the door behind them, they made their way down the swaying stairway to where William now slept. His large green chest swelled with each deep breath. The surrounding air was warm with the now-familiar charred scent. There was a scorched area on the ground directly in front of him.

"William," Iyla called out softly. "Wake up. Time to go."

The enormous beast opened his eyes and blinked in the daylight, his ears twitching. He raised his head, and his long neck extended up into the trees. He then bent down and came face to face with Aron.

He froze. "Shit," he said under his breath as William sniffed him from head to toe, his forceful breath blowing his cloak in a hot gust of wind. Aron pulled it tightly around him. "Nice boy," he said, holding out his hand.

"He won't hurt you," Iyla promised.

William finished scanning Aron and then stood up. He opened up his wings, and for the first time, Aron saw his enormous wingspan. The wings were very similar to oversized bat wings, but leathery and dark, shimmering green. William then shook his entire body and rose onto his hind legs to stretch. Aron backed up as he came down with a ground-shaking thud.

"OK, let's go!" Iyla called to Aron. William crouched down as Iyla climbed onto his back, using his hind leg and tail as support. Aron followed right behind and was surprised to find how smooth the dragon's scales felt on his palms.

"I don't think we're invisible," he noted.

"Not like you could tell anyway, but give it a minute."

William patrolled around the treehouse, continuing to stretch his legs and fan his wings between the trees. Then, with a heaving launch, they were airborne. William's powerful wings pulled them upward with every beat. Aron held tightly to Iyla, his legs tucked into a leather strap, until William's body leveled and they were moving smoothly in a horizontal direction.

They glided over an expansive, dark forest of mostly evergreens. The only bumps occurred when William would catch an air current, which then propelled them higher. In the distance and to the west, a body of water glistened, and beyond that, a clearing with rolling hills. To the east, it was all forest. To the north, more water. There was no sign of civilization.

Iyla turned around and leaned back, pointing to the water ahead. "Arillamon Sound!" she shouted. "On the other side of it is Oroc."

Aron nodded, taking in the panorama.

"Are there any cities?" he asked loudly. "You know, with buildings?"

"Not out here," she answered. "Men built up all of that in Seridon, but most everywhere else, we don't do things like that."

Aron wondered, where do people shop? Where do they work? The culture in this world, or at least this part of it, was a stark contrast to his life on Earth.

Life on Earth. It sounded like something an alien might say. And who's to say that these world-hopping Neclu Sapins never traveled to Earth, which meant Earth actually has had legitimate alien visitors?

"Iyla!" he called out, and she turned toward him. "What is your world called?"

She smiled. "Athemoni."

They were higher now, and Aron could see the opening of the Arillamon Sound to the east into the large blue ocean beyond the forest. Behind them, the fjords now looked small. It was peaceful high in the sky, riding William the Dragon. If he ever did get back home, no, *when* he got back home, he would now have his own stories to tell at the family holiday gatherings. But would anyone even believe him?

Chapter Five

WHEN THE WIND BLOWS

"**G**otta stop for a break." The chilly winds blew Iyla's words back toward Aron. The trees below grew larger as William descended, and the labyrinth of wide trails wound through the woods and across rolling hills, out toward the flatter lands beyond. As they crossed over the forest edge, a deep blue lake emerged between the first set of hills. The jagged cliffs and cotton-white clouds replicated on the water surface below. William glided over the calm waters, causing a rippling effect, but there was no reflection in the lake of a man and a Pelri riding a dragon.

Once they reached the southern edge of the lake, William plunged in, water spraying high above them. Finally on solid ground, it was the first time on this trip that Aron allowed his tense muscles to relax.

"This is Esippid Lake, a favorite dragon watering hole," Iyla announced. "Don't be surprised if we run into Seriah's dragon, Tenly. She tends to linger here since, well, you know."

"No one else took her in?"

Iyla shook her head. "Our dragons are loyal to only one in their lifetime. Once that bond is set, it's for life. And if they're ever separated, the dragon will remain in solitude until he or she dies. It's just their nature. Tenly is a true loner. This is the only place I've ever seen her," she explained.

Aron scanned his surroundings, somewhat unsettled. "Great. Another dragon… and this one is already a little pissed at humans for taking her Pelri. Just great."

Iyla laughed. "Relax. We're fine. She may not even be here at all, and she'll probably leave if she sees us." Iyla ran up to a large boulder wrapped in moss and disappeared behind it. Three seconds later, her head poked out, and she motioned him to follow.

"C'mon. William is going to need to take in a lot of water and eat. We can snack and rest here." Her tiny frame disappeared again.

Behind the boulder was a secluded area of stone and sand and a picture-perfect view of the clear blue water. Iyla had spread a blanket and was unpacking the food. "I came here a lot last year. This was my favorite picnic spot."

"Long way to go for a picnic. Especially if Tariadyn is even further than Kleey," Aron noted.

"Building a map in your head, I see," Iyla smiled. "No, we were living in Oroc at the time. My mom… passed away, and—" Aron heard her voice quiver, and Iyla turned away. "William likes it here. And it's a good place to just sit and think."

"It is beautiful," he agreed, thinking about his own mother, who had just passed. They sat in silence for a few minutes. A pleasant breeze found its way between the boulders.

"May I ask—" Aron started. "May I ask how she died?"

Iyla sighed before a small tear formed in her eye, and she turned away from him.

"You don't have to," Aron said quickly. "It's OK."

"No, I'm alright," she said as she looked out over the water. William was busy drinking from the small waterfall at the far end. "The humans took my mom about a year and a half ago. They starved her and beat her and experimented on her body."

"Iyla, my God! I am so sorry."

"When we got her back about a year ago, she was barely alive."

"How did you get her back?"

"William and I, along with my friend, Kenrick, and his dragon. We flew into Seridon and saved her. That's how Kenrick's dragon died," Iyla said. "But my mom, she was so weak. And at her age, she couldn't last much longer no matter what we did. Nature did what it could, but nothing helped."

"How old was she?" he asked.

"Fifty-one," Iyla answered.

"What a shame," he said. "Not very old."

"Not that old? She was way older than most Pelri. I felt fortunate that we had her as long as we did. Do humans on Earth usually live longer than that?"

"Yeah, usually. Most live into their seventies. My grandmother lived to her eighties."

"Wow, really? Humans here don't live that long. Pelri live longer. Elves, though, they live the longest."

Aron shrugged. "Yeah, thanks to you, I've got at least a good fifty years left, if not more."

Iyla's quizzical look told Aron she was doing the math in her head. "But that would mean you are in your twenties?"

"Twenty-four," he answered. "How old are you?"

"What? I thought we were closer in age. I'm eight."

"EIGHT?" he asked, eyes wide open. "That doesn't make any sense." Aron was feeling a bit uneasy. "There's no way you're eight. You look like a full-grown adult. How does an eight year old live on her own, cook her own food, *ride a dragon*?"

"What do you mean? I *am* an adult! But look at you! You look so young for twenty-four. No grey hair, no wrinkles, nothing! How is that possible?"

They both sat and looked at each other, trying to figure out how they could be so far apart in age. Aron wrestled with his own disturbing thoughts, feeling a little disgusted with himself, knowing the way he had looked at her in the treehouse. In silence, he collapsed back onto the flat stone behind him, clasping his hands behind his head. The sun was out, but he could still see the moons against the light blue sky. Those moons...

"Iyla," he said, as a thought occurred to him. "How many hours are in a day?"

"Twenty-four," she answered.

Aron thought for another second. "How many days are in a year?"

"1,020. Why?" Iyla replied.

"That's it!" Aron exclaimed, sitting up quickly. "Athemoni years are almost 3 times longer than Earth years. That would make us close to the same age. Now it makes sense!"

"How many days are in an Earth year?" Iyla asked.

"365."

Iyla thought about this a minute before attempting to hide a slight smile. "I get it."

"What a relief!" Aron said absentmindedly.

"Why a relief?" Iyla asked.

Aron felt his blood surge to his face. "Heh, never mind. I need a nap." He turned away and reached for his leather satchel as Iyla spread another blanket to lie down.

"Hey, Iyla? I'm really sorry about your mom. My mom passed away a few months ago, too. I know how bad it hurts."

"Thanks, Aron. I'm sorry about your mom, too."

Aron pulled the amulet out of the satchel and turned it over in his hands. The color variations in the wood ranged from blonde to a deep rich brown. The surface was so smooth to the touch. Iyla turned onto her side to face his direction.

"Hold on tight to that," she advised.

"Yeah," he said as his thumb and fingers fell into the familiar grooves. "I really hope we'll find some—"

And then the lake was gone. The sun was gone. There was no more sand, stone, or cliffs. There was no more William. There was no more Iyla.

He felt the sand and stone drop beneath him. Then came the quick icy chill before landing on something soft. He opened his eyes. Aron was on his bed, in his room in the townhouse he shared with Tora. "What the hell?" he muttered.

He stood up too quickly and felt a dizzy spell coming on. Stumbling, he paused and held on to the chest of drawers. He called out to Tora, but there was no answer. He hurried through the upper level, hoping to find her and the baby. There was no sign of either of them. In fact, there was no sign of a baby living there at all. No crib, no diapers, no toys. Everything was pretty much as he had left it.

In his hand, he still gripped the amulet. It wasn't a dream.

"*What is going on?*" he demanded, shaking the amulet in front of his face. Frustrated, he shoved it in his back pocket and descended the stairs to the living room. The blue and grey throw blanket was crumbled in a ball on Tora's favorite chair. In the kitchen, the keyring holder still hung on the wall, but there were no keys. *She's probably gone to the store*, he thought as he pulled a glass from the cabinet and filled it with ice and water from the refrigerator door. He grabbed the phone and dialed Tora's cell. It went immediately to voicemail.

"This voice mailbox is full..." Aron slammed the receiver back onto the hook.

A newspaper and several pieces of mail sat on the kitchen table, and an empty glass lay next to it. Aron picked up the newspaper and noticed it was an old one. He cocked his head a bit to the side as he thought. *Was this....? This could very well have been the same date his convoy was blown up in the desert, over two months ago.*

At that moment, he heard a key in the lock. *Tora*, he thought. But it wasn't Tora who walked through the door.

"Uncle Jeff?"

Tall and rugged, Uncle Jeff's grey hair never deviated from the classic high and tight. He froze mid-step. "Aron? Oh my God! I can't believe it! What the hell? Look at you! I can't believe it's you! Am I seeing a ghost?" Uncle Jeff embraced him tightly. "Oh my God!" he said again. Uncle Jeff was Aron's mother's younger brother. He lived out of state, but he and Aron had a close relationship, and he came to visit his sister and Aron often. "How is this possible? How are you here? We thought you were dead!" He embraced his nephew again. "When did you get back? My God, I can't believe it's you!"

"Nope, not dead! Although I thought I would've been too."

"We were told there was an attack on your convoy, that the only two who survived were then run down in a nearby town."

"Yeah, no, I survived. And you're never going to believe what happened. But where's Tora? I can tell you both everything. It was crazy!"

Uncle Jeff was immediately silent. His excitement at seeing Aron melted from his face as he stared back at him, not knowing what to say. "They didn't tell you?"

"Tell me what? What's wrong?" Aron felt a pang in his stomach.

"Aron, Tora was in an accident. She's gone."

The words echoed through his brain. *Tora is gone.* He dropped down onto the chair, ready to vomit.

"I'm so sorry, dude," his uncle consoled.

"How? When?" Aron's voice cracked as he spoke.

"It was over two months ago. Car accident. We were trying to contact you to let you know, and that's when we found out about the convoy attack. It was the same day."

"My God," was all that he could force from his lips.

"I'm so sorry," said Uncle Jeff. "I just came over to work on the house. I was going to put it on the market next month."

Aron continued to rub at his temples, attempting to thwart the inevitable tears. "This can't be." His father, his mother, and now his fiancée? And yet, *he* survives an enemy attack in a brutal war, not to mention traveling through a portal to an entirely new world?

Aron glanced up at his uncle. "What about the baby?"

His uncle seemed confused. "What baby?" he asked.

"Our baby, Tora's baby! Oh my God, the baby didn't survive, did he? Tora would've still been pregnant. The baby was due maybe a month ago." It was at that point that he could no longer hold back the tears. Aron jumped up and pounded on the door frame with his fist.

"Aron, I'm not sure I understand." His uncle hesitated. "There was no baby."

"She never told you? Tora was pregnant when I enlisted. We agreed she wouldn't tell anyone until after the first trimester. She told me she told her parents and you and Aunt Marianne." Aron paced the kitchen, nearly running into his uncle.

"Aron, she never told either of us anything about a pregnancy. I saw her several times after you enlisted. The last time was about a week before the accident. She was never pregnant."

Aron's mind was reeling. *Never pregnant? Did she lose the baby?* She would have told him if she had lost the baby.

Aron stood with his back to his uncle, leaning with his arms propped up against the wall, his body heaving. *She lied.* Tora lied to him about the pregnancy. Was it another attempt to stop him from enlisting? He thought they had worked through that. Was it because she wanted to get married? He knew he had dragged his feet on that, but with a baby coming... *But how can you lie about something like that? How? All I've been thinking about was getting back to my fiancée and my baby. Only to learn this bullshit! Why was I even brought back here? What am I supposed to do now?* His entire life had been flipped upside down in this last year. What was left for him?

"Anything else I need to know? What else has happened in these last few months that I don't know about?"

"Hey, bud," Uncle Jeff began. "I'm really sorry. I can't imagine what you are going through right now." He walked over to Aron and put his arm around him. Aron's body heaved with emotional exhaustion.

"You should know," Uncle Jeff started again. "We went ahead and filed a lawsuit against the drug company. If the judgment is in our favor, you will receive the compensation."

Again, Aron's jaw fell open. "What are you talking about?"

"Your mother," he said. "The autopsy results. The trace amounts of dimethylmercury in her body? They also found it in one of her medications."

Autopsy. Mercury.

"Mom," Aron whispered as his body wilted back into the chair, and they were both silent.

"Look, Aron, if you want to come and stay with us for a bit, you're more than welcome. Aunt Marianne—"

"No, I—" Aron was numb. "I... I better get back... I better report back to my company commander."

"Look, with all you've been through, I'm sure they will give you some time off," reasoned Uncle Jeff.

"I need to... get back. I've gotta get outta here." Aron stood up and embraced his uncle again, still in a fog of emotion. "Thanks... Uncle Jeff."

"So good to see you, bud." He handed Aron his house keys. "Call if you need anything. You understand?"

"I will. Keep the keys."

The door shut behind Uncle Jeff, and Aron stood there for a minute, absorbing the pain from the mountain of disturbing information that was dropped on him. Why did he not know about the autopsy? Why was there so much that didn't make sense?

The refrigerator hummed in the kitchen, and the crackle of the ice maker interrupted his thoughts. He turned on the coffeemaker and rummaged through the pantry for something edible. His chest ached. *What else?*

Aron walked back upstairs to his empty room and pulled the amulet from his back pocket. "Did you do this? Is this because of you? What the hell are you?" He growled and threw the amulet onto the bed.

He took a hot shower, dressed himself in fresh civilian clothes, and packed a bag of his mother's belongings that he had saved. Her wedding ring, a mostly empty perfume bottle, and the magazine she was reading the last time he talked to her. He slung the bag over his neck and across his chest, and sat on his bed with the amulet in his hand. *What the hell happened?*

Aron shoved the amulet into the bag. He needed answers.

It was a brisk Autumn afternoon, but he barely noticed the strong wind. A local bus had pulled over at the stop outside his neighborhood, and four strangers were loading their bags onto it.

"You pass the cemetery, right?"

The driver nodded.

Aron found a seat near the middle of the bus and sat down next to the window. He placed his bag on the seat next to him. The windows were smeared with grime and the entire bus smelled of gasoline and body odor. It was not a long ride.

Outside the cemetery, Aron took a deep breath. This would be the first time he visited his mother since her burial. *How could I have not known about the autopsy?*

Her gravestone was set under a large oak tree. He sat at the base of it, leaning against the trunk. It was peaceful.

"Mom." His breath hitched, and he paused. "I really wish you were here. This crazy crap has been happening, stuff you, you can't even imagine, and now," he paused again. "Now Tora is gone too." Aron wiped the corner of his eye. "I've always said I wanted to be just like dad. I wanted you to be proud, and I wanted to follow my dream. But this, this is some crazy shit happening, Mom. And it's not the army, which was its own shit show. Am I being punished for following my heart? Tora and I, we finally got to a good place. We found a way to meet in the middle. And I made the decision, Mom. You told me to make a decision, and I did. She was happy, and I was going to have a kid. It was the right thing to do. And now, now everyone is gone. Everything has been taken from me. God, I wish you were here to talk to me." His chest heaved with a sob, and he paused to gather himself.

"We're going to find out what happened to you, where that mercury came from. I promise you that, Mom. I need answers. I need to know what is going on, and I can't help but feel it's all connected somehow."

Aron reached for his bag and dumped it out behind the gravestone. The magazine pages flapped madly in the wind, and he trapped it under his leg. The glass detail of the perfume bottle caught the sunlight when the branches swayed.

"This thing." Aron picked up the wooden amulet. "I found it in a deserted town in Iraq when I was about to get blown up. I don't know what it is, Mom, but it has some kind of power, and it brought me to a different world. I know that sounds insane. But it's true. I was just there. I met people from there. I mean, they weren't human, but there was an elf and a Pelri which is like an elf, but not. And dragons, Mom! Dragons! Can you believe it? I swear, this all just happened! Then somehow this thing sent me back. And now I find out all this stuff about you. You, being poisoned. Tora, the car accident. And...I thought I was going to be a dad... This is nuts. Am I going insane?"

Aron paused and took a deep breath. "God, no one is going to believe this, are they?" He sat for a minute tapping the amulet onto his palm. *No one is going to believe me.* "But it happened, Mom. And this thing has something to do with all of it."

The paper subscription card escaped from the magazine and the wind took it a few gravesites down. Aron jumped up to retrieve it. A wind blew again just as he snatched it up, and in his other hand, the amulet felt warm to the touch. *Was it always that way?*

He glanced down at the gravestone where he now stood. *Tora Straught.*

"Oh, God." Aron sank to his knees.

Tora was gone. But the feeling in his gut wasn't the heartache that he expected. "Goddammit, this is your fault!" His right hand gripped the amulet tightly, and the deep red ruby almost seemed alive. He tried to drop it, but he couldn't let go. He was weightless.

"Fuck!"

Chapter Six

THE BOOKS IN THE CAVE

It was a rough landing this time as Aron's head hit the loose stones and sand at Esippid Lake. He sat up, rubbing his head.

"Dammit," he muttered, inhaling slowly to halt the double-breathing. His insides ached, still unable to fully process everything he had just learned. *God, I can't do this*, he thought.

He spotted Iyla by the water's edge with her back to him, tossing rocks into the lake. William, swimming at the far end, reminded Aron of the Loch Ness monster stories.

The amulet was still in his right hand, the subscription card in the sand beside him. Back to square one. He examined the deep red of the ruby, the smooth variations of the wood grain. He gripped it tightly, shook it, and then looked again. Nothing.

He took a minute to gather himself, to brace himself, before calling out to Iyla.

She spun around, her mouth open, and dropped her rock. Smiling, she ran toward him. "Aron! Thank the moons, you're back! What happened? One moment you were here and then bam, gone. If I didn't know better, I'd think you were a Sapin." She stepped back, eyeballing his fresh set of clothes. "And you've got socks now?" she said.

"Yeah. I guess the amulet decided I needed some answers from home. How long was I gone?"

"About two and a half hours," she replied, eyes narrowing. "So, you went home? I thought you didn't know how to make it work."

"I don't. This thing just sent me right to my house. Then I guess it decided to bring me back. I don't know what's going on. It's just... a mess." Aron frowned and ran his hand through his hair. "Were you waiting for me?"

"Puh, no. I was ready to head out a while ago. But William here refused to get out of the waterfall for the longest time. What happened during all that time? Did you see your fiancée and your new baby? And why'd the thing send you back?"

Aron felt the familiar pang in his stomach. He wasn't sure how to talk about that yet. "Later. Let's get going."

Iyla frowned, tilting her head slightly. "No. I think we should stay the night here and leave first thing in the morning. We've got a few hours to go, and I'd rather get there in the morning. Jens is busier later in the day."

"Yeah, sure, OK. But don't you think we should get there as soon as possible?"

"What's *your* rush? Apparently, you already know how to get home, and for some reason, you came back."

Aron frowned at her snappy retort. "I didn't–"

"I'm sorry. I'm just... really confused. I was starting to really trust you. The whole point in getting to Jens was so that we can figure out how to find Seriah, and then get you home. You got home. But you're back again. It just doesn't make sense to me. And you, shrugging off my questions, it makes me think you're hiding something."

Aron looked toward the clouds for a moment and sighed. He coyly poked Iyla on her shoulder as they walked. "I'm sorry. I didn't mean to brush you off. Look, I don't understand it either. I don't know how I got home, but when I was there," he paused briefly, "I learned a few things that were very upsetting. Monumental things. I don't know what's happening, Iyla, but I am not in control here. This wooden ruby stone thing, it's messing with me. From the moment I touched it, everything in my life has turned upside down. I'm not trying to hide anything from you. But I do think we need to find out what this thing is, and learn how to make it work. Maybe it has other powers or magic that we can use somehow. I just hope your elf friend knows something about how to control it. And I promise you, I'll help you find your friend."

Iyla softened her expression and turned toward the lake. "Well, if anyone knows anything about it, it would be Jens. Like I said, elves live a long time, and he's *old*, old. In the meantime, I'm going for a swim before dinner."

"You do that. I need a few minutes to think." There was something about Iyla that was so refreshing. At times, he thought it was the sweet aroma that naturally emanated from her. Was it something in her voice? She was kindhearted, generally good-natured, and clearly a loyal friend. *Why am I here?* he thought. *Is this my fate?* Tora was gone now. Gone. And a deep pit of uncertainty was left in her place. No squad, no mom, no Tora, no child. And no answers.

At sunset, William lit a bonfire outside of their camp spot, a hollowed-out section at the base of the cliff, although his body heat alone was enough to keep them warm through the night. Iyla's slight form was curled up against William's chest. Aron preferred to spread his blanket a little further away. Both he and Iyla kept a few flasks full of water beside them in case William's snores sparked a ground fire.

The stars twinkled in the sky like tiny Christmas lights turning on one by one. They were bigger and brighter than the stars he saw from home, but he could find no recognizable constellations. Aron was worlds away from

Earth, but the quiet tranquility of Esippid Lake was rather comforting.

"Iyla," he said quietly, unsure if she was awake.

"Yes," she whispered.

Slowly, Aron formed the words aloud. "My fiancée died in a car accident on the same day that you found me here in your world," he began, his voice faltering. "And as bad as that sounds, what hurt me the most was when I learned she had lied to me about being pregnant."

Iyla drew in a quick breath. "Oh, Aron," she breathed. "I am so sorry. I had no idea..."

"I know. It's a tough thing to swallow."

Iyla adjusted her position against William so she could see Aron better in the light of the moons and stars. "How do—" she hesitated. "Why would she lie about that?"

"Honestly, I don't even know what to think right now. Why would *anyone* lie about that? I mean, I know I'm not perfect. Everyone has their faults, and I had a hard time settling down, but–" Aron hesitated, stifling his emotions. "And now she's gone, and even if I did find my way home again, I can't even—"

"I'm sorry, Aron. You don't have to—"

"No, it's OK." Aron was silent for a moment, his gaze moving toward the night sky. "I have been mulling that over for these last several hours. Tora and I had a... unique relationship, which I suppose is a nice way of putting it. We'd known each other for several years. Have you ever been in a relationship with someone where you loved them, but maybe you weren't *in* love with them? I think that's where I was for a long time. I just had a certain level of love and companionship, and that satisfied me."

"Well, I can't say that I've ever been ready for binding yet, if that's what you're asking."

"Binding?"

"Yeah, just picking one person and promising to be with them for the rest of your life."

Aron smiled. "Right. We call that marriage. So maybe it was just that. She was ready, and I hadn't gotten there yet. I don't know why I didn't feel the need to take that step. I mean, I loved her, right? Then she tells me she's pregnant, and that was the kick in the butt. And I was really excited to be a dad."

"But you'd been together for a few years. How long would it normally take to get there, to know?"

"Yeah, and that's what my mother would say. She always got mad at me for being too complacent when it came to mine and Tora's relationship." He paused before letting out a small chuckle. "My mom didn't like her much. She would never admit it, but she didn't."

"Why not?" Iyla asked.

"Ah, well. Tora liked to have things her way, and she could usually manipulate a situation so she'd get what she wanted. I guess I was just used to her being her. We argued a lot. But I loved her and just—I don't know. My mom thought we didn't fit well together. For long term."

"Looks like your mom may have been right."

"But I could never see her doing something like that, though, lying about something that big. But, Tora... she never liked the idea of me joining the army. She could've been trying to manipulate me again and told me she was pregnant, thinking I wouldn't enlist."

"She sounds like a prize," Iyla muttered, and then immediately apologized.

"No, it's fine," he said. "I'm an idiot, and I really have no explanation other than I think I was just... comfortable with her. She was familiar. She was my constant, and we had a lot of years together. And I thought I loved her. I did love her. I was wrong for not seeing that maybe we weren't the best fit. Sometimes love does that. You don't really see things for what they are. And sometimes you're able to make it work anyway."

"Well, you're not an idiot. Except for when it comes to defending yourself against dragons." She winked.

"I didn't know!" Aron protested, remembering that terrifying feeling.

Iyla laughed. "You were holding a *frying pan*!" she teased.

He smiled, knowing how silly he must have looked. He listened as the lake water lapped at the shore. William was breathing heavily, and his warm breath felt good in the cool night air. "Do you think the wooden ruby might have other powers besides teleporting? I mean, what if it can time travel? There are a lot of things I would do differently."

"You're asking the wrong person. But what would you have done differently? And how do you know those other decisions would have improved your life or made you happier?"

"I don't know. But it would be nice to have my mom back."

"That's probably not something you could've changed."

"Is there a lot of magic in this world?"

"I guess, I don't know. If you're like the humans in Seridon, then I guess we have more than what you're used to. Humans don't seem to do anything special."

"So what else do the Pelri do, besides talking to nature and zipping across the planet with your burning pearls?"

"Hm, that's about it, really. The elves use more magic than we do. They have charms and enchantments and potions."

"And they train dragons..." Aron interjected.

"Well, *Jens* trains dragons."

"Yeah. Pretty cool." He scooted further down under his blanket and contemplated moving closer to William. He decided against it. "Good night, Iyla."

"Good night, Aron."

Dawn came quickly, and Iyla and Aron each took their turn showering in the waterfall before consuming a tarthberry and a few carrots for breakfast.

"Do you not eat meat?" Aron asked after his stomach growled a second time.

"Meat? What kind of meat?"

"Any kind. Beef. Do you have cows? Pork? Maybe you have deer?"

"Ew, no. But fish sometimes."

"What about the elves?"

"Why would we eat elves!?"

"I mean, do *they* eat meat?"

Iyla stopped and thought for a moment. "Yeah, I think so. Jens never offers it to me, though. Why?"

"Oh nothing. I was just thinking I could go for a nice plate of steak and eggs right about now."

"Go catch some fish in the lake."

Aron chuckled. "Nah, I'm alright. Fish in the morning isn't very appetizing."

"Why does it matter what time of day you eat certain foods?"

Aron thought for a moment. "I really don't know. Interesting point."

William was active that morning, swimming in the water and then flying the perimeter of the lake to dry his wings, but it wasn't long before they were climbing the wind currents toward the clouds into the morning sky.

Iyla pointed down at the lake, and Aron saw another dragon arriving just as they were on their way out. It was Seriah's dragon, Tenly. She was a beautiful silver and red iridescent dragon, larger than William. She had just made her landing with a splash into the water, her scales glistening in the morning sun as she showered under the waterfall. "She was probably waiting for us to leave," Iyla said.

There was more farmland in Oroc than what he had seen previously when flying from Kleey to Esippid Lake. Many goats and several unfamiliar animals grazed on the rolling hills. Fields of crops patterned the countryside.

As they rounded the northern tip of Arillamon Sound, the farmlands thinned out, and vast gorges approached in the distance. The steep rocky walls of the canyon were dotted with moss, ferns, and other green shrubs. As they advanced closer, Aron took in the many beautiful colors of the various wildflowers draping from the cliffs and rocks. It reminded him of the Spanish moss hanging from the trees in South Carolina, but this was much more colorful. There were long strands of pinks, blues, yellows, and purples spiraling far down into Ehn Ee Canyon.

William flew over the ridge and down into the gorge. The Rinn River below was bright turquoise, and shadows of fish and other water life swam beneath the surface. William headed upriver, flying low, just above the water. At times, his wings would cut into the rapids, effecting a cold spray that sluiced down their cloaks. The foliage tapered off, and large spans of blackened rock became more frequent. Caves cut into the walls, some low enough to fill with river water.

William, at last, landed atop a large boulder on the east side of the river where sand and rocks had amassed above the bank. Rearing up on his hind legs, he flapped his massive wings as Aron and Iyla held tight to the leather strap and a roaring inferno erupted from his powerful chops.

William came to rest on the sand, and the two climbed off his back. "Shit, William, what's all that about?" Aron said, his legs and backside aching from the long journey.

"Yeah, he does that every time," answered Iyla. "He was hatched here. He smells the scent of other dragons, so he's just making his presence known and marking his territory."

"Ah. And how many other dragons are we talking?"

"I'm pretty sure Jens has five at the moment. Two of them are his. The other three are the ones he's training. They're babies."

William opted to splash into the turquoise river and unwind from the long journey as Iyla and Aron climbed the narrow, rocky steps to a cave about twenty feet above them. Before they reached the opening, a grey-haired old elf emerged in a long, green, simple kaftan tied at the waist with a flat, braided rope. He probably would have been Aron's height if he wasn't bent forward at his shoulders. His long, straight hair was pulled back into a ponytail and hung to the backs of his knees. His wiry, grey beard was comparatively short, but still long enough to separate down the middle and tie off in two sections. The elf leaned on a tall wooden staff intricately carved with pictures of dragons and fire and the floral canyon.

"Iyla," he said, although he kept his eyes trained on Aron.

"Hi, Jens!" Iyla said and gave him a warm hug. Aron stepped back as Jens continued to study him.

"Sir," Aron said as he held out his right hand. The elf looked at Aron's outstretched hand suspiciously before turning to Iyla.

"Jens, this is my friend Aron. I brought him here because we have some things we'd like to talk to you about."

"Aron," he said, finally.

"Yes, sir," Aron responded. "I'm pleased to meet you."

Jens turned back to Iyla. "Iyla, I've received a supply of a rare dragon treat William might like. Go down to the feeding room and find some for him while I get to know Aron."

"Sure," she responded. "I'll be back soon."

Great, leave me alone with a magical elf who obviously wants to rip my head off.

"Come inside, Aron," the elf said as he turned around and led the way into the cave. Aron was surprised at how well-lit and clean it was. Cool, but not damp. Oil lamps and candles burned strategically around the small room, and two high-backed chairs lined the northern wall.

"Have a seat," Jens motioned to one chair, and Aron sat down. He then lumbered over to a cabinet to pull out a vessel made of an animal horn or tusk of some sort and filled it with a thick, warm wine.

"I must ask you," he began, handing the vessel to Aron and sitting down on the other chair. "Are you here of your own will?"

"Uh, yes? No. What do you mean? I didn't originally intend to come to this land, but to your canyon, yes."

"So, you are saying that Iyla has not forced you into anything, and she is not holding you captive by any means?"

"What? No! Well, not anymore."

"Not anymore? So, she has threatened you?"

"Well, initially, yes. But she actually saved my life, and I think we've come to terms with each other."

The elf took a long sip of his wine before continuing. "You know she has a history with humans. Most of us do, but especially Iyla. Ever since her mother's death, she has made it her purpose to find and rescue any missing of her kind. Her fellow Pelri do not know of this pursuit. She knows they would stop her. The Pelri are a gentle, kind, and peaceful type. She is brave, but she is also reckless."

"I see."

"Yes, a spirited one, my Iyla. Just like her mother," he said and paused. "But you, you are not from Seridon, I can see that." Jens tapped his staff lightly on the stone floor of the cave.

"No," Aron responded.

"You are from Ornott? Or from Earth?"

"Yes, Earth," Aron confirmed, intrigued by Jens' intuitiveness.

"Mm-hmm," Jens stood and walked into the next room, leaving Aron seated with his drink. He returned a moment later, holding a leather-bound book.

"And how is it that you have arrived here from Earth?" Jens asked.

"Well, that's why we're here, actually. Iyla thought you might be able to help us figure that out. We've kind of figured out the 'how,' but there's a lot we don't know. I promised to help her rescue her friend, and she would help me return home. It's important that I get home, sir. There's just so much that's happened, and I—"

Iyla appeared at the cave's opening, winded, after running up the narrow stone steps from the feeding room. "He loved it, Jens. What is it?"

"It is a new fruit grown from only a few trees in southern Parise. Excellent for training."

"Iyla says you have five dragons," Aron commented.

"I train dragons for whomever can afford the price," Jens said. "Well, almost. There aren't that many dragons available to begin with, and the responsibility of owning a dragon requires training. I have two that are mine, Kellery and Khennedy. Or, I should say, Kellery is mine. Khennedy won't leave Kellery's side, so I suppose that makes him mine too. I breed them as well. There are also two young dragons who are here, still in training, and another one that has yet to hatch. He or she has not yet been sold. I need to find patronage soon for bonding."

"Wow." Aron was fascinated.

Iyla grabbed a cushion and sat on the floor. "Did you show him the amulet?"

Jens' eyebrow raised slightly.

"We were just getting to that." Aron rummaged through his satchel and found the amulet at the bottom. The wood was warm again and the ruby even more so. Acutely aware of its power, he carefully passed it to Jens. "We don't know what it is, but when I held it in my hand, it brought me here to your world."

Jens examined the amulet cautiously and thoroughly. Turning it over in his hand, he held it up to the oil lamp above him. "How did you come across this object?" he asked.

"I was in the Middle East, fighting in a war. There was an explosion inside the building where I was hiding, and I grabbed onto it in the dark. Next thing I know, I'm here in your world lying beside a river with a pretty face looking down at me," he explained. Iyla's face turned red, and she rolled her eyes.

"Middle... East. Mm-hmm," he murmured, still examining every crevice of the amulet. Aron and Iyla sat in silence.

Turning to Iyla, he asked, "And how did you come across Aron?"

"William and I were journeying above Parise. We were over the Remmeline River, and William just took a nose-dive. I was trying to get him to go further north, but he wouldn't stop. As we got closer to the ground, I saw Aron lying next to the river with the wooden ruby in his hand. He fell unconscious, so I brought him home and took care of him until he was well. I figured I could get him to tell me where Seriah was, but it turns out, he's not even from our world. He's from Earth."

"Gems and jewels," Jens said quietly. "Dragons can spot them from miles away." Jens held the amulet loosely as he considered their accounts. Again, he stood up haltingly and disappeared to the back room, his staff clicking on the cave floor.

A sharp crackle outside startled them, and Iyla hurried to the opening of the cave.

Looking back at Aron, she put her finger to her lips. "There's three figures by the river wearing long, dark cloaks," she whispered. "I can't see their faces. Heads are covered. No dragons around."

"Why are you whispering?" Aron whispered back.

Jens returned from the back room. "Who's there?" he asked. "I don't have any appointments this morning."

Iyla shrugged her shoulders. "There's three of them," she replied quietly. "I think they're Sapins."

"Get in the back room, both of you." Jens handed the amulet back to Aron.

Aron moved to the entrance of the back room and saw that the walls were lined from floor to ceiling with hundreds, if not thousands, of old, leather-bound books. Some thick, some thin, each one neatly placed on the shelves. A chocolatey, musky smell lingered in the air.

A dark blue leather-bound book on the third shelf had a symbol on its spine that looked vaguely familiar to him. He reached for the book, but his fingers seemed to hit a glass window or shield. The room was dim, but he couldn't see the glass at all. Every book in the room was behind this invisible glass shield. Aron wisely decided that he should leave these books alone.

Jens slowly made his way down the stone stairway and met with the visitors. Iyla, who had not obeyed Jens' instructions, peered around the corner of the cave opening and motioned for Aron to come closer.

He could barely hear the conversation, but it appeared to be getting intense. One visitor glanced toward the opening to the cave, and Iyla cautiously moved out of view. When they dared to peer through the opening again, one of the cloaked figures was raising a finger to Jens' face. With lightning speed, Jens grabbed the hand and pushed it into its owner's face.

Jens' raised voice was clear. "I do not do business with humans or Neclu Sapins. Leave my canyon immediately."

"We are not leaving without the dragon!" yelled another cloaked figure.

A deafening roar reverberated throughout the canyon, an amalgamation of a shriek and a thunderous growl that vibrated through Aron's body. As a dark shadow fell over the gorge, a massive deep blue dragon swooped down toward Jens and the three figures, blowing forty-foot blasts of yellow and white fire from its powerful jaws, scorching the earth and rock and boiling the river water below them before landing forcefully on the bank.

"Kellery," whispered Iyla. "She's grown."

The dragon's dark blue scales shimmered silver as she charged the visitors, her menacing wings spread wide, her eyes flared, and two curls of smoke drifting upward from her nostrils. Jewels lined the outside edges of both her ears.

"Shit," said Aron, grateful he was not in her line of fire.

Jens turned away from the visitors and calmly walked back to the cave. Kellery didn't stop her advance toward them, her long spiked tail whipping through the air behind her. When she was within twenty feet of them, she stood on her hind legs, flapped her wings, and another ear-splitting sound shrieked from her lungs. Instantly, the visitors disappeared.

"They're gone! They just disappeared!" Aron said.

"Neclu Sapins," said Iyla, shaking her head. "At least one of them was, anyway. I can't always tell them apart from humans."

"They looked human to me. So Neclu Sapins are bad news too?" asked Aron.

"Most of them," answered Iyla. "The humans use them to do their bidding. They're always on some sort of devious errand for them."

"Are they dangerous, like your Seridon humans? Jens doesn't seem to be afraid of them."

Iyla smiled. "Jens isn't afraid of anyone. Anyways, they wouldn't hurt Jens, even if they could. He's way too valuable. They've been trying to get a dragon from him for years. And Jens is the only trainer around. They know they wouldn't be able to tame one without him."

Kellery, her fury subsided, took a quick swim in the river as the water simmered around her. Khennedy, who was silver and red like Seriah's dragon, Tenly, appeared from around the corner of the cliff and escorted her upriver and out of sight.

Jens entered the cave, and his brow furrowed at seeing Aron and Iyla. "I directed the two of you to wait in the back room. Why are you here?" he demanded.

Neither Iyla nor Aron answered. Their eyes met, but they sat and waited silently as Jens again retreated to the back room. For forty minutes, they sat and waited, listening to the sounds of the river outside.

Just when Aron was about to suggest they might need to check on him, Jens emerged, carrying four thick old books under his left arm. He stopped in the door frame, looking first at Aron, then at Iyla. Still using his staff, he eased himself into the empty chair. He placed the books on the floor beside him and again looked from Aron to Iyla and then back to Aron.

Jens drew in a deep breath, held it for three seconds, and began. "Elves," he said, looking at Aron, "live...an unreasonably long time. As such, over the centuries, we have taken it upon ourselves to be the custodians of historical records. These books tell the stories of Athemoni, the times of prosperity, the times of strife, and everything in between. These books have survived floods, fire, the onslaught of men, and magic. Over two hundred years ago, we moved the books to the caves here in Ehn Ee Canyon, guarded well by dragons, magic, and one very old elf. We elves guard and treasure every word that was written by each elf currently living or by our ancestors who have passed beyond.

"Never in my lifetime have these books been more valuable than they are on this day."

Chapter Seven

Devolution

"**I** am going to give you both a history lesson that even Iyla could learn from," said Jens, reaching for the second book in the stack on the floor. He dusted it off gently and continued. "This particular book was written by my grandfather, who lived through these events hundreds of years ago." He carefully placed the old book on his lap.

Aron glanced at Iyla, eyebrow raised. "I told you he's *old,*" she said. "And elves can sometimes live up to six hundred years!"

"Exactly how old are you, Sir?" Aron ventured.

Mildly amused, Jens replied, "Four hundred and three years."

"Whoa," said Aron under his breath, with a newfound reverence.

Jens cleared his throat. "Hundreds of years ago, Athemoni was a different world. There were very few humans here, forty to fifty. The gnomes and dryads all lived in the south: Parise, Tariadyn, Kleey, and Monteek. The elves inhabited Loriande and Bogarum, which are both north of the Telodot Sea; all of them, except for my grandfather who lived in Seridon, home of the Neclu Pelri."

Iyla cocked her head and interrupted. "Sapins, you mean. Neclu Sapins."

"I mean the Neclu Pelri," Jens corrected.

"Wait, Seridon? But that's where the humans live. And since when did the Pelri ever have *any* proper place to call home, much less Seridon?"

"I am telling you when," Jens responded. "You see, back then, Seridon was not called Seridon, and the Neclu Pelri were referred to only as 'Pelri.' Seridon's original name was Keyronai. Keyronai was the most exquisitely beautiful country in this world, from the colossal gemstones glistening in the mountains and waterfalls to the crystal-clear lakes and natural springs, white powdery beaches, and mighty moss-covered rock formations protruding from the ocean floor just off the coastline.

"Nature was one with the Pelri, and together they built Keyronai, the island country, into a paradise of splendor and peace."

"Jens, are you sure? This is Seridon you are talking about? Seridon *was* Keyronai? Keyronai was an actual place?" Iyla had told Aron of Seridon's dark and dirty lakes, the countless forests that were dead or destroyed, and the large cement buildings that crushed the landscape. Where the vegetation did grow, it was small, sickly, and weak. Flowers were sparse if they even grew at all.

Jens continued without responding to Iyla. "Unknown to most, there was a small band of Neclu Sapins living on one of the more minor islands of southern Keyronai. Though the Neclu Sapins are human-like in their appearance, they are also travelers, not only within our world but also to other worlds. They are a conniving, covetous breed, and they would travel and bring back whatever they could steal from other planets. This may have been what drew them and the humans together.

"The humans that were here, most likely brought here by the Sapins, were living in eastern Tariadyn. However, they coveted Keyronai, the wonderland of riches, beauty, and magic. So, the most ruthless of the humans formed a small armed force to invade Keyronai. What they did not realize in their initial drive, but promptly encountered, was that the country was protected by the extraordinary bond between nature and the Pelri. The land, in fact, provided its own protection, and at the moment that an enemy set foot on their land, nature intervened. Whether it was the tree branches and roots ensnaring their arms and legs and ripping them apart, or the sand giving way to swallow them whole, or the flowers spewing poisonous fumes; the land safeguarded the Pelri.

"During those times, the connection between Pelri and nature was formidable, much more deeply rooted than it is today. In current times, the Pelri communicate with nature, but on a lesser scale. They remain firm allies, but their enchanted connection was damaged." Jens paused and took a deep breath. Clutching his staff, he rose from his chair to move to the kitchen, where he pulled out the pitcher of wine and a wooden bowl of seasoned radish chips.

"I don't understand," said Aron. "If the land protected itself and the Pelri, how is it that the humans live there now? What happened?"

Jens re-filled Aron's vessel and his own and then poured a third drink for Iyla. After placing the bowl on the small table, he sat down again. Aron and Iyla both reached for a radish chip, and Jens resumed.

"Knowing now that they could not enter Keyronai on their own, the humans enlisted the Sapins, and together, they made a pact. The Sapins would help them take Keyronai in exchange for a portion of the country's riches.

"Now, the Sapins, similar to traveling, can also project themselves to another location in the image of another. So, while their Sapin form is not physically present at the projected location, their essence can move around as if they were actually there in an impersonated form. Of course, if their representation is killed before they return, they too, will die. It is by these means that the Sapins could pose as Pelri and move about within Keyronai to gather intelligence."

"Yes, I've seen them do it," Iyla interjected. "Once, when we were living in Parise, they tried to pose as my friend, Kenrick. The Sapin didn't realize that the real Kenrick was not over fifteen feet away behind a boulder. I saw them both at the same time. It was weird. That was when we had to move to Oroc."

"So, they aren't actually taking over their bodies, then," Aron reasoned.

"No, just an image, or replica, of their body. But you can't tell the difference between them."

"You can never trust the Neclu Sapins," Jens warned. "They are sly and deceitful, selfish creatures." He took a sip of his wine, caught up in his own thoughts as he wearily stared at the opening of the cave.

Jens began again. "The reconnaissance mission took some time before they found the answer, the source of the land's power. There was a pair of young Sapins who had relentlessly combed the country, exploring every inch, listening in on passing conversations, and following every lead. Finally, after two years, in the northern part of Keyronai, the Sapins arrived at the beautiful Urippa Spring."

Jens opened his grandfather's book and flipped to the middle. Reading from the book, Jens continued. "Adorned with colorful floating flowers, the steaming warm water of the spring was a curious, pale lavender. Large, glistening pearl-like stones had bubbled up through the fissures in the limestone and blanketed the spring floor, glowing white beneath the water's surface.

"In the center of this magnificent spring rose an enormous Tree. This majestic, vibrant Tree with its many branches reaching high and wide had stood in the center of this spring for many years, growing and fortifying the country and eventually outliving most of the descendants of the young elf who first planted her."

Jens closed the book while holding his place with his fingers. "This Tree," he said, "was a gift to the Pelri from a Bogarum Elf. The Elfblood Tree was a magical gift of security and protection that enhanced the intrinsic abilities of the Pelri to its superior level."

"The Elfblood Tree... why was it called that?" asked Aron.

"The Bogarum Elf, Levryn, the most powerful of all elves of that time, and probably even today, concocted an enchanted infusion. He soaked the tree seed in this brew and a pint of his own blood until it grew into a sapling. He was in love with a certain Pelri, and he gifted this Tree to her entire people to safeguard them and win her favor."

"Levryn, yes. He was in love with Miranda. My mom used to tell me about their love story when I was little," Iyla said. "So, it's true? They weren't just a story?"

Jens nodded. "They were real."

"But I've seen that Tree, Jens," said Iyla. "It's right in the middle of the spring. It's bare and grey. And the spring is dark with algae. William and I have flown over it many times. What happened to it?"

"It was those two Sapins, Norlon and Parfix, projecting as Pelri," continued Jens, "who had learned of the Tree in the spring as the source of the power, who destroyed it. At the direction of the humans, they brought down the entire country of Keyronai. Those two Sapins, in the dead of night, swam out to the Elfblood Tree and carved out her heart."

Iyla gasped. Aron's lips parted at Jens' ominous words.

"It was at that moment that Keyronai began its transformation to the desolate country that it is today." Jens opened the book to read again. "There was a sudden rolling of thunder that grew more deafening with every second, every minute, that passed. The ground shuddered, the forest shook, and the spring's water cooled to a frosty chill. The thunderous vibration continued for hours.

"The Pelri of Keyronai knew their safety was in jeopardy and swiftly rejoined their families. By the light of the moons, the two Sapins stood silently in the cold spring water, one with the Heart still in his hand, as they watched the country's fortification deteriorate. The Elfblood Tree shook as the leaves and twigs showered down from above. The Sapins lost their footing as the spring floor trembled beneath them. Just as Norlon stumbled and fell into the water, a massive explosion erupted from below. Parfix, holding the Elfblood Heart, instantly vanished as he launched himself into another world, narrowly escaping the blast.

"The explosion under Urippa Spring blasted the sparkling pearls from the spring's floor into the night sky, culminating in the final spectacular display of natural beauty to be seen in Keyronai. The pearls burst into flames and soared through the sky like thousands of brilliant shooting stars. Every eye in Keyronai witnessed the pearl explosion. The thunderous rumble ceased, and the air filled with thousands of musical notes as each pearl came to rest in the hands of a Pelri."

"The pearls..." whispered Iyla. "That's how we got our pearl drops."

"Yes," Jens confirmed. "When the last Pelri reached out for her pearl drop, every single 'Neclu' Pelri vanished from the beautiful Keyronai. They reassembled in Bogarum and began a new existence of elusive habitation."

"So, with nature's fortification gone, the humans moved in," Aron concluded.

Jens sipped his sweet wine as Aron and Iyla sat in silence, the weight of new awareness heavy in the air.

"And what became of the Sapins? The ones who killed the Elfblood Tree," Aron asked.

Jens paused a moment before answering. "It is assumed that Norlon was killed in the explosion from Urippa Spring.

He was not heard from again. The other, Parfix... it was rumored that he had escaped his fate by traveling. He returned years later, and as my grandfather sat in a small alehouse, he listened to Parfix bragging about his conquest over the Tree and conquering Keyronai but exasperated at losing his prized trophy. I am now certain that he traveled to Earth." Jens motioned to the wooden ruby amulet that Aron still held in his hand.

Aron slowly lowered his head and fixed his eyes on the amulet. "This is the Heart," he whispered. Unmistakable heat now emanated from it, and deep in the center, a tiny glimmer of light could be seen.

"The Heart of the Elfblood Tree," Iyla whispered.

Jens opened his grandfather's book again. Flipping through several pages, he came to a meticulously drawn picture of the majestic Tree.

"We have to fix her!" Iyla asserted. "We have to. That's why you're here, Aron. That's why I found you. That's why the Heart brought you back! We can return the Heart, and then I know I'll get Seriah back!"

Aron looked at Jens, searching for understanding.

"Aron," said Jens. "You are not of this world, but it is evident that our world has called on you and Iyla to restore the homeland of such worthy inhabitants of Athemoni. I hope you will heed its call."

Aron's own heart was beating in his throat. His blood surged through his veins. Never could he have imagined that his relentless yearning for adventure would lead him to the path that was now before him. Was it possible that it was Athemoni that had been calling him all this time?

"But sir, I was taken from my home, and I don't know how to get back. My mother, and... Tora, she... my life is there." Then again, what did he really have to go back to? "And this thing, this Tree Heart, ever since I touched it, my life has turned upside down. How can you be sure this isn't evil magic? How do you know these stories are true?"

"It is your decision, Aron. I trust my grandfather's words," said Jens. "I don't know what the little Elfblood magic that's left in this world has in store for you, but know that the Tree stemmed from love and was cultivated and enchanted for protection, not darkness. I have no doubt that its careful safeguarding will extend to you as well."

Iyla rose from her cushion on the floor and moved closer to Aron, her eyes focused on him, awaiting his response. She rested her small hand on his arm, and Aron felt a slight tremble.

The magnitude of this summons was staggering. And yet, the daily struggle he felt on Earth to satisfy the call of adventure made sense now. From Scout to Eagle Scout, his youth led him from hiking and rock-climbing to wildlife conservation trips in Namibia. He skied. He sky-dived. Scaled a Redwood and swam to Alcatraz. He could never settle down. It was never enough.

Aron was meant for something bigger. This was not just a yearning for excitement. His destiny was not to be found back home. His life there was, in effect, over. But here, on Athemoni, he could make a real difference. He was asked to not only save a Tree, but to reclaim the home of a diminishing race. A second chance in life. This was his calling. And maybe, just maybe, the Tree who pulled him to this world, would have some answers for him.

"Sir," Aron said. "Iyla has shown me her kind and generous spirit. And I owe her my life. I cannot refuse the opportunity to repay her for what she has given me. I'll do my best to help her and all the Neclu Pelri."

A small smile crept across Iyla's face as she reached for his hand, and he squeezed hers. Noting Jens' frown, he quickly let go.

"Alright. Well." Jens leaned on his staff and stood as quickly as his age would tolerate. "You are going to need provisions. Iyla, go to the cupboard and pull out what you will need. William should be well rested by this afternoon." Once again, Jens disappeared into the back room. He returned, carrying a sizeable, yellowed section of thick paper.

"We'll need to formulate a strategy," he said as he spread the paper on the table.

"A map! Finally!" exclaimed Aron.

Seridon, or Keyronai, was a large island country set east of Bogarum but just off the west coast of Neritte. It was made up of two large islands with the principal island to the north. The secondary island was about half the size of the northern one, and several smaller volcanic islands flanked each of them. Ehn Ee Canyon, where they were now located, was in the eastern part of Neritte, bordering Oroc. Their journey would take them across Neritte to the northern part of Seridon to find Urippa Spring. Flying with William, they would travel unseen to the center of the spring, where Aron would dismount and return the Heart to the Elfblood Tree.

"We also need a plan for afterward," advised Aron.

"After what?" asked Iyla.

"After we return her Heart. We don't know what will happen, do we? Will it even work? An exit strategy."

"Alright. You two talk about that, and I'll go check on William. He's about due for a good snack." Iyla stood and moved around the table. As she crossed the room, Aron's eyes followed her. Iyla was strong, confident, independent, and beautiful. A bond was forming that he had not felt before.

But as Iyla approached the opening to the cave, Aron felt as if his own heart had stopped. Something was wrong. She stepped out onto the narrow stone staircase and looked out over the Rinn River.

"Iyla, wait," he said.

And then a cloaked arm reached from outside the cave's opening, grabbed Iyla's shoulder, and she vanished.

Chapter Eight

Exiting Ehn Ee

"IYLA!" Aron exclaimed, running toward the cave opening. "She's gone, Jens!"

"STOP!" Aron froze at the strength and volume of Jens' voice. "Do not go near the entrance!" Jens' concerned expression shifted to anger as he hastened toward the mouth of the cave.

Aron's heart raced and the color drained from his face. *What the hell was that?* "What just happened? Was that a Sapin's arm? Where are the dragons?"

Halting just before the open air, Jens placed his fingers between his lips and signaled a deep, vibrating whistle. The low tone echoed throughout the canyon, getting louder as it reverberated. The thrashing whoosh of dragon wings preceded the thunderous rumbling and ground trembling, announcing the arrival of not only Kellery, Khennedy, and William, but also a smaller, young dragon trailing behind.

It was a magnificent sight, the four iridescent dragons splashing through the river and then perching atop the boulders on the canyon floor, their long, muscular tails whipping the wind and their glistening scales catching the bright sunlight. Jens crossed the threshold to the outside and scanned the canyon upriver and down.

"No sign of her." Jens' expression had returned to concern. "Wretched Sapins."

"Why weren't the dragons here before? Don't they guard this place?"

"This is a vast canyon, Aron. They, along with magic, guard the books and me, if it is ever needed. There was no reason to believe those Sapins even knew the two of you were here, especially since you were sent to the back room."

Aron's heart sank, recalling that they had disobeyed his command.

"Change of plans then," Aron responded, jamming the Heart into his satchel. "We're going after her. Tell me what I need to do. Tell me where we need to go. What are they going to do to her, Jens? Let's go after her, now!"

"Aron, listen to me." Jens placed a hand on his shoulder. "This is no doubt the work of the Sapins, but the humans could also be involved. And I don't know if they stole her simply because she is a Pelri or if they know about you being in this world with the Elfblood Heart."

"They couldn't know about me," said Aron. "No one has seen me. We've been careful."

"They have their ways, my son. We don't know how long they were standing outside the cave and whether they heard our conversation. Either way, Iyla is in grave danger, and you must go to Seridon immediately. You are human; you will blend in. I must remain here."

"You aren't coming? I don't know anything about this place. You've gotta at least give me some idea of what to expect."

"I am obligated to remain at the Canyon, but I will give you some instruction and protection."

"Sir, I will do everything I can to bring her back. I will. Just tell me what I need to know."

"I know you will. And I can see that you care for her, Aron. I do trust you," Jens said. "Iyla is like my own granddaughter. I cannot lose her." He paused, turning to hide his emotion. "And you cannot lose that Heart."

Clearing his throat, he instructed, "William will take you as he is familiar with you; however, you will part ways once you have arrived in Seridon. He will return here, and you will be on your own. Take the map. You should begin here at this point, south of Lupellerin Lake." Jens pointed to the southern coast of the main island. "William will fly well south and then come back up over the ocean to avoid being seen. This is where Iyla rescued her mother. We are certain this is where most captured Pelri are kept for initial experimentation."

"OK. I will find her," Aron's stomach tightened, remembering what Iyla had told him about her mother's capture.

"Humans and Sapins use money as a form of trade to acquire things. I assume you have a similar thing on Earth?" Aron nodded. Jens continued, "You are going to need it for food and supplies. The elves have collected a supply of money for urgent situations such as this." Jens shuffled his way back to the Elven library, and Aron followed close behind. He stood in the doorway as Jens reached deep into his pocket and pulled out a bronze key. This unusual key had three similar prongs, as if there were three different keys attached to only one handle. He held the key high to the ceiling and then pulled it down through the air to the floor, leaving a floating trail of glistening blue dust.

With the glass window gone, Jens pulled out several books from the middle of one bookcase to reveal a round wooden door on the back wall the size of a shield, with three keyholes. Rolling his key from right to left into the keyholes, he opened the round door. It creaked with age, and again the sweet, musky smell wafted around him.

Several stacks of square paper currency, along with silver and gold coins, were packed inside. "These are 'griggs,' Seridon money," said Jens, handing several stacks to Aron. "Pack these in your satchel. Use it for any necessities."

"Yes, thanks," said Aron.

"One more thing." Reaching again into the hidden door, he pulled out a triangular object about the same size as the key. It was black and made of iron. "A bit of Elven magic."

Jens placed the object in Aron's hand. It was cold with an uneven texture. "William cannot stay with you, as he is far too conspicuous. But if you are in danger, you can use this talisman as a signal, and I will send assistance. As you are not an elf, you will only be able to use it once, so choose that time wisely. And remember, Seridon is a country of humans and Sapins. You cannot trust them."

"Yes, right. OK. And what about clothes? Will I blend in with what I'm wearing? Do you think they'll ask questions?"

"You should be fine," Jens reassured. "You speak the same, your clothes are relatively similar. And you are from Parise, yes? Not many humans live in such remote areas so that should work. You are just passing through."

A chill ran up Aron's spine, but he was ready. He tucked the talisman into the inner pocket of his jacket and filled the remaining available space in his satchel with extra food and drink.

Aron and Jens made their way down the steep stone staircase. The four dragons remained perched on the boulders outside. Jens detoured to the right to stop by the food storage cave to gather several tarthberries, fish, and something that looked like a basketball-sized potato, to distribute to each one.

"Sir," Aron turned to Jens, and each dragon raised its head to look at him. "I've never actually flown a dragon myself."

Jens rested his hand on Aron's shoulder. "Unnecessary. William is well-trained. I'll tell him what he needs to do, and you just hold on tight to the straps. He understands Iyla is in trouble. They have a very close bond. He feels it."

Looking over toward the dragons finishing their meals and swimming in the water, he said, "This will be a long journey. Longer than the time it took for you to travel here. You will stop at the Neritte coastline close to the Kleey border to camp out and rest. The coastline is populated, but it will be late into the night already, so you will be well hidden. Then before sunrise, you will start again over the ocean and should arrive in Seridon, south of Lupellerin Lake, in the morning. William will know exactly where to go."

"Thank you, sir," Aron said. "I'll trust William."

William approached Aron and the old elf and curled his tail close to his body for Aron to use to climb onto his back. As Aron strapped himself on, Jens rested his forehead behind William's ear as his fingers drew signals onto his neck. No sooner did Jens back away when William rose onto his hind legs and flapped his strong wings, spewing a billowing torrent of yellow and white fire. Aron struggled to hang on to the leather straps as he felt the surge of William's body beneath him, hoisting them into the air.

Aron watched as Jens and the remaining three dragons grew smaller the higher they climbed. Kellery and Khennedy switched boulders to perch as sentries directly outside the opening to Jens' cave. Further upriver, Aron could see Jens' second young dragon, who never responded to his call, bathing in the water, seemingly oblivious to everything around him.

Beyond Ehn Ee Canyon, Neritte was a mountainous country, with tall snow-capped peaks and deep valleys populated with small clusters of villages. Aron could not determine what sort of people lived there from his altitude, but the homes were all small log cabin-like structures, most with a thin pillar of smoke rising out of their chimneys. He imagined they might be accustomed to dragons flying overhead as close as they were to Ehn Ee Canyon.

A few hours into their journey, dark grey clouds gathered around them, and he heard the faint sound of rolling thunder in the distance. Aron clung to William's heated armor as the cold air blew through his cloak. Tiny, gentle droplets morphed into pelting shards that bit his hands and face with the ice-cold rain. Sharp lightning stitched bright, menacing patterns across the night sky and then quickly disappeared before the thunderous rumble. Choking from the cloak that was tied at his neck, Aron winced as the leather riding straps tore into his hands and legs as he fought to lean into William as they hurtled across the angry wind currents. Aron struggled with the storm's relentless insistence to wrench his body from William's. But he held on.

Hours later, the clouds finally dissipated, and the moons shone brightly in the fresh starry sky. William began his descent with the dark seawater tossing and churning in the distance and Aron's heavy, rain-soaked cloak flapping behind him.

Hundreds of tiny lights dotted the landscape. Aron remembered Jens describing the coastline as populated, but William brought them down on a narrow remote beach, just over the edge of the tall jagged cliffs jutting out into the sea. Aron dismounted, and William lit a fire inside a small cove where they would camp for the night. Wincing at the pain, Aron rinsed his blistered, blood-streaked hands in the salty sea water before drying off by the fire and rationing his dinner. The sand was damp from the recent storm, so Aron's best option was to sleep on William's back, which, although warm, was most uncomfortable, especially after spending the last several hours strapped to him. William was also restless, and after dumping Aron off the side of him for the third time during the night, he and Aron both finally found comfort with William lying on his side and Aron tucked underneath William's left wing.

The rhythmic waves lulled him to sleep as he contemplated the possibilities of the impending events.

Chapter Nine

YETRIL'S EYES

A ron felt small under the giant wing of William. The precariousness of his position was unsettling, and he found it difficult to put out of his mind that he was sleeping on a dragon. However, the tumultuous events of the day had drained him, and sleep had come, if only for a few hours.

It was still dark when Aron once again tumbled from under William's wing to the wet sand below. There were voices. As William stretched and beat his wings, Aron gathered his satchel and cloak. He climbed onto William's back and strapped on just before William hoisted them into the cool twilight air.

"Dad! Look!" The faint words of a child drifted up behind them, but Aron and William were soon out of sight above the dark seawater, enveloped in the dense fog. *Shouldn't that kid be in bed?* he thought. But then memories of him and his dad waking up before dawn to go fishing flooded his mind. *He would've loved Athemoni.*

With Kleey now on their left and the ocean to the right, William traveled southward briefly before moving further out to sea and then changing directions to head north toward Seridon, just as Jens had delineated. Daylight was fast approaching, and it was fortunate that the fog concealed them before the morning sun broke through. The surf below was rough, and whitecaps speckled the dark blue ocean. To the far west, the southern volcanic islands emerged from the water in the distance. For a moment, Aron thought he saw a large dark form swimming beneath the surface before realizing it was only William's shadow.

Land was ahead. This was Seridon, originally Keyronai, the lost home of Iyla's people.

William touched down on the south side of a large protruding rock formation just steps from a desolate rocky beach. Aron dismounted and tossed the last few tarthberries to William for breakfast. As Aron ate, William paced slowly in front of him.

"I think this is where we part ways, buddy," Aron said. "Can't have you getting spotted with me."

William grunted and paced in the shallow water, and a few curls of smoke escaped his nostrils. He watched Aron closely, and Aron got the distinct feeling that he was trying to communicate something.

"Don't worry, buddy. I'll find her." Aron held out another tarthberry. "I'll find her and bring her back to ya. I promise."

William rose onto his hind legs, flapped his wings, and launched himself into the air. He looked back toward Aron and then quickly disappeared into the clouds.

"Thanks, bud," Aron whispered.

After taking a quick inventory of the contents of his satchel, Aron opened the map to plan his route, but with little detail on topography or populations, the most he could do was strategize for potential quandaries. He'd get a lay of the city, establish his base of operations, and procure weapons. In addition, he would be interacting with the Seridon humans and possibly Sapins. He needed to appear to be one of them, or at a minimum, a native inhabitant of Athemoni.

With renewed energy, he packed up his satchel, slung it over his shoulder, and waded into the knee-deep water toward the small, isolated beach. Beyond the beach, what had once been a dense grove of majestic palms, now stood towering, petrified forms shrouded in the grey veils of their own tattered branches. Refuse blanketed the terrain, and a probing stench of decay thickened the air. In the distance, Aron could barely make out the familiar sounds of a busy civilization.

A torn, discarded pamphlet wedged between two large stones caught his attention.

YERIL'S EYES

Faded and torn from weather, the words on the thick paper were still legible.

> *"Celebrate the Yeril Centenary at Yeril's Eyes! It's been one hundred years since Yeril gifted us with his vision of deliverance. What better way to honor our country's favorite seer than a festive jamboree at his namesake brewery! Head over to Radon Street and drink one for Yeril! All humans and Sapins are welcome. Entrance Fee: 15 Gg."*

Aron folded the pamphlet and tucked it into his pocket. A seer. Jens didn't cover that in his disrupted history lesson. As Aron trudged through the dead palms and debris, he saw several more copies of the tavern's flyer.

A half-mile in, Aron came to an actual paved road. It was in poor condition, but a road nonetheless, and a motivating discovery. The breezy air carried away the pungent scent of decay, although death was all around him. Forests were thick but brittle, grey and weak. Brown and grey; that was the range of the color palette surrounding him, not unlike the desert he had left behind. Every so often, he would see a more substantial, green shoot daring an attempt at life, but it was obviously an ill-fated gamble.

The low buzz of city noise was growing in the distance. The road was no longer in disrepair but now more significant and cleaner. Up ahead, lights and movement. An automobile was approaching, its coughing and sputtering motor growing louder. It passed him quickly and uneventfully. Aron breathed a quick sigh.

The dead forests gave way to dead grass, and across the flat land, the city burgeoned. Buildings and shops and people and several cars; it all seemed odd and out of place in this world, but almost encouraging in its familiarity. More cars passed in both directions, black smoke billowing behind them. They were similar to cars on Earth, but noisier and clunkier.

The city buildings, however, were a different story—and one of startling opulence. Among the noise and exhaust, beautiful structures made of white-washed stone and glossy marble emerged. Gold-framed windows and ornamental gemstones adorned every façade. Diamonds glistened on the walkways, and everywhere he looked, there were people. Lots of people walking and shopping and conversing. Their dress was quite similar to his own, and everyone seemed to be going about normal daily activities. Aron's apprehension at blending in was eased substantially.

Yeril's Eyes. The tavern was straight ahead, on the other side of the roundabout. The neon sign shone brightly above the boisterous patrons seated on the outside covered patio. Aron crossed the street and pressed his way through the crowded door. The thick stench of sweat mingling with the beer's malty aroma was strangely welcoming. Yeril's Eyes was your typical hole-in-the-wall tavern. A set of game tables was positioned along the south wall, largely ignored aside from one small party. A rowdy group in the back corner laughed and mocked the surrounding customers. Other than the waitress, there were no women in the tavern. Aron took a seat on the far side of the bar, facing the entrance.

The bartender nodded and handed him a menu. "Ya sightseein'?" he asked.

"What?" Aron was imperceptibly unnerved.

"You're not from here." The bartender noted.

Aron stiffened and then smiled. "Is it that obvious?"

"Well, I've never seen ya, ya got your pack over your shoulder, and to be honest, ya look like you could use a shower. What can I get ya?" He was a short man with jet-black hair, friendly and energetic.

Aron noticed a customer enter, fully covered in a dark, hooded cloak like the visitors at Ehn Ee Canyon. The customer sat down at a table on the opposite side of the bar.

"Give me the local favorite," Aron said.

"Where ya stayin'?"

"Uh, not sure yet. Got any recommendations? I've never been here before."

"Never been to Lupellerin? Quite the city, hunh?" asked the bartender as he dried a large glass with a towel.

"I've never been to any part of Seridon," he answered.

"Really? Thought everybody'd been to Seridon. Where ya from?" he asked, pouring a large mug of a dark caramel brew.

"Uh, western Parise. Born and raised."

"Hm. Long way from home. You're human, right? They don't got any Sapins out there, do they? Pretty remote out that way."

Aron was wondering where this line of questioning would go. "Haven't seen 'em. Then again, not sure I'd be able to tell."

"Meh, if you're around 'em enough, ya can tell. That one over there," the bartender nodded toward the new customer at the far table. "Typical Sapin. Easy one. And there's another over by the cronch table. He's not covered like the other one. And of course, ya know they all have the pale hair."

"Oh, no, I didn't realize that."

"Yeah. Sapins come here a lot. They're rude but useful. Should get yourself one. Take 'em back with ya."

"Get one?"

"Yah, why not? They're easily bribed."

"Why would I want one?"

"Man, they can get ya stuff. Maybe even take ya a few places. Get ya to where yer goin'."

Aron scanned the tavern. "So, they all usually wear the head-to-toe cloaks then." The Sapin customer who recently arrived was talking to a visibly irritated waitress, but he noticed he or she sent darting glances in Aron's direction.

"Usually, they do. Not always. They like to appear mysterious, I guess. Stupid. I know that guy, though, playing cronch. Rixly. He's alright." The blonde Sapin at the cronch table, who looked to be Aron's age, seemed as human as everyone else. Aron could easily picture the two of them in the U.S., going out for beers at the local Greene Turtle.

"Hm," Aron replied.

"Here," said the bartender, as he tossed a pencil to Aron. "Write this down. Faradell... Narrow."

Aron pulled out the old flyer he had found on the beach and unfolded it to write on.

"Aw, dude! Were ya 'round for that?"

"For what?" Aron asked.

"Yeril's Centenary! That's our flyer. That was like two months ago! It rocked, man, rocked! We had the biggest, baddest crowd in town! Had people come from all over."

"No," Aron replied. "I was in Parise still. Sounds like it was a blast, though." *This is weird.*

"Yeah? Did ya hear about it? 'Course, it turned into an even bigger bash than originally planned when we ended up gettin' that guy in the same year as the Centenary. Ya know they killed 'em, right? In the *same year* as Yeril's 100th anniversary of the foretelling. Pretty cool."

"Killed who?"

"Crakes. Don't ya hear about anything out there in western Parise? Yeril's foretelling! The guy he predicted would take Seridon. Dead. Gone. Killed at war, actually. On Earth. Yeah, that party rocked!"

Shit.

The blood in Aron's veins froze, and he felt sick to his stomach. He hid his pale expression by pretending to rummage through his satchel. The cloaked customer at the far table was watching him but turned away when Aron looked in that direction. His hooded head hung low, and Aron could see no face.

"Wow," Aron pretended to endorse the magnitude of the bartender's news. "That's huge! When was that?"

"Right before the Centenary. Awesome timing!" The bartender could barely contain his delight at the knowledge of this death. Raising a full mug, he shouted, "To Yeril!"

The crowded tavern responded, "To Yeril!"

Back in the corner, the rowdy, heavily intoxicated customers erupted, singing a celebrated bar ditty:

Old man, Yeril, lend your eyes
Tell us where our future lies
Seridon is doomed, he said
Unless the human from Earth is dead!

Trust my eyes, protect your home
I'll tell you what my eyes have known
Yeril's eyes, save our land
Save us from the Earthman's hand

All-knowing eyes, never lies!
Yeril's eyes! Yeril's eyes!

The men exploded into roars of laughter, and Aron shook his head, chuckling to himself.

"You know, back in the *really* remote parts of western Parise and Tondon, some people don't believe all that," Aron risked the confrontation.

The bartender stiffened. "You don't?"

"I'm not saying me."

"Not sure how ya wouldn't believe it when he got everything right."

"Everything?" Aron asked.

"He found the Tree Heart when stupid Parfix took off and lost it. Ol' Yeril knew when and where the Earthman would be born, where he lived. Knew what he looked like. Knew the Earthman'd be trying to get to that Heart every second of his life."

"Hm, true. Good thing he's dead." *Shit.* In the corner of his eye, he saw the cloaked Sapin get up from the table, take a last glance toward him, and exit the tavern.

Do not trust any of them. He had not forgotten Jens' words.

"So, Faradell Narrow?" Aron inquired.

"Oh yeah. Good place to stay the night. And not far down the road."

"Thanks." Aron handed him ten griggs. "By the way, who killed him?"

"Well, ya know the Sapins couldn't do it, or we'd be screwed. Not sure who exactly, but it happened in battle. His country was at war. Blew 'em up. Got him just in time, from what I heard."

"Excellent," Aron stood to leave. "And great brew. I'll be back again." The bartender raised his mug to Aron as he exited.

Outside, on the north side of the bar, a bull was roasting above an open-pit barbecue. It was still early afternoon, and the smokey, savory aroma filled the air. *Man, I gotta get home. They knew I was coming even though I didn't! What the hell kinda place did I fall into? Shit! Are these people responsible for the attack on my convoy? Were they working with the Iraqis?*

Aron stood in front of the roast for a bit to take in his surroundings. The sun was warm, and the light danced off the gemstones that swathed the city. Across the street, outside a small food store, a commotion between a haggard elderly man and a middle-aged woman drew his attention. Security had already arrived, and they restrained the man, face to the ground. The woman was crying and yelling at the man as the other security officer attempted to console her. A small crowd was gathering, and the man, with his hands bound behind his back, was forced into the back seat of the officer's vehicle before being driven away.

I gotta find Iyla. Aron approached an onlooker and asked where the police station was located.

"Police station?" The onlooker's brow furrowed.

Oh, crap, he thought, but pressed on. "The security headquarters? Law enforcement? Where did they take that man?"

"Peace Enforcement building?" the onlooker responded. "Go about three blocks in that direction, take a right, and it's about two blocks up. If you get to the sinkhole, you've gone too far. Be careful."

Sinkhole? "Great, thanks."

Aron could hear the onlooker muttering to his wife as he walked away. "What the hell is a police station?"

Aron decided to settle into a room at Faradell Narrow. He would set that up as his base of operations and clean himself up before moving forward. He didn't want to call any more attention to himself by looking like an outsider, since he blended in reasonably well here, and although it was more than unsettling to learn that another world had been plotting his death, the inhabitants believed their country was now safe, and they would not be looking for him. The cloaked Sapin's suspicious behavior in the tavern was also unnerving; however, Aron's current mission was to find Iyla, and he was well-trained to watch his back.

He found Faradell Narrow easily enough. It was, as the bartender stated, just down the road on the edge of the city. A stately white farmhouse with an oversized wrap-around veranda, it reminded Aron of a bed-and-breakfast where he had stayed with Tora in Georgia. While in Georgia, their bed-and-breakfast was set on a hill and surrounded by beautiful trees and gardens; here in Lupellerin, the house stood directly on the street, no foliage in sight.

The sign on the door said, "Please Enter." Aron opened the door and walked in, wiping his shoes on the floor mat.

"CLOSED!" shouted someone from behind a large desk, although he saw no one.

"Hello?" Aron asked. "I need a room for the night. Or maybe a couple nights."

A large, rough man in an unkempt shirt and pants appeared from under the desk. He was deeply tanned, almost bald, with an overgrown scruffy red beard. Sweat beaded over his tattoos, which covered every inch of visible skin.

"WE'RE CLOSED!" he yelled back at Aron.

"OK, alright!" he responded. "Any other places around here that—"

"WE'RE FULL! GET OUT!"

After a moment of hesitation, Aron turned and exited, closing the door behind him. *Why would the bartender have recommended this place?*

Aron turned the corner to head toward the Peace Enforcement building. Maybe he would find an alternative on the way.

Up ahead, he noticed the tail ends of a dark cloak fluttering and then disappearing behind a small jewelry store. It was the Sapin. Aron took off down the street to catch up to him, but he was no longer in sight.

Aron had the distinct impression that the Neclu Sapins, although powerful, were treated much like second-class citizens or servants here in Seridon. He recalled the bartender badmouthing them when he pointed them out to Aron in the bar, even though the one by the game table was supposedly 'alright.' He had seen a couple more in the street, always alone, no one really interacting with them. There were a few establishments that had posted signs stating, "Humans Only." If he approached this Sapin, who seemed intent on following him, it might not be out of the ordinary if it turned into an altercation.

The Peace Enforcement building was up ahead, but just beyond it was something even more intriguing. Several large tractors, cranes, and other machinery crowded the street for about four or five blocks. With pickup trucks and loud equipment, construction workers in neon vests and hard hats patiently stood on the edges of precisely what the onlooker had warned him about—a massive sinkhole.

Chapter Ten

All Humans are Bad

"Iyla, wait." Aron's voice echoed behind her, and a stiff, icy hand gripped her shoulder. Just as she was about to let out a scream, the river and canyon disappeared, and another hand covered her mouth as she was pulled back and wrapped in the dark, shrouded cloak of the figure behind her.

The Sapin's arm dug into her abdomen as grey darkness fell all around her. Her body tossed back and forth, and the air was almost too thick to breathe. A strange taste filled her mouth, bitter and then sour. When they emerged in Seridon, the Sapin's grip tightened around Iyla again before dragging her into a securely locked holding room.

The door slammed shut, and she was left in silence, surrounded by dull white walls and only one small window near the top of the door that led to the hallway, too high for her to peer through. Iyla knew this building.

This was it. They had captured her.

It had to be that Sapin that glanced her way earlier today in the canyon. The anticipation of their upcoming adventure was invigorating. But had she gotten careless? Distracted? The pieces had started coming together, and she was excited at the possibility of liberating her people from their transitory home life. And then she knew she'd find Seriah. But how was she going to do that now? *They're going to kill me.*

And what about Aron? What happened to him? Was he safe? *Did I ruin everything?* From their first meeting on the Remmeline River through their journey to Jens and learning more about the history of her race, she had grown to care about this man. This human. *Ugh! Why didn't I just listen to Jens and stay in the back room?*

The metal door opened, and a young, plump woman dressed entirely in light blue walked in with a tall water bottle and a folded gown. She studied Iyla curiously and cautiously approached her. *Was that fear in her eyes?*

"Please remove your clothing and put on the gown. Drink the water." After placing both items on the small table, she turned and left.

Iyla paced from one side of the room to the other. *Do they actually think I'm going to make this easy for them?* She thought about her mother and wondered if she, too, had been thrown into this same holding room. Did she stare at these same four walls, contemplating her escape? Did the same young woman bring her a gown and water and order her to change out of her clothes? Her mother would have fought. As old and frail as she was, she was strong in spirit. *I've gotta get out of here. They're not going to stop me.*

Voices filtered through the door. She jumped up to see through the window, but to no avail.

"Girl," said the voice. "She's a young one. I found her at the dragon canyon in Neritte." That was the Sapin.

"How old?" asked the second voice.

"I don't know. I didn't talk to her. Eight? Nine? Can't be ten."

There was a momentary pause. "And you just picked her up today?" Iyla guessed this must be the woman in blue that the Sapin was talking to.

"Yes, brought her straight here."

"Is that where she lives? In the canyon?"

"I don't think so. Only the dragons and the trainer live there. I was there with Richmon and Shiff. We need to get that dragon for the Commander. Jens is still being a shit about it." There was another pause.

"Do you know when she last ate?"

"No."

"Do you have her pearl drop?"

"No. She didn't have it on her."

"OK," the woman said suspiciously. "You'll need to report to body search on the fourth floor. And did anyone see you?" she asked.

"I nabbed her when she stepped out of the cave. The trainer was inside. Dragons were in a different part of the canyon. It was quick."

"Alright, I've got some paperwork here for you to fill out, a small container for your DNA sample—leave all of it at the front desk. We'll escort you to the fourth floor. If you leave your escort, payment is forfeited. The Commander thanks you for your service."

Iyla heard some shuffling after the woman and Sapin finished up their consultation. And then silence. She eyed the water bottle and gown that still sat on the table, untouched.

About twenty minutes passed before the door swung open once again. Blue clothes stood in the doorway, looked at the water bottle and gown, and then Iyla. She sighed dramatically and then turned and yelled, "HEDDAH!" before slamming the door shut behind her.

For the rest of the day, the door did not open, and Iyla sat in silence. She had to figure out how to escape. She scanned the room for anything she could use to rig the door lock. Nothing. Everything in the room was secured.

Thoughts of Aron and his safety hammered at her brain. If he wasn't taken, Jens would help him. Jens would figure out how to get the Heart back into the Elfblood Tree, hopefully before the humans killed her.

The door opened, and a different, older woman walked in with a tray of food. "Hey, honey! How're you doing in here? You alright? Well, aren't you just the prettiest little thing!" Then she whispered, "They didn't hurt you, did they?"

Iyla stared at her but said nothing. This woman had a kind face with thick brown hair that came to her shoulders. She seemed genuinely concerned about Iyla, but the blood spots on her pale blue uniform did not go unnoticed.

"I know you are probably frightened, and I'm so sorry for that, sweetie. Best advice I can give you is to just cooperate. There's really nothing else you can do, unfortunately. Can you do that? I'll be right here with you through all the tests."

Iyla did not respond, and the woman picked up the untouched water bottle and handed it to her.

"Please drink the water. You'll dehydrate. And look, I brought you some dinner. The chef here is actually pretty good. If you don't eat meat, I can get you a vegetarian option. Yes?"

Still, Iyla was silent.

The woman sighed. "I don't blame you for being guarded. I promise, there's nothing harmful in the food. It's just good food." Her hopeful but sad expression was almost comforting to Iyla.

Do not trust Seridon humans. Seridon humans...meeting Aron had now qualified Jens' warning.

"I'll leave you alone now, sweetie. Eat up, OK?" She left the room and closed the door softly.

Iyla had to admit the food did smell good, and she was famished. From her spot on the floor, she could see the steam rising from it. If she was going to die here, she might as well die with a full stomach.

The dinner tray was loaded with baked fish, a mound of mashed turnips, steamed frekka, which Aron always called "corn," and a small serving of raw praterbeans. It did taste good. If they didn't drug it, then at least it would give her some strength to fight.

About an hour later, the brown-haired woman returned. She stopped in the doorway, her eyes tired, but she smiled when she saw the empty dinner tray. "Aw, I'm glad to see you ate. I'm sure you feel a little better now?" Iyla had returned to her spot on the floor in the corner and said nothing.

"Well, I have a few questions for you, but I get the feeling that you probably won't want to answer them, hunh?" The woman nodded sympathetically. "I know how you must feel. The Pelri haven't been treated so well by us humans, and I am so sorry for that. You have every reason to be wary. But all I can do is try to make this process a little easier for you. I wish you didn't have to go through this at all, and I'm so sorry. Will you answer a few questions?"

Iyla stared at the woman as the anger intensified inside of her. *She knows what her people do to the Pelri. She knows it's wrong. Never trust a human, a Seridon human.*

"You killed my mother," Iyla murmured through gritted teeth.

"I'm sorry, sweetie, what was that?" asked the woman.

Iyla's eyes were narrow slits, and she could no longer suppress her fury. "You killed my mother and took my friends! Where's Seriah?" she screamed, jumping up and bolting for the door. The brown-haired woman was quick and caught her arm, gripping it tightly as Iyla pummeled her shoulder with her other fist.

"You killed my mother!" Tears were streaming down Iyla's cheeks. "Let me go!"

The woman reached into her pocket, pulled out a handful of fine pink powder, and tossed a cloud into Iyla's face. "I'm so sorry, doll. I have to," she whispered.

Iyla coughed and choked as the powder entered her lungs. Immediately, her legs buckled, and she crumpled onto the floor. The woman dove forward to catch Iyla's head as she fell.

Iyla couldn't move. She could breathe, and she could see, but her muscles would not respond.

"Aw, I'm so sorry little one. I wish I didn't have to do that. And now the tests will be skewed. We'll have to wait a little longer. Come on, now." She pulled Iyla's limp body out of the holding room and up onto a gurney. She tried to cry out, but her body responded to nothing.

The brown-haired woman removed Iyla's clothing, and once she was fully undressed, she clamped down her wrists and ankles to the sides of the bed. Her exposed body could still feel the chill in the air.

Another worker in blue clothes rounded the corner.

"Git! Git!" Brown-Hair shooed her away. "Can't you see she needs privacy? Git! Go!" She shook her head as the other worker backed out of the room and then pulled out a warm, wet cloth from the room behind her to wipe the powder from Iyla's face. She stood back and looked at Iyla lying helplessly on the gurney and sighed. "Poor thing." She pulled a white sheet over her body and face and wheeled her down the hall to another room. "Just hang in there, dear," she whispered.

Iyla's mind raced. Where were they going? What were they going to do to her? Again, she tried to cry out. Nothing. She couldn't move.

Through the sheet, Iyla could see the lights turn off. She heard the door shut, and all was quiet. Her eyes felt so sleepy. She didn't know if it was from actual fatigue or from the paralyzing powder she had inhaled. She fought to stay awake. She fought to scream. Desperately, she tried to move, but all she could really do was wait. *They're going to torture me.*

For two hours, she waited, her weary eyes stinging. Then he arrived.

The door swung open violently, and the knob slammed into the adjacent wall. The loud thud startled Iyla, and her skin prickled as blood surged through her veins.

"Sir," said Brown-Hair. "She's not decent at the moment!"

"I don't give a shit if she's not decent! Is this her?" The loud, gruff voice came from directly above her, just before the sheet was thrown off her body.

"Yes, sir. Sir? Please. I'll watch her."

"Move out of the way! Well, will you have a look at that...? She's a pretty one." He gazed down at her naked body. Iyla's heart pounded inside her chest, and she felt nauseous. It was him. What was he going to do? Goose bumps paraded across her bare body in the chilly air. *I gotta get out!* She strained to move her arms to cover herself, but it was no use.

He was a tall, husky man with black hair pulled back in a low ponytail, and he smiled a toothy smile. *Get away from me!* His mouth seemed too large relative to the rest of his tanned face. A long scar on the left side followed his hairline and black sideburns. And he reeked of old cheese. *Goddess, please don't let him touch me.*

"Commander... sir," said Brown-Hair. "She's got an appointment in the weight room."

"This is a good one. Have you started testing?" he asked.

"We need to get her to the weight room. And no, testing hasn't started yet. We had to use the powder, which, as you know—"

"Feisty one, hunh? I bet she is..."

"But I can handle her, sir, no problem. I can take care of her."

"Back off, Heddah! You are to manage her testing and research plan. Nothing else! After that, she's mine."

Iyla struggled to reconcile Heddah's concern with what she always knew: humans are bad. Who was this woman? Was she trying to shield her from him?

The Commander was head of Seridon's security and defensive strategies. He was the reason the Pelri were always in hiding. If only she could reach up to his dark head and rip his big mouth clear through to his eye sockets. The leader of Seridon, the most evil of all humans, who ordered the capture of all Pelri, the one responsible for the defiling and mutilation of her mother's frail body. *Get away from me!* Iyla cringed inside at the man's apparent fixation as Heddah retrieved the sheet to cover her. Her arms shivered as she fought to escape her own body.

"Start the testing. I want every result of every test as soon as you have it. Notify me immediately when the first round is done," he ordered.

"Yes, sir, but—"

"And make sure she eats. I don't like 'em too skinny."

"Yes," the woman whispered as she spotted a tear winding its way down from Iyla's eye.

Iyla heard them exit the room, and they shut the door behind them.

Again, she tried to move her legs and then her arms. Nothing. She was a prisoner in her own body. Her weary eyelids were so heavy, and it wasn't long before they closed, and she fell into a deep sleep.

Iyla awoke to a soft, warm hand stroking her hair. "You awake, doll?" asked the woman. "We need you awake and sitting up for these next few tests. It won't hurt, I promise."

"Just pull her up, Heddah, and push her head into the chin rest of the Tonometer. She's not your child. She's a Pelri." The man was reasonably young, slender, and wearing glasses. He was either a doctor or a scientist; Iyla couldn't tell. Two others were also in the room.

"She's still a living being that deserves kindness," Heddah responded. "You could afford to be a little more kind yourself, Teerint."

"Yes, I see how well that's worked out for you." His sarcasm prompted a few soft chuckles from the others. Heddah frowned as she rubbed her wrist.

Iyla was sitting upright when she noticed four wires connected to her chest and one connected to her neck. There was a bandage on her left hip. How long had she been sleeping, and what had they done to her body during that time? Heddah pulled the sheet around her.

"I have been here for over three years, Teerint. Three. I have worked on four Pelri, and not one of them was anywhere near as heartless as most humans I know. It's a shame what we put these sweet people through." Heddah guided Iyla's head to the chin rest.

"Well, I have been here for what, nine months, and this is my first opportunity to work on a Pelri, and I'm not going to screw it up. They'll be promoting me to Rakkarron Station soon enough, where I can study all the Pelri I want. They've got thirty-four live ones right now, I hear. I will find the key to their abilities; just wait. And when I do, Seridon will again be the prosperous and fruitful country it once was. It starts with this one. And it starts with me. But you keep talking like that, Heddah, and I wouldn't be surprised if it got you reported," warned Teerint. *Thirty-four Pelri?* Rakkarron Station, next stop. As soon as she escaped this building.

"It's just a shame, is all. What have they ever done to us? I mean, we humans took *their* land—and ruined it, mind you. I just hate to think about—"

"Seriously, Heddah. Do I need to assign a different research assistant to this job?"

Heddah sighed as she patted Iyla's thigh. And she could feel it. Iyla flexed her feet; she could move. The powder had worn off. Her eyes searched for the door. How fast were these humans? Could she outrun them? Heddah was undeniably strong, as she had clearly demonstrated in the holding room.

"Do you know her name?" asked Teerint. "Tell her to look straight ahead at the small light."

"No, I don't, but you have a mouth. What's keeping you from telling her? She's right here, sitting in front of you."

Teerint glared at Heddah.

"This won't hurt a bit, sweetie, just a little puff," Heddah comforted her as a puff of air stunned her eyeball. Iyla immediately jumped back.

"That's it, that's all it was."

Teerint used a bright light to peer closely into her eyes. He finished and glanced at Heddah, raising an eyebrow. "Is it just me, or does she smell like flowers?"

Heddah rolled her eyes. "Get your stuff. There's the door. I'm going to clean her up and get her dressed."

The room emptied, and Iyla was alone with Heddah. She had to make a break for it.

"I'm going to unhook these wires, and I'd like to get you in the shower if that's OK," she said. "Your legs are going to be a little unsteady, so just hold on to me, so you don't fall."

Iyla stared at her for a moment, not knowing how to respond. *All humans are bad*, she thought to herself. Could this Seridon human possibly be genuinely kind? Iyla didn't know what to make of Heddah. No. Never trust a Seridon human.

Iyla slid her feet down to touch the floor. Her knees buckled, just slightly, and Heddah wrapped her arm around her waist to support her. In this room, Iyla had a view of the outside, and the sky was dark. Clouds covered most of the stars, but the light of the moons broke through them. How long had she slept? Was it the same day?

"It's late, I know," said Heddah as she tested the shower water and helped Iyla step in and closed the curtain. "You just let me know if you need anything or if you're feeling light-headed."

Freshly showered and changed into a clean gown, Iyla sat down on the bed. "Why are you being nice to me?"

After the initial surprise at hearing Iyla speak, Heddah looked at her with her sad face and sighed. "Is there a reason I shouldn't be?"

"I know what goes on here and now at the Rakkarron Station. I know I probably won't ever leave this place, and my days are numbered. But why would a nice person work here, and why would you take part in the disgusting things that are done to the Pelri, and who knows who else?"

Heddah sat down next to her and patted Iyla's knee. She paused for a moment and then sighed again. "Well, that's probably a story for another day, sweet girl. Sometimes, we don't have a choice." Heddah's voice quivered slightly. She took a deep breath and seemed to drift off in thought, gazing across the sterile white room.

The equipment had been removed from the room. Aside from the bed she was sitting on and a small table and chair in the corner, the room was bare, although a slight upgrade from the preliminary holding room, which had no outside window or bathroom.

"I've got to head home, sweetie, but I'll be back in the morning. Get some rest." Heddah stood to leave. "Can I call you by your name?"

Iyla sat silent, even though she really didn't want Heddah to go.

"That's OK, honey. I understand."

She closed the door behind her as Iyla laid her head down on the clean pillow. Recalling the despicable conduct of the foul-smelling Commander, she pulled the covers up to her neck. She had to escape this evil place. She didn't want to die.

Chapter Eleven

The Sinkhole, the Sapin, and the Inn

A ron stood near the edge of the enormous sinkhole before him. Barriers were set up around the perimeter so that onlookers wouldn't tumble over the edge, but several made their way between them, regardless. He estimated it had to be at least two football fields wide. Peering over the jagged edge, Aron saw the wreckage of the homes, buildings, and vehicles that it had swallowed lying crumpled and destroyed at the bottom.

"I wanna see." Aron turned to the small boy behind him, probably about four or five Earth years old. He had skinned both his knees. "Can you hold me up so I can see?"

"You shouldn't be this close, little guy. Is your mom nearby?" Aron asked.

"She's working, but my aunt is over there by that building talking to the Peace Enforcement."

"You should probably go back over to her then."

"Why?" the little boy asked.

"She might get worried about you being so close to this sinkhole."

"Nah, I come look at it every day."

"Oh yeah? How long has it been here?"

"I don't know. A while. Is this the first time you're seeing it?" he asked.

"Yes. I don't live close by. I didn't know about this sinkhole until today," Aron answered.

"Can you get me closer?" he asked again.

Aron thought for a second. "How about if I pick you up and then take you over to your aunt? You can look real quick," he suggested. The little boy's face lit up as he nodded with excitement, and Aron bent down to scoop him up.

"Whoa!" exclaimed the boy. "So cool!"

With the boy in his arms, he wedged his way past the barriers again. Looking toward the Peace Enforcement building, he asked, "Which one is she?"

He pointed to a red-headed young woman about fifty yards away. "So, if you don't live here, where do you sleep at night?" asked the curious boy.

"Well, I'm not sure at the moment. I'm still looking for a room to stay in while I'm here."

"You should stay with us. We have room," the boy suggested.

Aron chuckled. "I'm not so sure your family would like that."

"Why not? We have people stay all the time. My house is an inn."

"Is it now?" Aron chuckled at his good luck.

The boy smiled. "Yes, just ask my aunt Leyna. She'll tell you."

"Well, thanks, little guy. I will."

Aunt Leyna finished her conversation with the Peace Enforcement officer and walked toward them. Aron set the boy down, and he ran ahead.

"Hi," she said to Aron.

"Hi," Aron smiled. "Found your nephew over by the sinkhole." Aron had learned at this point that handshaking was not a thing.

"Thank you," she replied, giving the boy a side-eye. "He's just fascinated by it."

"This man needs a place to stay," said the boy excitedly. "I told him he could stay at our inn."

"I see," said Leyna, reaching for his arm and pulling him to her side. "Nice to meet you. I hope he wasn't too much of a bother. I'm Leyna Farin."

"No, no. Not at all. Nice to meet you as well," said Aron. Pausing a quick moment, he added, "I'm Tony. Tony... Stark." *Sure, let's go with the Iron Man reference. Why not?* He rolled his eyes at his absurd alias.

"Oh, my brother's name is Anthony. He and I run the inn together, and we do have open rooms. It's right around the corner if you want to walk with us. And this little guy is Harvard."

"Harvard. Well, that's a cool name," Aron smiled at the boy as he grinned. Harvard ran ahead in the direction that Aron had come from.

"Not too far, Harvard!" Leyna called out. "Stay close!"

"Did you have a problem earlier?" Aron asked. "I saw you speaking with the Peace Enforcement officer. I don't mean to pry, I—"

"Yeah, no, no worries. Someone burglarized our inn this afternoon. Just a bit ago, actually."

"Oh, I'm sorry to hear that."

"I hope that doesn't change your mind about staying. It's a safe place, I promise. This doesn't usually happen. And they didn't take much. Just a couple griggs from the front desk. Anthony swears he doesn't remember leaving the front lobby area."

"Could it have been a guest?" asked Aron.

"Harvard! Stop!" Harvard had reached the end of the sidewalk and stopped just before the busy road in front of him.

Leyna continued. "We're actually empty right now. Everybody traveled here for the Centenary, and now they've all gone home. It's been really quiet the last few weeks. But at least that's given me some good quality time with Harvard. His mother works late hours, so I'm happy to help out. What brings you to Lupellerin?"

They had caught up to Harvard and made a right turn. "Just visiting. Haven't ever been here before, so... I'm looking for some old friends, and you know—exploring." The cover story was getting a little easier now.

"Well, that's nice." Leyna didn't press for any details.

It wasn't more than a few minutes when Leyna turned to follow Harvard up the steps to an inn: a large white house, with a wraparound veranda, situated directly on the street.

"Isn't this Faradell Narrow?" Aron raised an eyebrow.

"Yes, you've heard of us?"

"Uh, well, I was just here not more than an hour or two ago. I was told there were no rooms available."

"What?" She tilted her head slightly.

"Is Anthony a rather big guy? Bald, with a red beard?" Aron asked.

"No, why?"

"Well, that's who was behind the desk and told me you were full. Wasn't exactly polite about it either."

"And you're sure you were at *this* inn?" Leyna asked.

"Positive."

Leyna's brow furrowed. "That was probably the burglar! Anthony!" She threw open the front entry door, and the "Please Enter" sign clanged and swung from side to side. Aron and Harvard were close behind.

Anthony, several years older than Leyna, sat behind the desk. His brown hair was slightly shaggy, greying in a few spots, and his tired eyes were bloodshot.

"Daddy!" yelled Harvard. "Daddy! I saw the bottom of the sinkhole! There's a lot of stuff down there! I saw it!" Anthony picked up his son and sat him on his lap.

"Anthony, this is Tony." Leyna motioned for Aron to come closer. "He saw someone in here behind the desk not long ago."

"Good to meet you, Tony." Anthony assessed Aron suspiciously. "Can you describe him?"

"Yes, and good to meet you too," Aron again resisted the impulse to offer his hand. He detected a faint scent of alcohol on his breath. "He was sitting exactly where you are. Large guy, bald, red beard."

He looked at his sister, puzzled. "Did he have tattoos?"

"Yes," Aron answered. "All up and down his arms and around his neck."

Anthony sighed, rubbed his temples, and then his eyes narrowed, looking at Aron. "That's Bander, the pawnshop owner. His shop is on the other side of the road on the corner, and we've been friends for years, good guy. He'd never steal from us. Are you sure of that description?"

Aron sensed the mistrust. "All I can say is that he was here less than two hours ago, and he yelled at me to get out, that the inn was full."

Both Leyna and Anthony looked at each other, obviously finding it difficult to believe what they were hearing. Anthony rubbed his temples again and sighed.

And then it hit him. "Shit!" Aron said in a harsh whisper. "The Sapin!"

"What?"

"There was a Sapin. Right when I left here, I saw him running down the street and behind the store. It seemed suspicious, so I chased him but couldn't catch up." Aron neglected to disclose that this same Sapin had been following him most of the day.

"Anthony, the Sapin could have projected into the inn as Bander," Leyna said. "Maybe he was surprised when Tony walked in, and that's why he yelled for him to get out."

"Could be," Anthony conceded. "Of course, that means we'll never catch him." He placed Harvard back down on the floor.

"Well, it's not like Peace Enforcement was going to go looking for someone over a couple of griggs, anyway," Leyna reckoned.

Anthony shook his head, and Leyna sighed.

"C'mon, Tony, let's get you settled in," she said.

Momentarily forgetting his new moniker, Aron jumped to follow her up the staircase. "Thanks. Let me know if there's anything I can do to help."

Leyna led Aron to the third floor of the old inn. "Ah, the penthouse!" he kidded.

"The what?" Clearly, she didn't get it.

"Never mind. It's what they call the top floor back home. It's nice."

"So, you're OK with this, then?"

"Perfect. Thank you."

"Great. Dinner is at sunset in the table room if you're interested," she invited.

"Thanks, I'll be there," Aron replied gratefully as she turned to head back down the stairway. "Hey, uh, I'm sorry, but do you know anything about that sinkhole? When did it happen?"

"I think it's been here for about ten months, maybe. Why?"

"Just wondering. I haven't seen anything like that before. Does this happen in Seridon usually?"

Leyna thought for a quick second. "I wouldn't say 'usually,' but it's happened before—along with all the other freakish natural disasters. This is a big one, though. Can't imagine what a Sapin did this time."

"What do you mean?" Aron asked.

"What do I mean about what?"

"About the Sapins. Did they have something to do with it?"

Leyna was clearly puzzled. "Where are you from again?"

"Western Parise."

"Oh, wow. That *is* a long way. Don't they have Sapins out there?"

"Not typically," Aron explained. "I never see them."

"Hm, interesting. Well, Sapins do a lot of things, mostly at the bidding of humans. They do all these errands and missions for humans, but if they kill someone or something, our country suffers some sort of disaster. Tornado, tidal wave... sinkhole.

"It's always been that way," she continued. "Mythology has it that the Elfblood Tree cursed the Sapins when she was killed. You've heard of the Tree, right?"

Aron nodded. "Yes, the Elfblood Tree. Have you seen it?"

"Seen it? No, nobody goes there. Anyway, the Commander forbade the Sapins from killing anyone, anywhere, even when sending them out on missions, because of the tremendous damage they could cause. But it's not like the Sapins would *want* to, anyway. Their own family and things are always destroyed in the catastrophe. And if they have no family, the Sapin dies instantly."

"So, have they found the Sapin who caused that sinkhole? Do they know who was killed?" Aron couldn't remember how long ago it was that Iyla had said her friend, Seriah, had disappeared.

"Well, as I'm sure you know, it's pretty hard to catch a Sapin. I mean, this one has taken months already. Most likely, he or she has run off to some other country or some other world. But they usually pinpoint the offending Sapin based on who was killed in the subsequent disaster. Or by the Sapin's victim too, but if the Sapin killed someone in another world, it's not likely we'd know the victim unless it was mission-related."

"What about humans?" Aron asked. "Humans in Seridon kill Pelri and more. No repercussions for that?"

Leyna hesitated briefly, biting her bottom lip. Without meeting Aron's eyes, she said, "Well, obviously, killing is always wrong and usually illegal. But the natural disaster thing, that's specific to the Sapins."

There was a moment of awkward silence between them before Leyna broke it. "You—" she began and then stopped immediately. Aron looked at her and raised his eyebrows.

She began again. "You said 'humans in Seridon' kill Pelri. Are you saying humans in Parise live peacefully with the Pelri?"

"Pelri live with the Pelri. I'm saying I would never hurt one of them," Aron replied.

Leyna let out a deep breath. "OK, just so you know, you can't say that too loudly around here. Pelri sympathizers are arrested and punished severely. They are deemed 'traitors' to humanity."

"Incredible." Aron shook his head sadly, then quickly added, "I never understood that." He couldn't imagine what Iyla might be going through at that moment. Was she even alive?

"Don't worry, you're safe with us. My brother, well, he's sensitive about the issue. Our family was hit hard already simply for taking pity on the Pelri and how they're treated. My sister-in-law, *after* jail time served, she's now forced to work long hours at a... horrible place and will never receive wages again. Anthony has really been struggling to come to terms with not having her around very much. At least she's allowed to come home these days." Leyna paused as she gazed past him. "It's been my dream to move away from Seridon. I always thought Tariadyn would be nice. But I won't leave my family."

"I'm sorry, Leyna," Aron offered.

"Well, you get yourself settled in," she said, determined to change the subject. "I'll see you at dinner."

"Yes... thanks."

Aron scanned the charming, clean room. There was a large window opposite the door. From this level, he could see the outskirts of the city and the vast Lupellerin Lake in the distance. There were acres of irrigated fields between the lake and the city, their desperate attempt to grow… something.

According to Jens, the Seridon economy depended heavily on imports, along with anything the Sapins could steal. A steady stream of cargo ships made their way to their biggest port, southwest of Lupellerin, and then back across the ocean to Tariadyn and then inland through the Telodot Sea. Aron wondered whether the other countries had ever leveraged their trade dealings with Seridon. One would think they could band together, stonewall their exports, until the genocide stopped. But it might be worthwhile to have a look at these ports. They may need them for a covert escape.

After a quick shower, Aron figured he had just enough time before dinner to head back outside to stake out the Peace Enforcement building, and to see if he could pick up any intelligence on Iyla or other Pelri apprehensions. Leyna's warning had only confirmed what he knew already. It was too dangerous to mention Iyla, even to her.

Onlookers and construction workers still surrounded the sinkhole. Next to it, a high fence bordered the entire Peace Enforcement grounds. A steady stream of officers and citizens paraded in and out of the building's glass front doors.

Aron entered the single-story stone building. Inside, at the far end, one officer sat behind a thick, glass window, typing on a typewriter of sorts. Another was assisting someone. Two other people sat in chairs, waiting their turn. Next to the large, thick window, a concrete wall displayed paper flyers, announcements, and other literature. An old Yeril's Eyes centenary celebration flyer still hung near the bottom.

A full-color poster in the center of the wall caught his attention. It showed an illustration of a Pelri with identifying features highlighted. *PELRI WANTED*, it stated. *If Found, Notify Peace Enforcement Immediately.*

"Can I help you?" came a voice from behind Aron.

"Excuse me?" he said.

"Do you need assistance?" repeated the officer.

"Uh, yes," Aron stuttered. "What do I do if a Sapin stole from me?"

"A Sapin? How do you know? And what did he steal?"

"Well, I saw him do it, and it was a few griggs."

The officer smiled with a shade of condescension. "Seems to be a lot of that going around," he said. "I can take a report, but it ain't going to do much. Just be glad that's all it was."

Aron sighed as the officer turned away. "Oh, one more thing."

The officer was noticeably irritated.

"Catch any of these recently?" Aron asked, motioning to the poster of the Pelri.

The officer waved him off dismissively and mumbled "Confidential" as he turned the corner. Aron's brow furrowed, frustrated at the lack of intelligence available to find Iyla. *What now?*

Lost in thought, he made his way back to Faradell Narrow. He arrived a few minutes late for dinner, but the Farin family was hospitable and gracious. He ate in silence, struggling to figure out his next move. How do you find someone in an alien world when you can't even mention that you are looking for her?

"You doing alright?" Leyna asked.

Aron smiled. "Yes, the food is good. Do you have more corn? I mean, frekka?"

"Sure. Help yourself," she offered. "What's 'corn'? Is that a Parisean thing?"

Aron bit the inside of his lip. "Uh, yeah. Something we say back home."

"Hm, I always thought Pariseans used the same words as we do in Seridon." Leyna raised an eyebrow. "You seem a bit distracted. You alright?"

"Just having a hard time trying to locate one of my friends."

"What's their name? Maybe I can look them up in the registry for you," Leyna offered.

Aron's puzzled look prompted her to get up and retrieve a thick book from the lobby area.

"Oh, I don't know. Is that for people who live here? My friend doesn't live here either. Thanks, though."

"OK," she replied. "Well, let me know if I can help in any way."

Anthony stood up, wiping his mouth with the napkin. He raked his hand through his hair as he growled, "I know a few folks from Parise. I've never heard them use that word." He pulled out a slender, square-shaped bottle from a cabinet and retired to the back office. Leyna stared after him, her eyes tired.

"Uh, yeah. I'll definitely let you know. Once I get my bearings, I should have more luck. I'll start again in the morning."

Chapter Twelve

Heddah's Flowers

I yla awoke early the following morning to a severe pain extending diagonally across her abdomen. A large bandage covered her middle, and when she attempted to sit up, she found her wrists and ankles were again locked to the sides of the bed. Her heart pounded in her ears and her aching abdomen pulsated.

"Mornin', doll!" Heddah called softly as she opened the door. She strolled into the room carrying a small bouquet of flowers and an armful of towels and gowns. She noticed Iyla was secured to the bed and frowned. "Oh, dear moons. They didn't even unlock you." A tear formed at the corner of Iyla's eye. "Sweetie, are you OK? What's wrong? Are you hurting?"

Iyla nodded.

"Here, swallow these." Heddah handed her three soft green pills. "OK, that should help with the pain soon enough." Heddah unlocked the clamps and helped Iyla sit up. She set the linens in the bathroom and placed the flowers in a glass vase on the table beside her bed. "I got these for you on my way in."

"Since when did Seridon grow flowers?"

"Imported, directly from Neritte! Thought they might make you feel more relaxed." Iyla stared blankly at the pretty pink, yellow, and purple buds, their thick green stems immersed in the crystal-clear water.

"Can I look at your incision?" Heddah asked, allowing Iyla the opportunity to refuse.

Iyla looked down at the bandaging and the blood that was soaking through them. She nodded her head and carefully eased herself back down onto the bed. Removing the gauze, Heddah frowned at the lengthy incision and sloppy stitching.

"What did they do to me?" Iyla asked.

Heddah sighed. "Well, another one of their tests. They were taking cell samples from your organs with this one. I'm sorry I wasn't here for it. I would have insisted on a more experienced stitcher." Heddah poured a disinfectant on a clean towel and gently dabbed at the blood. "Try not to move too much. You don't want these stitches to tear."

Iyla stared up at the ceiling, desperately trying to hold back the tears. "Does it even matter?" she hissed, a tear escaping and dropping onto the sheet. "Why can't you just leave us all alone?"

"Doll, I've been asking that question for years." The words came out before Heddah even realized she was speaking aloud. "But you didn't hear me say that," she added quickly, glancing around all corners of the dull white room.

Iyla slowly turned on her side to face the wall, grimacing as the sheet pulled at her midsection. Heddah sighed and sat down on the edge of the bed. She ran her fingers through Iyla's hair, easing the strands off of her neck and spreading them like a fan across the pillow.

"Listen," she whispered, leaning in close to Iyla. "Today isn't going to be easy. The tests they run today will be very uncomfortable. I want you to know that I'm here for you. I can't do much, but I'll help you get through it in whatever way I can, OK? I'll take care of you."

Iyla stared at the wall.

"You should probably take off your necklace—"

"No." Iyla covered her pendant with her hand. "It was a gift. From my mother. I'm not taking it off."

"It's such an interesting design. Can I see?"

Iyla tentatively uncovered the worn stone pendant which hung from a crude chain. A curious outline was etched into the small black stone with a jade inlay.

"What is it exactly?" Heddah asked. "A cloud? But then what's that line? Maybe lightning? Hmm, no. Too straight."

"It's just a design. It's been in my family for years, passed down to all the daughters. My mother gave it to me right before she died. It kinda makes me feel closer to her."

"Well, then you keep it on, sweetie." Lowering her voice so that Iyla could barely hear her, Heddah said, "I hate what they do to the Pelri, what they're doing to you. I'm really sorry about all this."

Guarding her abdomen with one arm, Iyla eased back onto her back and looked up at her. Heddah had been nothing but kind to her since she arrived. Her warm brown eyes were misty as she cupped Iyla's cheek with her hand. This was the most time she had ever spent with humans. Well, other than Aron, but he didn't count. Could there be good humans here in Seridon?

Iyla dared to ask a question she'd been wondering about since the day before. "Did you know my mother?"

"Your mother?"

"I heard you say you've worked here for a while. My mother was held captive here over a year ago."

Heddah thought for a moment. "Well, let's see. The only female we've had here in the last three years... she was older. Mrinnia. Was she your mother?"

Another tear escaped Iyla's eye and trickled down her face as she nodded. The sound of her mother's name sent a wave of emotion through her body.

"Oh, she was an absolute dear. She got feisty at times... guess that's where you get it from," Heddah winked. "But a wonderful soul. Oh my, you're Mrinnia's daughter... so that means you must be Iyla."

Iyla nodded.

"She talked about you often," Heddah said with a smile.

"So, you were friends?"

"Oh, I loved sweet Mrinnia. Wasn't she released? I remember going to see her first thing one morning, but she was gone. She had such a rough time here, poor thing. She wasn't in good shape. Her chart said they released her. I didn't get to tell her goodbye."

"No," whispered Iyla. "She wasn't released. I took her back. I broke into this place and rescued her. She died soon after."

"Oh, heavens." Heddah covered her nose and mouth with her hand. "You took her back, yourself? Well, good for you! I bet they were trying to save face, telling us they released her. Oh, my dear. But we must keep this quiet, OK? Oh, and I'm so very sorry she passed. What a beautiful soul she was. Beautiful soul."

The door to the hallway swung open, and another technician came in with a breakfast tray. Heddah stood up quickly. "I'll be back in about an hour for your next set of tests."

The breakfast tray was placed in front of her, and then Iyla sat alone in the room, propped up against her pillow as she ate, increasingly anxious about the next round of testing, but cautiously comforted to have Heddah on her side. Her abdomen continued to throb as she admired the flowers by her bedside, already in full bloom. Their bright faces beamed with vibrant color.

As Iyla laid her head back down on the pillow, one yellow flower turned to watch her. She immediately propped herself up on one elbow to look more closely. In a language that was more music than words, Iyla said, "Can you hear me?"

The flowers stood motionless. Iyla sighed and closed her eyes, knowing they would be dead within a day here in this barren country. She had to find a way out of this place. She had to find Seriah. She had to help Aron save her people.

The door swung open again, and Teerint and two others strode into the room, with Heddah close behind. Iyla pulled the sheet up to her chin as they approached her. Teerint yanked the sheet out of her hands and grabbed her by the arm, pulling her off the bed. A searing pain shot through her abdomen as the skin and incision stretched and tore. She cried out as Heddah rushed to her.

"I've got her, I've got her," said Heddah. "Leave her be!"

Teerint released his grip as Heddah supported her under her arms. "C'mon, sweetie. We're walking into the next room. Easy does it."

The next room held a series of large, unidentifiable pieces of testing equipment. Metal machines with buttons and lights clicked and clacked around the room. Heddah helped her up onto one of the larger flat surfaces in the middle of the room before noticing the blood dripping from her incision. "Aw, now see what you did?" She scowled at Teerint before grabbing some more bandages from the cabinet and tending to Iyla's abdominal incision.

The menacing metal equipment she was lying on was hard and cold. There was a slight depression on one end in which her head rested. Above her was an ominous canopy of more heavy, complex equipment. Iyla felt dizzy.

After cleaning the blood off the floor, Heddah returned to Iyla's side. Leaning over her, she distracted her with her words as she locked her wrists down. "This is going to hurt a bit, but you will be fine, OK? Remember, I am right here, and I'll hold your hand if you like. Just breathe. I'll be here the whole time."

At the exact moment that she said "time," the heavy, black apparatus above her jerked and then descended slowly. Iyla heard a low whirring sound as one assistant was busily attaching wires to her head and neck. Iyla stared up at the bottom of the apparatus and the thousands of rounded pinpoints coming toward her. With one click, neon green lights illuminated each point.

"Pressure points are on," stated one assistant to Teerint.

Terrified, she turned to Heddah. "What's happening?"

"It's OK, sweetie. I'm right here. It won't be comfortable, but you will get through it."

From across the room, Teerint scowled. He approached the apparatus where Iyla lay and shoved Heddah aside. "Back off."

Heddah's face reddened. "I will not!" she said sternly and pushed herself back to Iyla's side. "I'm the only one keeping your subjects alive. You do your job, and I'll do mine!"

Teerint pursed his lips but retreated two steps. Another assistant inserted a needle into Iyla's arm. A thin tube connected the needle to a large bag of fluid hanging beside her. The large canopy continued to descend. The four monitors against the wall displayed a variation of neon green dots and lines. Some were blinking, others were making waves across the screens. The large apparatus was only about a foot above her, still inching its way down.

"Heddah!" Iyla shouted.

"Let me hold your hand," said Heddah, taking it and squeezing it tight.

The heavy canopy rested on top of her, from her neck down to her ankles. As it pressed down, it seemed to mold itself around her body. The whirring stopped. Teerint and his assistants were feverishly taking notes while watching the monitors.

"Pull and save those baseline results," directed Teerint as several sheets of paper dispensed from the machine. "Injection in the heel. Now."

A sharp pain in her left heel caused her to cry out again. Again, the assistants scrambled to jot down their findings, and the paper continued to dispense quickly from the machine. Two minutes later, the whirring sound started up again, and she could feel a tightening over every inch of her body. The machine pressed down further, and Iyla had trouble breathing. She gasped and coughed as Heddah tried to calm her. "Just breathe, doll. Just breathe."

"Watch the heartbeat and temperature," instructed Teerint, pointing to one monitor. "Did you see that?" Both assistants smiled and jotted down several more notes. "Now, let's do this."

Again, the machine pushed down, compressing her body until she felt her bones would shatter. Iyla cried out again, and a small tear fell from Heddah's eye. She swiped at it quickly as the machine finally halted its movement. A pool of blood had collected beneath her as it cascaded from her incision. Heddah pulled a cold, wet cloth out of a small plastic tub beside her and dabbed at Iyla's forehead. "OK," she said. "It's stopped. Just hang in there for a few more minutes."

"See?" said Teerint. "I knew it. Keep an eye on the electrocardiogram. Look at that rhythm. OK, again."

"No, Teerint, come on," Heddah cut in. "She's losing too much blood."

"She's fine. It'll stop."

"No! It's enough! Stop it, now!"

Teerint glared at Heddah. "Fine, just leave it there for a bit longer."

For twenty minutes, Iyla's body remained compressed. Her tears flowed as the pain intensified. Breathing was difficult, and the blood left inside her felt as if it was congealed in place, unable to flow freely through her veins. A stabbing pain in her chest was the last thing she felt before losing consciousness.

While Iyla slept, Heddah waited in the chair beside her bed, her face red and her eyes wet. Her heart hurt for this poor Pelri. She retrieved the pitcher of ice water and poured a glass for her, placing it on the bedside table. She glanced at the colorful flowers she had brought in this morning and checked her watch. It was early afternoon. Not only were these flowers still alive, they were brilliant and in full bloom. Hadn't she purchased six buds? Looking closely, Heddah noted there was now a seventh. One stem had double bloomed.

The Neclu Pelri had fascinated Heddah since she was a child. And now, here again, she had been given another opportunity to help one, and she was Mrinnia's daughter. She was heartbroken to hear of Mrinnia's passing, although not surprised. Humans didn't care about the life of a Pelri other than to study them, on their eternal quest to find their connection to nature, cloning it, and bringing Seridon back to the beautiful, bountiful, flourishing days of old. There had to be a way to get her out of here safely before she was transported to Rakkarron, or worse, killed, like so many other Pelri they had captured.

Iyla's eyelids fluttered, and then slowly opened. Heddah smiled as the Pelri turned to face her.

"Hey, little one. How do you feel? You alright?"

Iyla was quiet as she blinked her eyes in the afternoon sunlight spilling through the window.

"I know you're hurting, sweet girl. I'm so sorry. Here, drink this," said Heddah, handing her a small white cup. "I mixed it with a little water. It will help with the pain."

Iyla took the cup, half filled with a pale-yellow chalky liquid, and drank it down.

"Good job," said Heddah. "Give it about fifteen minutes, and you'll be able to move more easily. Just lie still for now."

"I feel completely flattened. I don't want to move."

"I've been monitoring you, and your vitals are good. A bit of compartment trauma, but the fluids mitigated that. I do want to get your limbs moving as soon as we can, though—get that blood circulating. You've got two cracked ribs, so don't twist your torso. How's your breathing?"

Iyla took a shallow breath.

"OK, let me know if your breathing gets difficult." Heddah pulled out an ice pack and placed it on top of Iyla's chest. She pulled the covers up over her again and sat back down on the chair. "Good news is, no more tests today."

"Heddah," Iyla whispered. "Please help me get out of here."

Heddah sighed and cautiously looked around the room. "Armed guards secure the entrances. They have guns, Iyla. You know what those are, right? They have bullets that will go right through your body. There are also undercover agents that roam the inside of this facility. All windows are locked. I'm just not sure how we would do it. If I get caught again—"

"I know about the entrance guards from when I rescued my mother. We won't get caught. I won't say anything. Please. We can do this. We'll be very careful."

Heddah paused, putting her hand to her forehead, and then swiping at a tear. Quietly, she said under her breath, "Oh, Iyla. I want to help you. Let me think about this for a bit, OK? Let me figure something out. I hate to see you go through this. Just rest, and I'll be back in about half an hour with your dinner and to walk you around."

Iyla half-closed her eyes. "We got my mom out. Please help me, Heddah."

Heddah turned away from Iyla and swiped at another tear before closing the door behind her. *How could I pull this off,* she thought.

The following morning, Heddah quietly entered Iyla's room with her breakfast. But Iyla's bed was empty and unmade. The bathroom door was open, but she wasn't there.

"Iyla?" The hairs on her arms stood on end as she listened for an answer. But there was no answer.

Heddah found her chart outside her room in the door pocket. The last entry affirmed that she had been taken to the hydro-immersion analysis room on the 6th floor late the previous night. She dropped the chart and ran to the stairwell.

At the far end of the hall, Heddah entered the quiet hydro-immersion analysis room. The lights were off, but the sun coming through the two small windows provided ample lighting. It was a large room, and on the outside wall sat two glass tanks, each the size of a compact car. They were both filled to the top with water.

There, floating in the tank on the right, was Iyla, naked and unconscious. A metal collar affixed to the rim of the tank surrounded her neck, keeping her head above water and preventing her from climbing out. Wires were attached to her head, neck, and torso, but all the machines had been turned off. The water was tinted pink from the blood escaping the incision on her abdomen.

"Iyla!" Heddah shouted and ran to her. The water was cold, and from the looks of her pruned skin, she had been in the tank all night.

Heddah pulled the drainage plug and detached the metal collar. She folded down the front side of the water tank, and Iyla's body collapsed onto her. Iyla's lips and fingers were blue. Heddah skillfully lifted her down from the tank and set her on the nearby gurney. Applying two fingers to the side of her neck, she confirmed Iyla was still alive. She found several blankets in the cabinet and laid them over her while rubbing her skin to warm her.

What were they thinking? Heddah thought to herself as she reapplied the disinfectant and bandages to her abdomen. *Oh, Iyla, I'm so sorry they've done this to you.*

She wheeled the gurney into the elevator to take Iyla back to her room, her face red with anger. Iyla was *her* charge, and she would not tolerate such carelessness and reckless neglect.

Back in the room, Heddah lifted her off the gurney and carried her wrapped body to the bed. She checked her breathing and used a stethoscope to listen to her lungs and her rapidly beating heart. After pulling another sheet over her, she sat down and rubbed Iyla's left hand between hers. The color had started to return to her nail beds. "That's it, pretty girl. Come on back to me. We've got plans to make. Come on, now."

Heddah sat back in the chair as her tense muscles relaxed slightly. Again, her gaze went back to the colorful blooms at Iyla's bedside, and through the clear vase, Heddah saw the long tangle of roots burgeoning from the lush green stems.

Chapter Thirteen

WHO ARE YOU?

A cool breeze found its way around the side of the stately old inn and through the open window of Aron's room. It was morbidly silent in the early morning before sunrise. There were no rustling leaves, no sounds of nature. Not even the typical sounds of a city, vehicles, or people. And that faint stench of mold and decay lingered in the air.

Aron heard the front door close as he descended the staircase, and through the lobby window, he watched as a dark-haired woman hurriedly crossed the street with her bag slung over her shoulder. Harvard's mother, most likely. He remembered Leyna mentioning her long work hours.

He grabbed the registry book Leyna had set on the small bookshelf. It resembled an old telephone book on Earth, with a bit more information per entry. He looked up "Farin, Leyna." The address for Faradell Narrow was listed, along with other indecipherable numbers and letters. Were these dates? Phone numbers? He had not yet seen any telephones.

He thumbed through the book's midsection, noting some unique and also ordinary names. Toward the back were the local business advertisements and coupons for fresh produce. He also noted the pawnshop address before coming across the registry's entry for Seridon's Office of Security and Defense. Certainly, a treasure trove of intelligence to be found there, if he could get inside. According to the small map, it was on the other side of the town center.

Movement upstairs prompted Aron to gather his things, step outside, and quietly close the door behind him. He had to make some headway today. And it was getting lighter out.

Once outside the pawnshop, he turned to look back at Faradell Narrow. Harvard was standing in the window waving to him. Smiling, he waved back. He was a good kid.

The sign in the pawnshop window stated it would open in two hours, but as he turned to walk away, he bumped shoulders with the same large, bearded man who had ordered him to leave Faradell Narrow the day before. This was Bander, the pawnshop owner. He had a large backpack slung over his back and keys in his hand.

"Hi," said Bander in a raspy voice. "Can I help you?"

"Uh, I was just checking your hours. I'll come back later," Aron responded.

"You're up early. You new around here?" His smile and friendly disposition were unexpected.

"Yeah. Just visiting," said Aron. "I think I met you yesterday, didn't I?"

Bander thought for a moment as the rising sun's rays danced off his sweaty, bald head.

"At Faradell Narrow?" Aron prompted.

"No, I haven't been by there this week. Is that where you're staying? Nice place. The Farins are great people. Why don't you come on in and look around? Anything specific you're looking for?" Bander unlocked the six bolts on the shop door and led him inside. "I've got jewelry and weapons in the back; tools, Pelri properties and furniture over there; electronics, and you see everything here in the front."

"Pelri properties?" Aron reacted.

"Yeah, you know, random things people have found that belonged to the Pelri. Little buggers are hard to find!" Bander chuckled.

Aron looked over the small stash of stolen belongings. "Have you got any of those pearls they use?" Aron inquired.

"Oh, no way, man. I'm not trying to get myself killed," Bander laughed. "The Commander would have my head if I kept one of those!"

"I bet," Aron agreed in his attempt to sound knowledgeable.

"Someone brought one in once. I reported it, of course. I'm not getting myself on the Commander's bad side, that's for sure."

"When did that happen?" Aron asked.

"Eh, couple years back. Really difficult to come by a Pelri, obviously."

"Right," Aron concurred. "Have you ever seen one?"

"Nah. You?"

"Pretty sure I have," Aron confessed.

"Did ya report it?"

"Report it?"

Bander paused skeptically. "Where did you say you're from?"

"I didn't. Western Parise. We don't have any reporting orders there."

"Hm. But you *are* human. Better be careful."

"This Commander," Aron began, but Bander interrupted.

"He'll cut off your head. Either that or slowly pierce every inch of your body with five hundred hot iron skewers; you know, whatever he's in the mood for."

"Sounds like a great guy." Aron's sarcasm was not lost on Bander, who immediately exploded into howling laughter.

"Have a look around. Let me know if you have questions."

Aron made his way to the back of the shop. A large display of weaponry covered three full aisles. Weathered, hand-forged swords in all sizes and designs. Some still had leather-bound handles, where on others, it had worn off. Spears jutted out from a wooden barrel. Daggers, maces, bows, crossbows, throwing discs, and shields lined the shelves. At the end of the second aisle, Aron stopped suddenly. He leaned in closer. On the third shelf was a 20-round box of Remington 9mm ammunition. On the bottom right corner of the box was a small red "Made in the USA" symbol.

"Holy shit," Aron whispered quietly.

Bander rounded the corner. "That's from Earth," he stated. "Guns are over here." He pointed to the next aisle over. "I've got two from Earth and three from Ornott. This one here is from Nekayah, but there's no ammunition for it."

Aron reached for the 9mm Glock.

"You know your guns," Bander observed.

Aron turned the gun over in his hands. "Sapins bring these in?"

"You know it!" he confirmed. "You have your pass?"

"Pass?"

"I need to see your pass to sell you the gun."

"We don't use those in Parise. How do I get one?" Aron asked.

Bander sighed. "The Commander issues them out of the Office of Security and Defense. But, uh, good luck with that. I told ya, he's a moody one."

Aron thought for a minute. "How much are you selling it for?"

"This one?" Bander looked it over. "750Gg."

Looking him in the eye, Aron countered, "Would you take double?"

Bander's eyes opened wide, his eyebrows raised. "Without a pass. Crakes, what are you doin'?"

"Look," said Aron. "I'm not a criminal. I'm not from here, and I believe a Sapin has been following me. I don't trust those bastards. Here, look me up. I'm clean. Do you keep records on this stuff?"

"1500Gg," Bander contemplated. Aron could tell the money was tempting, and he could easily make this sale under the table. "How long are you in town?"

"I'm meeting a friend of mine, and then we're heading out. So as soon as we find each other. I'm not sure how long it'll take, but you know where I'm staying—"

"Yeah, yeah, alright, but I'll be talking to the Farins. They're good friends of mine, and I want them to be aware of what's going on," Bander finally agreed. "But between us, this transaction did not happen."

"Yup, understood. We're good. Thank you."

"You know how to use this thing?" Bander asked.

"Yes, I have one back home."

Bander nodded. "I prefer the throwing discs myself. I've got a cabin out by the lake where I fish. That's where I practice. Let me know if you need more ammo. I've got extra in the back."

"Sure, thanks," Aron said, handing him the money. It seemed odd, the number of amicable people he had encountered in the short time he had spent in Seridon, land of the evil humans. He stashed the gun in the small of his back, nodding to Bander as he exited the shop.

It was a short walk to the city square, where he had first sat down for a beer at the tavern the day before. It was still too early for the other businesses in the area to open for the day. Nothing but quiet emptiness surrounded him, but he felt a little less vulnerable now. The Office of Security and Defense, the next destination, was a few miles away.

The main road through town diverged through a petrified wooded grove and then wound through a well-kept residential area. The concrete homes were small and plain. Here and there, a random jewel would sparkle and catch his eye, but it was nothing like what he had seen in the downtown area. He tried to imagine what Seridon had looked like before the humans took over, when it was still

Keyronai. The places he had seen already on Athemoni were beautiful, but he knew Keyronai would have been even more spectacular.

Several automobiles were traveling on the road now and passed him in both directions. Beyond the neighborhood and over a landscape of rolling hills, he could see a small farm and the workers tending to it. Four horses were pulling plows as a farmhand inspected an irrigation unit. On the far side, an interesting mechanical structure rose above and behind the barn, but he couldn't tell what it was. As Aron neared the farm, he saw the cornfield had reached the roadside. He pulled back the husk from a small ear. The kernels were hard and shriveled, and half of them were brown. Two strange insects emerged from the ear, and he quickly dropped it. *Yeah, they should just give up on that*, he thought. He knew they needed the Pelri to get this country to produce anything, and the Pelri were not inclined to give the humans any more than what they had already taken from them.

The farm workers watched him suspiciously as he passed. A blue sign signaled that the Office of Security and Defense was just ahead. A little pre-entrance surveillance had him pondering the sagaciousness of entering this building, armed and unlicensed.

Aron expected to see a typical concrete building. What he saw was more of a marble compound, set back from the road amidst a few rocky hills and fortified by a black iron gate. A large sign over the entrance to the compound ensured you knew where you were. There were approximately six buildings of varying sizes. Three of the buildings had no windows. Security guards in uniform roamed the grounds, two stationed at the entrance to the main building in the center.

Aron heard the sound of engines coming from behind him as a procession of dark blue vehicles approached and then passed. Slowly, the gate opened to allow them through and then closed behind the last one. They drove to one of the smaller windowless buildings, and the first to step out was a tall, dark-haired man with a low ponytail to whom the guards saluted. He barked a few orders at them, and three of them immediately dispersed.

The Commander? thought Aron.

Next were four young women, scantily clad and stumbling over each other. The Commander put his arm around the waist of one, while another ran to grab his free hand and kissed his neck. One wandered off as if she were chasing a butterfly and then abruptly hugged the flagpole. The fourth one carried her shoes as she stumbled behind them. *Were they drugged?* A guard casually pulled the wandering one back to join the group.

Two other guards opened the back end of a truck and pulled out a large cage. Inside was an old dwarf, yelling profanities. After unlocking the cage, they pulled the dwarf out and handcuffed him. He kicked the guards repeatedly until they tackled him to the ground and subsequently tied him at the ankles as well.

"Come on now, Thrivenbard! Just take it like a man," they mocked.

The Commander turned abruptly to address the commotion. "Thrivenbard! Cut the shit!"

The dwarf's following string of profanities brought the Commander to his side, who then kicked him until he fell over and rolled down the hill toward the awaiting women. The guards laughed as the old dwarf continued to roll until he rammed into a marble post. And still the cursing didn't stop, not until the Commander kicked him in the head, and he lay there unconscious.

"String him up!" he shouted to the guards.

One woman ran back to the vehicle, pulled out several multicolored balloons filled with helium, and then quickly returned to the others.

"Holy smokes," Aron said under his breath. It was a bizarre and sad scene, but they soon all disappeared into the small nondescript building, leaving the dwarf outside.

Movement from the corner of his eye caught Aron's attention. An abandoned rusty delivery truck was parked outside the compound on the other side of the road. Aron approached it with caution.

"Is someone there?" he called out.

There was a slight stirring.

"Come out from behind the truck," he said, his hand positioned and ready to draw the gun from the small of his back. He took a step closer but was hesitant to cause commotion directly across from the Security and Defense compound. Nothing.

Shifting position to peer between the cab and the trailer, he caught a glimpse of the familiar cloak. "I don't want to shoot. Come out from behind the truck," Aron ordered, acutely aware that the Sapin could simply teleport out of sight.

But he didn't. Instead, he made a run for it. Headed back in the direction from which he came, Aron took off after him. The Sapin was remarkably fast and Aron, having spent the last two months sleeping in a crate with leg and abdominal wounds, wasn't exactly in prime athletic condition.

He followed him off the main road and through a rocky, barren field. The field led to the opposite side of the small neighborhood he had passed earlier. Aron saw the Sapin dart behind the second home. *He'll slow down now,* Aron thought, assuming he would use the houses to hide and pause for a breath.

Aron stealthily weaved his way within the neighborhood boundaries between the houses, cars, and backyard sheds.

Two houses down, there was a fenced-in yard confining a strange animal making loud braying noises. To Aron, it looked like a cross between a cat and a koala bear, round, with thick black fur and a small head. Even as Aron neared the fence, the animal ignored him. Instead, it was only interested in what was outside the fence on the opposite side of the house.

Aron decided his best bet was to take the Sapin from the other side. At the corner of the house, he stopped to listen. Loud breathing. *He's tired. Why didn't he just teleport?* Aron paused another moment. He didn't want to shoot him, especially in this neighborhood. But he couldn't allow this Sapin to continue following him. No one would notice or care if he roughed him up a bit, though.

Still listening to the heavy breathing, Aron took a step forward, and the gravel crunched beneath his foot. Cursing his misstep, Aron whipped his gun around the corner just in time to see the Sapin jump to his feet and take off back alongside the gate with the peculiar crossbreed keeping pace. Aron caught a glimpse of his trademark blond hair blowing freely outside of his dark hood. The Sapin turned over two garbage cans to slow the chase, but Aron anticipated the move and hurdled over them.

Deep inside the neighborhood now, the Sapin rounded the next block but was slowing considerably. Aron cut through an open yard and ducked behind a storage shed. The Sapin was unaware of his shortcut and was headed down the street directly towards him. Just as he passed, Aron leaped out and seized him by the back of the neck, shoving the Sapin face-first onto the back wall of the shed.

He grabbed the Sapin's wrists with his right hand and then pushed him harder into the wall. "Why are you following me?" Aron demanded.

The Sapin didn't answer.

"Why are you following me?" he yelled. "Who are you, and who do you answer to?"

With his hand on the back of his hood, Aron pushed the Sapin's head and forced his face to the side. The Sapin cried out in pain. "Please stop," came the small voice.

Something wasn't right.

"Who are you?" Aron demanded once again.

His grip loosened somewhat on the Sapin's wrists, and with one swift movement, he yanked the Sapin's body around to face him. Long blond hair spilled out from inside the dark hood. He pulled the Sapin's hood back. Stunned, Aron immediately backed off, releasing her as he grasped his head with both hands. Thousands of thoughts flew through his mind at once as he tried to rationalize this body blow that he never saw coming.

This wasn't possible.

"Tora?"

Chapter Fourteen

PELTRI MAGIC

There was a strange peacefulness in the moment that Iyla awakened. Her eyes still closed, she savored the softness of the pillow, the warmth of the thick covers pulled up to her neck. It was quiet, except for the muffled whirring and blips of the mechanical equipment outside her room. And the sound of someone breathing. Carefully, she pushed on her bed frame to ease herself onto her other side. The bed creaked in protest and Heddah jolted awake in the chair beside her.

"You're back," Iyla murmured.

Heddah rubbed her neck, as well as the small of her back, as she grunted from sleeping in the rigid wooden chair. She placed the back of her hand on Iyla's forehead.

"Aw, sweet girl. You're awake. How are you feeling?"

"I... hurt." Iyla's fingers grazed the cuts on her neck. "My head... the incision."

"I know, sweetie. Let me take your temperature." Heddah pulled out a sterilized thermometer from her pocket and ripped off the protective paper wrap. Iyla noticed several more of these wraps already discarded on the floor.

"One hundred," she said with a satisfied smile.

"I am so sorry about last night," said Heddah. "I wish I had been here. They weren't supposed to do any more tests for a few days. They never should've left you in the tank." She examined Iyla's neck, where the metal collar from the water tank had torn her skin.

"I have to get out of here," Iyla whispered.

Heddah nodded. "Yes, I know. Working on it," she whispered. Then, a little more loudly, she announced, "Well, would you believe it's past lunchtime? I'm going to go get it for you, and then afterwards, we will get you walking. OK?"

"Please don't leave me, Heddah."

"Shh. No worries, I'm locking you in here, OK? Nobody will be able to come in."

Iyla nodded, and her gaze fell to Heddah's wrist.

"Heddah? What is that on your wrist?" Iyla had noticed two tiny metal squares embedded on the inside of her left wrist. In the center of each square was an amber-colored stone.

Heddah frowned, and her face reddened as she covered her wrist with her other hand.

"Heddah?"

"It's a locator device... a tracker."

Iyla stared at her intently, her dark grey eyes searching for understanding. Heddah sighed heavily and sat down in the chair. For the first time, Iyla noticed the weariness in her eyes.

"I... got myself into some trouble a few years ago."

"What kind of trouble?"

"Well, apparently, the unforgivable kind." Heddah half-smiled and shook her head. "Do you remember asking me why I work here?"

Iyla nodded.

"Maybe it's time I told you." Heddah raised her gaze toward the ceiling and took a deep breath before continuing. "When I first began working in this building years ago, it was just a part-time job in the money management division on the second floor. My family and I were starting our own business, and this was only supposed to be temporary as supplemental funds. It was during that time that I met my first Neclu Pelri. They had just begun taking in captives here since Rakkarron had filled to capacity. I wasn't aware of any experimentation done in this building when I took the job." Heddah paused for a moment. "Anyway, I was asked to deliver some documents to this very same floor, and I saw this poor young Pelri, half-clothed, bruised and beaten, and shivering in a cold, dark room. I felt so sorry for him. I mean, I knew the Pelri were mistreated, but to actually see it. That was different. It hurt my heart." Heddah's right hand patted her chest, and she looked to the window briefly before continuing.

"After that, I searched for excuses every day to return to this floor to see if I could help him in some way. We became secret friends, and I brought him food and medicine, and comfort items. I knew this was against the law, but I just felt so bad for him. He didn't deserve to be treated so terribly.

"And then I pushed it a little too far. I had tried to sneak him out of his room to see if I could get him outside for a bit. He hadn't seen the sunlight in months. The Master General found out and was so angry, he smashed the vials of chemicals he was carrying onto the floor. Glass was everywhere. The chemicals mixed and produced a toxic gas that permeated the entire floor and ended up killing the young Pelri. I was beaten and jailed, and now condemned to work in the very department I despised. I suppose it is their way of desensitizing me. It'll never work." Heddah's breath hitched, and her eyes darted quickly around the room. She leaned in closer to Iyla.

"I'll always regret my carelessness that led to that sweet Pelri's death. To this day, my heart still hurts for him. The only good to come out of it is that I am in a better position to help the poor captured souls, maybe making them a little more comfortable while they are here. I've been here long enough that most everyone tolerates me now, and I know they value the knowledge I've gained."

Iyla was quiet as she digested Heddah's recounting of her past. She felt the pain in Heddah's heart. This human has always been supportive of the Pelri. "I appreciate your trying to help us, Heddah."

"I will never apologize to them for trying to help him. I knew what could happen if I got caught. I just didn't think I would."

"I hate to ask for you to risk your life again, when—"

"Shh, stop. I make my own decisions. Come now. It's lunchtime, doll, and then I'll take you on a walk, and we can have a chat. Oh, did you see your flowers?" Heddah held the vase so Iyla could see it. "They've rooted!"

Iyla's eyes widened. "Heddah, can you break off a root for me?" She attempted to sit up, but couldn't.

"Break it? But, why?"

"Please."

Heddah pulled out one stem, snapped the root, and handed it to Iyla. She immediately bit into it and swallowed. Heddah's lips parted slightly as she whispered, "What are you doing?"

Iyla handed the remaining root to Heddah. "Can you take this and mash it into a paste?"

Heddah smiled and responded knowingly, "This is Pelri magic, isn't it..." and uncovered a bowl in one of the nearby cabinets.

When she brought the paste over, Iyla used her fingers to spread it across the length of the incision on her abdomen. Heddah watched intently as the redness subsided almost immediately. Strengthened by the proximity of the Pelri, those beautiful flowers were now returning the favor.

"Oh my, look at that! I knew it!" Heddah beamed.

And Iyla cracked a tiny smile.

"Well, blessed moons, I believe that's the first smile I've seen from you!" She helped Iyla sit up in the bed. "How do you do it?"

"It's not magic, but I should be good to go in a few hours. Let's go have that chat, Heddah."

"Shh, later," said Heddah. "You never know if they are listening. I'll be right back with your lunch."

The sunbeams caressed Iyla's face, and she relished every second of its touch after the many hours she had endured inside the stale, colorless room. The cool breeze that made its way over the thick walls of the courtyard gently tossed her hair and tickled her neck. She breathed in deeply, longing for the clean crisp smells of the forest. Was Aron out there? Was anyone searching for her? Clearly, there was no other exit from this courtyard, and she and Heddah reluctantly wended through the steel door and back into the dark hallway.

"What are you doing?" came a loud voice from behind them. They stopped immediately as Heddah wrapped her arm around Iyla's shoulders. The familiar tone was particularly unnerving. "Why do you have the Pelri?"

"Now, listen here, Teerint. Do you want to study a Pelri or not?" Heddah challenged. "You can't learn anything if she ain't alive! I'm bringing her in from an afternoon walk. Keepin' her blood flowing. You are well aware I won that battle."

Teerint's glasses rested on the end of his nose as he peered over them suspiciously. He scowled down at Iyla. She cringed and moved closer into Heddah.

Heddah wasn't done yet. "And speaking of which, who left her in the hydro-immersion tank, huh? Who?"

Teerint rolled his eyes. "My team had another case we were working on, Heddah."

"Oh, too busy? More important than the Pelri? How do you think that would go over with the Commander, letting a Pelri die not even fully tested? And you know he wants her. Think you'll get a pass? Think again. I told you no more tests for the remainder of the day! You ought to be thankful I found her in there and saved *your* rear end!"

"Whatever, Heddah. We all know you're a Pelri sympathizer. You never had the stomach to stand up to them and support your own kind!"

"Stand up to what? The Pelri don't bother us! At least I can look at myself in the mirror and know that I try my best to do what is decent and compassionate every single day."

Teerint threw up his hands in disgust as he stormed off down the hall. Iyla stared anxiously at Heddah. "Aren't you afraid of getting in trouble? For saying all that?"

"What's he going to do? Release me?" Heddah replied. "He's not my boss. He needs me. Come on, sweetie. Let's get you back in bed so you can rest. You can think about what we discussed on our walk."

"I will. I don't need rest, though. I'm doing much better now."

"Even so."

As they walked through the hallways, Iyla mentally logged the location of alcoves, stairwells, and exits. Busy workers infested every corridor, most of whom stared or grimaced at her presence. Such an evil place. The white walls were dull and dispiriting, and her heart craved the beauty and smells of verdant forests and natural landscapes. How would she get home, much less out of this building? Without trees, there was no way to signal William.

Heddah helped Iyla into the bed and opened her gown to check on her abdomen. She smiled. "Well, would you look at that." Iyla's incision had completely sealed. There was still a hint of red in one small area, but it was ready for the stitches to be removed. Heddah fetched the suture scissors and carefully removed each one.

"How does it feel?"

"Still sore, but I'm OK."

"We're going to leave the bandages on so as not to draw attention."

Iyla nodded and sat up again.

Heddah stood in front of Iyla with both hands on her hips. "Iyla," she paused. "Any chance you've got some sort of Pelri magic that would remove these?" she asked and motioned to the device embedded in her wrist.

"Heddah, are you serious?"

Glancing around the room, she said, "I need to get you out of here. And I'd like to go with you. I hate this place. And to have a chance to live a new life in a new place, where my family and I can be together. I won't ever get that here in Seridon."

Iyla sat for a minute, digesting her words. Heddah didn't know that everything was about to change as soon as she and Aron could get to Urippa Spring. What would happen to her and the rest of the humans when the Elfblood Tree's heart was restored? Would nature turn on them as it had done so long ago? Should she warn her? Maybe if she left Seridon before it happened, she would be safe.

Iyla reached for Heddah's wrist and inspected it. "No magic, but I could cut it out and stitch you back up. When the time is right, of course."

"Have you done this sort of thing before? What about your flower roots? Could they help?"

"I've removed other things, but not a tracking device. Not sure if the roots would help. I've only used them once on a human, and it helped, but not as quickly as it does on the Pelri. Of course, he was also in really bad shape."

"So, you've met another human? And you helped them?"

Iyla didn't answer.

"Well, I certainly hope he was decent to you."

"He's good."

Heddah smiled. "I'm glad there are others who realize that the Pelri don't deserve to be treated this way. There aren't many out there. Certainly, no one would admit to it. All I know is my family and maybe one or two others. But they've never mentioned meeting a Pelri, so—"

"You don't know him," Iyla interjected. "But he knows I've been taken, and we had some important plans, so I'm thinking he could be looking for me unless he's gone on without me, which is fine, but—"

"Oh, dear girl," Heddah said as she cupped Iyla's cheek. "I'm sure he's looking for you. And I'll keep my eye and ear out for him. Would you want to describe him, in case I see him?"

"No," said Iyla. "I just—"

"I know, sweetie," Heddah said thoughtfully. "I understand."

There was a brief silence as the two sat together.

"Have you seen a Pelri by the name of Seriah pass through here?"

"Seriah? Hmm. Male, right?"

"Yes. You've seen him?"

"Well, I'm not sure. We had a male come through here just several months ago."

"Yes! Seriah! Did he have light brown hair? About my age?"

"I'll have to check the log and see what I find. I didn't work with him, if it was. And he wasn't here long."

"Where is he now?"

"I'm not sure. They may have swapped him out with a Rakkarron Station resident. I'll see what I can find."

"Heddah?" said Iyla. "Thank you. And... I want you to be careful. And safe."

Heddah's warm smile always comforted Iyla. "I will. I need to be, for my family."

"Have you told them about me?"

"Yes."

Iyla stared down at the floor. The muffled sounds of footsteps and rhythmic bleeps and tones from outside the room leaked through the closed door.

"Promise me that once you and I are free from this place, you will leave Seridon immediately," Iyla stated. "Just grab your family and go."

"Well, that is my plan," replied Heddah.

"No, Heddah. You have to promise me you will do it right away."

Heddah studied Iyla's concerned expression. The weight of the conversation had grown from earnest to ominous in one sentence.

"Is there something you're not telling me, doll?"

"Please just trust me, OK? This is important."

"Well, whatever it is, I'm sure not going to lollygag around here if the tracker is out. You can be sure of it," Heddah reassured. "Now, I'm going to let you be for a bit. Remember what we talked about." She held up her index finger.

"One on the clock," Iyla mouthed back to her.

The door opened before Heddah reached for the knob. It was the young assistant who had first attempted to persuade Iyla to cooperate in the holding room. She glanced at Heddah and then over at Iyla before stowing the linens in the bathroom.

"Dakryn," Heddah said, "after I deliver the Pelri's dinner, I will lock her door with my restricted key. I don't want anyone commandeering another unscheduled test tonight. Her body is not ready. Understood?"

Dakryn nodded and hurried out of the room behind Heddah. A momentary smile slid across Iyla's lips as she fell back onto the pillow.

And all seven flowers turned toward her and smiled back.

Chapter Fifteen

It's Not What It Seems

"**I** can explain."

Retreating in disbelief, Aron grappled with finding anything comprehensible in what he saw in front of him.

"Aron, please," Tora implored.

"You... you're..."

"Aron, I can explain." Tora stepped toward him, but Aron held up his hand to block her.

"Stop," he growled, struggling to wrap his mind around the situation. "How—"

Tora interrupted, "It's not what it seems—"

"What isn't? That you're a Sapin? That you aren't actually dead and buried on Earth?" Aron's face was beet red as his eyes bored into her. "That you lied to me about getting pregnant? That you're not even human? What exactly isn't as it seems? My God, how is this even happening? I saw your headstone!"

Tora stood silent, mouth agape, the fiery rage on Aron's face, daring her to answer. His hands clenched, and his tense muscles contracted in his neck and jaw.

"I thought you were dead," Tora said quietly.

"Yes, apparently all of Seridon thinks I'm dead!" And there it was: the mental paradigm shift that allowed all the pieces to fall into place. "It was you. Me. I was your mission."

"No—"

"Yes. They sent you to Earth to keep me from coming here, as the seer predicted."

"You know about the—" she whispered with a raised eyebrow.

"Our entire life together has been a lie! Everything!" Aron snapped. "You knew I would find my way here if I joined the army. You knew it! And you used every trick in the book to manipulate me, to keep me from living my life the way I wanted! You never wanted me. I was nothing more to you than an assignment by the Commander!"

"No, that's not true! I loved you!" The tears cascaded down Tora's face. "That's not true."

"And then you told the Commander of Seridon that I was dead…"

Tora sank to her knees, crying. "Aron, please."

She crouched on the ground in front of him, her body heaving from the uncontrollable sobs. A whirlwind of memories sprinted through his mind. High school wrestling matches with Tora cheering for him on the sidelines, him cheering her on at track meets, summer drives to the beach, her gentle comfort when he lost his father, buying their first house together. She had been with him every step of the way. How could she have done this?

But his mother saw it. *There's just something… I'm just not confident that she's the right fit for you,* she had said on more than one occasion. The words echoed in his mind. And there were so many arguments, most of them centered on Tora pushing him in whatever direction she wanted him to go.

You should work for my dad, Aron.

No, don't enlist yet. Let's take that sky-diving trip.

We can afford it. I've always wanted to live in this neighborhood.

Will we ever get married?

Aron, I'm pregnant.

Her manipulation. All of it, a deceitful strategy with the solitary focus of keeping him away from any possibility of finding this world.

"So, what did you get out of all of this, Tora? What did they pay you to help the Commander hoard this stolen country?" Aron demanded.

"It wasn't like that!" she cried, her body hunched over in the fetal position with her face pressed to the dusty ground.

"You expect me to believe that you literally left your entire world to pretend to be someone else for years, on a mission for Seridon, for nothing? You think I would believe that? What did you get out of it, Tora?"

She pushed herself up from the ground. Still kneeling in front of him, she wiped her swollen, wet eyes with the back of her hand and shuddered as she looked up at him. "I got you. I thought I got you. But you never seemed satisfied with me. You were always looking for something more. I did those things to keep you close to me. I just wanted you."

Aron's stern face relaxed only slightly, and his arms fell loosely by his sides. This beautiful, strong woman whom he had once loved was now a frail, treacherous mess at his feet.

It was quiet on the road, all but the sound of each other's breathing. This woman had lied to him during the entire time that they knew each other. And he was going to marry her, this... Sapin. How could he not have known?

Sapins are a conniving, covetous breed, Jens had said. Abruptly, Aron turned on his heel and strode away from Tora, in the direction of the town center.

"No! Aron! Wait!"

"You don't have me, Tora," he yelled without looking back.

"But you don't understand," she pleaded.

"You're a liar. That's all I need to know." He wouldn't turn to look at her as he continued his pace.

Tora scrambled to her feet and hurried after him.

"Stay away from me," he warned.

"I loved you, Aron. Please listen," she said, trying to keep up with his quick pace. "Before I met you, I was just a dumb kid who ran away from home. I went to Earth with my friend, thinking it would be fun to track down the mystical 'man who would bring our country to its knees'. I didn't think I would actually find you. But I did." Tora paused. "Aron, can you please stop walking and listen to me?"

Aron stopped but didn't turn around.

"I fell in love with you, Aron. I wasn't on a mission. But my friend, she chickened out and went back to Seridon. Word got out that I had found you, and the Commander threatened me, saying he'd kill my family if I didn't cooperate. It all seemed well enough since all I had to do was keep you from going to the Middle East and finding the Heart. And keeping you from going there meant you would still be with me."

Aron's neck muscles tightened. He resumed walking.

"Aron, please!" she pleaded. "I can help you."

Aron spun around quickly. He looked down at her, his face only inches from hers. "Why would I ever trust you?"

Tora's face was streaked with dust and tears. Her body trembled. "Because my life is in danger, too. If the Commander finds out you're alive, he'll also come looking for me, for telling him you were dead when you weren't."

"What do you care? You can just travel to some other world and start over."

"I can't. It's... almost gone."

"What is?"

"Sapin magic dies. It's separate from our bodies and souls. It atrophies if it's not used, and it also weakens and dies if it's used... recklessly."

Aron sighed and shook his head. "Stay away from me, Tora."

Tears trickled slowly down her cheek as he walked away.

The streets and sidewalks had come alive with the late morning traffic, businesses, and pedestrians. Aron sat down on the ledge, surrounding an oversized marble statue in the center of the circle. He held his head in his hands, his fingers interlaced in his hair, struggling to suppress the grueling emotion of the last few hours. Tora was a Sapin. From the corner of his eye, he saw her lingering in the distance. His life had been a lie.

Aron missed Iyla. He needed to find her fast. He didn't want to think about what she might be going through. Would it be too risky to ask the Farins? And now, how did Tora's presence change things?

Commotion outside of Yeril's Eyes tavern redirected Aron's attention. After a loud crash, a clearly inebriated fellow carrying a box stumbled backward out of the door and fell down the two steps to the sidewalk. Two bouncers were yelling, and several passersby stopped to witness the action. But the dark-haired fellow got up, picked up his box, wiped his bloody brow with the back of his hand, and meandered down the sidewalk in the opposite direction.

Aron's stomach spurred him to head over to the tavern. He needed to think and hoped the same bartender was working today.

The tavern wasn't crowded, but broken glass and spilled beverages covered the bar top.

"Hey! You're back!" The bartender raised his mug to him as he took a seat at a nearby table. "I'll be with ya in a minute. You alright?"

Aron nodded. Would the bartender have any information? No, he immediately dismissed that notion, remembering he was not a friend to the Pelri.

He picked up the lunch menu and reviewed a short list of unfamiliar entrees and appetizers. A shadow fell over the menu, and he glanced up.

"I think you should hear me out." Tora was standing across from his table, and she slipped into the booth beside him.

Aron sighed. "Tora—"

"I can help you."

"Do you really think it's a good idea for either of us to be seen together?"

Tora paused a moment before answering. "There are no pictures of you, and you don't stand out physically. I mean, there are many people in the universe who are your relative size with dark hair. And the people of Seridon knew me only as a kid. After I passed on the news of your death, I faked my own."

The bartender approached, placing a mug on the table. "Everything alright over here?" he asked, glaring at Tora.

"It's fine. Just need a quick lunch. She's leaving soon," Aron responded, nodding his head in Tora's direction.

"Good. Well, ya gotta try this new brew. Very similar to yesterday's, but I added cinnamon and more variate."

"Thanks, bud. And if you could get me whatever lunch special is good, preferably beef, that would be great."

"And I'll have the fried rabbya," Tora injected. Both Aron and the bartender scowled as he wrote down the order.

"Gimme about ten minutes," he said and disappeared into the kitchen.

"I see you've made some friends," Tora said.

Aron ignored her remark. "Say what you want to say, and then go, please."

"Aron, I know Seridon. You don't. I know what you are here to do, and I can help you get there. You need to head a lot further north, and it's not an easy route. There are things... you haven't encountered before... things you don't know about. Let me help you get there. Let me make this up to you."

Aron paused momentarily. Tora's raised eyebrows and subtle smile was enough to show her renewed anticipation. "An about-face on the Commander's orders. Why?"

"What do I have to lose?"

"Your family? Friends?"

Tora lowered her head and swallowed. "No. They've... passed."

"So, I take it the family that I met was not actually your family."

Tora shook her head slowly.

"Did the Commander—?"

"No." Tora shook her head. "They were in... an accident. I don't want to talk about it."

"So, let me guess. You have no one else."

Tora's shoulders sagged, and she averted Aron's cynical glare.

"What do you know about the Pelri?" Aron gambled.

"The Pelri? What do you want to know?"

"Just tell me what you know about them."

Tora glanced around the bar quickly. "Well, I don't really know a lot about them. They're smaller than most Sapins and humans. They can travel within Athemoni. There are other magical talents that they have. I'm not really sure what, but it's got something to do with agriculture, I think. The Pelri are native to this country, and it hasn't been the same since they left, so the humans have been trying to capture them and analyze their powers to... to fix Seridon. Nothing grows here, as you can see. The Tree and the Pelri cursed the land on their way out. They have no intention of helping the humans, and I don't blame them, really. I mean, why would they, when humans and Sapins took their homeland away from them?"

"The Pelri cursed the land?"

"That's how the story goes."

"Puh," Aron scoffed. "What do you mean by 'analyze their powers'?"

"Experiments. A lot of scientific testing, trying to figure out what they've got that we don't... what gives them their abilities and they want to replicate them, I guess."

"Where do they do this testing?"

"Probably Rakkarron Station, after they're processed through, here in Lupellerin, of course. They process all Seridon visitors through Lupellerin. But that's where they keep all the captured Pelri. Rakkarron. It's on the east coast, just below the Isthmus of Asopo. Why?"

The bartender returned with their orders and an extra supply of napkins. "Another beer?" he asked Aron, completely ignoring Tora.

"Yeah, thanks."

"Hey, did you find Faradell Narrow? The owner was in here earlier. Picking up his Blue Blood rum. You just missed him. He buys in bulk, so we give him a good price."

"Yes, I found it. Nice place, thanks for the tip."

The bartender raised the empty beer bottle to Aron as he walked away.

To Tora, Aron said, "What's the best way to get there? To Rakkarron Station."

"Why do you want to go there? That's not where you're supposed to go, you know."

"It's not your concern. Just tell me how to get there," Aron insisted.

"I'll do better than that. I'll take you there. We'll have to find a vehicle, though."

Aron balked. "I don't need you to go with me. Just some good directions." This was the most significant breakthrough he'd gotten, but he didn't need a Sapin getting in the way—especially this Sapin.

"Aron!" Tora pleaded. "Let me help!"

"I don't want you anywhere near me."

"Aron, please. You can trust me."

"I can't, Tora! I can't trust you. Why don't you understand that? You've been lying to me since I first met you. How can you think I would ever trust you?"

"I just want to be with you, Aron. I want to earn your trust back. Please, let me try. I don't ever want to hurt you again."

Taking a bite of his sandwich, Aron contemplated his options. Tora knew the area, probably inside and out. She was also hell-bent on making amends. Maybe it would be worth his while to have her as a guide, just until he found Iyla.

"Can you teleport us there?" he asked, recalling the horrifying moment of witnessing the cloaked arm reaching out to Iyla's shoulder just before she disappeared.

Tora shook her head sadly.

"How long does it take to get there?"

"Maybe a day, if we have a car. We don't want to be traveling at night, though. The morcego wraiths nest close to there, and that's when they come out."

"Morcego wraiths?"

"Ugh, don't ask. There's nothing like it on Earth. You don't even want to know. And you still haven't told me why you want to go there."

"And it's still not your business," Aron retorted. "We leave in the morning. Do not follow me back to the inn. You can meet me around the corner from there, by the Peace Enforcement building. Find a vehicle." Aron stood up to leave, grabbing what was left of his sandwich and waving a few griggs at the bartender.

As he walked out the door, Tora sunk into the booth with a sigh, and a small smile slinked across her face.

On Aron's walk back to Faradell Narrow, he evaluated his new plan of action in his mind. In thirty-six hours, he should be in a position to rescue Iyla from her captors. They could then signal William and travel unseen northward to Urippa Spring.

"Tony!" Young Harvard came running full speed toward Aron as he walked through the front door of the inn. Aron dropped his backpack and held out his arms as Harvard jumped into them.

"Hey, bud, how's it going?"

"I saw the sinkhole again today!" he exclaimed.

"Did you?"

"Yes, Aunt Leyna lifted me up so I could look down into it again. The big cranes were pulling more stuff out of it."

"Wow! That's cool!" Aron laughed at the little boy's exuberance.

Harvard's dad, red-faced, entered the lobby with Leyna, unaware of Aron's presence and immersed in a quiet discussion. Aron wondered if Bander had already spoken to them about his gun purchase. Leyna noticed him first and smiled as he placed Harvard back on the floor.

"Hi, uh. So, it looks like tonight will be my last night here. I plan to be up early, so did you want me to go ahead and settle my bill now?"

"Oh, no!" Harvard pouted.

"Oh! Did you find your friend?" Leyna asked.

"Well, not yet, but I have a very good lead on where she might be."

"Aha, so it's a lady-friend." She winked at him. "Now it's all making sense."

Aron laughed. "No, it's not exactly like that," he said before noticing a fresh scrape above Anthony's eye. "Are you OK?" he asked, motioning to his injury.

"Yeah, yeah. I'm fine. Just a clumsy fall." Anthony moved to behind the desk, and Aron caught a pungent waft of alcohol. "I'll process you out over here, Tony," he said. "Are you having dinner here tonight again?"

"Yes, that would be great." Aron handed Anthony a small stack of griggs to cover his bill as Harvard cheered.

"It will be earlier than yesterday. Hope you're hungry. 'Cuz I sure don't know how I'll be hungry that early," he growled.

"Anthony, just stop." Leyna frowned.

"You can sit next to me!" yelled Harvard.

"You bet I will," Aron said with a laugh. "I'll be upstairs packing up a few things. Let me know if you need help with anything."

"Hey, uh, Tony. What do you know about Tariadyn? Leyna said you'd been there." Anthony asked.

Aron paused a moment at the bottom of the staircase. "What do *I* know? Well, I've passed through once or twice, but that's it. They have nice forests. It's a beautiful country, and uh, well, that's all I really know about it."

"Things definitely grow there, then."

"Oh, yes, definitely," Aron confirmed. "They've got great tarthberries."

Leyna and Anthony exchanged a raised eyebrow, which puzzled Aron.

"Looking to go on vacation?" he asked.

"We're not sure," Leyna interrupted. "Maybe we can talk more about it this afternoon."

It seemed strange that these people would ask him, someone not even from this world, about Tariadyn. Not that they had any idea where he was from. Aron smiled and then made his way up the staircase to his room. He opened the door and saw that it was just as he'd left it, the cool breeze still blowing through the open window. He unpacked his backpack and again took inventory. The Elfblood Tree's heart was at the bottom, safely wrapped in a smaller leather satchel. He still had plenty of currency. He refilled the three water flasks, tucked them in the outer pockets of the backpack, and then repacked everything, including the gun. Aron stowed the backpack under the bed while he showered and washed his clothes in the tub.

Pulling out Jens' map, Aron found Rakkarron on the eastern coast, where Tora had indicated. He deliberated over how much he could trust Tora and the intel he'd gathered from her about the Pelri. Jens was sure that Lupellerin was where Iyla would be held captive, just as her mother had been. God only knew what was happening to her right now. He had no time to waste.

A soft knock at the door pulled him out of his thoughts.

"Tony?" came the tiny voice.

He opened the door to see Harvard standing there holding an oversized blanket and a short stick. "Will you help me build a tent?"

Aron chuckled to himself. "Sure. It's almost dinnertime, though."

As they walked down the staircase, Aron overheard a hushed but heated discussion in the room below.

"Anthony, we have to," said Leyna. "There was no doubt in her voice, and I know she's going to do it. And if she does, we have to get out of here. She believes her, so I believe her. This is our opportunity, and I want us all to be together. Tell me you're on board." Aron paused on the staircase.

"I'm just so over this shit," Anthony answered through his teeth. "A life on the run? Again? Is that what we really want? Why she can't just leave well enough alone, I will never understand. Looks like we don't have much choice."

Aron cleared his throat and stomped noisily down the second half of the stairs. The discussion stopped as he and Harvard entered the room. Leyna smiled nervously, and they parted to opposite sides, pretending to look busy.

"Are you guys alright?" Aron ventured.

Anthony and Leyna glanced uneasily at each other and then at Aron. Anthony nodded his approval to his sister. "Look, Tony, you seem like a good guy, so we want to be upfront with you. We recently received some... disturbing news. You might call it a warning of sorts."

Here it comes, thought Aron. *They know about the gun.*

"Harvard, run up to your room and play for just a few minutes." Anthony guided his son back toward the stairs.

"But I wanna build a tent with Tony!"

"After dinner. Go on upstairs until it's ready."

Leyna waited until her nephew reached the next floor and then continued. "We think it's best that we leave Seridon, and sooner rather than later. And you might want to do the same."

Aron felt his nerves prickling on his arm. He wasn't expecting that. "Why? What was the warning? And from whom?"

Anthony again glanced at Leyna. "You know he's fine with them," she reassured her brother. "He's had tarthberries, for goodness' sake!"

Anthony motioned to the sofa and sat himself down in the chair across from it. He paused, running his hand through his shaggy hair, and Aron could see the sweat beading on his forehead. He cleared his throat. "My wife works at a facility that studies the Neclu Pelri. Now, understand, first of all, we don't agree with their practice. But, uh, they've recently captured a new one with whom she, my wife, has befriended. She, well, if you've met my wife, she has a heart of gold. But, uh, this Pelri—"

"What's her name?" Aron interrupted.

"My wife?"

"The Pelri. Do you know her name? Do you know what she looks like?"

Anthony looked to Leyna, who answered, "Uh… Iyla? I think that's what she said."

A surge of energy ran through Aron's body as he tried to remain composed. His heart pounded, and he felt every hair stand on end.

Anthony continued. "So, this Pelri, Iyla, and my wife have apparently agreed to help each other escape. You see, my wife is tracked by the government because of her compassion for the Pelri and some trouble she got into in the past. It's a long story… Anyway, the Pelri said that we would be in danger if we stayed in Seridon. She didn't say why, but—"

"Where is this facility where she works? Rakkarron Station?" Aron probed. Both Anthony and Leyna looked at him curiously.

"Uh, no. She works here in Lupellerin. Rakkarron Station is overloaded, so they've been keeping the newest captures here for a while now. Do you know this Pelri?"

"Holy shit," said Aron, standing up. "OK, this is good. This is good." He walked over to the nearest open window and moved the curtains aside to peer out and then shut it. "Do you mind?"

"No, go ahead," said Leyna, moving to the window on the opposite side of the room to shut that one as well.

"Is anyone else here?" Aron asked.

"No, still empty," answered Anthony.

"OK," Aron paced the room. "OK. Iyla is the friend that I've been looking for. Earlier today, I was led to believe that she might be at Rakkarron Station, which is why I needed to leave. But if she's here, if Iyla trusted your wife enough to warn her, then I will have to take that chance with the both of you. You see, I need to get Iyla out of there. We have... an important task to complete... and she's right; you're going to want to leave Seridon as soon as you can once we get them out."

"Why? What is happening?" asked Leyna.

"I don't really know exactly, but I know you are good people. You deserve a fair chance at a better life, which you won't ever have in Seridon. Please understand that I can't tell you everything just yet."

"Do you need any help? Maybe we can help you and Iyla. Are you in some kind of trouble? If this has anything to do with helping the Pelri, you know we're on board."

"I... I'm sorry. I can't ask anything more of you when I don't even know everything. But I want all of you to be safe. First, I just need to get to Iyla. I'll take all the help I can get with that."

"Well," said Anthony, "all I know is that she and my wife are still in the planning stages. The facility is well-guarded. My wife will be home later tonight. We can talk then?"

Muffled rustling in the lobby prompted all three of them to pivot toward the opening through the hallway. "Wrong! I'm home now!" came a lively voice.

Anthony and Leyna exchanged glances. "Mommy!" Harvard bounded down the stairs, throwing his small body into her.

"Hi sweetie, how's momma's boy been today?"

"Heddah! How did this happen?" Anthony beamed and strode over to his wife, planting a kiss on her cheek.

Heddah frowned and waved her hand in front of her face to disperse the odor. "Yeah, don't get too excited. I got an early leave tonight only because my little Pelri is sleeping, and I told them I had left something at home. You know that means they'll be tacking on extra hours before the end of the week. Well, who do we have here?" Her warm smile welcomed Aron as he entered the room behind Leyna.

Leyna motioned to Aron. "Heddah, this is our guest, Tony."

"Uh, actually... it's Aron. Sorry, I—"

"Don't even think about it. I get it," Leyna reassured. "Aron, huh?"

"Well, very nice to meet you, Aron. I hope you've been enjoying your stay," said Heddah. "What brings you to Lupellerin?"

"Heddah," said Leyna, "Aron is a friend of Iyla's. He knows."

A look of subtle surprise quickly turned to a knowing smile. "So, you're the good one," Heddah said. "I've heard about you."

"Have you?" Aron didn't think Iyla would have mentioned him under the circumstances. "Exactly what have you heard?" he tested.

"Oh, don't you worry. Your sweet girl is pretty tight-lipped. She just mentioned you might be looking for her." *Of course, he was looking for her*, he thought, wondering just how much Heddah knew about him. About either of them.

"How is she? Is she alright?"

"Well, she's been through the wringer with a couple of these experiments, especially this last one. The head researcher conducted a covert, over-night, unscheduled...oh, it makes me so angry! She's fairly well intact, considering, but I think she's trying to put on a strong front. I've got to get her out of there before the next round starts the day after tomorrow. I can't have her go through anything more, and I simply can't witness anymore of this cruelty. I can't do it. So, I've arranged for her to be able to slip out of her room tonight just for scoping out the building traffic during shift change down time. I think that might be our best chance, around one on the clock in the morning. We should all pack our bags. Tomorrow night we're doing it. We're leaving."

Aron's heart skipped a beat. Iyla was still alive. She had been found. And through a human family that actually cared for the Pelri. The plans were in place, and he would see her tomorrow. It had to have been some kind of miracle.

Chapter Sixteen

Nature's Bond

"Did you lock the door?" The night nurse was irritably demanding answers from Dakryn.

Iyla held her breath and dared not move as she crouched under the desk in a small office close to her room.

"No, ma'am," Dakryn responded. "It was Heddah. She said she was using her restricted key to lock her in so that they couldn't perform surprise testing overnight. She's trying to avoid another mishap like the other night."

Iyla ran her thumb and forefinger along the outer edges of the key that Heddah had left for her and then gripped it tightly. The night nurse sighed dramatically, and the rhythmic thud of her heavy footsteps faded as she exited the area down the hallway on the opposite side from where Iyla was hiding. The sound of papers rustling warned Iyla that Dakryn had not followed her. They were the only two remaining on this floor. Iyla wondered about the locked doors she had discovered and whether there were any other captives in this facility. And could she free them too, tomorrow night?

A sharp pain seared into Iyla's back as a bent metal seam on the underside of the desk pressed against her. She quietly readjusted her position.

It had been a productive night. At one on the clock, she had silently slipped out of her room and scouted the premises.

She found the laundry chute and the central vent to the air ducts that Heddah had suggested and determined the laundry chute would be the only option for escape since the air ducts reduced to a height that was not large enough for her to move through to the basement level.

There were very few workers at this hour, although the guard patrol still manned their posts. Several guards still on duty were playing cards in the break room. What if she just tried to get out now? No, the laundry room windows were locked. Breaking them would set off the alarms. She had to stick to the plan. The shift change tomorrow would provide the opportune time to make her way from her room to the laundry chute. She could easily slide down to the basement where Heddah would have left a small window open that faced the south side of the building. Once out, Heddah would meet her in the exterior stairwell on the west side and take her to her friend's cabin, where she would then remove Heddah's tracking device and be on her way.

The rustling of papers had stopped. The only sound was a steady double-tick from a nearby electronic device. Iyla cautiously moved out from under the desk to the office doorway. It was clear. She felt the blood coursing through her veins. Swiftly darting between desks and chairs, she stealthily made her way down the hallway.

She passed the doorway to the room where she was taken after the pink powder had paralyzed her that first day, that terrifying day when that disgusting Commander came in to view her. Her stomach turned at the thought of him, his ugly face and his stink.

Iyla swiftly hurried to her room. She locked herself in and then stowed Heddah's key inside the bathroom cabinet. *Tomorrow night.* She was getting out. Satisfied with her reconnaissance mission, she flopped onto the bed.

Iyla's bedside flowers, whose blooms had closed in slumber, opened wide, acknowledging her arrival. "Don't worry," said Iyla. "I won't leave you behind."

Twice that night, the nightmares tore through her mind. She woke up screaming, recalling the experiments she had just endured. And the tears flowed for her late mother, after undergoing only a small piece of the horrors that she had suffered.

"Iyla? You doing OK? I've got breakfast." Heddah asked softly after peeking through the door. Iyla had just finished her shower and was toweling off her hair. The warm, sweet smells from Heddah's tray invited Iyla to soothe the rumble in her stomach.

"I'm so tired."

"You didn't sleep well? I can imagine. Oh, how I wish I could just walk you out of here and welcome you into my home, away from all this evil."

Iyla cracked a small smile. "You know, I might actually miss this food," she said softly. "Nothing else, though."

Heddah smiled. "Chef Barrod. He's got connections to the good stuff."

"We're still getting out of here, right?"

"Shh." Heddah nodded. "But sweetie, first I've got some news for you."

Iyla reluctantly put her fork down. Heddah sat on the bed, smoothed the fabric of her pants with both her hands, and sighed with a gleaming smile.

"I met Aron."

With a slight pang in her stomach, Iyla's lips parted slightly, and she blinked her eyes, attempting to clear the confusion. "You met... Aron?"

"Yes. He's staying at my family's inn. He's been looking for you!"

"How—"

"I know. How crazy is that? I'm telling you, the moons are on your side, sweet girl."

"What exactly did he tell you?"

"Oh, you kids, I know you're up to something!" Heddah chuckled. "So guarded, both of you. He's come to rescue you. That's all I know. Oh, and he confirmed your warning that we should leave Seridon. Whatever is going on, Iyla, you do know I want to help, right? My whole family does. I know good people when I meet 'em!"

"Heddah, you've already done so much. I don't want to put you in any more danger... being around me. You don't want to stay too close to us."

"I know, I know. But listen, shh. Aron will meet you in the outside stairwell on the side of the building, not me. I will stay at home, so the tracking log doesn't look suspicious. Makes sense, right?"

"OK."

Heddah's smile brightened the dismal room. Iyla was more reserved, and a calmness had fallen over her. They were getting out. Aron had come to help her.

"Thank you, Heddah," she said sincerely. "Thank you for helping me and taking this risk."

"Oh, doll," Heddah responded, as she placed her hand on Iyla's cheek. "I just feel so fortunate to be able to help. Finally, really helping a little Pelri. Now, I've got to get a few things done, and I'll be back in about an hour. You're still in recovery, so no tests scheduled. Do you need anything?"

Iyla shook her head as Heddah stood up and pulled the chart from the outside door pocket. Her bright excitement quickly turned to serious concern. "This isn't right. What is going on now? Teerint!" Turning to Iyla, she said, "I'll be right back."

Teerint rounded the corner with an assistant, just as Heddah's second bellowing of his name exploded from her lungs.

"What is this?" Heddah demanded, pounding her index finger on the chart. She had left Iyla's door open and had stopped him mid-stride. "What is this? I said no testing until tomorrow! She is still recovering!"

"Sorry, the Commander is coming to take her this afternoon. We need to get one more test in first," he explained coolly.

"What are you talking about? Why is he coming? Why don't I know about this? We're... we're not even halfway through the standards with her!"

"Well, Heddah," Teerint patronized, "the Commander doesn't answer to you. He does as he pleases. Were you not aware of that either? He wants the Pelri, and he'll be here this afternoon. And don't blame me. I need more time with her too. Testing starts at two on the clock."

Iyla felt the shot of panic burn through her middle like an acid injection. Heddah turned to her as she stood in the doorway. *The Commander wanted the Pelri.* She knew what that meant.

"Fine. But I'm going home for lunch. You'll have to find someone to cover for me." Heddah emphatically exited the conversation, stormed off in the opposite direction, and left Iyla staring at Teerint. He scowled at her and shut the door.

Iyla rushed to the bathroom cabinet and confirmed the restricted key was still there. Where was Heddah going? The thought of the Commander placing his hands on her, besides the painful testing, was bad enough. But the timing of it all couldn't be worse. She had to get out of there, and it had to be soon.

Looking around the room, she saw nothing to pack other than the seven flowers on her bedside table. Their vibrant beauty had helped to keep her spirits up, and her hope alive while in this dull and dreary room. What used to be six scrawny stems had burst into a flourishing, leafy bouquet with colorful blooms. Their sweet fragrance invigorated her senses and reminded her of home. Yes, she would change out of her gown, back into her freshly washed clothes, and then she could easily tuck them into her side belt.

Iyla spent the rest of the morning thinking about Heddah and what her plan might be. She said she was leaving for lunch. But they had just eaten breakfast. She must be going to Aron to arrange a change of plans. Iyla figured she'd wait until after lunch, and if there was no sign of Heddah, she would go through with the original plan in broad daylight. She paced the room, going over the plan in her head, before flopping down on the soft bed. She was so tired, and a very faint sound of familiar music lulled her to sleep.

About two hours later, the door swung open, and a red-haired technician strode in with clean linens and placed half of them in the bathroom. Iyla sat up quickly and looked out the small window. The sun appeared to be high in the sky. Returning to the room but keeping her distance, the technician said to Iyla, "I'll need you to get up from the bed. I need to... change..."

Suddenly, the technician's eyes rolled back into her head as she swayed dizzily from side to side. Stumbling, she grasped the edge of the wall cabinet as Iyla rushed to catch her. The technician fell to the floor, still breathing but unconscious.

What do I do? They're going to think I did something.

Iyla checked her pulse. Her body convulsed as Iyla pressed down on her torso, trying to keep her still. *They're going to think I did it. They're going to kill me for sure, now.*

"Help!" she yelled. "Someone, help, please!" Iyla rolled her to her side as the pungent acidic odor of vomit filled the room.

A young assistant poked his head through the doorway. Iyla recognized him as one of Teerint's assistants who had helped with the pressure testing. "What's going on?"

"Help her!" pleaded Iyla. "I think she's having a seizure!"

The assistant's eyes widened as he gasped and then crouched down by the technician to check her breathing. "What did you do to her?"

"I didn't! I'm trying to help her! Can you please do something or find someone who can?"

The assistant opened the technician's eyelids to check her pupils. Slowly, his head lifted, and his gaze met Iyla's. He stared at her for longer than what was comfortable. He blinked, and his body shuddered before he collapsed on top of the technician.

"What is happening?" Iyla yelled. The assistant's body continued to shake as Iyla pulled him off the technician and laid him on his side.

"Iyla? What is going on?" Heddah had returned.

"Stay back! Get out! I don't know what's happening. They both came into the room and started shaking." Iyla ran to Heddah to push her back.

"Let me help them!" Heddah pushed Iyla aside and placed her hand on the assistant's forehead just before the vomit spewed from his mouth. "I'll get someone."

She hurried out of the room and quickly returned with a scientist who worked on the floor below them. The two bodies lay motionless on the floor. He kneeled to examine them as Iyla tried to mop up the vomit with a bathroom towel. Heddah hovered behind him. "We need to get them to the hospital. Does your floor have a Sapin runner?"

"Yes," Heddah answered. "I'll... Krekleer? Hey!"

The scientist's eyes were locked onto the wall behind Heddah as he swayed and then stumbled to the floor, slamming his head on the corner of the counter on the way down. Blood flowed down his face and pooled on the floor.

"Oh my, Krekleer?" Heddah rubbed his arm as he began to convulse. She looked at Iyla.

"What do we do? They're going to think I did this!"

"Grab another towel." Heddah motioned to the cabinet.

Iyla ran to Krekleer's side and pressed the towel onto his head. As Heddah rummaged through the cabinets, Iyla heard a single faint musical chord coming from the corner of the room. Was someone calling her name?

Her bedside flowers moved in unison to look at her, and Iyla was certain they each gave her a wink.

"Heddah! The flowers!"

"What about the flowers?"

"They're doing this! I think they're trying to help me get out of here!" Memories of Jens' stories flashed through her mind. How the bond between Pelri and nature used to be back when Seridon was Keyronai and the land protected her ancestors.

Heddah stood beside Iyla. "Blessed moons! Are you sure?"

"They are! They're doing this!"

"Have mercy. OK, sweetie, this is it," she said and rushed to close the door. "Are you ready? Easy now."

Iyla nodded.

"Grab the technician's coat, and here, take Krekleer's glasses. Pull your hair down and cover your ears."

Iyla did as she was told, while Heddah checked the pulse of all three motionless bodies on the floor.

Heddah sighed. "I don't know," she said, shaking her head. Then to Iyla, "I already spoke with Aron. The laundry room is jam-packed with workers this time of day, so I'll take you out to the courtyard. Aron will be there to help us get you over the wall."

"And you?"

"As long as we get there unnoticed, I'll go back inside and then break for lunch. I'll lock this door with the restricted key. We don't want them to know you're not in here. It should buy us a little time. I'll meet you and Aron at the inn."

"Got it," Iyla confirmed.

"You go first. Go to the north stairwell. I'll hang back a little, so I can be sure you get to the exit," said Heddah as she cracked the door open and noted the four workers in the immediate vicinity. "Here, hold this chart and stand tall. Walk with a purpose."

Iyla pulled the flowers out of the vase and tucked them into her side belt under the technician's coat before reaching for the chart. "Let's go."

She opened the door wide and strode confidently, but not too hurriedly, toward the hallway that led to the north stairwell. Two workers were conversing near the last desk in the room. They glanced up briefly as Iyla passed, but she continued on.

"Ugh, I don't feel well," Iyla heard one of them say.

As she turned the corner to the hallway, she heard her room door shut and knew that Heddah was following. The entrance to the stairwell was at the far end of the hall. She focused on the bright window ahead, where she could see the end of a flagpole and a red, gold, and silver striped flag fluttering in the breeze.

The stairwell door opened, and a guard strolled into the hallway toward her. Iyla stiffened her small frame, and her breath hitched. He eyed her curiously, slowing his pace as he passed, and then stumbled to catch his footing. His hand clasped his forehead as he recovered from his dizzy spell, but he continued down the hallway.

"You alright there, sir?" Heddah asked. He didn't respond and disappeared around the corner.

She was almost there.

"Heddah, come here a moment." It was Teerint. "These documents needed to go to the communications department. Wait, Heddah, who is that?"

No! Iyla could feel his eyes burning into the back of her. Should she make a run for it?

"Oh, Teerint, yes, yes, yes. I know. I'll do it," Heddah positioned herself between him and Iyla. "Also, I need you to go over these testing forms."

"Heddah, move. Who is that?" He skirted around Heddah and quickened his pace toward Iyla.

"Teerint!" Heddah yelled as Iyla glanced behind her and saw the recognition on his face.

"Guards!" he bellowed.

Iyla ran toward the stairwell, but Teerint anticipated her direction and moved between her and the door, grasping the doorknob and holding it shut. In a moment, Heddah was behind her. She yanked the technician's coat off Iyla, exposing the potent flowers nestled securely in her belt.

Almost simultaneously, Teerint doubled over as if someone had punched him in the gut. He reached for Iyla as he staggered toward her, gripping her arm. Heddah quickly slammed her elbow into Teerint's arm, forcing him to release his hold.

Spinning around, Iyla rushed to the window. Forcing the window open and gripping the flagpole, she wriggled through the frame and out onto the narrow ledge on the roof.

"Iyla!" Heddah shouted just as Teerint hurled himself toward the window and fell to his knees. Iyla saw his body begin to convulse, and his eyes rolled back into his head as he fell to the floor.

Three guards rushed into the hallway.

"Help! He's seizing!" Heddah exclaimed as she rolled him to his side. "I saw him vomiting out the window, and then he fell to the floor."

"Get the Sapin runner," one guard said to another. "Tell him we need a doctor immediately."

Iyla stood outside on the narrow ledge with her back pressed up against the steep-pitched roof of the alcove. She needed to get further up to be out of sight. She could hear Heddah and the guards tending to Teerint inside. Iyla knew she didn't have much time. They would soon discover she was missing.

A gust of wind blew her hair into her face. She gripped the corner drainpipe and tugged it to test its strength. She looked out over the city below her. Several buildings sparkled with brilliant gemstone hues. Quite a few pedestrians were making their way about the city sidewalks, as well as the many vehicles clunking through the streets. She was eight stories above ground level.

Holding onto the drainpipe, Iyla was able to swivel her position to face the corner, placing each foot on the narrow ledge of the connecting walls. She pulled herself up onto the hot roof and swiftly hunkered into the shaded valley of the two adjoining roof lines on the other side. She was well-hidden from eyes on the ground, providing her the opportunity to catch her breath.

Heddah had told her that Aron would meet her in the courtyard, which meant she needed to crawl over the roof wall and across the rooftop to get there. Iyla could still hear shouting from the open window below her. But not Heddah.

Carefully, Iyla stretched to grasp a roof tile and pulled herself up toward the roof's safety wall. Another gust of wind whipped around her, and she placed her hand protectively on the flowers tucked in her side belt. Positioning her right foot on the ridge of the alcove roof, she swiftly cleared the safety wall and crouched low into the side.

Quiet.

Other than the high-pitched whistle of the wind, there was no sound on the roof below the rim of the wall. She waited. Slowly, Iyla removed Krekleer's glasses and peered over the edge to the ground below. Among the blended busy movement, her eyes diverted to one form, darting across the street. It was Heddah. She was out.

Now, it was up to her to get down to the ground, where Aron would meet her. Across the rooftop was a collection of large, metal mechanical units, solar panels, thick pipes, vents, and two chimneys. A door facing her led to the building interior.

Crouching low, she dashed to the opposite side of the building and kneeled behind the wall. Peering over again, she could see the courtyard. It was empty. It wasn't much to look at other than cracked concrete and stone. The walls of the courtyard were high and wide. On the east side was an old fountain that no longer held water. A marble image of the Commander rose from the middle of it, but years of neglect had led to a cracked leg, a missing arm, and discoloration.

Iyla noticed one guard was patrolling inside. She watched and waited. The guard remained on the east side, near the entrance of the facility. Appearing anxious, he occasionally glanced about as if looking for potential threats and yet not wanting to be noticed. Someone had lassoed a chain around the neck of the statue of the Commander and left it hanging down its side. *That wasn't there when I was last in the courtyard.* Two steel poles lay on the ground outside the fountain.

Again, the guard furtively glanced about and then turned his gaze upward. He saw her. And that was no guard. *Aron!* He was here. He'd made it. Aron quickly moved to position himself against the building wall around the corner from the entrance, where she could just barely see him. He covertly motioned to the roof of the east wall. A narrow steel caged ladder was fixed to the outside of the building and ran from the roof down to the ground just outside the courtyard wall. She smiled and nodded.

Iyla jolted at the sound of a loud slam on the other side of the metal units and pipes. The door to the roof! Someone was coming. She ran to the ladder as a flurry of footsteps pounded across the rooftop. She nimbly climbed over the short rooftop wall, secured her footing, and ducked into the frame of the hot metal ladder. Had they seen her?

Two stifled pops and a hissing whiz near her ear confirmed that they had.

Chapter Seventeen

Let's Go

Tora, fully cloaked, stood alone at the edge of the sinkhole, staring down into the deep pit of debris. Aron looked on as she turned to see him approaching her, her face red. It was early, just after sunrise. The moons were still visible between the grey clouds, and the air was dank from the overnight rain showers. Her glum expression instantly transformed into a smile of relief.

"No need," Aron said abruptly. "Plans have changed."

"What? What do you mean?"

"Look, I'm only meeting you here because I told you I would. But plans have changed, and I no longer need your services."

She winced. "Aron, how are you going to get through all of Seridon without my help?"

"I have all the help I need." His response was cold and firm.

"Aron," she pleaded, placing her pale hand on his arm. "Please don't leave me here by myself."

"Tora, there's no reason for you to come with me. In fact, I don't want you anywhere near me. Find a shelter if you are so worried." Aron was now numb to her signature subterfuge. Callous, maybe, but this was her doing. He couldn't trust her.

"A shelter? Aron, they don't have that kind of thing here."

"Goodbye, Tora," he said, turning to walk away.

"ARON!" Her futile pleading veered to venomous desperation. "I'll report you."

Aron stiffened. Red anger colored his face and ears.

"I will, Aron. Without you, what does it matter if I live or die? I'll tell the Commander you're alive and that you're here in Seridon, and you'll never get near that Tree. You'll die at his hand. And this country will remain as lifeless as it is now until all the Pelri are dead."

The master manipulator had reached a new low. Aron's fingers dug into his palms as the anger smoldered inside him. Slowly, he turned to face her.

"And there it is." His shrewd tone tempered his seething fury. "The real Tora has finally fully emerged. You have a very sick way of showing your love. For years, I cared for you, Tora. I loved you. I went along with all that you wanted, ceded to every lie and every manipulation—until I didn't. And it has all brought me to this moment. *This* moment, in this strange world, as you stand in front of me, a traitor not only to your country but even to the two of us.

"Your power may be dying, Tora, but mine is not. You do not know what I am capable of. I have contacts here who are genuinely honorable people. And I won't let you hurt them. I don't want you near us, and," he hesitated, "I will never trust you."

Aron raked his hand through his hair before leaning his back against the stone house just in front of the Peace Enforcement building. *How can I possibly bring her along?* he thought. *But if she tells the Commander, we're doomed.* "If I say you can come with me and you make one move to hurt any of them, you, Tora, will know what true agony is. Do you understand what I am telling you?"

Tora nodded. "This is the right thing, Aron. You'll see. I promise. Everything will be OK."

"You make me sick." Aron scowled in disgust as he walked away.

"Where will I meet you?" she asked.

Aron spun on his heel. "We both know you'll find me," he retorted.

Tora clenched her teeth and set off in the opposite direction. Aron listened to her footsteps fading quickly as he made his way back to Faradell Narrow. The light breeze could not cool his anger. How would he explain Tora to the Farins, to Iyla? How could he ensure Tora wouldn't destroy their plan and the future of the Pelri?

Aron just missed Heddah leaving for work as he entered the inn. Warm, inviting smells were coming from the kitchen, and he could hear Harvard playing in the next room.

"Aron, is that you?" Leyna called. "Breakfast will be ready soon."

"OK, thanks. I'll be back down in a minute." Aron headed upstairs to take inventory, as was his usual routine any time he left his belongings behind.

At the top of the stairs, he noticed the door to his room was ajar. He had closed and locked it before he left. He was sure of it. Panic coursed through his veins when he saw that his backpack was opened up and sitting on top of his bed. He hurriedly sifted through the pack. The money, the gun; it was still there. His map and the elf's iron talisman; all there. Reaching for the satchel at the bottom, every hair on his arms stood on end. He felt his heart clamoring to escape from his chest. It was gone.

He closed up the backpack and shoved it far under the bed against the wall. Rapidly descending the staircase, he called out to Leyna just as Harvard crossed the hallway at the bottom.

"Harvard, wait!" A thousand scenarios zipped through Aron's mind, seeing the Heart in the small boy's hands.

"Look, Aunt Leyna," Harvard said. "It's warm!"

"Where did you get this?" Leyna asked Harvard just as Aron rounded the corner.

She now held the Heart of the Elfblood Tree.

"Uh, excuse me. I need that back." He reached out, and Leyna promptly handed it to him.

"Harvard! Did you take this from our guest?" she scolded. "Aron, I'm sorry."

"It's fine; it's OK." Palpable relief washed over his face. It's safe. We're safe. Breathe.

"You're as white as a ghost! Harvard, you apologize to Aron for getting into his things, and then you go to your room."

"Sorry, Tony-Aron." Aron couldn't help chuckling at his new nickname as Harvard trudged up the stairs.

Leyna shook her head. "He gets into the keys at the desk and thinks every room is his own new adventure."

"Don't worry about it. It didn't go far, thank God."

"What is that, anyway? Interesting-looking object... beautiful, really."

"Uh, well, story for another day, I think? What's for breakfast?" He couldn't put it off much longer. Eventually, they would need to know the whole truth. They deserved that much.

Leyna brushed off his blatant change of topic. "Lucky for us, the market just got a fresh shipment of fruit yesterday. I mean, they're no tarthberries, but they're from Parise!" She brought out a large bowl of colorful fruit cut into bite-size pieces, along with blueberry muffins with butter and mashed cassava.

"Looks great!"

"So, Aron. You've really had tarthberries?"

"Oh, yeah. They're fantastic! Haven't you had them before?"

"Well, no," she answered, marginally confused. "But how? I mean, since they only grow where the Pelri live, how did you... have you been to where they live? Are they in Tariadyn? How long did you say you've known Iyla, exactly?"

"Oh, wow. I didn't know. I haven't known Iyla very long. No, they're no longer in Tariadyn. They're always moving, you know."

"Yes, and tarthberry bushes won't survive a day without them no matter what country you're in, so you had to have been to where they live."

"Uh, yeah," said Aron, not sure how much he should reveal.

"Wow." Leyna sank back into her chair. "That's amazing that you've been that close to a Pelri village. Did you just, sort of, stumble upon it?"

"Uh, kind of. Iyla basically saved my life." Aron thought back to waking from a two-month coma, locked in a wooden crate. And then he smiled to himself, thinking about Iyla's cute face looking down at him, serving him soup in her extraordinary treehouse overlooking the lagoon. How is it that it seemed so long ago?

"Really? How did that happen?"

Aron contemplated his response for a brief moment. "I'm not sure that you'd believe me if I told you."

"Sure, I would." She smiled. "So, how many Pelri are you friends with?"

"Just Iyla. I haven't met any others."

Leyna smiled. "Sorry for all the questions. We're just fascinated by them. I'm looking forward to meeting Iyla. Are you ready for tonight?"

"Bag is packed. You?"

"Yes. I'll pack Harvard's bag while he naps, and that's it, really. So, you'll stop here first, to remove Heddah's tracker, and then we head out."

"Will Tariadyn be your final destination?"

"We're not sure yet." Leyna bit her bottom lip.

The front door opened, then slammed shut, and both Leyna and Aron rose from their chairs.

"Anthony! Leyna!" came Heddah's voice.

"Heddah, aren't you supposed to be at work still? What's going on?"

"Where's Anthony? This is important."

"He's out back. Are you OK?"

"I'll get him," said Aron just as Anthony rounded the corner.

"No, I'm not OK. They're screwing things up over there again!"

"Heddah? What's going on?" Anthony looked like he had just gotten out of bed.

Heddah and Leyna both glared at him.

"OK, everyone, listen. Iyla's chart now has testing scheduled for this afternoon. I tried to get them to cancel it, but the Commander is headed here to take her! We've got to get that girl out of there, quick. Oh, the thought of that nasty Commander with my sweet girl... it cannot happen. We have to move the timeline up." Heddah was near tears as she busily sorted through a bag that was stashed behind the front desk. "I don't know what we're going to do. I don't know how to get her out of there in the middle of the day! That darn Teerint. I bet he knew about this long ago." She pulled out a tissue and blew her nose.

"Heddah, come here," Anthony stepped toward her, but his shoulder rammed into the door frame. He reached out to Heddah, pulled her into his arms, and held her tight. "Just breathe. You'll figure this out."

"Right. I will. Because it certainly won't be you!" She pushed herself away from her husband. "And we don't have time to breathe! I need to go back there with a plan! And you need to take a cold shower!"

Anthony retreated and sighed, running his fingers through his hair.

"OK, let's just think this through," said Aron. "You said there's a courtyard, right? You've taken Iyla to walk there. If you can get her there again, I can take it from there."

"Yes. OK, yes. So, I can get you into the courtyard first before I leave for lunch. But there's no gate or door from there directly outside. We need to plan a way for you to climb over the wall and get out of there with Iyla, because you'll never get her out if you take her through the building."

"Just leave that part to me. All you have to do is get her there, and then when you go on lunch break, we'll meet you here. You two, make sure you and Harvard are ready to go," Aron said to Anthony and Leyna. "Have some boiled water ready for Iyla to get the tracker out. I don't know what all she'll need, but that just seems logical, right? A sharp knife, needle, thread…"

"I'll see if I can find some actual surgical instruments and supplies at work," said Heddah.

"Great," said Aron. "Heddah, let's go."

Chapter Eighteen

In the Pit

"**S**he's going down the ladder!"

Aron heard several more pops as the darts whizzed past Iyla's head. The cramped cage surrounding the ladder hindered her pace considerably. *C'mon Iyla.*

"You! Go down after her! Do not kill her! The rest of us will meet you at the bottom." Four uniformed guards appeared at the rooftop safety wall and three quickly disappeared again.

With Iyla's ladder taking her to the outside of the courtyard, he needed to scale the wall to recover her. He needed a bridge. Aron grasped one of the steel poles and used it to swing at the disintegrating legs of the Commander's statue. On the fourth swing, a sizeable chunk of one leg sailed to the ground. Again, he swung at the figure, and the second leg shattered to pieces.

Using the chain lassoed around the statue's neck, Aron pulled the marble structure over. Its head smashed into the courtyard wall, providing him a solid ramp to climb over it. *The guards had to have heard that, dammit.* He swiftly scaled the toppled statue up to the broad flat coping stones on the top of the wall.

The east side of the facility where Iyla was descending on the ladder was fifty yards away. Aron skillfully dodged the flying darts as he scrambled along the top of the wall toward her. Iyla had reached the end of the ladder and took the last five-foot leap to the ground.

The courtyard wall was about six feet back from the ladder, but Aron jumped from the wall, grasping onto the ladder as two darts whizzed past either side of his face. He climbed down several rungs and then jumped to the ground, where Iyla was pressed up against the side of the building, waiting for him.

A slight smile of relief crossed each of their faces before Aron grabbed Iyla's hand and darted back along the outside of the courtyard.

"Halt!"

Iyla fell to the ground, yanking Aron downward and grabbing her left shoulder blade. She reached around and plucked out the dart. "I'm hit!"

"Are you OK? Can you run?" Aron pulled her to her feet. An alarm sounding from inside the building heralded their escape. "C'mon, I got you." Just as her knees buckled, Aron lifted her over his shoulder and her eyes closed.

Faradell Narrow was only about a mile and a half from the facility, but the guards weren't far behind. Aron knew they needed to find cover to shake them. He rounded the far corner of the courtyard just as the three other guards appeared from the front exit of the building. He was a solid hundred yards ahead. Several vehicles were parked behind the courtyard, but he couldn't take the chance to find one unlocked. He bolted for a small dump truck on the other side, quickly ducked behind it, and then gently laid Iyla on the ground.

Climbing up the side of the truck, he was able to unlatch the back to ease down the tailgate. He scooped Iyla up and placed her in the truck bed. Swiftly and quietly, he climbed in and pulled the chain to close the tailgate. He moved several boxes and cinder blocks and pulled Iyla all the way up toward the cab. A thick, waxy drop cloth provided ample coverage for both of them.

He checked Iyla's breathing and the entry wound on her shoulder blade. She seemed in good shape aside from the tranquilizer shot and several bruises, although he was puzzled by the bouquet of flowers tucked at her hip.

"Check over there! We're going to head in this direction!" Aron heard the guards scurrying between the parked vehicles and then outside the truck. He dared not flinch.

"Open up the drain cover," one guard demanded.

Aron heard the clanking of a manhole cover about ten yards away.

"Crakes!"

There was a bit more shuffling, the manhole cover clanking again, the thud of three sets of fading footsteps, and then nothing. Aron remained still, although he was dripping with sweat under the drop cloth with the scorching sun pounding down on the steel truck.

Iyla lay peacefully beside him, sweat beading on her upper lip and at her hairline. He was so glad to see her. He moved a few strands of hair from her face and allowed one finger to caress her cheek.

A car engine started in the parking lot. The tires crunched on the gravel, and then the engine noise faded into the distance. They had to get to Faradell Narrow before Heddah would be expected back at work. With the tracker still attached to her wrist, the authorities would surely be knocking at her door in no time.

Aron pulled back the drop cloth. The slight breeze was a welcome reprieve. The alarm continued to sound from inside the building, but the guards were nowhere in sight. Looking behind him, through the two windows of the cab, Aron saw a familiar procession of vehicles pulling up and disappearing to the front of the facility. The Commander had arrived.

Aron carefully unlatched the tailgate and carried Iyla out of the truck bed. Instead of taking the main road, he headed south toward a warehouse and then down a less-traveled road leading to a sparse residential area. Heddah had provided detailed directions for the detour, but with little cover, Aron kept to the side of the road and hid behind any structures he came across. Iyla's slight frame was relatively easy to manage.

"So, this is what you're still here for," came a voice behind him, and he swiveled to confront it. "Is this why you were asking me about the Pelri?"

Aron was surprised at his relief. *Of course.* "Still not your business, Tora."

"How did you find a Pelri? And what are you doing with her?" She continued to walk about five paces behind him. "I saw you help her escape."

"Are you going to use that against me, too?" Aron quickened his stride. "Tell the Commander I'm a Pelri sympathizer?"

"Nope. I'm just here to help."

"I told you I don't need your help. And I still don't know how I'm going to explain you to my friends, so back off."

"You could just tell them the truth," Tora suggested.

"You fail to realize that you don't come off so well in that story."

"Do they even know who you really are? What you're here to do? I can't imagine any humans in Seridon would want to help you take their country away from them."

"Tora. Just back away for now. You know where I'm staying, and you know where I'm going. Just give me some time to figure out how to make this all work for everyone."

Tora slowed her pace and then stopped as Aron continued down the dirt road. Several people were crossing the road up ahead, and he dipped behind a parked vehicle and waited for them to pass. He could see Faradell Narrow just across the street. With a swift heave, he threw Iyla over his shoulder and made a run for it.

Heddah was standing at the entrance and opened the door to let them in.

"What happened to her? Is she OK?" She put her two fingers to Iyla's neck to check for a pulse as Aron laid her down on the lobby sofa.

Leyna entered from the kitchen and locked the front doors before handing a glass of water to Aron. "She'll be fine," said Aron. "She was on the roof and was shot by a tranquilizer dart on the way out. They're looking for us. We don't have much time."

"But we need her to get Heddah's tracker out. If we don't take it out, they'll be right on our tails every step of the way."

"Aw, sweet girl," Heddah rubbed her cheek and then pressed her hand to Iyla's forehead.

"What's wrong with her, Tony-Aron?" Harvard scooted up to the edge of the sofa and poked Iyla's shoulder with his small finger.

"She'll be OK. She's not feeling well and needs to sleep."

"Where's Anthony?" Heddah asked.

Leyna rolled her eyes and nodded to the back office.

"Again?" Heddah sighed, and her tired eyes closed as she bit the inside of her cheek.

Aron gently tapped Iyla's chin to wake her, but she continued to sleep. "Have you got everything ready? The boiled water and all that?" he asked. "We may have to take it with us."

"I've got it," replied Heddah and hurried to the kitchen. She returned almost immediately. "Aron, her flowers! Does she still have them?"

"What, these?" Aron carefully released the flowers, which were wilting from the pinch of Iyla's belt.

"Yes! Leyna, get a bowl and something to crush the roots with." Heddah took the flowers from Aron and his glass of water and immersed them.

"What are you doing?" he asked.

"I don't know if it'll work, but Iyla did this the other day after a difficult testing day." Heddah broke a few roots off and crushed them into a paste. She gently pushed the root paste onto Iyla's tongue using a small spoon and then closed her mouth.

"What does it do?" Leyna asked.

"It was like some magical medicinal root. It healed her up quick. I hope it works." The three of them, plus Harvard, stared down at Iyla, looking for any sign of change.

"Here," said Heddah. "Hold some roots under her nose."

The room was quiet, but they each heard the faint sound of an alarm in the distance through the open window. Leyna had pulled the lobby curtains shut. A crash came from the back office, and Heddah rolled her eyes, her face flushed.

"Should I–?" Aron started.

"No, just leave him be. He'll be fine." Heddah shook her head.

Iyla's nose wrinkled, and she swatted at the roots under her nose.

Aron, Leyna, and Heddah smiled with a sigh of relief. Iyla opened her eyes and was startled to see all the faces watching her.

"It's OK!" said Aron. "You're OK." He helped her to sit up, and Heddah went to the kitchen for another glass of water. Leyna and Harvard just stared at her.

"Hi, Iyla. I'm Leyna. And this is my nephew, Harvard. Heddah's son. We're so glad to meet you."

"We're at Faradell Narrow, where Heddah lives," said Aron.

"Well, I figured that!" said Iyla, wiping the sweat from her brow. "I'm fine, I'm fine. You can all back up now. Hi Leyna. Hi Harvard."

"OK, then," said Aron, as Heddah handed Iyla the water. "Here's the deal. The guards are searching for us, and I'm sure this place is not far down on their list, so we need to bug outta here. But we've got to get Heddah's tracker out first, so they don't follow us. Are you OK? Can you do this?"

"Yes, I know. Let's do it," said Iyla.

Leyna retrieved the instruments and bandages that Heddah had lifted from her work and the boiled water sitting on the stove. Iyla held her seven blooms close to her as they soaked up the water they craved. She took in the sweet aroma as she examined Heddah's tracker.

Aron stepped aside to pull back the curtain and peered out the window. "Guys, we've gotta go."

"Aron, I haven't even started. Give me five minutes," said Iyla.

"We don't have one minute. They're here. They're marching up the street right now."

Heddah and Leyna both turned to face each other.

"Take everyone down to the pit," Heddah said to Leyna. "I'll get Anthony. Iyla, can you walk?"

Leyna helped Iyla off the sofa and grabbed Harvard's hand. "Aron, grab the water and our bags by the back door. I've got the rest of this stuff." She led them out the back door and across the narrow yard to the large tool shed. Inside, on the shed floor, was an old, worn rug, which Leyna pulled aside. Camouflaged into the wooden floor was a three-foot square door that opened into the ground. Aron held the door up as Iyla and Leyna, holding Harvard, climbed down into the hole.

"Harvard," Leyna whispered. "Remember how we practiced being quiet down in the pit? We have to be very quiet now."

"Where's mommy and daddy?" His frightened voice tugged at Aron's heartstrings.

"Shh," whispered Leyna. "They're coming."

Aron could hear Heddah arguing with Anthony in the back office.

"Anthony! Get yourself together! We have to go down to the pit!"

"No!" he shouted. "I'm not going! I'm done with this." His words were garbled and slow.

"Just come with me, with Harvard," said Heddah. "The guards are almost at our door."

"No. I'm not hiding. I'm not… running. Just go. I'm not doing… that… again."

Aron cringed as the sound of shattering glass sliced through the air into his ears. There was more shuffling and muffled voices, and then Heddah was running toward him.

"Get in!" she whispered. She climbed down after Aron and pulled the rug over before shutting the door and bolting it from the inside.

A wooden ladder led to the cramped stone interior of the "pit." It was cool and damp, but the air was thick and smelled of earth. A small lantern sat in the corner and struggled to light the room. The five of them just barely fit in that five-foot by eight-foot space. Iyla and Leyna, with Harvard on her lap, were sitting on a small stone bench in front of Aron. He couldn't stand up straight with the ceiling only five and a half feet high.

Aron set the bags and the pot of water down and sat on his heels on the cold stone floor as Heddah continued to secure the entrance.

"Where's Anthony?" asked Leyna.

"He's not coming. He says he's done running from the government. Stupid liquor talking. He says he'll steer them away from the inn."

"But he's the one who built the pit! For this very reason!" Leyna exclaimed.

"He's drunk, Leyna! He's not thinking straight! He's certainly not in a good place. I couldn't get him to come down here. They're not after him, anyway." Heddah pulled Harvard into her.

"What about our plans to get out of Seridon? You can't stay now."

"I'm not staying. You're not staying. And neither is he. He'll sober up. He'll be fine." Heddah tried to rationalize. "For now, we need to just get this thing out of my wrist."

"Won't they be able to track your path down here?" Aron asked.

"The tracker isn't that precise. They never bothered to upgrade the technology, fortunately. You've got the water, Aron? Iyla, sweetie, how are you doing? You think you can get this out of me down here?"

"Yeah, sure. Did you bring a sharp knife? And I'll need something to tie you off." Heddah handed her the surgical supplies and six clean rags. Leyna distracted Harvard in the opposite corner while Aron watched Iyla skillfully draw the knife down into Heddah's wrist. Blood spilled freely, and Aron sopped up what he could with one of the rags. Heddah's frame stiffened, but she did not make a sound.

"I'm trying not to hit a major artery or slice a muscle or tendon," Iyla said, "but... it looks like they wrapped the implant around one."

"Probably an added safeguard to prevent its extraction," said Aron.

"Definitely. It's literally a ring welded closed around it. I'm not sure how to remove it without snipping the tendon to slide it off. Heddah, you OK? Do you remember when they implanted this?"

"I was unconscious. I didn't see anything. And I'm alright, but the quicker, the better. Clip the tendon if you have to." The light from the lantern accentuated Heddah's face, wincing in pain.

"You'll lose mobility in your hand, Heddah."

"Just do it, sweetie."

"Aron," said Iyla, unable to hide her concern, "break off a bit of root from one of my flowers. Heddah, you're going to need to bite down on this." Heddah opened her mouth for Iyla to insert a rag.

Thud. There was movement above them. Each one of them inside the pit froze in place. Intentional shuffling and another thud made Aron's skin prickle.

A faint, muffled voice said, "She ain't here, I tol' ya. Jus' me and my Blue." Both Leyna and Heddah rolled their eyes, shaking their heads. "We don't never see her, anyway. Always working at your damn facility. She was here for five minutes for lunch, yelled at me for spending time with my friend, Blue Blood, here, then, back to work! Did ya check there? What ya want her for, anyway?"

"Crakes," whispered Leyna.

"Is that daddy?" said Harvard.

Both Heddah and Leyna quickly shushed him. Iyla silently bowed her head as she continued to apply pressure to Heddah's wrist. After another minute of scuffling, it was quiet again. They each looked around the pit at each other.

Aron handed the root fragment to Iyla. She released the pressure, pulled back the rag, and inserted the root into her incision. "Bite down."

Heddah groaned into the rag as Iyla clipped the tendon, pulled the skin away from the tracker, and slid it off. Tears came to Heddah's eyes, and she swayed side to side before reaching for Aron to steady herself as the pain rolled through her. She repositioned herself on the floor, lying her head on the bag. Aron handed Iyla the pre-threaded needles, and Iyla skillfully sewed up the tendon, closed the incision, and bandaged her wrist tightly with a splint. "Try not to move your hand at all for a while."

"My moons, I can't believe it's out!" Her face was red and wet. "Thank you, Iyla."

Iyla smiled. "Make sure you keep it clean. I hope the root helps you heal faster, and it should keep the infection away."

"How do you know how to do this, Iyla?" asked Leyna.

Iyla shrugged. "Most Pelri know the basics of fixing our bodies."

Leyna laughed. "I'd hardly call that 'basic.' You're an angel!"

"Aron, can you hand me that stone?" Heddah pointed to the corner nearest him, where a pile of six or seven stones about the size of a grapefruit sat unobtrusively. Using the stone in her good hand, she pounded the tracking device until it was flat. It was done. Heddah slumped into the wall nearest her and wiped her sweaty brow.

The small room fell silent again as they listened for any movement above. It had been still for several minutes.

Aron spoke up. "I think they've left."

"Let's give it several more minutes," suggested Leyna.

"I don't think we should leave this pit until nightfall," said Aron. Iyla nodded.

"What about Anthony?" asked Leyna.

"Hopefully, he'll be sober by then." Heddah didn't even try to hide the snarky tone. "Let's try and get some sleep, then. We'll have more energy for the hike out to the cabin."

Chapter Nineteen

THE CABIN ON LUPELLERIN LAKE

S leeping on the damp, hard stone was difficult, but add to it the cramped quarters and a young child who didn't know what was going on, and it was near impossible. Aron was lying on the floor on the end next to the wall, using his bag as his pillow. Iyla was next to him, with Heddah to her left. She was restless and unable to settle into a comfortable position, while Harvard, who was between Heddah and Leyna, had finally fallen asleep.

"Are you doing OK?" Aron whispered.

"Yes, I'm fine," Iyla replied. "I'm glad you came, Aron. How did you get here?"

"William," Aron said with a smirk.

"Nice."

"I couldn't bring him, because well, you know. He's a big one. Jens gave me a talisman with Elven magic if we need help, but we can only use it once."

"OK. We have a long trek ahead of us, you know. And without the trees, I can't call William. But let's not use the talisman unless we have absolutely no other choice."

"Oh. Right." He had forgotten that they needed the trees to signal William. He could hear her fingers tapping on her leather belt.

"These are good people, Aron."

"I know."

Iyla paused before adding, "I know they're human–Seridon humans–but we can't let them get hurt. We're going to have to tell them."

"Yeah, I'm just a little worried about Anthony," said Aron. "I mean, I think his intentions are good, but he definitely has some demons he's dealing with. I don't think he's got himself together. Not sure if we can really put our trust in him."

"But Heddah, she'll keep him in line. I just don't want anything to happen to them."

"Yeah." Aron laid on his back, staring up into the darkness. Without the tiny lantern, it was pitch black inside the stone pit. The earthy odor was strong, and the damp air hovered around him. At times, it was almost suffocating. Or maybe it was just the heavy weight of what he needed to disclose to Iyla.

"Iyla, I have to tell you some things that I found out while I was searching for you."

"OK," she said, barely above a whisper.

Aron took a deep breath and softly cleared his throat. He turned on his side so that his body faced toward hers. "Tora is here, in Lupellerin."

"Tora? As in, your fiancée, Tora? How's that even possible? You told me she died in an accident."

"I know. That's what I was told. But that's not all." Aron hesitated briefly. "She's a Sapin."

"A Sapin?" Hearing a measured level of movement on the other side of her, Aron reminded her to keep her voice low.

"Yeah. I'm still having a hard time wrapping my head around it. But then, it does make sense. When we were together, back in the States—or, on Earth—she was deliberately keeping me from getting to—"

"Shh. Don't say it. Not yet," Iyla warned. Aron could hear her soft breathing as she tried to take it all in. "So, she found you? Did you talk to her?"

"Yes. She didn't know I was here, in your world, until the other day. She thought I was dead as well. And then she saw me here in Lupellerin. She's now in hiding because she mistakenly told the Commander of Seridon that I was gone and was no longer a threat to their country. Apparently, there was some sort of prophecy and a huge country-wide celebration. But she's still her same manipulative self. Now she says she wants to come with us—me—to the Tree because she has nothing left here in Seridon. It seems she is still trying to hold on to the relationship we once had. She said if she can't come with me, then she doesn't care if the Commander knows I'm alive. She's even threatened to tell him herself if I don't let her."

Iyla exhaled slowly. Against the other wall, Leyna shifted, and Harvard made a quick squeaking sound as he slept.

"And... how do you feel about this? Her."

Aron sighed. "I can't trust her. Not after all the lies she told and the manipulation. Whatever her intentions may have been, I can't be with someone who did what she did. It's clear that she was never the right person for me. I'm so angry."

"Where is she now?" Iyla asked.

"I don't know. But she knows exactly where we are, and she'll be following us. I told her to give me some time, and that she was not to touch any of you. Honestly, I think she's just miserable and lonely, but I don't trust her at all."

"She's a Sapin. If she gets near any of us, she could just whisk us off to the Commander's headquarters."

"I don't think she can. She said her magic is dying from misuse. I asked her to teleport me to Rakkarron Station when I thought you were there, and she said she couldn't do it, even after telling me she wanted to come with me. She barely has anything left."

"And you believe that? I mean, I've heard that Sapin magic can die, but why would you believe her?"

"She has no family or friends keeping her here. If I were in her position, I would have left Athemoni altogether. But she didn't. She's here. I don't think she's got enough magic to get herself out of here."

Heddah shifted her position, so that she was facing Iyla. "Crakes, these stones are hard! And my wrist is pounding," she whispered loudly. "I should have remembered to throw some mats down here. What are you two lovebirds chatting about?"

"Just catching up," said Iyla. "And I told you—"

"I know what you told me," Heddah interrupted.

"Yeah, I guess we need to get to sleep." Aron was grateful that no one could see his red face. He faked a yawn and resettled his head on his bag. Iyla turned onto her back, and a lock of her long brown hair fell just in front of his nose. He had missed that sweet, peaceful aroma.

A few hours passed, and once Harvard was awake, it was apparent that no one else was going to get any more sleep. Leyna lit the lantern and, one by one, they each stood up inside the stone pit and stretched their aching muscles. Harvard complained he was hungry, and Iyla yawned as she rubbed her neck and shoulders. Heddah climbed up to the door of the pit to unlatch the bolts, then remembered her left hand was out of commission, so Leyna took over.

Cautiously, they exited the pit and the shed and stepped into the early night air. A soft drizzle dampened their faces as they crossed the yard to the double door in the back of the Inn. Aside from the noise of a few vehicles, they only heard the faint sound of music and laughter coming from a tavern down the street.

"Heddah, you all stay here while Harvard and I go inside to get Anthony and a bag of snacks. Then we'll be on our way," said Leyna.

"Wait," whispered Aron, pointing toward the street in front of the inn. Light from the street lantern filtered through the trees where a lone guard paced sleepily.

"Leyna, Harvard. Shh!" Heddah motioned for them to get down.

Everyone froze.

"Leyna, go quickly and quietly. We'll wait for you up at the end of the road."

Leyna nodded and slipped inside through the back door. Heddah reached for Harvard's hand and nodded to Aron and Iyla.

Successfully reaching the end of the road undetected, they stopped to wait behind an abandoned vehicle. Heddah winced when Harvard accidentally pulled on her left hand.

"Does it hurt?" asked Iyla. Without waiting for an answer, she broke off a small piece of root from the flowers that were tucked back into her side belt. She had wrapped them in a wet rag and tied them together with a string that she had found on the floor of the shed. "Here, suck on this for a little while."

Heddah chuckled softly. "You really are the botanical queen."

"And don't forget—skilled surgeon!" Aron injected.

They both smiled as Iyla rolled her eyes.

After a few moments, they saw movement just behind them. It was Leyna, waving a small square of blue paper. "He's gone. They took Anthony to jail."

"Blessed moons!" Heddah sighed, and through the shadows, Aron saw her toss her bag to the ground.

"Why would they arrest him?" asked Aron.

"Probably for all that drinking. Who knows? Maybe they just didn't like the way he looked at them, or they didn't want to go back empty-handed. They don't need a reason."

Leyna handed a bag of snack food to Aron. "You all go on ahead. I'll go bail out Anthony, and we'll catch up."

"Sweetie, I'm not going to leave you behind," said Heddah.

"The three of you need to get out of here. I'm the only one who can go bail him out without getting arrested myself. Just go. We won't be far behind."

"But daddy!" Harvard wailed. "I want daddy to come!"

Heddah knelt in front of him. "Sweetie, he'll be coming with us. Aunt Leyna is going to get him right now. We'll see him at the cabin."

Aron glanced at Iyla and Heddah and then slung his bag onto his back. Iyla held out her hand to the pouting Harvard, and his face lit up as she took his hand in hers. "Let's go, Heddah," she said as she grabbed another bag.

Heddah gave Leyna a tight hug before starting on their way. "We're headed north. The cabin is on the lake. Bander should already be there. It'll take us—"

"Bander?" Aron turned to Heddah behind him. "This is Bander's cabin?"

"Oh, that's right. I heard you had met him. He's been a family friend for a long time. He told Anthony you had purchased a gun at his store."

"Yes," said Aron.

"Well, you don't need to worry about him. He's one of us," assured Heddah.

The gentle drizzle had upgraded to a light rain as they hiked along the dirt—now mud—road and then through the same withered and sickly farming fields that Aron had seen through his window at Faradell Narrow. The pipe sprinkler irrigation systems continued to spray water on the crops even as the rain fell. Heddah fashioned a sling to carry

Harvard on her back through the mud as their wet clothes got heavier.

They trudged on, mostly in silence, with Heddah leading the way. Aron and Iyla followed a few yards behind. Lupellerin, the city, was adjacent to Lupellerin Lake. However, Bander's cabin was on the west side of the lake, so this leg of the journey would take several hours by foot.

Eventually, the rain stopped, and a few dark clouds parted to reveal a beautiful, starry sky. The moons were bright and low on the horizon. All three were much closer to each other this night.

"Those moons are just wild," Aron remarked under his breath.

"What, you don't have moons where you're from?" Iyla chuckled.

"Shh." Aron motioned toward Heddah. "Not three. We only have one."

"Well, it should only be two moons, really. That smaller one is actually a piece of that other one next to it."

"What? Seriously? How did that happen?"

"Look, you can tell it's not round. Jens' history books will tell you that there was a collision with an asteroid or some celestial object many years ago that broke it apart. He was four years old when it happened."

Aron readily worked out the calculation in his head. "So that would make him about eleven or twelve in Earth years. Old enough to realize what was going on. That's crazy."

Iyla nodded. "The largest moon is named Neoma. That one there, the one that broke, is named Secoriea. Jens said that the piece that broke off didn't get a name until several years after the event. His name is Rikkipal."

"Interesting. Ours is just called 'the moon,'" Aron said with a smile.

"The Neclu Pelri believe that Diana, goddess of the moons, sent the asteroid to destroy Seridon and all of its human corruption. She had a temper. With her strength and fury, all of Athemoni could have been destroyed. But Secoriea took the hit, throwing the asteroid off-course and protecting our world from total annihilation."

"Diana..." Aron murmured. "I want to say that Roman mythology has a moon goddess named Diana. Not sure, though. I wasn't really into that stuff."

"Well, I don't know what Roman mythology is, but that's what we believe."

Aron smiled at Iyla. She was beautiful even with her dark, wet hair plastered to her head and the streaks of dirt on her face from the floor of the pit. There was certainly no denying that some divine power, whether it was the Elfblood Tree, or something else, had brought their worlds together.

"Hey. Are you doing OK?" Aron asked. "At the facility, did they hurt you?"

Iyla shrugged. "I don't...I can't—"

"You don't have to talk about it. I know you woke up a few times last night. You were gripping my arm. Just want you to know that I'm here for you, OK? We'll talk when you're ready."

Iyla nodded as a tear glistened in the moonlight.

"Better not see any smooching back there!" Heddah called behind her. "Got some young eyes here with me."

"Heddah!" Iyla exclaimed. "We're not doing that!"

Aron laughed and was glad to see a smile on Iyla's face.

"Oh, never mind! He's asleep," Heddah said after craning her neck to check on Harvard. "Carry on!"

Mortified, Iyla glanced at Aron, then quickened her pace to catch up to Heddah. Aron could hear Iyla's persistent denials as Heddah continued to tease.

They had reached the lake, and the cabin was only another hour and a half or so westward. Their feet ached, and they paused briefly to switch sleeping Harvard over to Aron's back. Iyla checked on Heddah's sutures and re-wrapped the bandage tightly around the splint.

"What do you think the Commander is going to do?" Iyla asked Heddah.

"Well," she answered, "he's going to be pissed. A lot of people at the facility will lose their job. He's going to send out a search party to look for you, and of course, they will look for me as well as I'm sure they've put two and two together. I'm hoping you and Aron will do what you need to do and then get out of Seridon yourselves."

"Where will you go?"

"Well, we've always talked about Tariadyn. We'll rest up at Bander's cabin and then set out again. Seridon's largest port is west of here, so we'll see if we can get on a ship without attracting too much attention."

As they all stood to resume their hike, Aron said, "Heddah, I want you to know how much we appreciate what you and your family have done for us. We couldn't have gotten this far without you."

"Think nothing of it," said Heddah. "You know how we feel about the Pelri. And a friend of the Pelri is a friend of ours. I wish there was more that we could do for all of your kind, Iyla."

Iyla reached out to Heddah and embraced her.

A light fog blanketed the lake and slinked inland amongst the modest cabins and beach-style dwellings along the lakeshore. Eventually, the number of homes dwindled, some separated by at least a mile. The moons and stars illuminated the path to the last lone cabin that rested at the edge of the western end of Lupellerin Lake.

The cabin was old but well-kept and sat out on the end of a tiny peninsula. Smoke curled out of the chimney, and a light was on in one window. A long dock extending into the waters behind the cabin was home to two boats: a simple 12-foot fishing boat, and the other, a majestic sailboat, triple in size.

Answering Heddah's knock, Bander opened the door, and his smile greeted them warmly.

"Bander," said Aron.

"Heddah filled me in," said Bander with a swift pat on Aron's shoulder. "Glad you arrived safely."

Aron turned and placed his arm behind Iyla. "I'd like you to meet my friend, Iyla."

"Iyla. Absolute pleasure." Bander tentatively opened up his arms and then embraced Iyla, and she smiled appreciatively.

With a pot of tea on the stove, the soggy travelers finally sat comfortably on a sofa in front of the dwindling flames. Heddah tucked Harvard in on a small cot in the next room and then sat down next to Iyla.

"I was expecting all of you earlier. I'm glad you made it. What about Anthony and Leyna?"

"They're not far behind. We had an incident earlier today." Heddah apprised him of the day's events as Bander stood by the fire and shook his head. His thick red beard twitched now and then as her account unfolded. He was a husky man, and his short sleeves revealed his bulky muscles decorated with various multi-colored images.

"Well," he said, "I know you must be hungry. I've got plenty of sandwiches, and the tea is hot." He passed around a tray of sandwiches and several unusual vegetables. Heddah poured the tea.

"You all will have to double up on the rooms, but there are plenty of beds and cots," Bander directed. "Iyla, when Leyna gets here, why don't the two of you take the room next to Harvard. Aron, you can bunk in my room."

"Bander," said Aron, "if you don't mind, Iyla and I need to be together. We've got some things we need to catch up on before we head out."

"Sure. Up to you. Doesn't matter to me." Bander took a large bite out of his sandwich. "So, what exactly is this thing you need to do? Heddah said you had some sort of job to finish? And why would this little one risk so much here in Seridon?" he asked, referring to Iyla.

Aron raised his head to the ceiling and sighed. He glanced over at Heddah, who was watching him thoughtfully and then at Iyla sitting next to her. She nodded ever so slightly. He sighed again.

"OK," he began. "Iyla and I were talking earlier and decided that for your own sakes, we needed to fill you in. We both told you that you should all leave Seridon as soon as possible. I really don't know what is going to happen, but we need to tell you why. You may want to sit down, Bander."

The creases in Bander's brow deepened as he pulled a stool closer to the fireplace and sat. Heddah's usual warmth had transitioned to concern and curiosity as she sat on the edge of the sofa and finished her tea. Iyla was visibly exhausted, but she repositioned herself to face Heddah and Bander.

"I'm not really sure where to begin... or how you're going to even take this... or if we should even be telling you this at all," Aron said.

But a knock at the door startled all four of them.

"Oh good, they're here!" Heddah sang out as she jumped up to answer the door. But it wasn't Anthony and Leyna standing on the other side of it. It was a pale-haired, fully cloaked, wet Sapin. It was Tora.

Chapter Twenty

Unveilment

Frozen in place, Heddah shut the door. Tora continued to knock from the outside as Heddah slowly turned toward the group.

"Bander? Why would a Sapin be so far away from the city and knocking on your cabin door? Do you think she's working for the facility? Or for the Commander?"

"Tora," Aron growled. Hurrying to Heddah's side, he opened the door again. "What are you doing?" he demanded.

Bander remained silent on his stool, partially hidden by the armoire to his left. Fire crackled in the fireplace as Iyla slunk down into the sofa.

Heddah's wary expression turned to surprise as Aron moved past her. "I'll be right back. Just give me a minute." He stole a glance at Iyla before gripping Tora's arm and ushering her a few steps backward. *Shit, what are they thinking now?*

Heddah left the door cracked behind them, and Aron glanced through the window to gauge any reaction. Nervously biting the inside of her lip, Heddah sighed and took her seat back on the sofa. Faint lines drew across her brow. She reached for her tea as Bander shot her a disapproving glare, and then she turned to Iyla. "Don't worry, sweetie. They all have a past." Iyla sat up uncomfortably.

"Aron!" Tora stomped her foot.

"Shh! Just wait!" Aron stood back from the window, out of view from those inside.

"What are you talking about?" Bander almost shouted at Heddah. "What is he doing associating with a Sapin? And yes, she could be working for the Commander!"

Dammit!

"It's his ex-fiancée," Iyla injected. "He didn't know she was a Sapin until recently."

Heddah raised an eyebrow.

"Didn't know?" Bander exclaimed. "How do you not know?"

Iyla sighed, and the group waited in silence.

Aron turned to Tora. "What are you doing?" he seethed.

"I gave you time, Aron. You've had hours and hours to loop me in. I had to take matters into my own hands."

"You will not take matters into your own hands. I don't even want you here. You are lucky I'm letting you travel with us at all! These are my friends, and we do this my way. Do you understand?"

Tora frowned, but she shook it off, and forced a pleasant smile. "Fine."

Aron opened the door again and strode in with Tora following on his heels.

"I don't want a Sapin in my cabin, Aron," Bander warned.

"Let me explain," said Aron. "It's not what you think."

"Aron..." Iyla murmured, shaking her head.

"Just hang on. Tora," he put his hand on her shoulder and guided her back to the doorframe of the kitchen. "Stand here. Do not move."

Facing the others, Aron cleared his throat and began again. "I was about to fill you in on some details that I—Iyla and I—feel you should know. First, we can't even begin to tell you how much we appreciate your help these last few days. We want you to know the entire truth, to understand what we're doing, and you deserve the opportunity to do what you need to with that information. We hope you'll be able to support us, but we understand if that will be difficult for you. Either way, I'm asking that you allow us to continue to move forward.

"So, here goes." He paused and took a deep breath. "Iyla found me in Parise when she was looking for her friend, Seriah, who is still missing. However, I am not from there. I'm not from Parise. In fact, I'm not from Athemoni. My full name is Aron Coverstone." Aron paused, waiting for a reaction from Bander and Heddah, but they listened patiently. "I'm from Earth." Still, no response. He continued. "I lived there with Tora. She and I have known each other for several years, and we were engaged. What I didn't know was that she was not from Earth, that she wasn't like every other human I knew. She lied to me, because she was trying to keep me from coming here, to Athemoni. To Seridon."

"That's not exactly, I—" Tora started, before Aron turned and raised his palm to silence her.

"Whatever story she may tell you," said Aron, "her primary goal was to keep me from this world. From your world. I didn't even know your world existed."

Aron reached for his bag that was next to Iyla. He unzipped it and pulled out the Heart. "Leyna asked me what this was the other day when Harvard found it in my bag. This is why I am here. This is the Heart of the Elfblood Tree."

Heddah's mouth parted. Bander's head tilted to the side slightly as he squinted his eyes. Iyla and Aron watched as understanding washed across their faces.

Heddah spoke first. "You—if you're—aren't you supposed to be dead?"

Aron motioned to Tora. "*She* thought I was dead, and that's what she told the Commander. And now she claims she could be in danger if the Commander knows I'm not dead, that I'm here and alive. She wants to come with me to the

Tree. I don't want her to come, but she's threatened to report me if I refuse."

Heddah's glare could cut glass.

"What's going to happen when you bring back the Heart?" asked Bander.

Iyla rose from the sofa and stood next to Aron. "We don't know what will happen. Maybe nothing at all. As far as we know, the Elfblood Tree could be forever gone. But we don't know. That's why we asked that you leave Seridon to ensure your safety, in case something does happen."

"Is she the Sapin that was following you? How can you trust her?" Bander asked Aron, motioning to Tora.

"Yes, and I don't. Not at all. But she's put me in a difficult situation for the moment. Her magic is almost gone, but I've told her she is not to go near any of you. She won't be staying here, Bander."

The room fell silent for several seconds as the two grappled with this new knowledge.

Aron continued. "The Pelri are entitled to their homeland that humans and Sapins ruthlessly stole from them so many years ago, and I'm certain that this Heart, or the Tree, brought me here to help them get it back."

Heddah glanced at Aron and then at Iyla. A tear came to her eye as she stood up and embraced her Pelri friend. "So do I," she said. "And I'm coming with you."

"What?" Iyla and Aron said in unison. Tora's eye roll didn't go unnoticed as she stood behind them in the door frame.

"Well, this is certainly a bigger deal than what I expected, but you're going to need someone you can trust to help you navigate," said Heddah, throwing an icy glance in Tora's direction.

Until this point, Bander had remained seated on his stool between the fireplace and the armoire. But a subtle smile slowly inched across his bearded face. Heddah turned to him, eyebrow raised.

"Crakes, yeah!" Bander exclaimed suddenly. "I'm up for an adventure! You're going to need a boat ride across the lake and up the Galvenais River, right?"

Iyla quickly wiped at a tear. "Thank you. Thank you, both."

Bander chuckled and delivered a bear hug to both Iyla and Aron.

"What if this ends up being a major historical event that brings humans and Pelri together? Wouldn't that be wonderful?" Heddah professed.

"Don't hold your breath," came Tora's voice from the kitchen, abruptly deflating the spirited tone of the room.

"But we still have the problem of the Sapin," Bander reinforced. "She needs to be secured. You can't trust a Sapin. I don't care if she says she's low on magic."

"Yes," said Aron. "I'm working on that."

"So, what are you going to do? Can't exactly tie her down."

"Oh, blessed moons! Come on in here, Tora!" called Heddah.

Startled and marginally confused, Tora glanced at each one in the room and slowly approached the four friends.

"What is your agenda, Tora?" Heddah asked pointedly.

"What do you mean?" Tora responded in a small voice.

"Are you going to whisk one or all of us away when you get the chance? Why do you want to go to the Tree? And why are you blackmailing Aron to allow you to accompany him? Are you going to try to steal the Heart? Give us an explanation. Why are you here?"

"OK. Uh, no, I don't have enough magic left to whisk anyone anywhere. I haven't used my magic responsibly," she explained as her eyes shifted about the room. "And as I've told Aron, I just want to help. I did deceive him, and I want to make it up to him. I want him to believe that I'm not a bad person."

Aron sighed and shook his head.

"Alright then," said Heddah. "Prove it to us. But just know you're not getting a free pass. You need to know that we won't blindly trust you, and you'll need to keep your distance, and we'll have to take precautionary measures. Understood?"

"Yes," said Tora. "I understand. I can earn your trust. I will."

Iyla eyed Tora warily. She stepped back from the group and stood on the other side of Heddah.

Still frowning, Bander said, "There's a small tackle shed about fifty yards from the cabin, closer to the dock. You can sleep there for the night."

"Thank you. That will be just fine." Tora glanced at Aron before heading to the door of the cabin.

"OK! So that's that. We'll need to get up by sunrise. How about we all get some sleep?" Heddah said.

"What about Leyna and Anthony?" asked Aron.

"Yeah, I really hope they show up soon. If worse comes to worst, they can just sleep in the boat, and we'll fill them in later. Tora, did you happen to see my husband and his sister anywhere out there?"

"No, I'm sorry. I haven't seen them."

"Alright. Everyone to bed then. Big day tomorrow."

The scant moonlit hours quickly passed. Both Iyla and Aron awoke to the sound of whispered conversation coming from the kitchen. Listening intently, they still couldn't decipher the words.

"Anthony and Leyna," said Aron. Iyla nodded.

After tucking her flowers into her belt, Iyla and Aron emerged from their room to greet them. Heddah stood at the sink, rinsing and wringing a washcloth a little more forcefully than necessary, and Anthony and Leyna were seated at the table. They looked up when the floor creaked as they entered.

Leyna looked exhausted, but Anthony's swollen black eye and bruised neck were most concerning. Dried blood caked on his bottom lip and behind his ear. His shirt was torn, and there were bloodstains on his shoulder.

Iyla drew in her breath. "What happened?"

"They just arrived about half an hour ago," said Heddah. "I've told them… what you told us. Although I'm really second-guessing that decision with mister drunk blabber over here." Her face was red as she threw the wet washcloth onto the table in front of Anthony.

"Are you OK?" Iyla asked, breaking off a flower root and handing it to Heddah. Heddah promptly put on a pot of water to make a tea.

"Courtesy of the Commander himself," said Anthony, gesturing to his wounds. "I'm so sorry."

"He told them about you, Iyla," Leyna cut in. "He'd had too much to drink, as you know, and… well, after they arrested him, the Commander showed up at the Peace Enforcement building, demanding to know where you were. Anthony's been having some… problems."

"I'm so sorry, really." Anthony struggled to make eye contact. "I'm just—I'm sorry."

"When I got there to bail him out," Leyna continued, "I told them we would lead them to you. We escaped when we stopped to camp for the night. We had them heading further south toward Port Maneruck, but we all have to go. We have to leave. Now."

Iyla and Aron exchanged a worried glance.

"What about Aron?" Iyla asked.

"I don't think they know about him. It didn't seem like it, anyway. And, obviously, *we* are only just finding out now, so," replied Leyna.

Aron searched Leyna's face for any sign of judgment or anger.

"We're coming with you, too," Leyna reassured them. "We've suffered long enough under this Commander's thumb. This country belongs to the Pelri."

"Now, hold on there—" Anthony interrupted. "I'm all about the Pelri and all, and again, I'm so sorry, but Heddah and I, we have a small son. I don't want Harvard in any danger."

"I understand that completely," replied Aron. "I would never ask you to put your son in harm's way. And I can't tell you what these next few weeks will bring."

Heddah moved closer to Anthony and rested her hand on his shoulder. "Anthony, I'm going. Harvard loves his new friend, Aron, and we'll be passing right by my brother's home on the other side of the lake. I'm sure Darrett and Brynn will be happy to take him and keep him safe until our return. And if you want to stay behind with them, you be my guest. I need to do this."

Anthony stood up from the table. He reached back and grasped the back of his neck with a frustrated sigh as he left the room.

Heddah looked over at Aron and Iyla apologetically. "He really does feel bad about all this. Doesn't make me less angry."

The front door opened, and Bander strode in with a layer of sweat on his brow. "The boat's ready to go," he announced. "Aron, I found these clamps. If she gets out of them, well, obviously we shouldn't have trusted her, and she has more magic than she's letting on."

"I'll go wake Harvard," said Heddah as Aron reached to take the clamps from Bander.

Chapter Twenty-One

The Farmhouse on the Hill

Aron sat portside on the deck, while Tora sat quietly at the stern of the boat, her cloak wrapped tightly around her, covering the clamps that secured her at her wrists. As Bander manned the sails in the moderate winds, she didn't seem fazed by the cautious glares he threw her way. The soft cadence of conversation surfaced from the cabin below. They had been sailing on the Lupellerin Lake for almost three hours.

Leyna and Anthony slept, Heddah was cleaning the galley, and Aron could just barely see the top of Iyla's head as she gazed out the cabin windows, unresponsive to Harvard's chatter. Only Aron noticed when Harvard climbed the ladder to the deck, and sidled up next to Tora. Aron promptly placed his hand on his shoulder and channeled him back a few feet.

Harvard glanced up at Aron as Tora rolled her eyes.

"But I want to say hi to her," he said.

"Hello there." Tora smiled at Harvard.

"I'm Harvard. What's your name?"

"My name is Tora."

Harvard smiled back. "How come I haven't seen you before?"

"Well, I arrived at Bander's cabin last night after you were asleep."

"Are you friends with Bander?"

"Come now, Harvard," Aron interjected.

"I just met him," Tora answered. "But I've known Aron for a few years." Harvard's eyes lit up.

"Harvard!" yelled Bander as he rushed toward him and grabbed him behind the neck. "Get down in the cabin with your mother!"

"He's fine," said Aron. "I was watching."

Heddah's frightened face popped up over the top of the metal ladder. "Harvard! Come here!"

"What did I do?" His voice trailed as he descended the ladder.

Tora sighed and dejectedly leaned over the boat's edge to stare at the wake. When she looked up, Aron was standing above her. "I didn't—"

"I know. But everyone really needs you to keep your distance."

"We're on a boat, Aron. And he came to me."

"Maybe another half hour or so, and we'll be at Heddah's brother's house. Just sit tight."

"Where am I going to go?" Tora shrugged him off as he turned to head toward the hatch. "I've never felt so callously isolated in such close quarters," she mumbled.

"Everything OK?" asked Iyla as she reached the top of the ladder.

"It's fine; everyone's fine." Aron rubbed his forehead.

Leyna and Anthony had woken up, and they too climbed the ladder up to the deck to sit on the small cushioned bench on the port side. Anthony's swelling had gone down substantially, and even the bruising had subsided.

"Bottle of Blue would be great about now..." he remarked with a smirk. Tora rolled her eyes again.

"Don't even think about it," Heddah replied with a sharp glare. "It's not funny, and that stupid bottle almost got us all in the Commander's prison, if not killed on the spot. Not funny at all."

"Really, Anthony? Just stop." Leyna got up and moved to the starboard side. Her red hair was tousled in the back, and she still had creases on her face from sleeping on the narrow bunk.

Iyla peeled off a petal from one of her flowers and handed it to Anthony. "Let this sit under your tongue for a while. Might help."

"And here. Eat the sandwiches," Heddah brought up a tray piled high with a tasty lunch. "I've got a few catilla eggs cooking in the oven. They'll be ready in a minute." She made her way back down into the cabin.

"I'll help you, Heddah," Iyla volunteered.

"Ugh, eggs," he complained.

"Anthony!" came a call from the bow.

Aron followed Anthony to see what Bander needed. Tora scooted closer to the end of the bench.

Bander was looking out across the cerulean water. "Something doesn't seem right."

In the distance was the shoreline of the northeastern rim of the lake. Beyond that was what appeared to be a farm of some sort, but it was too far to see it clearly. Anthony shielded the sun from his eyes as he looked out in the direction where Bander was pointing.

"Oh, we're almost there," he stated.

"No, look closely," Bander instructed. "It doesn't look right. I mean, normally we'd see some animals at this point, but there's nothing. Almost seems deserted."

"Yeah, but—" Anthony paused. "His house used to be yellow. Same with the barn and boathouse. Where is the boathouse?"

"How long's it been since you been out here?"

"Half a year? Maybe more than that," replied Anthony. "You're right, though. Something's not right."

All three men stood quietly for a few minutes, watching as they gradually neared Darrett and Brynn's farm. The sound of flapping prompted Bander to grasp the rigging and redirect the sails.

"Bander," said Anthony, "it's been torched."

"What?" yelled Bander.

"The house, the barn. They're burned. The boathouse is completely gone."

Bander returned to the bow to stand beside Anthony. He, too, shielded his eyes from the glare as the boat glided closer to the shore.

"Crakes…" he whispered.

"They were here."

The charming, old yellow house that once stood firmly on the small hill above the lake was now black with soot, a gaping hole in the lower part of the roof, and glass from the broken windows was strewn across the scorched acreage. Dark grey smoke disseminated into the breeze that moved above the lingering embers. Further back behind the house was the remains of the large barn.

"Aron," said Tora. "Is everything OK?"

"Anthony?" Heddah, who had just emerged from the cabin below, reached for Anthony's arm and stared blankly at the disturbing scene they were approaching. A tear trickled down the right side of her cheek as Anthony embraced her tightly.

"We're going to go check it out. You stay here with Harvard and the Pelri. Stay down inside the cabin."

"They're looking for me, Anthony! This is because of me."

"We don't know what happened yet. Just stay down in the cabin, and we'll be right back."

Bander anchored the boat near the remains of the sunken dock. Tora followed Aron up the hill to the farm, while Leyna remained behind in the cabin with Heddah, Harvard, and Iyla.

The smell of burnt wood and blood filled the air, and Tora gasped when she caught up to Aron, her wrists still bound in front of her. The bodies of two cats, a dog, and four catillas lay lifeless just beyond the narrow sandy beach, affording the scavenging critters a considerable feast. They paused at the scene before making their way to the broken-down doorway of the farmhouse.

"Tell me you had nothing to do with this," demanded Aron under his breath.

Chapter Twenty-Two

DARRETT AND BRYNN

Tora's hurt look seemed genuine, but any remnant of trust Aron had for her was long gone. "Tell me you didn't speak to anyone about Heddah, Iyla, or me!"

"I—" she hesitated. "No!"

"You're lying!" Aron hissed.

"I didn't even know who Heddah and Iyla were! I didn't!"

"And me? Did you talk to anyone about me?"

"I—not exactly—I never mentioned your name."

"TORA! To who? What exactly did you say?" Aron gripped her shoulder and pressed her against the tall picket fence.

"It was an old acquaintance I bumped into right after I saw you in Seridon the first time. I was such a mess of emotions and crying in an alley. I just said that I was told my fiancé had died, and then I just saw you and thought you had faked your death."

Aron rolled his eyes at the ignorance and irony of Tora's lie. "Does he know who I am?"

"You mean that you're the one that Yeril forewarned us about? I don't think so."

"You don't think so? What do you mean? Does he know or not?"

"Well, I didn't *tell* him you were!"

"Tora, don't you think he might put two and two together? You've been gone for years, on a mission for the Commander.

Seridon hears that I'm dead, and then you return, giving him that story. Damn it, Tora! What the hell were you thinking?"

"I was upset, Aron! And I barely knew him. He couldn't know."

"You've probably got every one of us killed. Stay back," Aron ordered as he strode through the gate toward the front door. Tora obediently remained a fair distance behind the rest of the travelers.

There wasn't much left of the farmhouse, and the stairs were too dangerous to climb. Black soot covered the few walls that remained, and the floorboards smoldered beneath their feet. The charred smell reminded Aron of his first meeting with William, and his stomach was just as unsettled as it was then. There was nothing salvageable inside and no sign of Darrett or Brynn.

"Do you think they may have hidden near the barn?" Bander asked. "Or maybe they weren't here when they showed up."

"The barn is burned too," replied Anthony, his brow furrowed. "They probably took them prisoner." His soot-blackened hand pressed against his forehead and through his sweaty hair.

"Yeah, but you remember the boulders and cliff bank out behind there? It's worth a look. We've gotta find them. This is gonna kill Heddah."

The barn was on the west side of the hill, not far from the farmhouse, and the stench of death grew stronger as they passed several slaughtered cows, pigs, and goats, all covered in blood with wooden stakes driven through their bodies.

"Who would do this?" Aron said as he stepped over the carcasses, flies swarming above them.

"Has to be the Commander," said Bander. "Whoever it was, they were certainly trying to make a point. This is disgusting. Just evil."

Anthony halted just before entering the barn. He extended his arms, preventing the others from passing. His gaze went beyond the barn, to the north side. "Crakes…"

Aron turned to Tora and motioned to her to remain where she was, about fifty feet behind. A large wooden structure loomed from the hill behind the barn. From their position, they could only see the top of it, which was in the shape of the letter T. The men rounded the far corner of the barn, where they could see the structure in its entirety. From either side hung a large flag, the same flag that flew from the facility where Heddah worked, where Iyla had been held captive. Its red, silver, and gold colors flapped wildly in the breeze. But what hung from the rope below each flag made each of them take in their breath. Anthony's knees buckled, and he fell to the ground alongside the nearby boulders. Bander immediately bowed his head, covering his face with one hand as he stumbled into the doorframe of the barn. Avoiding the scene, he then turned back toward his boat that was docked a fair distance behind them.

Strapped and suspended below each flag, was Darrett and Brynn. With their arms tied at the wrist, they had been stripped of their garments, and their lifeless bodies dangled above pools of their own blood. They were barely recognizable as blood continued to seep from large gashes in their thighs, throat, and mouth. Brynn's long blonde braided hair was soaked to a deep burgundy, and her head was thrown back, exposing her gouged neck.

"We need to get them down," said Aron as he felt a sickening turn in his stomach. "My God…"

Anthony bent over the side of the nearest boulder to vomit. Regrouping, he nodded and pulled a knife from his belt. After testing for stability, he climbed to the highest point of the remains of the barn, where he leaned over to cut the ropes. Aron caught the mutilated, bloody bodies as Bander retrieved a shovel from the garden shed and began digging two deep holes. Aron saw two tears slip from the corners of Bander's eyes which he quickly wiped away.

The three men stood mutely beside the new gravesites. Tora, who had witnessed the burials from a short distance, sat on the seat of the couple's disposed farm equipment, trying to swallow the lump in her throat. Aron bent toward the ground, his hands to his knees, in an effort to mitigate the nausea. Anthony cleared his throat several times.

"They were good people," Bander said finally, his voice cracking. "Good people. No one deserves this. Especially them."

"Were they looking for Heddah and Iyla?" Aron asked. "Is that why they did this?"

"No doubt," Anthony answered, clearing his throat once again. Aron could see the wetness in his eyes as well. "But then, Brynn was half-elf. You may not know this, but for common Seridon citizens, interracial bindings are not permitted. She, herself, was born of an interracial union and then, her being with Darrett... it's why they lived far from the city. But they came here looking for Heddah and Iyla, no question. No other reason for them to come this far out. Crakes, I thought we steered them south!" Anthony pounded the side of the boulder. "The Commander is not going to let up. I know he wants Iyla. And this here, this was him making a statement."

Aron and the rest of the somber group sat quietly in the cabin of the boat as Harvard napped. Heddah remained in the back, staring blankly out the small window. Her brother and beautiful sister-in-law had paid for her offenses.

"Don't go there, Heddah." Leyna brought her some tea and a bowl of radish chips. "There was no way to know his vengeance would overcome us so quickly."

"But how? You and Anthony had led them south. How could they have gotten so far ahead of us? My brother is gone! Dead! And sweet Brynn. Oh, poor sweet Brynn! I did this! I did this to them!"

"You can't put this on yourself, Heddah. Darrett and Brynn had their own violations as well. No one deserves what they went through, but they knew the risk. And this had to have been a separate search party."

"Leyna, the Commander never would have gone looking if it weren't for me. My brother and Brynn were wonderful people. Never hurt a soul. This is my fault." Heddah's voice broke as another tear streamed down and fell onto her lap.

"They were," reassured Leyna. "I know they were. They will be missed, surely."

"Heddah," said Aron, "I'm so sorry for your loss. I...I don't even know what to say, other than I know what it's like. To lose those you love. This is truly horrific."

Iyla appeared from behind Leyna and sat down next to Heddah. She placed her hand over the top of Heddah's. "I'm so sorry. I will understand if you all don't want to pursue this further. Aron and I, we need to keep going, but if this is too much—"

"Definitely not!" Heddah retorted, wiping her face and shaking out her hands. "My family will not have died in vain. We *will* get you to Urippa Spring. You and Aron. We're gonna make this world right. I just need... I just need to be by myself for a little bit."

Chapter Twenty-Three

THE CONFESSION

D eath was sobering.

The melancholy group had reached the mouth of the Galvenais River, and the boat could not sail further. Bander, Anthony, and Aron anchored and secured the boat while Leyna, Heddah, and Iyla gathered their belongings and other necessities. Tora remained on deck as far from the rest of them as Aron saw fit.

Something had shifted within Anthony, and Aron detected a newfound strength emanating from his core. Anthony was a decent man, or at least he used to be. There was a renewed focus in his eyes, and where many would have been at their absolute breaking point, Anthony seemed to have found his fortitude.

The small band of humans, Pelri, and Sapin would trek on foot, following the river northward and over the mountains. They quietly disembarked and set their sights toward the brown fields ahead and the mountains in the distance, as most of them battled in vain to escape the horrific memory of Darrett and Brynn's ruthless murders.

"You know, if we follow this river to its source, we're bound to find Mad Menrich," Tora called from a few yards behind.

Iyla was the only one who turned to acknowledge her, albeit with a suspicious glare.

"Who's Mad Menrich?" Aron asked quietly as he kept pace with Iyla and Heddah.

"I don't know," said Iyla.

"He's a former captain under the Commander," Heddah answered. "They say he made a dirty deal with a demon many years ago and is now cursed."

"Demon? You're kidding, right?" asked Aron.

"No. He lives in a cave up in those mountains," said Heddah. "He was cursed by the demon, and once every two weeks or so, he'll throw himself off the mountain. He'll lie crippled at the foot of it where a mammoth serpent will swallow him whole and then promptly burst into flames. The following rainfall washes his ashes into the river, where he is made whole again. He heals up through the next several days, and then it happens all over again. It's driven him mad, and travelers, if they don't come across him, will report hearing his shrieks from miles away."

"How does one not die after all that?" Aron was suspicious at the mention of a demon, although under the circumstances, he wasn't sure why.

"It's the curse. And if anyone else kills him, his curse will be theirs. So they say."

"So, is this true, or just a myth?"

"It's true," Tora called from behind. "We'll hear him."

"Are there many demons on Athemoni?" asked Aron.

"We've never seen any," said Heddah. "Have you, Iyla?"

"No," she answered. "A few mad trolls, maybe. But no demons."

The group trudged forward in silence. Bander and Anthony, with Harvard on his shoulders, led them over a stretch of rocky terrain, keeping the river at a distance down to their left. Eventually, they stood atop a ridge, looking down at a small village spread across the valley below. It reminded Aron of the miniature Christmas town that his mother displayed above the fireplace over the holiday season. He had always admired the detail of each tiny house and his mother would talk about each resident who might have lived there.

The mountains loomed beyond the town, casting their shadow over the village at their feet. Curls of smoke rose out of the chimneys of every home. A bonfire in the center of the village glowed in the warm evening air.

"We should camp here for the night, don't you think? Not go any further tonight. I don't want to take any chances with the residents of that village." Aron suggested. "Do you know anything about them?"

"No," said Bander. "There will be a few of these small towns along the way, but I don't think they have much contact with Lupellerin. And that was probably their intent when settling out here. But you're right. Best to approach them in the light of morning."

Tora, always several yards behind, sat down on a nearby rock overlooking the tiny village in the distance. Anthony eyed her warily as he lifted Harvard off his shoulders, and as the others set up camp, Harvard quietly slipped over to the other side of the large rock and sat down beside Tora. Aron lingered just behind them to discreetly supervise the interaction.

"I'm not supposed to talk to you," he said.

"I know," Tora replied.

"Do you know why?"

"Well, I suppose it's because they don't trust me yet. But I think they will come around soon." Tora straightened her posture with feigned assurance.

"I think you seem nice. And I like your hair." Harvard smiled widely, reaching out to touch a blonde strand.

"Harvard," warned Aron, shaking his head, and Harvard withdrew with a frown.

Tora turned back to Aron. "He's fine."

Harvard smiled again. "Do you want to come help set up the tents, Tora?"

"I think I will stay over here for now. Thanks, though."

Harvard leaned forward to peer over the precipice into the vale below. "This reminds me of my sinkhole! There's a sinkhole right near my house! It's so cool, and Tony-Aron helped me see over the edge! That's where I met him. How did you meet him?"

Aron smiled to himself.

Tora's sudden crestfallen expression dampened Harvard's enthusiasm, and a small tear formed in the corner of her eye.

"What's wrong? Are you OK?" Harvard asked.

Tora immediately wiped at her eye and turned to look out toward the valley and the dancing smoke lines. "I'm OK."

"No, you're not. I can tell you're sad."

Aron leaned closer to listen.

Tora sighed and wiped again at her other eye. "My family... they died in that sinkhole."

The crunch of gravel behind them startled Tora.

"*You?*" Heddah hissed loudly at Tora as she picked Harvard up with her good arm and backed away. Aron didn't realize that Heddah had drawn close and was standing beside him. "*You* caused that sinkhole? *Who did you kill, Tora?*"

"No! I didn't!" Tora responded, sparking the attention of the rest of the group. Aron instinctively moved between Heddah and Tora as Iyla rushed to Heddah's side.

"Who was it, Tora?" Heddah demanded.

"Wait. Tora, what's going on?" Aron asked, attempting to defuse the situation.

"It's not like that! I didn't mean to!" Tora exclaimed.

"So, you did then! *Who was it?*"

A look of terror washed over Tora's face as Aron and Heddah demanded answers. Iyla stood just behind Aron, and Anthony, his sister, and Bander sauntered over, alarmed at the sound of their heated voices.

"Did what? Heddah, what are you talking about? Tora?" asked Aron.

"*She* is the Sapin who caused that sinkhole! Who did you kill, Tora?"

"Wait, Heddah. Hold on. How do you know she did it?" Aron was confused.

"I just heard her tell my son that her family was killed in the sinkhole. You were standing right there. You had to have heard her too. That's how you know which Sapin caused the disaster! Family and friends, it's always the link. You, yourself, said that she had no family left here! She just said her family was killed in the sinkhole! She is the Sapin who caused it!"

"Now, hold on, Heddah," said Aron. "Leyna said that the sinkhole broke open around ten or so months ago. Tora was with me in my home on Earth at that time. I would think I would've known if she'd done something so horrible as killing someone. I mean, Tora, did you come back here while you were living with me?"

Iyla cautiously reached for Aron's hand and squeezed it gently, pulling him toward her. "Aron—" her voice cracking slightly. She took a deep breath and looked up into his stormy eyes. After glancing aside quickly toward Tora, she asked, "Aron, didn't you tell me your mother died around that time?"

Aron stiffened. Her words cut through his heart and lungs as he stepped back, letting go of Iyla's grasp.

Dimethylmercury.

The silence of the evening air was deafening, and his mind scrambled to make sense of these last several months, these last several words. *How could—?* "No," he murmured, shaking his head.

They also found it in one of her medications.

"Aron," Tora cried, reeling forward. But Anthony stepped between them, blocking her reach.

"No... no. Tora, tell me you didn't do this. My mother. Tell me you didn't kill my mother!" Aron's face burned red.

Tora shook her head. "No," she sobbed.

Aron stared at Tora and the rest of the group. Heddah's livid expression matched the depth of Iyla's compassion. Leyna's concern galvanized as she pulled Harvard closer to her. Anthony and Bander: strong, resolute, and protective.

And Tora. He found it curious that it was she who was the stranger. His Tora, the one he knew for many years, certainly had her faults. But murder? Dimethylmercury in her medication, Uncle Jeff had said. Another piercing knife to the heart pushed him against the large boulders behind him.

"How could—" he began weakly. "My mother died at the same time the sinkhole opened up. You're a Sapin, and your family was killed in that sinkhole!"

"Aron, please!" Tora cried out. "I didn't mean to! It was an accident!"

"My God." He sank to the ground as Iyla hurried to his side. He couldn't see. It was as if he was looking through a fishbowl; watery colors and figures all around him. And then the numbness enveloped him.

"Aron! I'm so sorry!"

Anthony grasped Tora's arm firmly and suggested she leave immediately.

"No! Leave me alone!" Tora struggled to break free of Anthony's grip. "Aron! It was an accident! I'm so sorry!"

Heddah took hold of Tora's elbow, which she was using to batter Anthony. "You need to go."

"ARON!"

"Get away from me." His words were like shards of ice on his lips. "I never want to see you again." His face fell, and Iyla wrapped her arms around him.

Tora's wide eyes abruptly narrowed, and her face hardened. "You will regret this, Aron," she seethed. "Every one of you will be sorry you turned me out!" Her eyes bored into Iyla as she sneered, "Especially you." Her threatening glare was like a dagger, penetrating each one, and in an instant, she vanished, her wrist clamps clinking on the ground.

The campfire provided little comfort to Aron. With Iyla on one side, her arm wrapped supportively around him, and Heddah and a sleepy Harvard on his other, he allowed his mind and his emotions to dwell in the torment of the earth-shattering confession earlier that evening. One thing was clear. Tora was never the person he thought she was, and the revelation of the depth of her depraved deception only solidified his resolve. *Sapins are sly and deceitful, selfish creatures*, Jens had said. Never trust a Sapin.

Anthony poked at the fire as Leyna turned the meat that was grilling above it. Bander lit his pipe and quietly studied the stars.

"Can't help but wonder where she's headed," he began. "Ya know? Eventually, the Commander'll know everything if he doesn't already. She knows our plan, our route."

"We'll deviate," said Anthony. "Find better cover; avoid all roads. We've got a long way to go."

"What about disguises?" suggested Leyna.

"Yeah, it may come to that." Anthony stood up and handed Aron his meat tucked in what appeared to be a piece of cardboard folded in half.

"Thanks," Aron said. "Look, are you sure you all want to continue? Your lives are certainly in danger, even more so now. You've already lost so much. You never asked for this."

"Just shut it," said Bander, and Aron managed a half smile to break through the pain ripping through his heart.

The crackle and hiss of the campfire managed to sing Harvard to sleep. Iyla was resting on Aron's shoulder. He could hear her soft breathing, and her sweet fragrance helped to relax his tense muscles.

"We should get to the south side of that village well before noon tomorrow," said Anthony. "We can look for some means of transportation and stock up on any additional supplies we may need before heading into the mountains."

Exhausted from the emotions of the day, the group drifted into restless sleep in the clear, cool air.

Chapter Twenty-Four

KENDAL

I t was just after noon when they reached the tall wooden gates of the small village in the valley. Several bags of trash sat against the stone walls, a pungent stench permeating the air and thousands of flies competing for the most delectable position. A sign that read "Kendal" arched across the boarded entryway.

Red-faced and dripping with sweat, Bander reached for the oversized gate knocker and whacked it loudly several times. He set down his backpack, and they waited and listened.

Anthony carried Harvard on his shoulders, and his shirt was as wet as if he had just run through a tropical rainstorm. Exhausted, Heddah and Leyna collapsed down onto their bags to wait. Even Iyla and Aron had reached their limit. The entire group was emotionally drained.

The sun was glaring that day, and their trek was long and rocky. They were out of water as the river had been too far down the steep, entangled gorge to access. Now that they had reached the valley and the village, they would fill up their canteens and restock their supplies.

Bander knocked again.

"You'd think they'd have a gatekeeper, small as this town is," Anthony commented.

"Are they not a fan of visitors?" offered Aron.

"Most small towns will welcome non-threatening visitors for trade and news reports," said Heddah.

Bander knocked a third time, this time more forcefully, and the gate fell ajar. There was no one on the other side. No lock? Bander pushed the door a bit more and poked his head in, then looked back at the others and shrugged.

"No one?" asked Aron. Bander shook his head, and the travelers gathered their belongings and cautiously entered the village of Kendal.

A cobblestoned courtyard with a modest central fountain greeted the visitors, although the fountain pool was roped off and covered over with a brown tarp. To the left of the fountain was a line of simple shops and trading booths. Their shelves were primarily bare, and no merchants were to be found. It was eerily quiet. A rather dank odor mixed with smoke filled the air.

There was a corridor to the right that was dark but clean. After making their way through it, they came upon their first Kendal inhabitants—a mother, about thirty yards away, pulling her small crying child into her residence just as a catilla jumped through the open window.

Two young men pulling a wagon piled with dirty linens disappeared around the corner.

"Hey," Aron spoke up. "Did you notice these people we've seen? They're all wearing a mask over their face."

"Oh, blessed moons!" Heddah exclaimed, just as a middle-aged woman approached them with her arms full of water jugs. A dark mask covered her face as well, and her clothes needed a wash.

"You people don't live here. Why're you here? You need to go," she advised. "It's the buqume virus; it has devastated our town. You catch it; you'll surely die! You need to leave!"

The travelers glanced around at each other as they pulled their shirts up to cover their nose and mouth.

"Ma'am," Anthony began, "is there somewhere that we can purchase supplies and fill up our canteens before we travel through?"

"You need to go now if you don't want to die! I just lost my brother and my niece! All the bodies are being burned in the center of town to help stop the spread. You should really go. Upriver. Get your water upriver."

"Crakes," said Bander. "Let's get outta here."

"C'mon," said Leyna as they reversed course and headed back to the unlocked gate.

They immediately approached another cart, this one pulled by an elderly man. His aged wife lay lifeless, partially covered by the stained sheets on top of her. Her wrinkled skin had large dark and leathery splotches covered with hive-like scars, oozing a thick orange substance. Noticing the tears in his eyes, they stopped to allow him to pass. The stench of disease and death followed him to the town center bonfire, where he would say his final farewell.

Closing the gate behind them, the ragged friends again put down their packs and glanced around at each other.

"We need to bathe—quickly," said Heddah. "Anthony, can you start a fire? We all need to change clothes." Bander, Aron, and Iyla gathered straw and fire stones while Heddah and Leyna made their way with Harvard down the gorge's steep walls to the river below.

"We've still got plenty of daylight left," Aron remarked as he knocked a few fire stones together, the way Iyla had shown him during their short time in Oroc. The stones immediately caught fire and burned a bright yellow and green. "We should keep moving."

Bander tossed an armful of fire stones into the pile next to Anthony before acknowledging Aron's comment. "You don't want to mess with the buqume virus. It's highly contagious and obviously deadly. We're going to need to flush out our bodies immediately. We'll set out again after we've burned our clothes."

"*Burn* our clothes?"

"You come down with it; you'll never get to the Tree. Go on down to the river and wash while we build this up," Bander said.

Iyla and Aron carefully made their way down into the gorge, carrying their packs on their back. Heddah, Leyna and Harvard were further downriver, out of earshot. "I can't believe that virus is still around. I thought it was eradicated a few years ago," said Iyla.

"So, you've heard of this?"

"Oh yeah. Bander's right; it's pretty bad. It even hit our Pelri community when we were in Oroc. Very painful virus. We lost eleven."

"That's terrible. I'm so sorry."

"I was very young. I barely remember it."

"Hey, Iyla." Aron stopped and reached for Iyla's arm. "You doing alright? You've been very quiet."

Iyla smiled. "Don't you worry about me, Earth-man," she said, punching him playfully.

"Iyla, come on. I know you're brave. I know you're determined. But you've also been through a lot, and it's OK if you're not OK. I know you aren't sleeping well. You don't have to put on a front. I'm here for you, so just talk to me."

Iyla was silent for a few moments. "I know," she said quietly.

"Did they hurt you?"

Iyla nodded, her lips pressed together.

"Experiments?"

"Yeah. Some were no big deal. Others…I thought I was going to die there. But Heddah, she always took care of me when she could."

"Thankfully, she was there." Aron paused before asking his next question. "The Commander, did he see you?"

Iyla nodded her head again. "But he didn't, he didn't, um… we got out just in time."

Aron sighed. "I'm sorry I couldn't find you sooner. I hate that they hurt you."

Iyla turned her head and wiped a tear. "I'm so glad you happened to stay at the inn."

"I know! What a lucky break," Aron agreed. "I'm glad we're doing this together."

"Me too."

Returning her smile, Aron said, "You know we've both got a target on our backs now, in enemy territory. I mean, we're lucky to have met the Farins, and they're great, but this is our mission, our journey, and you're my primary concern. Tora, she—"

"I'm not worried about Tora," she interrupted.

"Well, I am. She's obviously not the person I knew. And now she's shown all of her colors. She knows our whereabouts, our intention, and she has the connections to not only stop us—get us killed—but also to once again prevent your people from having the home that belongs to them."

"I don't know, Aron. I saw the way she looked at you. She does genuinely love you in some sort of way." Iyla bit the inside of her cheek as she glanced upriver. "And honestly, that's what bugged me the most."

"That she loved me? She has an appalling way of showing it. I may have known her for a long time, but there is nothing left for me with her. I look in her eyes, and I see nothing but a vacant stranger." Aron kicked at the stone by his feet. How could he have missed the staggering number of lies Tora had woven around herself? How could he have loved someone who could do what she did? He tilted his head up slightly to Iyla, who was perched a bit higher on a rock. "So, what bugged you about it?" Aron smiled.

Iyla rolled her eyes slightly and smiled back. "Let's just say I could never treat you the way she did, and we'll leave it at that."

Aron laughed and held out his hand to help her down the last few feet of the gorge. That beautiful, floral fragrance radiated from her lips, her hair. "So, I can assume you've been in love then? Boyfriend? Other than William, that is?"

Iyla giggled at the reference to Aron and William's first meeting. "I have. And the relationship was most definitely not based on lies."

"Well, then you have certainly come out ahead," Aron agreed. "So, what's become of this boyfriend, the one you treated so well...?" He continued to hold her hand in his, even though they had reached the river bank.

"He's fine, as far as I know. We parted on fairly good terms about half a year ago. He was a bit of a homebody; I liked to explore the world."

"Bet it could be difficult being both a homebody and a Pelri, with your... wandering ways."

"Yeah. But he was a good guy."

"So, he was a Pelri, then?" Aron verified.

"Of course."

"Of course? What do you mean, 'of course'?"

"Well, Pelri stick with the Pelri. For the most part," Iyla responded, and added a wink.

"And for the lesser part?"

"Hmm," Iyla contemplated as she watched the other three climbing back up the gorge. "It's rare. *We're* rare. We need to keep our kind going."

"Aha," Aron acknowledged and slowly released her hand. "I see. So, it's frowned upon." He paused a moment before adding, "I wonder if that way of thinking will change when the Pelri get their homeland back and are allowed to thrive."

"Don't count on it. Not after what happened with my sister."

"Sister? I didn't know you had a sister."

"Half-sister, Rivianne," Iyla corrected. "She's two years older than me. We have the same father, but her mother is human."

Aron raised his eyebrows, calculating the age difference in Earth years. "Wow, why didn't you tell me this before?"

"I didn't know I needed to." Iyla smiled and dove into the river ahead of Aron, splashing him. Below the surface, she removed her contaminated clothing and scrubbed herself down with the soap that Leyna had packed. She wiped the water from her face as she emerged. "I haven't spoken to her in a few years. Her mother was a spy for the Commander. She came across my dad one day in Neritte and got... overly friendly, and then disappeared in the night. Rivianne was born and didn't seem to inherit any of the Pelri traits, so the Commander tossed her to the garbage when she was about one year old. Jens helped my dad find her, but he had to keep her hidden from the rest of the world, basically. He didn't know how the rest of the Pelri would handle her, either. But eventually, it came out, and there was definitely an adjustment period for everyone. He raised her for a short time before she eventually took off."

"Took off where? She knows she has you, her sister, right? And what happened to her mother? And your dad?"

"The Commander had her mother killed. She was just a tool to him. And yes, Rivianne knows of me. We never had much of a relationship. She wanted nothing to do with me, and she never really fit in with any of the Pelri. She can't travel or talk to nature the way Pelri do, so I think she always felt like an outsider. She may have been jealous that she wasn't a full-blood, and it was difficult for her. She caused a lot of trouble in our community—fights, theft, and in one case, arson. Then one day, she was gone, and nobody's heard from her since. Not even Jens. My dad died not long after she disappeared. Then it was just my mom and me."

"Well, Rivianne has missed out on a lot then," said Aron. "It's sad, really."

"Yeah. It's sad, but it seemed she was determined to make things worse than what they needed to be." Iyla motioned for Aron to turn around as she stepped out of the water and dressed in fresh clothes.

"Aron?" she asked. "Do you think we're going to make this happen? The Heart and getting Keyronai back?"

Aron wiped the water from his face before answering. "No doubt in my mind. And now I've got even more incentive." He winked before he ducked back under the current.

After the fire consumed the last of their contaminated garments, the freshly dressed group filled up on the remaining meat and dried fruit. Bander estimated that the next town, which was located at the base of the mountain, would be several hours' hike from their current whereabouts.

"The sun won't be up much longer," he said. "We need to set out."

Chapter Twenty-Five

Be Strong

"If we continue up the Galvenais River, we'll go through the western side of the mountains," said Anthony. "The terrain is more difficult to hike, but it's slightly less distance to cover than if we took a turn to the east toward Rakkarron."

The group had found accommodations in the village of Ingreso. They stocked up on food, clothing, additional weapons, and supplies as they prepped for the next leg of their journey into the mountains ahead of them.

"Yeah, but Tora expects us to stay to the west," Bander stated. "Mad Menrich? Remember? It's a little more populous to the east. Maybe easier to hide in plain sight? And we'll bump right into the Tarkien River. We're going to risk the morcego wraiths either way."

"What exactly are these morcego wraiths?" asked Aron. "I take it probably not as friendly as your catillas?"

Bander and Anthony both looked at each other, somewhat confused.

"Catillas?" asked Bander. "You don't have catillas on Earth either?"

"No."

"Well, you're definitely not going to like the morcego wraiths," Bander laughed as Iyla sidled over to join them. "You have bats? Small dragon-winged rodents with fangs?"

"Yes."

"Bats, but no catillas? Crakes. OK, morcego wraiths are like oversized bats. Or, more like evil spirit oversized bats. With several long tails, maybe five, sometimes up to ten tails."

"Spirits of bats? You mean like, ghosts?"

"I think 'ghosts' would imply that they were once alive and have died, and this was what is left behind. So, no. They are born as these spirit-bats and are very much alive," Bander assured Aron. "Grow to be about as big as we are. Oh, and they feed on bugs and flesh."

"Ah! Of course, they do!"

"They're only found in the central part of Seridon," Iyla added. "No one has ever found any other nests anywhere on Athemoni. I've seen them once before when I was with William, but only once. And I'd like to keep it that way."

"Chlorophyll allergies," said Bander.

"Seriously?" Aron raised his eyebrows.

"That's what they say. Crazy, right?"

The three men stared down at the map in silence for a moment. Aron was still trying to picture these creatures in his head.

"Your jeep sure would've come in handy now, Anthony."

"Jeep?" exclaimed Aron. "You have a jeep?"

"*Had,*" Anthony clarified. "The Commander's guards took it when Heddah was sent to prison. But I thought jeeps were from Nedaria, not Earth."

"Earth. Definitely Earth."

"Vehicles are pretty hard to come by. The inn was just starting to do well, and the Commander had employed quite a few Sapins to bring them back from Earth, Ornott, and Nedaria. They were paid hundreds of griggs for every vehicle they brought back. But the push had wiped out the magic of a ton of Sapins, so they quit the program. Even after they tried just bringing over the parts. Not enough manpower to keep the ones we got running, so the government seized a lot of them from the Seridon citizens."

"And nobody rides horses?"

"Yeah, some do. And laredars, but in Seridon, it's pretty expensive to keep animals fed, so only those who can afford it."

"And laredars are... what, exactly?"

Bander thought for a moment. "Kinda like a horse, I guess. Taller. Much longer neck. But they have a large hump on their back. Not flat like a horse."

"Oh, you mean a camel!"

"Camel?"

In the opposite corner of the room, Leyna sat with Harvard on her lap, and Heddah stood to her right, preparing sandwiches. Harvard's face was sleepy as he leaned back against his aunt, not even cracking a smile for his favorite friend, Tony-Aron.

"Mom-m-my," he whimpered, reaching for Heddah and tugging on her shirt. She casually rubbed his cheek and then bent down to look into his eyes.

"Does he look a little flushed to you?" she asked Leyna. Anthony swiveled in his seat to examine his son.

"His eyes are a little red," said his dad as he placed a hand to his forehead. "Yeah. He's warm."

"Harvard, how are you feeling? Are you doing OK?" Leyna nudged her nephew playfully.

"I'm cold. Mommy, hold me," Harvard cried.

Heddah picked up her son and wrapped him in a cotton blanket from the bed. "I'm going to take off your shoes and make you something yummy to drink, OK?"

He closed his eyes as Heddah laid him down on the small sofa.

Aron and Iyla exchanged concerned glances, prompting Iyla to break apart generous portions of her flower root. Handing two to Heddah, she nodded, saying, "Just in case."

Each traveler silently consumed the root and wrapped a tight-knit cloth around their face. Heddah caught her breath when she pulled Harvard's shirt up, revealing three large red splotches covering the left side of his back. "Dear moons," she sighed and buried her face in his neck. "No! Please, no!"

Anthony wrapped his arms around his wife and son. "It's going to be alright. Children handle this better than adults."

Bander stood up and began packing some of his things in a bag. "We're going to have to leave at first light. We don't want to contaminate this town and have the virus blow up here as well, if that's what he has."

"Yeah, but we also need a solid night's rest before moving on, especially Harvard," said Leyna.

Aron agreed. "So, we head east first thing in the morning, then."

"I'll be sure to have plenty of roots with us," Iyla injected.

With gear and belongings packed, they each settled into their beds. But as Harvard's temperature rose, Aron couldn't help but worry about his little friend. Heddah and Leyna continued the tea treatment with Iyla's roots, but the rash continued to spread, and his breathing became difficult. Heddah gently rubbed the root paste over his torso, and several times, Aron heard the frantic gasping as young Harvard tried to breathe in sufficient oxygen. Eventually, they graduated from the cold washcloth on his forehead to a cool bath in their attempt to lower his fever. Feeling powerless, Aron sat on the sidelines as Iyla helped to spread the root paste over Harvard's small body.

The following morning wasn't much easier to manage. With Harvard strapped tightly to Anthony, the group quietly exited Ingreso. Although his fever had dropped to just above normal, the angry red splotches stretched across Harvard's body, and the extreme fatigue kept him from opening his eyes for more than a few minutes. The others continued to wear coverings over their face and drank the flower root tea every two hours to evade the grasp of the deadly virus.

"I'm so tired, Momma."

Heddah cradled Harvard close to her as they paused to rest and eat. Iyla wrapped her arm around Heddah as a tear trickled down her cheek. Harvard's weak body was still wrapped in the cotton blanket, even though the sun was high in the cloudless sky.

"Be strong, Heddah," said Iyla, as she reached to hold his cold, small hand in hers. "He's got a lot of life ahead of him."

Heddah's breath hitched as she turned her face away from Iyla and Harvard. It was heartbreaking to see such a tough, vibrant, and compassionate person feeling powerless to help the ones she loved most.

It would be another three days before they reached the Tarkien River and the next town. They pitched their tents in a well-concealed gap between several fallen boulders. As the day retreated, the rain pattered down on the thick canvas, Aron's thoughts were with little Harvard and his family. With the sacrifices this family had made for him and for Iyla, he just hoped they were on the right path and that in the end, these losses and this heartache wouldn't be for nothing. He needed to make sure that the Pelri would get their homeland back, that Iyla would find her friend, and all his new friends would be safe.

The damp air and quiet night invited Aron's nose to partake in the array of aromas surrounding him. While the memory of the dry air of the Middle Eastern desert bore hints of thyme and sesame seeds, and the breezy air of Tariadyn and Kleey was crisp and sweet like a fresh apple, the melancholic air in rural Seridon was noticeably different. For some reason, it reminded him of sitting in his mother's hospital room when he kissed the tears on her cheek for the last time.

Chapter Twenty-Six

PASSERSBY

H arvard faded in and out of consciousness over the next six days as they trudged on through the pelting rainfall. The group now waded through stretches of dark, dense mud and rock. They had reached the Tarkien River a few days ago and were headed due north in the steep, mountainous terrain. A few waterfalls had provided some necessary showers, and they were fortunate enough to come upon an exposed hot water vein outside one town. Heddah pointed out that natural hot water vein holes were fairly prevalent on Athemoni, particularly in Seridon, where the ground had opened up in small gaps, and sometimes more significant gaps, to reveal these minor underground streams. The subterranean fires and molten lava heated the streams below the rocky iron layer, just under Athemoni's crust. These convenient water veins came in handy to wash their clothes and tents; not to mention, Harvard got a good, therapeutic soaking bath.

The group passed several towns, but they were careful not to cross over the town limits. They avoided any human interaction for fear of viral spread and unnecessary chatter that might find its way back to the Commander.

Meanwhile, Heddah tended to her son, keeping him dry, wrapped, and warm, dosing him with root tea, and exercising his weak limbs to work out the stiffness in his swollen joints. His breathing had improved, but his bones and muscles ached, and he did little more than sleep as they continued their journey into the mountains. Heddah had been unusually quiet these last few days.

As nightfall loomed, the group found a secluded alcove beneath a large rock formation that jutted out from the side of the mountain. It not only provided shelter from the rain, but also adequately camouflaged their campsite.

The dampness in the air intensified the colder mountain temperatures. They stayed together under one tent to share the warmth, and Aron listened as the rain spattered heavily on the rock.

Once again, using his pack for a pillow, Aron reached inside for his routine self-reassurance that everything was still there. There was no shortage of money. Jens had stocked him well. The Elven talisman remained safely tucked in the inside pocket. His gun, ammunition—all there. And the Heart. He took it out of the small satchel at the bottom of his bag. His touch seemed to activate the red glow, and organic heat steadily emanated from its core. He was careful not to allow his thumb and fingers to fall into its smooth recessions.

"Heddah." Aron quietly broke the silence. "Why don't you lay Harvard over here with me? I've got a great heat source." He partially uncovered the Heart from his pack, shielding the radiant glow. They could all hear a faint, pulsating puh-dum, puh-dum, puh-dum.

Heddah looked first toward her husband and then to Iyla, then back to Aron. "Do you think it's... safe?"

"I believe so. Even just having him closer to it, he'll stay warmer. Maybe even sweat it out. I'll keep it in the leather satchel."

Iyla agreed. "I think that's a great idea."

"Yeah, but I don't want you catching it either."

"I'm still wearing the mask, drinking the tea, and I think if any of us were to get it, we would have by now."

Heddah lifted her son from her lap and laid him down next to Aron with the Heart wrapped in the blanket between them. Iyla made room for Heddah and moved to Aron's other side as he zipped up his pack.

A tentative smile crept across Harvard's pale face when he saw Aron beside him. His tired eyes closed once again as his breathing slowed to a steady pace. His small, flaccid body was so frail.

"You know," said Iyla, "he hasn't gotten the jaundice or the orange excretions. That's a good sign."

Heddah nodded, and Aron knew she was afraid to concede any inkling of hope.

The rain slowed considerably as the rest of the group slept. Aron, unable to sleep, listened intently as a dull, thumping sound in the distance drew closer and then faded again. The crunch of gravel at a steady pace told Aron they were not alone in this mountain bypass. Bears? Mountain lions? He wondered at the type of creatures that could be lurking outside in this world. He certainly wasn't looking forward to meeting any oversized bat wraiths.

Wait. Was that shouting? He sat up slowly. Muffled in the distance, he heard it again. It was a male voice. And again, the sound of crunching gravel. And another voice.

Anthony sat up quickly, tilting his head to listen. Bander snored next to him, and Anthony jabbed him in the side. He grunted irritably, but Anthony immediately covered his mouth. Bander sat up slowly, eyeing both Aron and Anthony.

Another voice, female. They were closer. Both Leyna and Iyla awoke, and Aron put his finger to his lips.

"Keep moving!" That was the male.

"I think it's as good as any place to camp for the night." Another male voice. They were significantly closer.

"Keep moving! We're not stopping before we reach Bedrock Ridge. How else do you think we will catch up?"

"I'm exhausted." That was the female voice. Aron could tell they were about to pass below them.

"Shut up! Keep moving!"

Their gravelly footsteps were directly below them.

"Crakes," whispered Bander. "That's the Commander."

There was a scuffle of crunching gravel—several thumps and bumps. Aron estimated a minimum of ten people passing on the path about twenty feet below.

The noise faded.

"Shit," said Aron. "You sure that was him?"

"I'd recognize that raspy, gnarled voice anywhere. The girl, you think that was Tora?"

"I don't know. Shit," Aron whispered again. "We need to lie low. Everyone, stay quiet. There could be another squad following them."

Harvard was the only one sleeping at this point. Heddah reached to tuck the blanket tightly around him.

"What's going on?" she whispered.

Iyla put her finger to her lips and motioned outside. There were several minutes of silence where only the wind dared to whisper. A light pattering of raindrops on the rocks began once again.

"Pretty sure they've passed," said Anthony.

Aron carefully stood up and stepped over the sleeping Harvard. "I'll have a look around."

"Yup," said Bander. "I'm going with you."

"Me too," said Iyla.

Aron objected. "Stay here. It's safer hidden back here."

"Really? Did you really just say that?" said Iyla, continuing toward the opening of the tent. "Quite sure I can handle myself."

"Iyla," Aron gripped her arm lightly, and feeling his chest tighten, he realized the emotional hold she had on him. "Obviously, you can handle yourself. But, the fewer of us we have running around out there, the better, for the moment.

Just stay with the Heart. Bander and I will be back in twenty minutes, OK?"

"Truth be told, *you* really shouldn't be running around out there either," said Bander. "I have no intention of making a liar out of old man, Yeril. You should stay back safely in the tent. Anthony and I will go."

"Psh, screw that!" Aron scoffed. "I'm military trained. The Tree brought me to this world and damned if I'm not going to do my job."

Bander scowled, glancing at Iyla and shaking his head.

The three men scoured the surrounding area, finding only footprints headed north.

"So now we are following them." Bander shook his head. "We don't have an alternative route at this point. We all have to pass across the isthmus, and now it looks as if they will get to the Tree before we do."

"Why wouldn't they have used their vehicles? I thought they had them all."

"Cars are loud, not dependable in the mountains, especially. It's not surprising."

"You all really could use a skilled mechanic in these parts," Aron remarked, primarily to himself. "We're not in a good position, you're right, but we all still have a ways to go. We'll have to follow them closely and then pass them when they set up camp. Where's Bedrock Ridge?"

"It's not much further north of us. Maybe a few miles."

"We don't want to get any closer at this point, then. Let's rest a few more hours, and then we'll bypass them before sunrise."

Back in the tent, Aron relayed the plan to the others and took his place between Harvard and Iyla to rest.

Iyla, lying on her side with her head resting on her hand, whispered to Aron. "Aron? What about Jens' talisman?"

"What about it?"

"I mean, I feel like we're trapped with the Commander between the Tree and us. Don't you think this would be a good time to call for help? We have no other way to Urippa Spring."

Aron paused before answering. "We can only use the talisman once. Is this really the greatest time of need? I think we still have a chance of getting there on our own."

"But if we can get help—"

"I don't think the talisman was meant to be used lightly. And I don't know what kind of help he meant."

Iyla sighed as she laid back down. Aron turned on his side toward her. He could barely make out the profile of her face in the dark.

It wasn't long before all eyes were closed again.

"Tony-Aron? Tony-Aron? TOE-NEE-AIR-RIN!"

Aron could feel small fingers pulling at his left ear and then squeezing his nose. When he opened his eyes, a smiling Harvard was looking down at him.

"Hey, bud! You're looking pretty good this morning! You feeling better?"

"Yup!"

Hearing their chatter, Heddah awoke, and a smile spread across her tired face. "Harvard! Come, let momma feel your head."

One by one, although still dark, the travelers arose. They cheerfully embraced Harvard and gratefully removed their face coverings. Harvard had beaten the buqume virus.

"My sweet baby! He's going to be alright!" Heddah and Anthony held each other close, grateful to have averted losing their only child. She grabbed her small son and pummeled him with kisses. "My precious boy!"

They each quickly gathered their gear and packed up the tent before unfolding a quick meal and setting out in the damp morning hours.

It was eerily quiet in the early darkness. The clouds mostly covered the moons and stars, and the only sounds were the shuffling of their footsteps. The rocky, mountainous terrain was difficult to traverse, and they all kept a watchful eye for the Commander and his party's campsite.

Bander, leading the way, paused as the largest moon, Neoma, peeked through the clearing skies. He dug his walking stick into the face of the cliff beside him and looked toward the crest nearly a hundred yards above them. He motioned for everyone to stay quiet and pointed upward. Heddah immediately gathered Harvard in her arms and moved to Anthony's side.

"Wraith nest," Iyla whispered to Aron. "Just move slowly and stay as quiet as possible. They don't hear or see very well."

"Shit," said Aron.

"I know," said Iyla. "I was hoping they'd all be higher up."

"How many are we talking about here?"

"There's usually two to three to a nest. I can see three nests from here."

"Three?! I thought it was just that one up there."

"Just keeping going. The more distance we put between them and us, the better."

The group carefully made their way around the side of the mountain and down into the narrow valley. They couldn't help but notice the disturbing litter of human belongings on their path.

Once they crossed the chasm, they made their way westward and came to a wide clearing on the north side. Aron glanced back at the rocky mountain through which they had just traversed. He could easily see the three dark cavities about a third of the way up the mountainside from this distant position.

"Fifty griggs says they're here. The Commander." Bander dared to speak just above a whisper. "Eyes open."

"Hold up," said Aron. "We can't just go walking out into that open field. If you suspect they're here, we need cover."

"Look." Iyla pointed across the clearing to a tiny bright light in the distance. "Campfire."

"I guess the morcego wraiths haven't found them yet. Awfully close to their nests for a campsite," said Aron.

"Or maybe the wraiths have already had their fill, and it's only what's left of their squad sittin' 'round that campfire. Could be why we haven't seen any yet."

Aron weighed Bander's theory and shuddered.

"Well, come on now, let's keep moving!" said Heddah. "It's just about daybreak. How are we going to pass their camp?"

"I see they've got the wide-open field to the west, and they are right up against the rocky terrain to the east. Are those more mountains? I can't see it too well." Scanning the panorama before him, Aron strategized their next move.

"Yeah," Bander answered. "If we go back behind those mountains, they will certainly get to the Tree before we do."

Anthony and Heddah, with Harvard on her back, climbed onto the large flat rock in front of them for a better view. The group was fairly well hidden behind the many boulders that spread across the base of the mountain. It was easy to see there had been multiple rock slides that had built up over many years.

"There's nothing," said Anthony. "There's no cover to the west of their camp."

Heddah put her son down to stretch out her back muscles and massage her wrist.

"Then we are going to have to hurry before the sun comes up," said Aron. "We can keep a good distance away from them, and they'll have a hard time seeing us. Let's move. Stay low."

"You guys aren't going anywhere," came an unfamiliar voice from behind them.

Chapter Twenty-Seven

Elven Magic

A burning twinge traveled through Aron's spine, and the hairs on the back of his neck stood on end. With his hand on his gun, he pivoted slowly toward the direction of the voice behind him. Through the dim light of the stars and moons, he saw Leyna and Bander, each in a headlock by a uniformed soldier, with a weapon pointed at their temples.

Iyla's breath hitched just before Harvard cried out to his mother. Heddah shushed him quickly. They stood frozen on the rocky overlook as Bander and Leyna struggled to free themselves.

"Don't move," one soldier growled at Bander. "Unless you want to feel your brain explode!"

Anthony stepped forward slowly. "Please, let them go. They've done nothing. Please."

"Stay back, or I pull the trigger!"

Aron raised both his hands so they could see them. "Sir, please, let them go. They've done nothing."

"Which one of you is Aron Coverstone?"

An icy breeze brushed through the travelers, and Aron half expected to hear the rustling of leaves and tree branches. But it was dead silent. Tora had indeed sold him out.

"I am," said Aron, taking a step toward them.

"No," Iyla whispered as she reached to grab his arm.

"And that's the Pelri, right over there." The soldier holding Leyna motioned to Iyla. This was the female voice they had heard late in the night. Aron could just make out her profile through the shadows of the early morning.

"I'm Aron," he repeated. "Please, let them go."

Iyla stepped forward, and her necklace glimmered in the moonlight. The female soldier's lips parted slightly, and she caught her breath.

"Rivianne?"

The female soldier's eyes widened and then quickly narrowed as she clenched her jaw.

"I want the four of you, and the kid, up against that boulder." The first soldier shoved Bander toward the boulders. Harvard began to cry. The female soldier hesitated before pushing Leyna up against the boulder next to Bander.

"Rivianne!" cried Iyla. "What are you doing? You know who I am!"

"Riv, who is this person?" barked the first soldier.

Rivianne glanced back and fixed her eyes on Iyla. "She's no one. She's the Pelri we've been looking for."

Iyla's face fell. "Rivianne, how can you do this?"

The wind picked up considerably and at a similar pace to the increasing volume of Harvard's howling.

"Shut that kid up and get your backs to the rock. *Now!*"

Heddah picked up her son and pressed him close to her. His wailing sounded more like screams. The pitch was higher and more piercing to Aron's ears, the louder it became. A bitter cold gust of wind moved through their bodies, and they realized the screaming wasn't Harvard.

Iyla muttered under her breath and grabbed Aron's hand as he reached to cover his ears.

"What is it?" he yelled above the noise as the rest of the group turned back toward the mountains.

"Wraiths!" she cried as a filmy darkness swept toward them. The two soldiers pushed Bander and Leyna behind the boulder just before Iyla and Aron flattened themselves to the ground. It streaked above their backs, leaving an icy, viscous chill in its wake.

Aron reached into his pack and pulled out the Elven talisman before the wraith could double back. Across the open field, he saw the soldiers about thirty yards in the distance, dragging Bander and Leyna toward the Commander's camp.

The wraith headed toward them once again. Aron pushed Iyla back to the ground and raised the talisman above his head, squeezing it tight. An electrical current traveled through his body as a bolt of lightning surged from the talisman into the moonlit sky.

The high, piercing screech of the wraith reverberated through his brain as he held the iron talisman firmly in his grasp. The wraith dove toward Heddah and Harvard just as Anthony pushed his family off the boulder to the ground about four feet below. But the wraith immediately adjusted course and swooped toward Anthony.

"No!" Aron could hear Heddah's screams over the wraith's screech. She shielded Harvard's view as she cried out from between two boulders. Heddah dropped to the ground, holding Harvard tightly to her chest. Her sobs blended with her son's as the wraith enveloped Anthony into its icy black film. "No! Anthony!"

Anthony's body collapsed within its grip, his skin shriveling and then hardening before finally crumbling into the darkness of the wraith.

"Anthony!" Heddah continued to hold Harvard close as she remained on all fours, her body heaving with every sob. Harvard cried out to his father, but Heddah again pulled his face into her, curtaining his view. Aron felt her agony in his stomach and up through to his heart as he held tight to the talisman.

A second wraith was soaring toward them. Aron tried to redirect the lightning bolt toward it, but he couldn't deviate from his position. He yelled at Iyla to stay down just before a billowing blast of fire scorched through the sky in front of them. Aron fell to the ground as the talisman extinguished its power.

The first wraith retreated toward the mountains as another blast of dragon fire pummeled the second wraith fifty yards in front of them. Dragon fire.

William.

"Heddah!" Iyla yelled as Aron reached down to pull her and Harvard from the rocks below them.

Her face was red and streaked with dusty tears. She collapsed onto the gravel next to Aron. "They took Anthony!" she cried.

"I know," said Aron, trying to avoid seeing the pain in her face.

"They took him! We have to save him!"

"Heddah," Iyla placed her hand on her cheek and looked into her watery eyes. "Heddah, he's gone."

"No! He can't!"

"Heddah—"

Harvard sat on the ground crying into Heddah's lap. Her breath hitched as her eyes darted, quickly scanning the area. "Where's Leyna? And Bander?" she asked. "Did they get them too? Oh, dear moons, no!"

Iyla paused before answering. "The soldiers took them to their camp."

Heddah stared at Iyla, whispering as her body shuddered. "No. My family..." Her frame sank into Aron's, trembling. Another unconscionable loss for this honorable family.

The air had warmed some, and the sun had just peeked over the horizon. A ground-shaking thump followed the sound of wind behind them.

"Crakes!" said Heddah, a fresh wave of terror surfacing. "It's a blessed dragon!" She pulled her son onto her lap, wrapping her arms around his sobbing form.

"It's OK, Heddah. It's William. He's my dragon. He won't hurt you."

"Your...?" Her voice trailed off as she stared at the beast about twenty-five yards away.

Harvard sat up slowly, wiping his tears, and peeked out from his mother's embrace. "Whoa..." he whispered between shudders. His small hands gripped Heddah's arm, his eyes wide.

"We have to get out of here, Heddah. William is here to help."

"C'mon, Heddah! Hold on to Harvard. We've gotta get out of here!" Aron stepped onto the dragon's tail and climbed up his rear leg onto his back behind Iyla. "Climb up on his tail and hand Harvard to me. Then I'll help pull you up."

"Blessed moons!" Heddah swore as she handed her tear-streaked son to Aron. "This can't be safe."

"Don't worry, Heddah," Iyla reassured. "William is a lot safer than you'd think. In fact, on his back is probably the safest place to be right now."

"But Leyna, and Bander, if the Commander's got them..."

"We're going to take a look," said Aron. "His men won't see us when we're on William."

Heddah's anxious expression didn't change. Aron showed her the leather leg straps and instructed her on how to secure herself and Harvard. No sooner had she pulled the last strap and William launched into the air. They felt the pull of the ascent with every beat of his massive wings. Heddah looked back toward the ground, to the spot where she had lost her husband.

"Aron! They're coming!"

Two large morcego wraiths were headed after them. William made an abrupt roll to face the oncoming wraiths.

For Aron, the feeling was not unlike riding a roller coaster at the many theme parks in his world. The riders, nearly upside-down, felt the swell of William's lungs and tightening of his muscles before the dragon blew a mammoth surge of roaring fire, enveloping the wraiths. Their forms crackled and hissed as they disintegrated in the morning light.

A third wraith that was further back slowed considerably and then changed direction, no longer able to see the Pelri and her friends riding astride the dragon.

Within moments, they passed over the Commander's camp. Circling twice, they noted the sixteen smaller tents and one large tent in the center. The smoldering campfires and the harried activity told them they were packing up to set out again. There was no sign of Bander or Leyna.

While he was thankful for the unexpected comfort that William brought, Aron couldn't help but reflect on what this journey had cost. Iyla had been kidnapped, threatened, and tortured. Heddah had not only lost her brother and sister-in-law, but nearly her son, and her husband was gone. Bander and Leyna were now held captive by the tyrannical Commander. They had all lost their homes and businesses. His mother. They had placed all of their faith in Aron's hands to deliver the Heart back to the Elfblood Tree, not even knowing what that really meant for any of them.

"Do you see them?" asked Heddah.

"No."

"I don't see them, Heddah," said Iyla.

Heddah rested her head on Aron's back, with Harvard between them. Aron sensed a quick sniffle before Heddah continued. "We need to move forward. We need to keep going."

"What?" Iyla turned and called back to Heddah over the wind. "Are you sure?"

"Yes. We need to get this done. They're tough. The two of them can hold their own. They won't kill them. They will use them to get to us, to you and Aron. I think the best plan would be to complete this mission. Everything else will fall into place after that."

"Now wait," Aron interrupted. "We can get closer. While we're riding William with Iyla, we're invisible to them. Let's give it one more shot. We can get a better look coasting just above their heads."

William circled widely in his descent above the remaining tents that had not yet been packed up. He brought them close, just above the campsite. The wind gusts from his strong wings blew one tent over and caused a ripple effect on the large one in the center. A few outside soldiers held tightly to their jackets and belongings as they looked upward at the clear morning sky.

"Momma!" Harvard yelled and pointed at the single old laredar used to haul the gear. Two soldiers spun on their heels to locate the source of the child's voice. Heddah covered his mouth quickly as William continued past the large tent.

"There!" whispered Iyla, pointing toward the foot of the mountain. Bander and Leyna sat in a heavily guarded caged cart with their hands tied behind their backs.

"They don't look injured," Aron remarked.

Heddah sighed as a tear rolled down her cheek, relieved they were still alive. "Well, they couldn't have gotten here long before we did."

"We're not going to be able to get to them unnoticed with all those soldiers guarding," said Iyla.

"What if William walks us over to the back side?" Aron suggested.

Iyla shook her head. "William isn't the most graceful creature on the ground. Besides, then what? Anything we try to do, they'll hear us. They're right there next to them. And they won't be leaving their side for the rest of their journey; I can tell you that."

"She's right," added Heddah. "Our best bet is to press forward as fast as we're able."

The thrust of William's wings pulled them back up high above the campsite. Each rider bowed their head into the back of the one in front of them, doggedly enduring the pain in the pit of their stomach.

"They'll be OK," Heddah said, wiping the corners of her eyes. "We'll get them back."

Heddah was a strong woman. She had lost the most of all of them, yet she steadfastly continued to fight for the Pelri and what was right. Aron couldn't help but admire such a remarkable woman.

They circled twice more before heading north toward the Isthmus of Asopo.

Chapter Twenty-Eight

Under the Sand

The air was chilly above the clouds over Seridon. Iyla, Aron, Heddah, and Harvard huddled together on William's back. None of them knew what to say. Anthony was gone, and they had left their friends with the Commander. Guilt gnawed at Aron, as Heddah clung to her son, the only family she had left.

The dragon brought them down at the central-eastern side of the Isthmus of Asopo. They tumbled off his back before he hurried to swim and drink from the Sea of Hovelik. It was a sunny day with a strong warm wind that whipped up the sand, stinging their exposed skin. Miniature twisters sprung up and dissipated every few minutes as they skipped from the beach out to the water.

"Poor guy really needed a rest," said Iyla, regarding William.

"Yeah, well, we're far ahead of the Commander's squad now. They won't be catching up anytime soon." Aron rummaged through his pack for the map that he had borrowed from Jens. "Still a ways to go, but we can do that in no time, now that we've got William."

Iyla had removed her outerwear and followed William into the water. "It's warm!"

Aron watched as she cupped her hand and splashed water on her bronze face. Her dark hair blew wildly as a small twister fizzled out beside her.

"I'm going to take Harvard out of the sand." Heddah scooped up her son and wrapped him in her cloak before hurrying off the beach.

"No!" Harvard yelled. "I wanna watch the dragon!" But Heddah didn't stop, carrying him to the only shelter she could find.

An old, abandoned stone structure stood about fifty yards inland, and Heddah slipped inside. It immediately reminded Aron of the ruins of the Alamo. He and Tora had explored the grounds not long ago when visiting friends in San Antonio. The similarities were remarkable, and after glancing back at Iyla, he strode toward the building.

It was constructed of a coarse white stone and mortar that rose about twenty feet high. The side walls were crumbling, and there was a partial rear wall remaining, but no roof. The front was reasonably intact, with only a door frame, no door. Intricate designs had been carved into the framework, but the many years of wind and weather had taken their toll. What was once a meticulously landscaped, wooded garden surrounded the structure. Palms, much like the ones he saw when he first set foot on the beaches of Lupellerin, now petrified, still left behind a stately stone majesty.

Pausing in the doorway, he noticed Heddah sitting inside against the wall with Harvard curled up beside her, drawing dragon doodles in the sand. She had been crying.

"Heddah?" he whispered.

She quickly wiped at her face. "It's OK. I'm OK. I needed to get it out and just needed a quiet place by myself."

"I'm sorry," Aron replied. "I'll leave you alone."

"No, I'm fine. Just stay."

Aron sat down beside her and reached for her hand. "I need to thank you, Heddah, for your friendship and for taking care of Iyla. You have given so much, and subsequently, you've lost so much. I'm incredibly grateful to you."

"Aron, I believe in you, and I believe in Iyla. Yes, the Pelri deserve to have their homeland back. But, while I truly believe this has been my purpose, to help the Pelri," she paused. "I... I'm not sure I can go on. I... I need to keep my son safe."

"Heddah," Aron gave her hand a squeeze. "I understand, completely."

"I'm sorry I couldn't get you all the way there."

"Don't," Aron interrupted. "You have done so much for us. We'll get you both to a safe place. The Commander's men will be marching straight through here. We'll find a safe place for you."

"Momma?" Harvard had made his way to the center of the open room and was sprawled out on the sandy floor, brushing it into piles with his arms.

"Harvard! We're going to have to throw you into the sea to get all that sand off you!"

"Momma, what does this say?" He was pointing to the floor where the sand had been cleared away.

Aron and Heddah both made their way across the room to see what Harvard had found.

"Hey, guys! The water feels great on sore muscles! You should come for a swim." Iyla strolled through the open doorframe, soaking wet and face glowing. "What's going on in here?"

"Well, apparently, my son has chosen a career path as an archaeologist. Take a look at this." An inscription had been chiseled into the stone floor.

"That looks like Elven. Maybe the Bogarum vernacular?" Iyla presumed.

Aron raised his eyebrows. "Do you speak Elven?"

"Not much. I just travel a lot." Iyla winked, and Aron smiled.

Heddah brushed more of the sand to the side. "Look! Iyla, look at this symbol. Isn't that what's on your pendant?"

Aron took a closer look. "Jens' book..."

"Whoa," said Iyla, fumbling with her necklace. "It's the same symbol. I've never seen it anywhere before."

"Iyla, this same symbol was on one of Jens' books in his library cave. I thought it looked familiar, so I went to pull the book from the shelf, but I couldn't touch any of them because of that invisible barrier."

"There must be some meaning behind it. Why wouldn't he have mentioned that to me?"

"I don't know. But I agree. It has to have some significance, to be engraved here, and Jens' book, and on your necklace."

"I thought it looked like a cloud," said Heddah.

The three stood silently for a moment, studying the engraved stone floor.

"A tree," said Aron. "It's a tree. Look, this top part, that's the leaves and this line curving down, is the trunk. Do you see it?"

"I think you're right! Of course, it's a tree! Makes total sense now. The Elfblood Tree! It has to be!" Heddah exclaimed.

"What does this mean?" Iyla shivered, and Aron noticed goosebumps prickling her skin. "My mother gave me this necklace."

"I don't think any of this is a coincidence," said Aron. "In the same way that the Tree brought me to your world, I think it also meant for you to be part of this. All of us. I think whatever magic Levryn put on that Tree, it purposely brought us all together to save it. To save Keyronai."

"Right here, the Isthmus of Asopo, this is where they met," said Iyla. "Levryn and Miranda. According to the stories my mom would tell me, anyway. This must've been some sort of memorial to them."

"That would make sense," Aron and Heddah agreed.

"Who's Levilyn and Manda?"

They all smiled at Harvard.

"Levryn was a Bogarum Elf and Miranda was a Pelri, and they were bound to each other and they lived here a long, long time ago," Iyla replied.

They each looked around at the remains of this centuries-old structure. A quiet reverence moved through them, and simultaneously, they cleared away the rest of the sand that carpeted the stone floor. Iyla could pick out a word or two of the lengthy inscription that she recognized, but not enough to understand all that was written.

"A… something… beginning… something-something… light. In the morning… uh, the Pelri… I don't know. Something about nature."

"Is there anything else you remember from your mom's stories?" asked Aron.

"Not anything significant, I don't think. I mean, Levryn and Miranda met here. I think they were bound here as well. You call it 'married', right? They had three children, two boys, and a girl, all of whom inherited Miranda's Pelri features and traits. Everyone loved them, all the elves, and all the Pelri, and they were revered like royalty. Together, they kept their people safe and their countries prosperous."

After a brief pause, Heddah asked, "Do you know what became of the children?"

"Well, as I said, they were royalty, so they eventually took their parents' place. I'm guessing the monarchy must have fizzled out after the Heart was stolen, if not before. We don't have any of that now. The Pelri have been hunted by the humans and Sapins pretty much since we left them behind with a barren country."

There were a few moments of silence before Aron suggested they set up camp. That evening, as they prepared dinner over the campfire, Aron pointed out that they didn't have a new plan of action for the return of the Heart.

"And Heddah, you and Harvard... we really don't know what's going to happen when we do the—you know—when we give the Heart back. I don't know how long it's going to take or what's going to happen. I want to be sure you are both in a safe place first."

"You do realize," Iyla quipped, "it's not like we'll be doing open-heart surgery, right? I'm sure it's just a matter of maybe getting it close to the Tree."

Aron raised an eyebrow at her. "And you know this how?"

"Well, I don't *know*. I'm just saying it *is* magic, and I don't think we would've been selected to do this if we needed all those technical skills. We're not doctors or arborists."

"Well, I'm not, anyway," Aron added. "I think we should take you both to Tariadyn first, or wherever it is you wanted to go."

"Tariadyn is a good ways away now. Why don't you set us down a small distance north of the Tree? Once the deed is done, you'll be able to easily circle around and pick us up."

"There's mostly flatlands surrounding Urippa Spring," said Iyla. "Not a great location for hiding. We'd have to work fast. William can get us up close to the Tree, and Aron, you can just jump off and do it while I circle around and then pick you up. Then we'll scoop up Heddah and Harvard and go. Easy as chips. And that way, no one will be able to see William either."

"Easy as chips?" Aron raised his eyebrows. "Maybe a little too easy. I guess we'll see when we get there. If there's a safe place to drop off Heddah and Harvard, we'll do that. For now, I think this is a good place to sleep for the night. Leaving in the early morning, right?"

"Yup, we should get there before noon if we do."

After a meager supper, the group settled inside the stone ruin. Aron's mind raced with the prospects of tomorrow, and he felt anxious about the safety of his friends. Their plan seemed simple enough. Would they finally succeed at repairing the Tree and bringing the Pelri back to their homeland? What would become of the humans? What would become of him?

Chapter Twenty-Nine

Operation: Elfblood Heart

N o one saw them that night as they doused their campfire before retiring to their tents pitched inside the stone memorial. No one saw them the next day as the green dragon launched his large, iridescent form and his four riders into the brisk morning air. And no one watched as a gentle breeze blew across the isthmus, carrying the white sand through the empty ruin and once again shrouding the Elven inscription and symbols on the old stone-paved floor.

It was the last stretch of their journey to the Elfblood Tree to return her Heart. Harvard, who had woken several times throughout the night with nightmares about his father, was groggy. But he perked up a bit at the excitement of riding a dragon once again. "This is way better than my sinkhole!" he called to Iyla, sitting in front of him. His mother wrapped her arms around her small boy and held tight to Iyla while Aron brought up the rear.

It was a cloudless sky over Seridon, and Aron could smell a faint, sweet fragrance floating among the wind currents, a welcome relief from the stench of the dry decay below. The Sea of Hovelik extended to the east and the Anget Ocean to the west. The vast water bodies of Athemoni had such depth of color. Blue, but the richness of it, almost a living blue, was a stark contrast to the dull beiges, browns, and greys of the wasteland that was Seridon. The northern half of the island above the isthmus was unpopulated. The rough but primarily flat terrain was thick with petrified debris.

Puh-dum, puh-dum, puh-dum. The rhythmic beat of the Heart was strong, and Aron could feel each pulse through his backpack. The sound seemed to energize William as his wings beat in time.

"Aron!" Iyla pointed down to a clearing not far ahead of them. About twenty soldiers were marching northward, armed and ready for battle.

"Seridon soldiers. The Commander's men," said Heddah. "Do they have Leyna and Bander?"

"Shit. They can't be the ones we left at Bedrock Ridge. This is a different squad he must have sent ahead." Aron pressed his lips together, and his brow furrowed as they passed them. "Iyla, how much further?"

"Not long at all. They can't see us. We'll get there long before they do."

"Up ahead!" Heddah pointed further north. Another squad of ten soldiers escorted a herd of black, four-legged animals that were definitely not horses. They had canine legs and paws, but their heads were flat, slender, and smooth like a snake. Their body and tail reminded Aron of an armadillo.

"What are those?"

"Vexlores," replied Heddah. "Their bites are deadly, as are their tails if they pierce your skin. Good thing is, the Tree is in the middle of the spring, and they don't swim."

"Or fly," added Iyla.

"Thank God for William."

Iyla chuckled. "They must think you are some powerful warlord or something. Bring out the vexlores; the human from Earth is coming...!"

"Hey, they are looking for you too, a tiny Pelri, so..." They both laughed.

"Guys—" Heddah interrupted and squeezed Iyla's arms.

Up ahead marched yet another fairly large body of troops. Like the previous smaller squads, they were headed north, fully armed and ready for battle.

Their laughing ceased. Aron's stomach tightened. How many more troops were making their way to Urippa Spring?

One dragon, three adults, and a child were up against a trained layered army. Aron couldn't begin to evaluate the opposition. Sure, William was formidable, but the Commander had the numbers and the weapons. They just needed to get there first.

It wasn't long before they could see in the distance a break in the eternal forest of broken tree statues. Aron's heart pounded in his chest, and Iyla glanced back at him and nodded. Although not as beautiful as it once was, the muddled waters of Urippa Spring were just ahead. In the center, they could just make out the contour of a tall, shapely Tree stretching its bare branches out over the water. It, too, looked more like an old sculpture, hardened, discolored, and lifeless.

"What's all that around the edges of the spring?" Heddah asked.

"I don't know," Iyla replied. "I can't tell from here. I don't remember there being anything there. Just the dead Tree in the muddy water."

"It looks like it's moving."

They rode silently for the next few minutes as William brought them closer and lower. Then they realized what they were seeing. Both Iyla and Heddah drew in their breath at the exact moment that Aron said what they were all thinking.

"The Commander's army." It was a full-on battalion of approximately five hundred troops. "How? How could they have gotten here before us? It's impossible."

"Sapins," said Heddah. "It's the only way."

"Tora betrayed us all," said Aron. "Can't say I'm surprised at this point."

Heddah nodded. "The Commander would have immediately started using the Sapins to transport his army here, ready and waiting for us, and then sent his backup troops to scour the path hoping to catch up to us before we even got here. Obviously, they didn't factor in an invisible dragon. But now what are we going to do?"

They were now flying directly over the spring and the Tree, circling above the armed troops. With guns, swords, spears, crossbows, and other unfamiliar weapons pulled from other worlds at the ready, they surrounded the spring, each soldier with their back to the Tree standing in the center.

"As long as Iyla is riding William, they can't see us," said Aron. "Heddah, there's nowhere to hide you and Harvard. You're going to have to hold on tight. If we can get William to just take us down as close to the Tree as possible, I'll jump off into the water. They won't even see me coming until I'm in the water. Once I've got the Heart back in the Tree, you'll swoop down and pick me up."

There was a momentary pause before Heddah squeezed Iyla's shoulder. "It's the only way. We've gotta do it."

William circled Urippa Spring, the Elfblood Tree, and the battalion a few more times, searching for the best angle. Each soldier was poised to fight, but none were entirely sure of their focus. The Heart was pulsating loudly in Aron's backpack, and he could only believe that the soldiers could hear it too. William swerved just above their heads, and the wind from his beating wings pushed some of them backward. Awkwardly regaining their balance, they searched the skies for the source of the heated gust, firing their weapons into the air.

"C'mon, William. I'm ready," said Aron, and William not-so-gracefully brought them in as close to the Tree as he could, hovering briefly before Aron unstrapped himself and dove into the water toward the Tree.

Under the water, it was cool, quiet, and dark. It wasn't as deep as he expected, but he remained below the surface and swam directly to the base of the Tree. Had they seen him?

The root system of the giant Tree was partially above the floor of the spring, and they spread like tentacles on an octopus. With his leg wrapped around one, he pulled open the small bag he had taken from his backpack that contained the Heart. It was hot, and the sound of its beating reverberated in his ears. It pulsated in his hand as it warmed the water around him.

He needed air, but he still had to locate where to place the Heart. His chest was tightening, and he couldn't breathe. He had to get above the water's surface. Slowly, holding on to the trunk of the Tree, he edged his way up and desperately tried not to gasp as his lungs were finally assuaged with fresh oxygen.

Gunfire.

"Shit." He couldn't see William. He ducked down into the water just as two fiery arrows streaked by his head. They'd seen him.

He had to get the Heart into the Tree and quickly. He swam below again, searching for holes or marks. It was difficult to see more than a few inches in front of him, and he found nothing through the murky water.

There were several rounds of gunfire, some louder than others. Were they still aiming at him? And that's when he heard a screeching roar.

Chapter Thirty

It Takes Two

A bove the water, Iyla guided William upward as soon as Aron jumped off. His splash surprised the troops, who didn't hesitate to commence fire on the rippling water surface.

"No!" Heddah screamed as the bullets and arrows struck the waters near where Aron had disappeared.

Iyla's heart sank, and she prayed they didn't find their target. *C'mon, Aron. You're OK under there. I know you are.*

Several troops rushed to the side of the spring where they heard the splash near the Tree. William abruptly swiveled about a hundred yards above the army and then took an immediate nosedive toward the ground. He spewed a torrent of raging inferno onto the soldiers, who ran shrieking toward the water. Those who jumped in, fizzled, and as the steam rose, their bodies promptly floated to the surface. Stunned, but unable to see where the fire originated, the surrounding soldiers began firing aimlessly into the air. Heddah covered her son as William dodged the onslaught.

Iyla flattened herself tightly against the base of William's neck. Her heart pounded as the bullets, arrows, fireballs, and lasers skimmed past her. Or was it William's heart that she felt? She glanced over William's side as an arrow whizzed by, just missing her head. Aron again rose to the surface and then quickly went under. *Something's wrong.*

William dove back toward the soldiers, discharging a second firestorm into the battalion. Iyla felt a surge of heat on her chest. But it was not from William. She glanced downward and saw that the jade symbol of the Tree on her necklace was glowing and pulsating.

"Heddah!" she called behind her. And then an ear-splitting shriek yanked her attention to the eastern sky.

Emerging from several low-hanging clouds were two unexpected forms gliding their way. Kellery and Khennedy.

"Thank you, Jens," Iyla whispered.

Their iridescent armor sparkled in the bright sun as they headed straight for the battalion stationed around the spring. Nostrils flaring, the torrents of flames that shot from them scorched everything in their path. Not far behind, a much smaller dragon followed, adding his own shower of flames.

"Blessed moons! There's more!" Heddah shouted as the battalion retreated behind their shields and then fired upon the three dragons. Harvard clung to Iyla, sheltered by his mother's frame.

"Heddah!" Iyla yelled. "I have to go in and help Aron!"

"Iyla, your pendant! It's glowing!"

"I know. I've gotta go in. Once I'm off William, they're gonna be able to see you. Hang tight to William!"

Heddah nodded, reaching for the straps in front of her son.

William brought them down close to the water's surface as Iyla swiveled her position and looked out over the sea of soldiers battling the three dragons before dropping into the shallow, muddy waters near the Tree. At the very moment that she lost contact with William, his form, along with Heddah's and Harvard's, materialized. And it was at that same moment that she saw on the opposite side of the spring, a familiar silhouette. Her stomach tightened.

"Rivianne," Iyla whispered under her breath. Poised at the water's edge, Rivianne wielded her scintillgur, one of the most powerful weapons on Athemoni. The swords, stolen from Nedaria by the Sapins, shot electrical currents and blue fire at lightning speed. There were possibly only half a dozen skilled swordsmen trained to use it.

And Rivianne was one of them.

William immediately launched upward, but his sudden appearance caught Rivianne's eye, and her focus and her aim honed in on him.

"Rivianne, NO!" Iyla shouted as the surge of electricity and fire shot into the air. William dodged the strike, but her second shot came too quick.

"NO! Rivianne, STOP!"

The searing streak of burning electricity lacerated the dragon's armor underneath his right foreleg and burned clean through to the other side.

"NO!" Iyla screamed as the heavy beast plummeted from above. "William!"

Heddah clung tightly to her son and to William's neck as they spiraled downward at increasing speed. The scintillgur had also scorched his right wing, but he arduously fought to slow the descent. Iyla could see the look of terror on Heddah's face. They were going to hit the shallow water hard and fast. "No," she whispered.

It was at that moment, a massive silver and red form swooped up from behind William and snatched Heddah and Harvard from his back.

"Tenly...!" Iyla said under her breath, her mouth slightly agape as she stared in disbelief at the dramatic scene playing out in front of her. Seriah's dragon had returned to fight for her and the remaining Pelri.

The thunderous crash of William hitting the shallow waters of Urippa Spring jolted Iyla into focus. Her stomach clenched as another pang shot through it, and a tear flowed from the corner of her eye. Her own half-sister had struck down her long-time best friend and guardian.

Rivianne gloated in satisfaction at the water's edge, watching as William writhed in agony. He continued to emit streams of blazing flames, and Iyla could no longer hold back her grief. Rivianne glanced her way, and her empty expression told Iyla everything.

Suddenly, Aron emerged from below the water's surface, gasping for air.

"I can't find it," he panted.

Iyla wiped at her eyes. "What do you mean? You can't find the Heart?"

"I can't find where to put the Heart. I can't see much through this water. There's a large scar about three feet below the surface. I thought that's where it would go in, where it was cut out of her, but it won't go in."

From the corner of her eye, Iyla saw Rivianne taking aim with her scintillgur. She was going for Aron.

"Get down!" Iyla pushed Aron back down under the surface, and they both swam down to the floor and between the tangled root system. A bright bolt of lightning broke through under the surface where they had just been. Anticipating a paralyzing shock to their system or even death, Iyla felt only a minor twinge, and then the lightning bolt solidified under the water. A dense jagged light form broke off from its source and floated gently to the spring floor.

Light! Iyla immediately swam toward it and tentatively touched its outer surface. It was... cold? The mystical waters of the spring had frozen the light. She picked it up and quickly swam back to Aron.

Aron reached out and pulled Iyla toward the large scar near the base of the Tree. With the light in her hands, they could see every cut and crevice of the brutal scar left by the Sapin so many years ago. Her pendant glowing, she reached for the Heart in Aron's hand, and together, they pressed it into the Elfblood Tree.

Another slight tingly feeling spread through her body before the Heart melded into the tree trunk. The surrounding bark darkened, and living color expanded from the Heart's position. Aron looked at Iyla, and they smiled through the murky water. He reached for her hand and pulled her up to the surface.

The ground trembled as the deep brown color traveled up the thick trunk of the Elfblood Tree and spread outward to the tips of every branch like a glorious invigorating stretch after a long sleep. The smaller limbs twitched and shook, sprouting forth tiny green shoots that unfurled into lush green leaves. And then there was more. Verdant foliage quickly formed a magnificent canopy, a deep violet edging each leaf with color so vivid it gleamed. The Tree creaked and groaned as fresh sap traveled through its old vascular system, warming the trunk and in turn, disseminating the heat throughout the spring waters.

Jens' three dragons disappeared on the horizon. The Commander's battalion, those who weren't already dead or frozen in fear, dispersed quickly, many leaving their weapons behind. Those remaining stared wide-eyed as the Tree grew both in height and vibrancy. Rivianne was nowhere to be found.

Aron and Iyla stood by the Tree and watched as Urippa Spring transformed. The ground continued to shudder and tremble. The waters of the spring warmed steadily as the vibrations rippled along the surface, and a faint lavender color pushed through the murk. It spread quickly through the water to the far end, where William lay. His body, partially submerged, heaved in quick breaths as spiraling tendrils of smoke slipped out of his nostrils.

"William!" Iyla slogged through the waters to reach her friend.

"Shit! What happened? And where's Heddah and Harvard?"

"He was struck by the scintillgur. It may have gone through his chest. It was Rivianne. She did it."

Iyla knelt down in the water beside William's head and stroked his jeweled ears, as her tears dropped onto his sad face. "William, please."

William grunted as Aron doggedly shouldered him to roll onto his back.

"All the dragons came, Aron. All of them. Jens' dragons, they came and fought the soldiers. And Tenly, she saved Heddah and Harvard, when my William was struck."

"Tenly was here too? Where are they now?"

"I don't know. I didn't see, after William..."

Iyla bent down to bury her face in William's. Aron continued to push on him.

Then the ground shook like an earthquake with a loud rumble. The floor of the spring shoved Iyla upward as William's body lurched.

"William!" Iyla cried.

The heavy dragon rolled to his other side, exposing his large wound beneath his foreleg.

"Iyla, wait! It stopped." They quickly balanced themselves in the water. Although the ground still rumbled, they stood solidly on the floor of the spring. "Let me look at his wound."

Blood spilled into the water as Aron and Iyla tended to William. Iyla frantically patted her sides, searching for her seven blooms. "My flowers! Aron, they're gone!" Aron's brow furrowed as he pressed down on the wound. Iyla collapsed into William, stroking his neck and face.

"Is there anything here we could use to sew him up?" Aron asked. Both he and Iyla scanned their surroundings and then back toward the Tree. Its branches were now filled with large, green leaves extending further across the water. "What about the stems of the Tree's leaves? Or something to bandage him?"

"It's not strong enough. His armor is too thick."

"But maybe Elfblood leaf stems are stronger."

A pang shot through Iyla's stomach. She couldn't lose her best friend.

Wait. "Aron, look." She gently stroked William's chest. "I don't think we need to sew him up," said Iyla.

William was still, but breathing heavily as the lavender water lapped at his sides. The bloody water had dissipated. He grunted when Aron carefully removed the pressure. A long clean tear traveled from the dragon's side, up under his foreleg, and then toward the base of his neck. But the bleeding had stopped. Methodically, each scale was knitting itself to the adjacent one bordering the long laceration. The waters of Urippa Spring had not only washed it clean, sealing the wound, but had fused his armor together as well.

"Whoa, look at it." Aron reached for Iyla and pulled her close as William snorted loudly, lifted his foreleg, and then rolled back to submerge his wound in the water.

Iyla turned to Aron and smiled. William would survive. A new world was beginning for the Pelri, and she was grateful to have him and Aron here beside her. Aron smiled back and did not hesitate when she planted a soft, fragrant kiss on his lips.

Chapter Thirty-One

DOWN WILL COME SETIDON

L ilacs. Aron thought back to the last time he was with his mother, in her room playing checkers, and he remembered the vase of lilacs that was always on her nightstand. She had planted six lilac bushes surrounding her house nine years ago. "It's just a wonderfully familiar, sweet fragrance that reminds me of purity and a renewal of life," she had told him. Lilacs.

William snorted as Aron and Iyla, hand in hand, watched the Elfblood Tree explode in color, more than doubling in size. The lavender water warmed on their legs as pink, yellow, and white lilies popped up from beneath the surface of the water. The surrounding air was breezy and fragrant. Beyond the spring, beautiful trees and sprays of kaleidoscopic flowers enveloped the hardened statuary, framing the swollen ground in the distance as it disgorged streams of sparkling gemstones.

Again, the earth trembled, and the rush of excitement coursed through Aron's veins. This was it. They had done it.

He took Iyla's left hand into his and moved behind her before wrapping his arms around her tiny frame and holding her close as they witnessed the transformation.

The scent of smoke wafted by, and William stretched, letting out a long, blazing roar. He boldly flapped his wings and spewed a skyward inferno.

"C'mon!" Iyla urged. "Let's follow it!"

They mounted the dragon, and William launched them upward, effortlessly climbing the wind gusts into the now cloudless cerulean sky.

From their vantage point, they watched first-hand the beautiful new life bursting forth onto a desolate land. Like the waves that wash up onto the beach, a sea of brilliant color pushed through the petrified countryside as the dead statues shook, crumbled, and collapsed.

The earth quaked and rumbled. In the distance, they saw people running southward as fissures opened up all around them. It was the soldiers, humans and Sapins; the land was swallowing its enemy. Aron and Iyla watched from above as the fractured earth sealed itself once again, lacing its scars with lush foliage, flowers, and trees.

Up ahead, two heavily armed men scrambled up the rocky hillside as more cracks followed them.

"The Commander!" Iyla shouted, pointing down at them, and then cringed as the greenery wrapped its vines around the men's limbs and torsos, penetrating their skin. The trees snaked their slender new branches down each man's throat before tossing them into the opened bowels of the angry earth.

"Holy shit," Aron whispered under his breath.

The sentient landscape and botanical guardians had returned, primed to fight for their rightful countrymen.

William continued to glide southward, trailing the wave of green. Beyond the isthmus and Bedrock Ridge, passed the jagged mountains harboring the morcego wraiths, they veered eastward.

"It's Rakkarron!" Iyla shouted as miles of brown valley transformed into a dazzling verdant landscape. A large stone building, dull and decrepit, loomed in the distance. The rumbling earth shook the old building as pieces fell on one side.

The dragons were there, circling the building, glittering in the bright afternoon sun and spewing their fire.

"Aron, that's Rakkarron Station! Look, the dragons are freeing the Pelri!" And sure enough, the small and sickly Pelri were mounting the dragons from the windows on the sides of the building. They faded and then materialized once again as they dismounted in a grassy clearing a short distance away.

William brought them down to the field, where Iyla and Aron climbed off. Iyla scanned the small group of Pelri until her eyes finally rested on that one friend she was hoping to see.

"Seriah!" Iyla bolted over to a small Pelri group, embracing her long-time friend, and Aron couldn't help but smile. "Finally! I can't believe it!"

"Iyla! This was you? You did this?" Seriah's thin face revealed not only surprise but also the deep lines of his recent pain. He hugged her again.

"I couldn't have done it without my friend, Aron." Iyla turned and pulled Aron to her. "Aron, this is Seriah."

"Yes, I gathered," Aron laughed. "Great to finally meet you."

"But you're human," he said, raising an eyebrow.

"He's not like that," Iyla interjected. "There are actually quite a few really exceptional humans, Seriah."

"Tony-Aron! Iyla!" came a small voice both Aron and Iyla recognized. "I'm riding another dragon!"

Harvard.

"Yes!" Aron triumphantly punched his fist into the air, a wave of relief washing over him as Tenly landed with not just Harvard, but Heddah, Bander and Leyna.

"Great moons, it's Tenly!" Seriah dashed to her side as she lowered herself for her new human friends to dismount. "Aw, Tenly." He chuckled as the oversized beast nuzzled him vigorously.

"I'm so glad you're alright." Aron gave Leyna a hug as Iyla threw her arms around Heddah and Harvard. "So good to see you."

"Yeah, we're all good!" Heddah shouted. "And William! He's OK!"

"We saved the Pelri, Tony-Aron!"

"That's wonderful! I'm so proud of you!" Aron lifted Harvard into his arms as Bander affably grasped Aron's shoulder. They embraced each other warmly before Bander turned and pointed to the old building. "It's going down."

They watched as first the northern side, and then the rest of Rakkarron Station, crumbled to the ground, and a cloud of dust and debris billowed into the air. A cheer exploded from the stronger Pelri in the field. Within minutes, the ground opened up, and the remains of the Pelri prison were swallowed into the earth. The ground closed again but continued to rumble; the surface bubbling like boiling water. The dragons dispersed, and within seconds, a mountain formation of diamonds, crystal, and veins of gold shot up from below the earth. The tall formation rose, climbing thousands of feet into the air, with jagged peaks and shimmering clarity. The dragons circled the beautiful structure as it grew, the sunlight glimmering through every facet and bouncing off the brilliant colors. Sapphires, rubies, and emeralds lined the base in a fantastic display of rich, sparkling splendor.

When it had reached its final stature, each of Jens' three dragons took their place perched on a diamond peak. With wings spread, they blasted a culminating inferno as the Pelri continued to cheer.

There was nothing like it. The extravagance of the man-made buildings in Lupellerin paled compared to nature's masterpiece mixed with a bit of old Elven magic.

"Blessed moons! Who would have thought I would have seen this day!" Heddah stood in awe at the glistening grandeur before her.

Iyla grabbed Aron's hand and pulled him onto William's back. "C'mon, Seriah, let's keep following it!"

Seriah smiled as he mounted Tenly.

"We'll come too!" called Leyna.

Nature's wave had gotten ahead of them, and for a while, all they could see was the beauty it left in its wake. There were miles of flowers in colors that Aron had never seen before. Lush trees in all shapes and sizes and a fresh green carpet swathed the countryside once again.

Veering toward the west, they passed over what was once the tiny disease-ridden town of Kendal, now a valley of wildflowers. Soon enough, they caught up with the green wave just before the city of Lupellerin. The lake was shimmering and churning as the ground continued to rumble and crack.

"Do you hear that?" Iyla whispered. "In the distance."

Aron listened as the spine-chilling sounds reached his ears. "It's screaming," Aron acknowledged as his arms prickled. Iyla nodded, horror washing across her face.

"This is awful. Maybe we should turn back."

The taller buildings of Lupellerin were shaking and swaying, and Aron began to wonder what had become of the friendly bartender at Yeril's Eyes, Iyla's sister, Rivianne, and Tora, his ex-fiancée. And what would become of him? As a human, was he safe? He didn't even belong to this world. And then there was Heddah, Harvard, Leyna, and Bander; did they have this same concern? Would any humans or Sapins be safe? Surely, at least the innocent ones would survive nature's purge.

As they approached the city, the tallest of the marble buildings began to crumble. The sound was deafening as it crashed to the ground and the earth opened and swallowed it up. One by one, each building fell, homes and businesses alike. Bander's pawn shop, Yeril's Eyes, and Faradell Narrow were now all piles of rubble. The peace enforcement building collapsed down into the nearby sinkhole, which finally sealed over, and in so doing, erased the glaring symbol of his mother's passing.

Heddah's facility where Iyla was detained came down simultaneously with the massive statue of the Commander at the center of the city. The Commander's compound was the last to go. Again, the ground opened up, pulled in the debris, and sealed it within itself. In its place, a rose garden was sewn, with young oak trees in the northeast corner and dogwoods to the south. Sprays of pink clematis swathed the granite rock on the western border.

And Seridon was Keyronai again.

Chapter Thirty-Two

Almost Everything

They now stood in what was previously the town center, where the fountain and Commander's statue once loomed over the busy circle. Seriah, Heddah, Leyna, Bander and Harvard dismounted the dragons, taking in their new surroundings. Aron had never seen such beauty. Deep, rich greens and sparkling gemstones were almost everywhere he turned. Where there was once a cluster of stores, now stood a grove of tall, stately Aspen trees, skirted by rhododendrons and juniper shrubs. Lined by three weeping spruce trees, a grand exhibition of ironstone rock, exposing colorful flashes of opal, nestled itself into the lot that was once Bander's pawn shop. To the northeast, the intense blue of Lupellerin Lake and its powdery beaches all but pleaded with him to take a swim from several miles away.

But standing in front of him was an entirely different kind of beauty. Iyla's beauty was not only on the outside, but it radiated from within her. She was brave and kind, funny and smart. It was her compassion and bravery that had brought them together, which, in turn, saved her entire Pelri community from extinction. It was she and the Elfblood Tree that saved him from a lifetime of lies. And now, as she stood in front of him, Aron noticed a fresh glow, a literal radiance emanating from her.

"It was all in the books," came a voice from behind them.

"Jens!" Iyla ran to embrace her oldest friend.

"You did well, Iyla. As did you, son," he added, nodding to Aron as he held Iyla close.

"So, you knew all of this would happen?" Aron asked.

Jens paused briefly as he took in the brilliant landscape. Then, turning back to Aron, he said, "Do you see what Iyla wears around her neck? That pendant has been passed down from mother to first-born daughter through many generations. It was originally crafted by Levryn and given to Miranda as his promise of love and safekeeping."

Iyla gently fondled the pendant, the engraved symbol now only faintly illuminated. Her lips parted slightly. "Are you saying that I am a direct descendant of Levryn and Miranda?"

"You are. 'A new beginning is only one sunrise away. I commit myself to you with every ray of light in every morning forward, and the Pelri will forever reign as stewards of nature and of Keyronai.'"

"The inscription on the ruin's floor in Asopo!" Iyla whispered.

"Yes."

"And you knew all along that Iyla would be the one to save her people and her country? And that the Tree would bring me here?"

"Not exactly. I knew it would be someone in her lineage. And when she brought you to Ehn Ee Canyon, it appeared that everything was beginning to line up for Iyla and you to change the course of this country, and all of Athemoni, for that matter. And for Iyla to take her place as Keyronai's next crowned Kaiserin."

"Wait, what?" they both said in unison.

"And restoring Keyronai is not the only reason you were brought to our world, Aron. The Tree is even more powerful than you think and probably knows you and Iyla more than you know yourselves." Jens nodded toward Iyla as her face flushed.

"Whoa," said Aron and took Iyla's hand. "But why didn't you tell us this when we were at the Canyon?"

Jens spread his arms wide. "This is Iyla's inheritance, her birthright. You, Aron, are not from this world. But you do have a choice. You always had a choice, whether you wanted to heed the call of the Tree or return to your Earth."

Aron stood beside Iyla, his hand squeezing hers. Behind Jens, three dragons rolled in the lush new grass while Harvard, eyes wide, stared up at him. With Bander's arm around her, Heddah wrapped hers around Leyna as they anxiously listened to the old elf. The sound of the rumbling earth was slowly fading.

"I've lived a life full of lies for the last several years. And every decision I made was based on a distortion by someone whom I thought I loved and whom I thought loved me. But I never felt settled. I never felt complete. I was always craving a new adventure, a new... something. Never could I have imagined it was another world calling me home. Your world, your Tree, has brought me here, where I've found the most selfless, bravest person I have ever met, and for that, I'm so grateful. I owe Iyla my life, and I'd be damned if I didn't choose to spend the rest of my life working to not only repay her but to help her live her best life. I've found amazing new friends. I have finally found the life for which I was destined."

Iyla pulled Aron's face down toward her and gently planted a sweet kiss on his lips. He smiled. *Lilacs. Familiar, purity, and a renewal of life.*

"I knew it!" Heddah shouted as both Iyla's and Aron's faces flushed.

Jens turned to the four humans standing behind him. "Introductions, please."

Iyla scrambled to Heddah's side. "Jens, these are very good friends who helped us get the Heart to the Elfblood Tree. This is Heddah. She helped me escape from the humans in the detainment facility. I couldn't have done it without her.

And Harvard here is her son who bravely rode a dragon and saved his mother." She winked at Harvard, who threw his shoulders back with a big smile. "Leyna is Harvard's aunt, and she owned the inn where Aron stayed while he looked for me. And Bander, he not only ferried us across the lake but escorted us through the mountains with the morcego wraiths. They're great friends to the Pelri. Not all Seridon humans are bad, Jens.

"And everyone," Iyla continued. "This is my oldest friend, Jens. He knows... almost everything."

"Blessed to meet you," said Heddah. "Thank you for all that you've done."

"I should thank you. It seems the four of you have shown unusual kindness to my favorite Pelri. And it seems Keyronai and its magic has spared you."

"We love the Pelri, sir," said Leyna, her voice cracking.

Jens' rigid gaze moved to the grassy turf behind Aron. Silence fell, and 210 small bright lights illuminated simultaneously in the dusk, only fifty yards in front of them, and 210 Pelri appeared in the field. Not far behind, an additional twenty-seven Pelri from Rakkarron marched over the hill to join them.

"It seems a ceremony is in order," Jens announced with a rare smile.

Several magnolia trees sprang up from the grass behind the humans to form a lush backdrop to the beautiful setting, their oversized white flowers decorating their veil of branches and thick leaves. Two of them bent their branches down and intertwined to fashion an intricate, but solid bench where Leyna and Heddah guided Iyla to sit before rejoining Aron, Harvard and Bander to watch from alongside the Pelri, whose pearl drops continued to glow.

The cool floral breeze carried a peaceful melody through the tree branches that Aron barely recognized. The trees were speaking, and more of them sprang up in the distance. A grove of sinewy maples swayed behind the Pelri gathering, and a thicket of rosebushes grew in front of a mound of glimmering white topaz. Birch and oak trees rose and stood guard, encircling the congregation.

"A new chapter begins for Keyronai," Jens began, "and our Pelri have returned home."

Aron's arms prickled at the excitement flowing throughout the group and whispers of "Iyla" skittered among the Pelri.

"Some of you may have forgotten the days of old, when Levryn and Miranda, together, pioneered this country to reach a level of opulence, of prosperity and security, that this world has never seen. Their skillful guidance was passed down through their lineage until the fateful day when the Heart of the Elfblood Tree was stolen." Jens paused, all eyes focused on him. "Though much of your past has been forgotten, the tenacious Pelri lived on. You all have survived, including Levryn and Miranda's progeny, Iyla, daughter of Mrinnia."

Whispers and murmurs spread throughout the group.

"Seriah?" Jens turned to him, standing at the edge of the group. "Please, you have some words?"

Seriah respectfully approached and turned to stand beside Jens and address his countrymen. "We all know Iyla very well. She has a good heart, a quick wit, and she's a loyal friend. What you may not know is that she has spent the last year, since Mrinnia's death, searching for our lost ones. I was helping her, the day that I was taken, and she didn't tell you because she knew you'd object. She knew you'd try to stop her. The humans, they are... were... they were so evil. But Iyla always puts others before herself. She's an exceptional, resourceful, and compassionate soul, and I should be honored to have her represent us in our new Keyronai."

A cheer rose up from the small Pelri crowd and Aron breathed a sigh as he watched Iyla smiling from her tree bench. The soft music in the air grew slightly louder and more distinct as the breeze blew through the tree leaves.

As the coronation continued, Jens described the events of the day and previous weeks, and two young Pelri from the front row approached Iyla with a gift: a crown formed using branches of the Elfblood Tree itself. They placed the crown on her head as the new Kaiserin, Iyla of Keyronai.

The sun sat just below the horizon while Neoma, Secoriea, and Rikkipal began to shine in the early evening sky, illuminating the extraordinary colors and sparkling gems of the new Keyronai.

Aron looked out over the small crowd of Pelri, whose expressions of hope and relief were undeniable, much like the connection he felt to them.

The connection. That's what's been missing his whole life. He was connected to this world, and this was where he belonged. He was finally at peace, where the only pull he felt was the captivating lure of a Pelri named Iyla.

He saw Heddah smiling from ear to ear, while wide-eyed Harvard found it challenging to sit still. Leyna and Bander were tired but proudly supporting their new friends. Five dragons now circled above, and in the distance, Aron caught sight of a tall, pale-haired Sapin disappearing behind a large quartz rock.

About the Author

Born and raised in Maryland, Kristin wrote her first book in third grade. Yes, she drew the pictures herself, hand-sewed the pages together, and wrapped the cover with a fabric remnant; but it still counts. After many years of exploring every creative endeavor imaginable, she finally experienced the pinnacle of artistry and created a world: Athemoni, in the fantasy novel, *When the Tree Calls*. (It counts.) These days you'll find Kristin at home with her husband, still exploring every creative endeavor imaginable, trying to type with a dog's head on her lap, and looking forward to the next time she'll see her precious grandbabies.

WANT MORE?

Thank you for reading my first novel, *When the Tree Calls*. I hope you enjoyed exploring Athemoni and connecting with Aron, Iyla, and the rest of the gang.

Want more? Please visit my website and join the mailing list to stay on top of the lastest news, freebies, and new release announcements. Just scan or click the QR code below:

Reviews are gold in the indie publishing world! Please consider submitting an honest review on Amazon or any other platform. Thank you so much for your support!

KRISTIN WAHLNE